About the author

The author was born in Scotland and, after serving in the Army, embarked on a career in industry.

He has worked in several different sectors in senior roles and was latterly CEO of a large international data capture company.

He retired for the first time in 1995 to take on a consultancy designed to help new businesses become established.

In 2018, he finally retired from business life to become a full-time author.

John lives in Scotland and Portugal with his wife, and they have two grown-up sons.

THE VOICE
The fifth DCI Burt murder mystery

JOHN REID

THE VOICE

The fifth DCI Burt murder mystery

Vanguard Press

A CIP catalogue record for this title is
available from the British Library.

ISBN 978 1 80016 317 1

Vanguard Press is an imprint of
Pegasus Elliot MacKenzie Publishers Ltd
www.pegasuspublishers.com

First Published in 2022

Vanguard Press
Sheraton House, Castle Park
Cambridge England

Printed & Bound in Great Britain

Dedication

To my wife for her continued support and assistance in writing this novel and also to my reading forum for their sometimes humorous but always constructive comments.

Also from the DCI Steve Burt Series by John Reid

The Forgotten Gun
The Auction
The Disciples
The Watchers

Coming soon in the same series

The Norwich Murders
The Abduction

Chapter One

It was a wet and wild early March night as the small Ford van bucked and slid along the rough path that had been cut into the lightly wooded area atop the railway embankment. It was after midnight and the lights on the van only just showed the path. With a steep drop on his right, the driver was being ultra-careful.

The path was designed for walkers and the occasional railway maintenance crew vehicle but tonight it served as the route for a crime.

There were two hooded men in the front of the van. Both were lightweight career criminals guilty of nothing more than being lazy and thinking those with wealth owed them a living. The title 'career criminal' flattered them as they had been involved in nothing more serious than botched burglaries and failed scams. They were well known in the lower courts, and it was only their combined tally of court appearances that afforded them their title of career criminals.

Neither was very bright and that suited the person they worked for. Their boss was the genuine article and did merit the title of career criminal. He was an unscrupulous rogue who had committed most crimes in his long career, including murder. Over the years and when the pair weren't in jail, he used them to run errands and do the heavy lifting that he was too idle to do himself.

As the pair made their way further into the trees, they looked out for the pedestrian bridge that crossed the railway line into Victoria Station. The lights from the track helped them see and just as the bridge came into view, they stopped the van. Their boss had been very specific as to where they should stop, and without knowing it, commit the most serious crime in their so far unspectacular criminal careers.

Both men got out and looked around. This part of London was heavily populated, and they had been warned not to be spotted. Happy that they hadn't been seen, they opened the back doors. Their boss had given them the van keys with the parcel already loaded in the back. All they had to do was dump it down the embankment at the selected spot. One of them pulled out the object which seemed to be wrapped in a rough old grey woollen blanket. From the weight, size and shape, the one pulling immediately realised it was a body. This caused him to drop the object and stand back.

"Bloody hell, Bert, it's a stiff!"

"Yeah." Bert was a man of few words.

"What do we do? I sure as hell didn't sign up to get involved in dumping bodies." Reality struck the second man. "Suppose we'd been pulled over by the cops and they found this in the van." He was sweating and panicking at the same time. "We'd be in all kinds of shit."

"Yeah." This seemed to be Bert's only response. "I suppose there's nothing we can do except dump the bloody thing and get the hell out of here." This was the most Bert had spoken since they set off on their mission. Not only was Bert a man of few words but he did nothing in a hurry.

Frankie, Bert's partner, was the smarter of the two, but only just. "You're right; come on, let's get it out."

They pulled the wrapped body from the van. As they did, they noticed it had been carefully bound with plastic ties. For no reason, Frankie counted them. One secured the blanket over the head, the second the chest, the third the hips, the fourth the knees and the fifth the ankles.

"Whoever made up this poor sod as a package did a right good job. They've bound him five times."

Frankie took the head while Bert took the feet. As they shuffled sideways under the weight of the body, Frankie spoke up. "Bert, this poor bugger isn't long dead." At this Bert dropped his end and jumped back.

"What are you doing?" Frankie had kept hold of the head, so the feet were now sitting in a puddle. "I only meant it's stiff. See, it didn't even bend when you dropped your end; that means rigor mortis has set in, so he's been dead less than 24 hours. Now come on, pick up the feet."

Bert did as he was told. The pair had been told exactly where to throw the package down the embankment. Their boss had chosen the spot because, apart from a few shrubby trees on the bank, the bottom was covered in thick undergrowth. The package would be well hidden and not discovered for months.

"Right Bert, we'll swing it between us and on the count of three let it go."

"Right."

Frankie smiled to himself despite the gravity of their situation. "One…" He started to swing the head as he stood ninety degrees on to it. It reminded him of playing with a skipping rope. As he swung his end, Bert dropped the feet again.

"I wasn't ready, let me count."

"OK. You sure you can count to three?"

Bert didn't reply. He picked up his end and counted. "One… two… three!"

The package sailed into the air and tumbled down the bank. They had put so much force into their swing that it accelerated as it tumbled down towards the undergrowth and the security fence at the bottom.

Both men stood and watched. Frankie had a torch and shone it after the body. He couldn't see the blanket and assumed they had done their job. The body bound in the grey blanket was hidden.

As they made their way back along the track, the more educated Frankie spoke. "If that body had been murdered, you realise we could be done as accessories?"

"Yeah. I suppose."

Having successfully navigated their return along the path and turned onto the main road, the pair drove on in silence until Bert spoke up. "What's rigor mortis and how come you know so much?"

"I seen it on television. One of those post-mortem programmes. It said when you kill somebody, they is limp in the beginning, then this thing called rigor mortis sets in and it makes the body stiff like a lump of wood, but it doesn't last. After, say, a day or less, it goes limp again see, so our body was stiff, so it stands to reason. It hadn't been dead for a day."

Frankie looked across at his partner as he drove, convinced he was smarter than Bert. He quickly saw the error in his thinking. Everyone was smarter than Bert.

They drove on and would report their mission completed in the morning. Frankie and Bert were due a bonus for their night's work.

Chapter Two

DCI Steve Burt was late into his office on Thursday the 12th of March. He was attending an Army reunion in the evening and had visited a dress hire shop on his way to work. He wasn't keen to go especially given the circumstances that had led up to him resigning his commission some eighteen years previously. He admitted to being curious as to how his ex-colleagues had faired in the intervening years, and his wife had persuaded him he needed a good night out. She was due to deliver their first child and Steve was reluctant to leave her in case the baby arrived early. She reminded him she was a doctor and a woman and told him the baby wouldn't arrive for days. Reluctantly and at the last minute, he'd agreed to go but had to take what the hire company had available at short notice. He told himself it was fine and although the dinner jacket was a bit big, the trousers were a perfect fit. The DCI thought this was testament to his wife's cooking and his expanding waistline.

Carrying his suit bag, he walked in to find his team hard at work.

After solving a triple murder and a gold bullion heist some six months ago, the powers that be had increased his staff and extended the remit of Steve's Special Resolutions Unit, giving him free rein to get involved with all units in the Metropolitan Police Service at New Scotland Yard. This change had brought difficulties; not least, bedding in a new and larger team. It hadn't been easy, but each new member was keen, and they were beginning to gel as a harmonious unit.

As he said good morning to everyone, he adjourned to his office to find a cup of now lukewarm coffee on his desk. He dropped his suit hire bag on a chair and sat behind his desk drinking the tepid liquid. He listened to his team in the outer office and allowed himself a few minutes to reminisce.

For some reason, Detective Constable Amelia Cooper — known as Poppy — had taken umbrage at another female detective constable being brought in, especially as DC Mary Dougan was assigned to active cases while Poppy was stuck on administrative duties, but both Poppy and Mary were bright and had soon made up their differences, and they were now good friends.

The two female officers were very different. Mary was a deep thinker while Poppy was more scatter-brained. Mary was over five foot ten while Poppy was a bit shorter, at five foot eight. Poppy was blonde and Mary was dark. Poppy wore stylish fashions while Mary always wore the same light grey trouser suit.

Steve sighed and thought a lot of water had passed under the bridge in six months. They'd solved over ten high-profile cases in that time and earned each other's respect. He shook himself out of his daydream and called his team into his office.

"Right. Where are we with the current cases?"

Since acquiring his larger team, the DCI had to admit his life had become easier. Six months previously, he'd been disappointed to lose his friend and long-standing colleague, DI Abul Ishmal. Abul had been with him from the start of the establishment of the Special Resolutions Unit and Steve was sorry to see him transferred to other duties. He'd known for some time his friend wasn't really up to the task of being his number two, but he felt somehow he'd let Abul down. Having said that, he admitted the new manning level worked well and the addition of Detective Inspector Peter Jones and Detective Sergeant Matt Conway made his life a lot easier. Mary Dougan was inexperienced and a graduate entrant while the two male officers were very experienced, and the DCI had worked with them before.

"Poppy. Anything outstanding?"

"No sir. Sorry to say everything is up to date. You three have court duties tomorrow." Poppy pointed her pen indicating, in turn, the DCI, Peter and Matt. "It's that bullion case from months back. I've got the file ready for you."

"Thanks, Poppy."

Everyone looked pleased. They were on top of their caseloads.

"Peter. Where are we with the carjacking?"

"All done, Steve. The two guys are charged and on remand."

"Matt?"

"I've finished the porn case. The CPS has approved the charges, soliciting for prostitution. There should be no problems. The other case, that's the lorry hijacking, is ongoing. I've got the driver and his mate in central. I'm due to go with Mary to interview them and charge them later this morning."

"Good. So that's it?" Steve liked Matt and knew him to be a competent officer.

"Yes. All under control. Unless we get an influx of cases, we might all get some leave."

The group nodded. "Good idea."

The DCI smiled. "Well, if you've got any left you can try, but no guarantees. Right, everybody, carry on."

The DCI had a few files on his desk he needed to review and reluctantly opened the top one. As he did, he shouted through to the outer office. "Is anyone going to get me a cup of hot coffee?"

***

DCI Burt was ordering his coffee as Frankie and Bert drove up to a portacabin parked in a rundown industrial estate beside Heathrow airport. It was a second-hand car lot.

They opened the door and a cloud of cigarette smoke wafted over them, polluting that part of west London. Inside the cabin, it looked as though a fog had descended just inside this one unit.

"Brought the van back, boss." Frankie held the keys in front of him and dropped them on the desk occupied by their sometime employer.

"Everything go OK?"

"Sweet as a nut, boss, but you didn't tell us it was a body."

The boss whose name was Eddie Randall stared at Frankie. In a voice that resonated with threats, he spoke slowly and deliberately. "It wasn't a body. Got it? It was a parcel of rubbish. Don't you ever forget it, or *you* might be the next parcel."

Frankie went pale. At five foot seven and weighing in at around 140 pounds he never looked healthy, but the loss of colour coupled with a week's stubble on his face rendered him looking decidedly ill.

"Sorry Eddie, I can't even remember where we were last night." He turned to Bert. "That right Bert?"

Bert the man of few words looked blankly at his friend. "If you say so, Frankie."

"See, boss, nothing to worry about."

Eddie Randall stood and produced a roll of fifty-pound notes from his back pocket. He peeled two off and threw them onto his desk. "There, that's your bonus. I'll be in touch when I need you again."

Frankie went forward and retrieved the money. As he turned, he saw a figure in the corner slouched in an old armchair. He immediately recognised the man he knew as the Blade. He was an enforcer for their boss, and he liked to cut people using a very sharp flick knife. Frankie noticed he was playing with his knife, twirling it between his fingers. He was very afraid of the Blade and physically trembled in his presence. Frankie had seen some of the Blade's handiwork and knew he was pure evil. In fact, he was probably mad. Frankie pulled Bert out the door and almost ran from the office.

After the pair had gone, the Blade stood up. "Why do you use these clowns?"

"They're useful. Besides, you don't question my decisions. You do as I tell you."

"Yeah. Yeah. All that bull, but remember I know you're not the kingpin around here. I know you take orders just like me."

Eddie Randall was a big man. His shaven head and various tattoos on his head and neck gave him a sinister appearance. His height and weight made him a fearsome-looking character and few men would cross him and expect not to finish up in hospital, or worse.

The Blade wasn't that brave, but he knew Eddie's background and knew he had enough on the big man to cause him trouble. For this reason, he felt able to push his luck on occasions.

"Listen, I do as I'm told, but the guy I listen to is the main man. He's kept this little organisation going with jobs and money, plus he's kept the cops off our backs. If it wasn't for him, we'd all be on holiday at Her Majesty's pleasure, so you leave the organisation to me and our patron. You just do as I tell you. Got it?"

The Blade knew that there was someone important pulling Eddie's strings, but this was the first time he'd heard the big man admit it. He decided to back off.

"Whatever you say. You're the boss."

***

As had become common practice and only when caseloads permitted, the DCI and his senior detective had lunch in the canteen in New Scotland Yard. They'd worked and solved many cases over the past six months, but the DCI felt his number two hadn't really settled, even after six months.

Over a plate of sausage, egg and chips, Peter Jones and Steve discussed a wide variety of topics. Over these lunches, Steve had learnt that his almost six foot tall and very slim colleague was not only Welsh but an avid rugby man. The DCI had teased him about his lack of bulk and Peter had replied he was 150 pounds of pure muscle. He allowed the conversation to open up and encouraged Peter to talk about himself.

"One reason I wanted to work with you, Steve, is that you are seen to get results and anyone working with you is bound to be noticed." Peter had confided. "Of course, being on your team also means you get the bigger more difficult cases, so it's great experience."

Steve knew his reputation among junior officers and accepted most officers who were assigned to his unit would be transient. He thought at least Peter was being honest. At this particular lunchtime, the conversation drifted into more personal territory triggered by a question about why the DCI had the need to hire an evening suit.

Steve found Peter easy to talk to and opened up a little about his life before the police. He hoped sharing personal information might allow the Welshman to feel more at home.

"I used to be in the Army, 2nd Parachute Regiment. I loved it you know, as a young man full of testosterone and fit as a butcher's dog. It was a great life, but something happened, and I left. It was after leaving the Army that I joined the police." The DCI wasn't prepared to go into any more detail.

"I got an invite out of the blue inviting me to a regimental reunion. I've had others but my wife has persuaded me to go to this one." Steve finished his coffee and pushed his empty plate aside. "God only knows who'll be there. It's getting on for eighteen years since I resigned my commission. I was twenty-five when I left. I suppose some of my contemporaries might be there, but the older officers are probably dead or in nursing homes." Steve stood up. "I'll see tonight. I'm disappearing early today. Can you hold the fort, but call me if anything important comes in?"

The DI also stood. "I will but reluctantly; go off and enjoy yourself tonight. We can cope."

***

Steve arrived home in good time to organise himself. His wife, Dr Alison Mills, was sitting in the reception area of her ground-floor medical practice talking to an earnest-looking middle-aged man Steve knew was her new locum. With the imminent birth of their first child, Alison had recruited another doctor to take care of her practice until she was ready to return to work after the birth. Steve acknowledged both of them as he climbed the stairs to their upper floor apartment. He knew Alison didn't like being disturbed when talking about medical matters. As he passed Steve thought his heavily pregnant wife was looking radiant but huge. He didn't know much about childbirth but thought he might be a father any minute.

Once suited and booted and having his wife again convince him she was not about to drop their child, the DCI reluctantly climbed into his taxi and headed off to the Ashley Hotel just off Milton Road in West London.

It was 6.35 p.m. when Steve exited the taxi, and even from outside he could hear loud voices bellowing out of the open windows on the first floor. He paid off his taxi and with a resigned sigh, marched into the hotel and up to the first floor.

Steve was surprised by how many people were present. At first, he didn't recognise anyone. He wandered around the edge of the room and accepted a glass of whisky from a white-coated waiter. He saw several officers in their mess kit so assumed they were serving officers. He didn't recognise any of them.

As he stood sipping his whisky, he was tapped on the shoulder from behind. He turned to see a very dapper man with slicked-back grey hair and an imposing bearing. Neither man spoke for a few seconds until the stranger grabbed Steve's hand and shook it vigorously.

"You don't remember me, do you?"

An embarrassed DCI racked his brains. "Yes! Yes, I do, it's Major Hope."

"Got it in one. How the hell are you, Steve? You haven't been to one of these bashes before. I saw you come in and couldn't believe my eyes."

Major Robert Hope had been Captain Steve Burt's Company Commander during his time with the Paras. He wasn't the dashing figure Steve remembered but he reminded himself the last time he had seen the major was 18 years ago and they were both steaming drunk.

The pair stood examining each other and asking questions. "I saw you got an MBE for police services. I suppose you're some high-flyer in New Scotland Yard now?"

"No. Just an ordinary working copper. But what about you? Are you still serving?"

"Christ no! I've been out to pasture for the past twelve years. My boy's serving though, he graduated Sandhurst a few years ago now." The Major laughed. "It's a bit of a coincidence but he's commissioned into the Military Police."

"Well, good for him. What about your wife?"

"Still going strong. Still telling me I drink too much and still ruling the roost, but I couldn't bear to be without her. What about you. Married?"

"Yes. She's a doctor and we're about to have our first child."

At this, Robert Hope shook Steve's hand again and stopped a white-coated waiter and relieved him of four whiskies. He decanted two into one and handed Steve what was now a very large tot. "Congratulations, old boy." They clinked glasses together and the Major drank heartily. Steve took a drink that was larger than he'd intended.

The evening progressed. Ex-Captain Burt met a few people he'd served with and enjoyed catching up with them. The dinner gong sounded, and thirty-six not-too-sober ex and current officers filed in to eat. As was normal, the decibel level was high. The more alcohol that was consumed, the louder the table became.

The speeches were heard more or less in silence and the colonel, whom Steve had also served under and who had eased his exit from the regiment, made the toast to the Queen, the regiment and fallen comrades.

This was the sign for the real festivities to begin. Wine gave way to brandy. Whisky gave way to more whisky, and people began removing their jackets and undoing their bowties. Small groups formed around the table and some officers went back to the room they had first congregated in as it had a series of more comfortable sofas and armchairs.

Steve was with a group of people he'd served with towards the end of his career. One of them, now a full Colonel who was still serving, touched upon Steve's exit from the regiment. Several of the group were still serving and had been present when Steve punched a major at a formal event because Steve was bedding his wife.

"I prefer not to talk about that."

"Well," said the colonel who had also been a Captain with Steve, "if it's any consolation to you, that sexy she-wolf of a walking whore got banged up by a corporal and departed the scene overnight. The hubby resigned his commission and was last heard of selling used cars in Glasgow."

The group broke instantly into riotous laughter.

And so, the evening went on, more booze, more stories both true and exaggerated and everyone building up to a first-class hangover in the morning.

Major Hope sought out Steve and guided him away from his group.

"Can we talk, Steve? I think I might need your help."

With his senses dulled due to an excess intake of single malt, Steve agreed. The pair unsteadily made their way to the outer room, but Robert

Hope thought it too busy and noisy and suggested they adjourn to the hotel bar.

Seated at a corner table in the more refined atmosphere of the bar, Robert looked at Steve and refocused his eyes. He'd had a lot to drink but had been legendary in his day for his capacity to hold his liquor. It seemed nothing had changed. The waiter brought yet another whisky for the Major and soda water for Steve. The DCI reluctantly reminded himself he had to work tomorrow and decided to start his sobering-up process now.

"Steve. I told you that my boy Alex was in the Service, in the RMP."

"Yes. He's done well."

"I only told you half the story. He's seconded to the SIB. You know, plain clothes, just like you, a detective. He came to see me a couple of months ago. Said he had been given a special assignment and he was going undercover. He couldn't say what it was about, but he said he'd call or text every opportunity he could so his mother and I would know he was all right." The Major drank a large slug of his scotch.

"For the first few weeks, we had regular texts and even the odd phone call. Then six weeks ago nothing, he just disappeared. I knew it might be nothing to worry about, but his mother is concerned. I called the MOD, but they gave me the run-around. Because Alex is SIB and on operations, I can't even speak to his commanding officer." The Major finished his whisky.

"It's over six weeks, Steve, and not a word. I know you're high up in the police and wondered if you could somehow look into it. You know, put our minds at rest?"

Robert Hope was clearly distressed. His body language was that of a defeated man.

"Bob, I'd like to help but it's military, I can't get involved. Have you reported it to the police as a missing person?"

"Yes, but they gave me the brush-off as well. They said it was military."

Steve thought back to the last time he'd looked into a missing person as a favour and remembered the trouble it had brought him.

"Look Bob," Steve produced one of his business cards from his wallet, "here's my card. If you haven't heard anything by this time next week, give me a call." This was all the DCI could think to do to offer his ex-Company Commander some hope.

As an afterthought, Steve asked, "Was your son's undercover job in the UK?"

"Yes, he was clear on that when he came to see me."

"Mmm." The DCI suspected he would become involved in the Captain Alex Hope case. He just didn't know how.

Both men returned to the party that was beginning to wind down. Steve was ready to call it a night.

Chapter Three

The next morning, Friday the 13th of March, the DCI had breakfast with his wife and was only vaguely conscious of feeling a bit liverish from the excess alcohol of the previous evening. Even his wife was impressed considering she had seen the state he was in when he had returned from the reunion.

"You must have a very strong liver."

"No, I just didn't drink too much," he lied.

"Remember I saw you get into bed, but don't worry, I won't report you for being drunk and disorderly." Alison laughed. "You should have seen yourself trying to undo your shoelaces, I wish I'd had my camera."

Steve was a bit embarrassed and didn't like being reminded he'd lost a bit of control last night.

He changed the subject to their usual morning topic of conversation.

"Will our child arrive today?"

"I've told you; it will come in its own time. Yes, it's due today but babies have their own agenda. Don't worry, I'll call you if it starts."

Steve ate his last piece of toast and finished his coffee. As he was leaving, he stopped to kiss his wife. "You know it's Friday the 13th. I'm not sure I want our child born on that date and Friday the 13th always seems to throw up some funny cases." He kissed her again and left for the Yard. He knew the walk would be as good a hangover cure as anything else.

As he walked, he recalled the events of last night. He'd enjoyed himself more than he thought he would but his meeting with his old Company Commander played on his mind. He couldn't shake off the feeling that he would be involved.

He walked briskly as it was chilly and as he arrived at the Yard he noticed he was breathing only marginally heavily. The DCI pushed out his chest as he thought, *Not bad for a forty-four-year-old man.*

Eddie Randall was in his portacabin office early on this dry but cold Friday morning. He'd had a coded message from the man who gave him his orders. He'd never met his controller. A friend of Eddie's had acted as an intermediary and set up the first contact. Since the man had taken over Eddie's life some six months ago, he hadn't been arrested or questioned by the police despite carrying out some serious crimes on his controller's instructions. He had, however, been well rewarded for his troubles as compensation for giving up the freedom to act on his own initiative. His controller sent him coded messages by text when he needed to speak to him, and Eddie obeyed by being where he was told and on time ready to receive each call.

Eddie was early and pondered who his controller or, as he called him, the Voice, might be. He was obviously well connected but Eddie felt he was ruthless. Apart from the two recent murders Eddie had been ordered to carry out, including the killing of his friend who had set him up with the Voice, he'd been ordered to collect protection money, set fire to a factory and even do a jewel smash-and-grab during which a shop assistant was killed.

Eddie's car emporium consisted of half a dozen failed MOT cars and a couple of stolen cars their owners were glad to get rid of. The phone rang at exactly nine a.m. Eddie picked up on the first ring. "Yes?"

The Voice, as always, was disguised. His controller used some form of an electronic device to disguise his voice. "Good, you're there. An envelope will be delivered to you this morning by post. In it, you'll find instructions and photographs of the person you are to remove." There was a slight pause from the electronic voice. "Permanently... Your fee will be paid as usual on completion of the job. Is that clear?"

"Yes." Eddie was desperate to ask who he was, but he had tried it in the early days of their arrangement, and it was made clear if he continued to ask the question his days of breathing in the contaminated air of his portacabin office would be limited.

"Good. I want this to be public. I want people to see this man has been murdered. It's by way of a warning to others. Do you understand?"

After Eddie had acknowledged his understanding, the Voice carried on.

"Now I have another job for you; you'll receive another envelope on Monday. Be in your office at the same time next Tuesday for instructions. Is that clear?"

Eddie just had time to confirm before the line went dead.

***

With a relatively clear head, the DCI entered his office. He knew he had court today as did Peter and Matt. Poppy sat at her desk with neatly stacked files in front of her.

"The CPS called. They want you at the Bailey by ten this morning. I tried to get out of them when you'd be called but they wouldn't say. You're to meet with the QC before the court sits and go over your evidence."

"Right. Any sign of Peter or Matt?"

"No sir but it's only 08.05."

Not long after, both detectives turned up carrying the first of the day's caffeine intake. They took a file each from Poppy, listened to the same speech Poppy had given the DCI and settled down to remind themselves what had happened during the case.

At 09.53, the three detectives walked into the grand entrance of the Old Bailey. This was the UK's best known criminal court in the country and had witnessed almost every criminal undertaking ever prosecuted.

The three made their way to a room on the first floor. As they walked in, the lead prosecuting QC, Sir Richard Barber, was already dressed in his court clothes and was donning his wig while talking to a man Steve knew as Erskine Smyth, a solicitor for the CPS.

Sir Richard stopped talking when he heard the door open. "Ah! You must be the police and I'm guessing you are DCI Burt?" Sir Richard headed toward Steve.

They shook hands warmly and Steve introduced his colleagues. Before Sir Richard could continue, the door opened again and in stepped Detective Inspector Abul Ishmal.

Abul had been a permanent member of Steve's team during the gold bullion heist and had in fact been the SIO on the case. Unfortunately, the complexity of the case brought to the fore Abul's weaknesses, and it had been decided to transfer him to other duties. Steve hadn't fought the transfer of his friend, realising the senior officers who recommended Abul's transfer were right in their assessment of his abilities. Still, Steve felt guilty although Abul seemed to hold no ill-feeling towards his ex-boss.

With all four officers present, Sir Richard ran through his timetable and his strategy for the day ahead. "I know it's boring just hanging about but the four of you are the key, so your evidence is vital."

They spent a good thirty minutes going over who said what and when. At precisely ten-thirty, a clerk knocked on the door to inform Sir Richard the judge was ready.

All four detectives had the outline timetable from Sir Richard. They knew the running order and knew they had time for a coffee in the grandly named restaurant which in fact looked more like a down-market canteen.

All four men had worked on the case so knew each other but over a coffee, each divulged more of himself as part of a 'get to know you better' exercise. As Steve finished his coffee, his phone buzzed. He looked at the screen and saw it was Alison.

"Hi, what's up?"

"Now don't panic. The baby is on its way. I've ordered a taxi, phoned the hospital, my suitcase is packed and I'm in the practice reception so everything's in hand."

Steve was dumbstruck. He'd roleplayed this moment in his head a hundred times but now it was happening he didn't know what to say.

"Are you still there?"

"Er, yes. I'll get over to the hospital and meet you there."

"No, there's no need. It could be hours yet and you're not attending the birth so just you enjoy your day and come and see me when you can." There was a pause. "Steve, that's the taxi. I've got to go. See you later and I love you." The line went dead.

His three companions all knew he was about to become a father and worked out from Steve's end of the conversation that things were happening. He confirmed his wife was about to give birth, but he said he would stay and give his evidence before going to the hospital.

Fortunately, the DCI was first onto the stand. It took Sir Richard forty-six minutes to expertly draw Steve's evidence from him before passing the DCI over to the defence QC.

Steve didn't know the defence QC, but he didn't seem overly concerned about getting his client acquitted. He only asked Steve three questions and dismissed him as a witness. The whole exercise took just over one hour.

The DCI sent a note to Sir Richard and Erskine Smyth of the CPS saying he had to leave the building and explained why. He added his mobile number to the note and dashed back to the Yard to collect his car.

***

Eddie Randall received his post just before ten o'clock. In it was the large brown envelope he was expecting. He examined it for clues as to who the Voice might be or at least where the envelope had been posted from. He failed on both counts. Reluctantly, he opened the envelope and withdrew the contents.

There were two grainy photographs of a middle-aged man with a mane of grey hair tied in a ponytail getting into a car. His face was clear enough for recognition. Also, in the envelope was a typed sheet of A4 paper. It gave the grey-haired man's name as Cameron Bowie and his address as The Crystal Motor Company in Mile End Road, East London.

Eddie noticed also typed on the page was an additional instruction. It said the deed had to be done at the premises during working hours. Eddie pondered this for a few minutes. He'd never had such strict instructions from the Voice before and wondered why the killing had to be so public. He called out to Frankie and Bert. They were washing his stock of clapped-out cars for sale.

"Get yourselves into the office, I've got a job for you."

Eddie used his laptop to look up Crystal Motors. He discovered it was owned and run by a Cameron Bowie, that it specialised in vintage and high-end sports cars and it had been running for the last eleven years.

He looked at the motors for sale and thought if the payment from the Voice was enough, he might buy something.

Frankie and Bert arrived a few minutes later. Both were wet through and Bert in particular was dripping water on the portacabin floor. As usual, they looked a mess even when wet. Eddie thought maybe the Blade was right. These two looked like something from a refugee camp but not one of the better ones. Bert had taken to not shaving, like Frankie, and Eddie noticed his once white tennis shoes had holes in them. He also saw Bert seemed to prefer string to a belt to hold up his oversized jeans.

With a sigh, he started. "Right, I want you to keep watch on this fella." He handed over the pictures. "His name is Cameron Bowie, and he runs a garage on the Mile End Road. I only want you to see what he does during the day. If he goes out, do not follow him. Is that clear?"

Frankie was excited. "Yes boss, only watch him when he's in the garage." Frankie appeared to be a bit confused and before Eddie could reply, he added, "But what do you want us to do?"

Eddie's tolerance for stupidity was low but this seemed unreal. He made a great effort to stay calm and be patient with his two employees even though they were self-employed.

"I want you to watch him inside his garage. I want you to note what he does and when. I want you to write everything down. I especially want to know how many times he's on his own and at what times." Eddie spoke to the two as though they were children. "Now do you understand?"

This time Bert replied. "Got it, everything you said but what do we write on?"

Patience was stretching now. "Here." Eddie threw an A4 pad at Bert followed by a pen from his desk.

Bert picked them up and smiled, giving Eddie a nod.

"Boss." It was Frankie's turn to test Eddie's patience. "When we've written everything down. Then what?"

"You bring the paper to me and explain it. You only stay watching until Mr Bowie leaves. Then you come back here. Got it?" Eddie was trying hard not to explode.

"Right you are. We write everything down and come back here. How do we get there?"

Eddie threw the keys for the Ford van the pair had driven yesterday. With a mighty effort, Eddie smiled. "Anything else gents?"

"Well, boss," Frankie spoke up. "Do we get a bonus for this?"

"No Frankie, you only get a bonus if you're employed." Eddie tried to explain things as simply as he could. "Neither of you works for me so if anybody asks, you *don't* work for me. Got it? You're not on the payroll. Only people on payrolls get bonuses if they do something well. You get backhanders. Tax-free cash when you do me a little service like disposing of some trash the other night, and this little observation job I've just given you."

"Yeah. Right, so we don't get wages, but you pay us?"

Eddie gave up. "That's right, Frankie. This job should last for two days." Eddie pulled some money from his pocket. "Here. There's forty quid to tide you over. If you do good, I'll pay you even more. Now get out of here but don't get caught doing anything you shouldn't."

The pair, now forty pounds richer, armed with a notepad and pen plus a set of wheels, left to carry out their boss's wishes or at least what they thought were their boss's wishes.

***

Steve arrived at the private maternity hospital at 12.45 p.m. just after Bert and Frankie had set off to find the car showroom on Mile End Road. He explained who he was and was shown into a plush waiting room especially furnished for expectant fathers. There were two other men in the room. The nurse who had shown Steve into the room said she'd find out how Mrs Burt was doing and come back and tell him.

He acknowledged the other two men, one of whom was pacing the floor. Several copies of the day's newspapers were on a coffee table, and he picked one up. He didn't really focus on the printed page. His anxiety level was off the scale, and he could feel a bout of acid reflux coming on. Steve was just about to stand and join the other man in pacing the floor when a different nurse arrived and asked for Mr Burt. She led Steve along a wide, brightly lit corridor and ushered him into a private side room.

There sitting up in bed was his wife, cradling a bundle in a pink knitted blanket. Steve, who wasn't naturally emotional, started to cry as he approached the edge of the bed. He was speechless. Wiping away his tears, he kissed Alison gently on the lips and stood back looking at the little face that was sound asleep, peeping out of the shawl.

"You have a daughter, DCI Burt. She's seven pounds six ounces and the most beautiful baby in the world." Alison was now also crying to keep her husband company.

Steve still could not find his voice. He kissed his wife again and pulled back a corner of the pink shawl. He stared, mesmerised by this little human being that was his daughter. He stroked her cheek and felt how soft and spongy it was.

For some reason, he couldn't explain, when he found his voice the first thing he said was, "Does she have any hair?"

Alison tried to break into laughter, but her recent experience meant she could only giggle and then gently. "You silly detective, her hair will grow in and probably change colour anyway." Alison looked lovingly at Steve. "Are you pleased? I know you wanted a boy and that's why we didn't want to know the sex until now."

The DCI started crying again. He leant over, moving his daughter nearer her mother so he could put his arm around Alison. "Don't be silly; this is the best day of my life."

"You also didn't want our baby born on Friday the 13th."

"I don't care. I'm just glad she's here and you're both well." He kissed his wife again.

The door opened and a tall, very beautiful nurse with a strong Irish accent arrived. "I've come to take Baby to the nursery. You, Dr Mills, need your rest, and you, Mr Burt, need to leave. Visiting is from six tonight. Now be off with you and give this good woman some rest."

Alison handed over their daughter. Steve embraced his wife and held her. It was clear to Alison he didn't want to leave. "You heard the nurse. Come back at six tonight and bring me something nice."

The DCI pulled away and stood. "OK, I'll surprise you. Oh! By the way, what are we going to call her?"

"I've no idea. Now let me get some rest. It's been a hectic day so far."

***

Bert and Frankie fought their way through the traffic and after more than a few wrong turns eventually found themselves on the Mile End Road. They cruised, or rather, stopped and started along the road to the annoyance of other motorists in their quest to find Crystal Motors.

Eventually, they spotted a filling station and to the side a large hangar-like building with the sign CRYSTAL MOTORS, QUALITY USED CARS emblazoned above the glass sliding doors that faced the road. Not knowing what else to do, Frankie drove onto the forecourt of the filling station and parked away from the petrol pumps.

"What do we do now, Frankie?"

Frankie, the more intellectual one of the pair, didn't have a clue, but couldn't admit this to Bert.

"Maybe we just go into the showroom and say we're interested in buying a motor."

"Yeah. Good idea, what about the van?"

Bert, although in Frankie's eyes wasn't as sharp as himself, had a knack of spotting flaws in Frankie's plans.

"Tell you what. Let's drive around. See if we can find a place to park then we'll come back."

They left the filling station forecourt and turned right. It was obvious there was nowhere they could park the van and see the garage. After about a quarter of a mile, a narrow lane appeared on their right-hand side. Frankie turned in and stopped. There were cars parked and signs that said permit parking only. Frankie parked in the first vacant space.

"It says permits, Frankie."

"Oh yeah. Well, it's eleven-thirty and people round here with permits is at work. You heard Eddie. We've to finish when this geezer goes home and that's got to be around five." Frankie stood tall, amazed at his logic. "So, them folks with a permit are out until they get home and that'll be well after we've gone. No sweat. This'll do us."

The two emaciated individuals in their cheap and scruffy ill-fitting clothes made their way back to Crystal Motors. Bert was in charge of the notepad and pen. Without a second thought, they walked straight into the showroom. Although it was typical of thousands of such places up and down the country, Frankie and Bert had never been in such a place. They stood mouths open in genuine awe of this gleaming monument to the car.

32

Frankie nudged Bert out of his trance. The pair walked further into the temple to opulence, admiring the highly polished metal and even higher polish to the floor. They looked around but saw no one resembling their quarry. They spotted two young men in flash suits sitting at a desk chatting away but apart from them, the place was empty. One of the well-dressed youths stood and approached the pair. He clearly didn't like what he saw. Two gormless dirty weeds of men standing in his showroom where the cheapest car was fifteen grand. He doubted this pair had fifteen pennies.

"Yes gents, can I help you?" The salesman was covering his bets. He could be wrong, and they might be eccentric millionaires, but he doubted it. However, just in case he'd be polite until he found out if they were.

"No." A startled Frankie spoke up. "We're just browsing, thank you." Frankie thought he'd answered in his best, most cultured voice. His confidence wasn't helped by having Bert by his side giggling at Frankie's attempt to impress.

"What kind of car were you thinking about? We've got a very nice Austin Allegro. It's just come in, only one careful lady owner. She was a vicar. It's only done 5000 miles from new, a real snip at thirty thousand."

Frankie, as the designated mouthpiece, smiled at the salesman. "Yes, I'm not sure about that. Maybe we can just look around?" Frankie felt he had taken on the accent of a country gentleman quite well, but Bert didn't.

"I'm sorry sir, but unless you are a serious buyer, I'll have to ask you to leave. We have a delivery expected any time now and it would be dangerous for you to be in here."

The salesman was reluctant to touch either Frankie or Bert so settled for pointing to the front of the showroom.

Bert just to prove he was as smart as Frankie asked "Is Mr Bowie in?"

The salesman stood back astonished that either of these two scruffs would know the name of his boss. "No, he's out."

Bert was on a roll. "When will he be back?"

"Around two o'clock. Why?"

This caught Bert out. He'd used up whatever power was left in his brain cell. Frankie answered, still talking in his perceived upper-class accent. "Oh! No reason, we were told he could do us a good deal on a motor."

The pair left. Opposite the garage, they saw a greasy spoon café. "We'll get a table by the window and watch out for the ponytail man to get back." Frankie had reverted to his normal cockney accent.

"Good idea. We can have something to eat at the same time."

***

It was after two o'clock when Cameron Bowie was spotted returning to his showroom. The pair of spies couldn't see from their position in the window of the café, so Frankie sent Bert to have a look. Bert was gone twenty minutes.

"He's in an office at the back but it's funny. I walked up the side of the building and it goes a long way back. The bit at the front with the cars is only about a third of it. I saw a lot of mechanic type guys outside having a smoke, but the inside of the garage was empty."

"Right. That'll impress the boss. Write it in your report."

"I can't."

"Why not?"

"I can't write. I thought you'd do it."

"Not me. Last time I was inside, the Education Officer said I should learn. It got me off the work detail, but I couldn't make anything of it."

Bert looked concerned. "What do we do? Eddie wanted a written report."

"Yeah, and who asked for paper and pencil." Frankie was pointing at Bert. "You did; why did you do that. Now Eddie thinks we can write."

"Could we not ask somebody to write it for us?"

"Great. Just go out onto the road and stop someone. Explain we're a couple of criminals staking out the car showroom and can you please put something on our paper." Frankie sneered at Bert who was lost.

Frankie sighed and stood up. "Come on. Let's see if we can spot our man inside and see what he's doing. We'll just have to come clean with Eddie."

The pair strolled across the road and took up a position outside the glass doors trying to look inconspicuous.

Cameron Bowie was unaware of being under surveillance. Today was like most working days. He'd taken the morning off to meet his mates for a round of golf and spent the afternoon sitting in his office, answering telephone calls, drinking tea and occasionally trying to sell a customer one of his overpriced second-hand cars. At five o'clock, he always counted any takings for the day and locked them in his safe. After saying goodnight to his sales team, he drove off and went home. This Friday was no different from any other day.

As they saw their target drive off, Frankie had an idea. "Wait here." Bert had no choice as Frankie hurried into the showroom. He found the same overdressed salesman.

"Does Mr Bowie work weekends?"

"No. Not usually. Why?"

"Oh! Nothing. Just wondered."

Leaving his best posh voice hanging in the air Frankie re-joined Bert and the two headed back to their van.

Unknown to the pair, the Blade had driven past the car showroom not only to check on the two, in his eyes, incompetents but to see for himself the lay of the land.

After all, he had a murder to commit on Monday.

Chapter Four

Steve arrived at the hospital just before six o'clock. It was still Friday the 13th but he felt he'd been on the go for days. As he walked through the main entrance, he was surprised to see Twiggy, Poppy and Matt Conway sitting in the reception area. The coffee table between the seats appeared to be covered in bunches of flowers, parcels of various sizes and an enormous teddy bear.

"What are you all doing here?" Steve was surprised but pleased to see his colleagues.

Matt spoke for the group. "Well, I told Poppy you were now a father." Like a variety act, Matt handed over to Poppy.

"And I called Flo because I know your wife would want her to know."

Steve opened his mouth but before any sound came out Poppy was talking again. "Don't ask, sir, it's a girl thing."

Twiggy was next in line to speak. "And I suggested some of us should visit Alison and your baby tonight."

"And I persuaded Matt to drive us here." Poppy looked pleased with herself.

Steve was lost for words and a plan. He hadn't thought anyone from the team would visit the hospital. "Well, thanks. Look, let me go to see Alison and tell her you're here. I think visiting on the day of a birth is limited to an hour so give me a while and I'll come and get you."

Steve approached the bed and gave his wife a hug and a long, slow kiss. "Slow down, boy. You've had your way with me before and that's why I'm here." She kissed him on the cheek. "I'm not ready just yet. You'll have to give me a few days." They both laughed and Steve hugged his wife again. He lay on the bed beside her and put his arm around her.

"How are you feeling?"

"I'm fine, just a bit tired. They've told you I'll get home on Monday. Because I'm regarded as an older mother, they'll keep me in an extra day."

Steve just nodded.

"I brought you flowers and chocolates." She could see that as he'd laid them on a corner chair as he entered the room. He became more serious. "Have you thought of a name yet?"

"Well, I thought maybe after my mother. She was called Isobel."

"Hm. Isobel Burt. Not bad."

"You never told me your mother's name."

"It was Rosemary."

Alison sounded the words. "Rosemary Burt. It has a certain ring to it." Alison pulled slightly away from her husband's embrace. "What about Rosemary Isobel Burt?"

The pair were now looking directly at each other their faces only inches apart. "Yes, I like that."

"Is that it then? We've named our baby?"

Alison giggled and kissed her husband hard on the lips. "Yes." She seemed very happy. "We'll call her Rosie."

Steve could see his wife was overjoyed and admitted he felt the same. Little Rosie would change their lives, but for the better.

"Oh! You've got visitors, I'll just get them." Steve left his wife wondering who might visit her in hospital.

Twiggy was first in, followed by Poppy and Matt. Alison knew Twiggy very well and apart from being her patient, they were firm friends. Poppy and Matt were less well known to her, but she was pleased to see them. The DCI stood back and let the visitors do the talking and ask their questions. He heard Alison say, "Seven pounds six ounces.

The scrum around Alison's bed continued until the pretty Irish nurse arrived to herd them out. On the chair in the corner of the room were several gift-wrapped boxes, two bunches of flowers and two teddy bears. One was bigger than Rosie and the other was the size of Steve's hand. The nurse said she would be back to sort out what she called "The mess on the chair". Steve was last to leave, saying he'd be back tomorrow.

In the reception area the team stood talking until Matt said "Boss, there's a great pub around the corner. Why don't we go and wet your daughter's head?"

Twiggy spoke first. "Great idea but I can't; I don't drink and I've an appointment in half an hour with my personal trainer."

Poppy said she had to be somewhere else and as Matt had suggested it Steve felt obliged to go.

"Well, it seems it's only us, Matt, let's go."

The pair adjourned to the Anchor Pub just around the corner from the hospital. Matt bought the beer and as it was delivered to their table he toasted the DCI, his wife and their new baby.

Steve was touched and after his first mouthful of beer realised how thirsty he was and how uptight he'd become over the past twelve hours. He visibly relaxed in Matt's company, sunk his pint and ordered two more.

As the evening and the third pint progressed, Steve asked Matt about himself. He saw in front of him a well-built man in his late twenties or early thirties, with a full head of black hair and a round face verging on flabby. Steve knew he was five foot nine inches tall and estimated his weight at around 160 lbs. As always, he was wearing a light sports jacket, white shirt, and his favoured, chino trousers.

"Well, I've always been a copper. I left school and joined as a cadet. I'm now 29 years old and after eleven years I've reached the dizzy rank of sergeant." Matt was staring into his beer. "Peter Jones is younger than me and he's already an inspector purely because he's a fast-track graduate entrant." Matt looked squarely at the DCI. "Please don't think I'm moaning, sir. It's just every so often I get a bit down thinking of my career prospects. I suppose that's why I wanted to be on your team. I don't know if you know it, but guys like me are clamouring to get into Special Resolutions. They know we get the difficult cases and that our clear-up rate's the best in the Met. The general feeling is if anyone does well in your unit they get noticed. Look at Andy Mills. He was a constable but got noticed and is now a DS with Inspector on the horizon. I could go on but I'm very happy to be here sir and happy to have the opportunity to show you what I can do."

Steve drained his beer. "Matt. First, it's Steve when we're away from the crowd. Second, we're a team so you should avoid grandstanding thinking it'll get you noticed. It won't, maybe even the reverse and third it's my shout. Same again?"

The evening ended after the fourth pint. Matt told his boss more about his private life which he admitted was pretty boring. He didn't have a steady girlfriend and lived in a two-bedroom flat that he rented.

Only Matt had his car but decided to leave it parked and collect it the next day. Both men went home in separate taxis.

***

Steve visited his wife twice on Saturday and unknown to her he'd bought a five-litre tub of bright pink paint and had started re-painting the nursery. They had decided to paint it in a neutral colour to suit either sex, but Steve wanted Rosie to be all-female right from the start, hence his newly acquired DIY painting skills.

He was able to hold his daughter for long periods during his Saturday visits and loved every second of it before she was snatched away to the nursery which seemed to happen at regular intervals. Alison had had a long hot bath after breakfast and in Steve's eyes looked stunning, and he told her so.

"Well thank you, sir, but don't think I don't need help with Rosie. You'd better take at least a week's paternity leave."

"A week, but I'm allowed months!"

"Listen, DCI Burt, I'm the mother of your child. You can't fool me. After a week you'll get withdrawal symptoms and need to go chasing bad guys again. So, you're on warning, I need you for one week and then you can go back." Alison was smiling fondly at her husband. Rosie was in the nursery. Steve held his wife tightly and kissed her passionately on the lips. "What did I do to deserve you, Dr Mills?"

Alison returned his kiss, pushed him away and told him his time was up but not before telling him. "You're not the only one who got lucky. And by the way, I hope you've not got pink paint all over the nursery carpet?"

Steve was surprised. He'd hoped to keep his DIY activities a secret and a surprise. "How the hell did you know?"

"I'm married to a detective. You've got pink paint under your nails and on the back of your hands." Alison was giggling. "I've got you bang to rights, mister."

***

Sunday the 15th of March saw Steve collect his wife and daughter from the hospital, and drive them home. He knew as soon as they entered their apartment that life as they'd known it would never be the same. He tried to help but knew he was getting in the way of Alison's carefully rehearsed plans.

"Go and sit down. Open a bottle of wine or something. I have everything covered."

And so, it went on for a week, Steve helping where he could especially if Rosie cried out during the night. Alison was occasionally exasperated by his clumsy attempts to help but in the evenings after Rosie had been fed and prepared for bed the pair sat with their daughter just enjoying each other company and marvelling at the new human being resting on Steve's lap.

Steve had called Commander Alfie Brooks and told him he would be back on Monday the 23rd of March. He called Poppy with the good news and asked her to arrange for Peter, Matt and Mary to be in at nine for a briefing.

The DCI felt refreshed from his break and his newly found domestic contentment.

If he had known what awaited him on his return to work, he might not have been so keen to cut short his paternity leave.

***

As the DCI was getting used to having a baby in the house, the Voice was switching off his mobile phone. It was a pay as you go, and he knew such phones were referred to as burner phones.

He'd just finished a short but profitable conversation with his contact in Russia. He looked at the writing pad on his desk on which he'd written three lines. Each line read the same. Make of car and model, colour and maximum mileage. Such calls were becoming more frequent as was the seventy-five thousand pounds the Voice would receive for shipping these three cars albeit in parts.

He sat back in his plush executive leather chair and allowed himself to daydream. He saw himself as a self-made man, a man of the people and an example of what hard work and street-smart intelligence could achieve. He was 52 years old, stood five foot ten inches, still had a full mane of soft greying hair and was remarkably slim still fitting into 33-inch waist trousers. He was wealthy by any standards. He lived well, was well regarded within his circle, was seen to be successful but he recognised his character flaw. He was the type of person who would take a shortcut if he saw one and didn't mind breaking the law to achieve his aims. He also recognised a ruthlessness in his character that so far had served him well.

He had several business ventures on the go but his latest deal with the Russian had proven the most lucrative. He knew his public profile was admired and people close to him had him earmarked for great things. However, while his main business interest was publishing, he was aware that lately, he'd become involved in the seamier and illegal side of making money.

He'd met Vlad at a trade show a few months ago although he suspected Vlad wasn't his real name. The Russian spoke perfect English and was touting for work representing British firms in Russia. The Voice took an immediate liking to Vlad and the two got on well.

He allowed himself to drift into another world of reminiscences and opportunities. He recalled Vlad suggesting they have dinner for which he paid. He remembered Vlad drinking vodka by the bucket and himself joining in. The clear liquid was like a fire going down his throat and although he didn't drink anything like the volume Vlad had drunk, he was nonetheless very merry as they left the restaurant. Vlad insisted they move on to a gentlemen's club he knew and after more vodka and scantily dressed girls sitting on his knee, the Voice and Vlad took a room in a nearby hotel for the night, each accompanied by a girl from the club.

The Voice didn't normally allow himself to get so drunk, but he remembered his delight through his drunken haze at the prospect of enjoying his companion's body. He allowed a slight smile to appear on his face as he remembered the girl. She was large in all the right places and was obviously no stranger to the nude male torso.

Then he remembered the ending of his drunken night of passion with some regret and a feeling of shame. The girl had started performing a sex act on him that seemed impossible. Just as she got herself into some contorted position over him a flash exploded in his eye. Someone had taken a photograph of him and the girl. At that point, he jumped out of bed, but the photographer was gone, and he couldn't give chase due to his lack of clothes. For a moment he thought about the girl and wondered how her impossibly contorted position hovering over him would have finished up. With a shrug, he told himself he'd never know.

Next morning nursing a bad hangover, the Voice met Vlad for breakfast in the hotel dining room. It was obvious Vlad was behind the photograph and that the whole evening had been a set-up.

He recalled the conversation. Vlad had explained that he could be useful to him on several fronts. They were to work together, and that the photograph would never be sent to the newspapers, so long as he cooperated. Vlad knew the Voice couldn't afford a scandal.

"So, what do I have to do?"

"Nothing except get even richer than you are now." Vlad settled back in his chair but kept his voice low. "You see in my country we have very wealthy people who crave the luxuries of the West. Especially motor cars but the west doesn't like us and makes it difficult for these people to have what they want." Vlad paused to look at the Voice to see if he was following this narrative.

Satisfied Vlad carried on. "I am a member of a group dedicated to supplying our rich brothers with their hearts' desires, especially cars. Unfortunately, all the cars these people desire are here in England. What we need is to have someone here who can…" Vlad raised his eyebrows in a conspiratorial manner "… *liberate* these desirable pieces of metal and ship them to Mother Russia. It's simple and we'll pay a great fee for each car we receive."

Each man stared at the other. Vlad with a grin on his face; the Voice deep in thought.

"Are you mad? You expect me to go out and steal cars and ship them to you?" He recalled how taken aback he was by Vlad's proposal.

"Yes, but my friend, *you* don't do the work. Go out and find someone who knows cars and can be persuaded to help you."

As he slowly surfaced from his nostalgic moments, he recalled that Vlad had been insistent and had reminded him of the existence of the photograph. He also remembered Vlad mentioning that he could be useful to his associates in other areas as yet unspecified.

The Voice shook himself back to the present, opened the bottom drawer of his desk and retrieved a small portable typewriter. He pulled on latex gloves, retrieved a piece of A4 paper and inserted it into the machine. He typed using one finger exactly what Vlad had said during the phone call. That done, he inserted a label into the typewriter and again with one finger typed out Eddie Randall's address. He attached it to an envelope, placed the single sheet of paper into the envelope and sealed it without leaving any DNA that might be salvaged later.

By posting it early on this Saturday morning Eddie would receive it by Monday and another illegal venture would be set in motion.

***

The Voice walked to the post box, noticing how quiet this part of London was. Meanwhile, Eddie Randall was in his office having a beer with the Blade. He knew the owner of the car showroom had to be killed Monday, and that the Blade would have to do it. Eddie wanted to discuss the plan.

Eddie explained how he wanted the killing to look. "Nothing subtle, this is a message. People have to see and know this geezer was murdered. You got it?"

The Blade was as usual sprawled over the armchair using his flick knife to clean his nails. "Yeah. I get it. But why?"

"Never you mind. That's how I want it." There was silence in the so-called office as both men sized each other up. It was clear the Blade didn't trust Eddie, but it was Eddie who paid him. He concluded that if he were careful then Eddie couldn't do him any harm.

Based on the intelligence or lack of it that Bert and Frankie had gathered, Eddie proceeded to brief the Blade.

"The guy should be in his office after two o'clock. I've had Frankie and Bert look the place over. They say there are two half-glass offices along the back wall. The showroom's like a hanger, you know long and narrow. The target uses the right-hand office as you look in from the road. There's a filling station right next door."

"Yeah. I know, I took a drive over there to check up on your two idiots. It's my neck if I get caught and I'm not about to put any faith in those two clowns. I didn't stop but I drove past a few times."

"Good. So, here's the plan. Frankie and Bert will drive you over to Mile End in that Granada I just took in. It has false plates so there's no danger of it being linked back here. I figure if you leave the car, and it waits by the kerb you should be in and out in less than a minute. Frankie's a good driver so once you've done the deed, you're out and away. If you leave here around two tomorrow afternoon, the geezer you're after should be there."

The Blade was sceptical. It sounded too easy, but he had to agree it was a simple plan except for the part involving the two clowns. Eddie saw the worry on the Blade's face. "Don't worry, I'll put the fear of God in both of them. They'll do exactly as they're told."

The Blade unwound himself from his chair and stood up. He tossed his beer can into a bin in the corner. "They'd better do as they're told. I'm not doing a life stretch just because they screwed up. If I'm caught, I won't stay quiet."

Eddie was alarmed by this statement but pretended not to be concerned. "They'll be fine. Just be here on Monday before two o'clock and get the job done. There's ten grand in it for you."

The mention of money cheered the Blade up. He left smiling saying he'd be back on Monday.

Eddie wasn't normally given over to worrying but the Blade's remark about squealing if he were caught had unnerved him. He realised he was the man in the middle. If the police ever called, he would have no idea who this Voice was. He recalled the ruthlessness of the man when he ordered the killing of Vince Maguire.

Vince had, in a way, introduced the Voice to Eddie. The Voice had asked if Vince knew a reliable and trustworthy person who didn't mind bending the rules for money and knew about cars, and Vince had given him Eddie's number.

The Voice had called a few days later and asked if Eddie could steal a 7 series BMW in metallic grey with less than 5000 miles on the clock. If he could he'd be paid three thousand pounds.

"I'll call you in 24 hours. If you have the car, I'll tell you where to deliver it. If you don't, you won't hear from me again."

Nicking the car was easy. All Eddie did was cruise the West End until he spotted a car that matched what he needed. He got lucky when he drove it away as it showed only 3219 miles on the clock. Frankie and Bert drove Eddie to the West End and took his car back to the compound following the Beemer.

Since then, Eddie hadn't had to steal a car for the Voice but had been ordered to do some dangerous things like killing Vince Maguire. The Voice explained through his electronic voice distorter: "I can't have any loose ends, Eddie. Just take care of Vince and as he's a friend of yours I'll double the fee to twenty grand."

Eddie remembered the killing and the Blade's pure joy as he sank his stiletto blade into Vince's neck. It was Vince's body that Frankie and Bert had disposed of down the railway embankment.

Eddie shuddered at the thought. He was glad he wouldn't be present at this second killing ordered by the Voice. But Eddie couldn't work out why this Cameron Bowie had to die. He thought about it, and concluded, *Maybe I'll find out soon.*

Chapter Five

An envelope was delivered to Eddie Randall on Monday the 16th of March as promised by the Voice. Again, Eddie examined it for clues but could find nothing to indicate who the Voice might be or help track him down.

Yet again there was a single piece of paper, and on it were just three lines of type.

AUDI Q8 — DARK COLOUR — NO MORE THAN 5000 MILES
LAND ROVER DEFENDER — GREY COLOUR — NO MORE THAN 2000 MILES
JAGUAR — RED COLOUR — NO MORE THAN 5000 MILES.

Eddie studied the paper. It was clear these were cars the Voice wanted Eddie to steal, just like the BMW he'd nicked a couple of weeks ago.

Eddie put the paper back in the envelope and placed it in the top drawer of his desk. It was 10.25 a.m. He hadn't seen the Blade, and he had to brief Bert and Frankie on what he wanted them to do in the afternoon. He stepped up to his office door and saw his two key workers leaning against an old Ford Cortina, smoking.

As the boss he needed more productivity from these two, even though, as he'd explained to them, they weren't on his payroll. "Get that Granada washed." Eddie pointed to the biggest car on his lot. "I've got a job for you this afternoon. Come and see me when it's clean."

The two not overly bright key employees sauntered away from the Cortina in the direction of the Granada mumbling about not being appreciated.

***

46

DI Peter Jones was finishing a team meeting with the officers in DCI Burt's team as Eddie struggled on with his day ahead. Peter was now the acknowledged number two and he'd been instructed by Commander Alfie Brooks to keep everyone busy.

Alfie had ensured the team had enough to do but avoided giving them any high-profile cases. Although he felt the team had potential, he knew that without Steve Burt to lead them they might flounder if given any of the usual difficult cases the DCI's unit was used to.

So, while Steve was away, it was a week of tidying up other departments more straightforward cases. They were handling a case of a suspicious death that the perpetrator had already confessed to, a serial robbery case where the culprit was targeting low-end hotels, they had a case of pilfering at a high-end electronics manufacturing company and a hit and run. It was the latter that was proving the most difficult and therefore interesting.

Commander Brooks knew the unit known as Special Resolutions was better than these cases and suspected the team would complain, but not to him. Steve would get an earful on his return.

DI Jones had allocated tasks covering the investigations into all four cases and the team were now working on those. Peter Jones felt it would be a slow week.

***

Frankie and Bert finished washing the Ford Granada and once seated in Eddie's office reminded him washing alone wouldn't remove the rust from the car nor fill in the rust holes on the wings.

Eddie ignored their comments. "Right. Now, at about two o'clock the Blade needs you to drive to that garage in Mile End Road. He's got a job to do so you two had better not screw up." He stared at both his key workers who stared blankly back.

"You're to pull up kerb-side in front of the showroom. Keep the engine running and be ready to pull away as soon as the Blade gets back in." Eddie again stared at the pair but got no sign that they understood. An exasperated Eddie shouted, "Do you bloody understand?"

In unison, the pair nodded and together said, "Yes, yes."

Eddie wasn't sure they did understand so went over it again. "You take the Blade from here to the showroom in Mile End Road you checked out on Friday. You pull up at the kerb. The Blade will get out. He'll go into the showroom, do what he has to do and return to the car. As soon as he gets back in, you pull away and drive here as quickly as you can, but don't break the speed limit and don't get pulled over by the old bill. Now have you got that?"

Bert looked a bit vacant, but Frankie was keen to impress. "Got it boss; no problems." He looked at his partner who nodded. "Do we get a bonus?"

Eddie had expected this and took the easy way out. With a sigh, he answered. "Yes Frankie, you'll both get a hundred quid each. But remember, no slip-ups."

Frankie and Bert didn't hear anything after the 'one hundred pounds each' bonus. They both stood in a daze at the thought of all that money. "Which car do we take, boss?"

Eddie wondered why he used this pair of idiots, but just said, "The Granada." Then he answered his own question realising they were cheap.

The Blade arrived as planned just before two. The four conspirators held a final briefing led by Eddie. The Blade again stated that he didn't really want Frankie and Bert anywhere near the job but was overridden by Eddie.

The Ford Granada with its rusted bodywork and rust holes in the wings set off at 2.14 p.m. looking less like a gangster's getaway car and more like a car on its way to the scrapyard.

***

On Monday afternoon, the 16th of March at exactly 3.03 p.m., Frankie parked the Granada beside the kerb outside the showrooms of the Crystal Motor Company.

The Blade reminded them. "Keep the engine running. I'll be about three minutes at most."

The Blade exited the car and held the switchblade comfortably in his hand inside the right-hand pocket of his jacket. He approached the open glass doors and entered. He saw the two salesmen sitting at a desk toward the back of the showroom. They seemed to be concentrating on a game on their mobile phones. Neither looked up as the Blade, staying close to the right-hand wall, made his way towards his victim's office. He could see a grey-haired man sitting behind a desk apparently reading a newspaper. The Blade gripped his knife tightly as he felt the adrenaline rush, he always felt at such moments, course through his veins. One last glance towards the two salesmen and the Blade opened the office door and entered. The office was built using the building's two outside walls for support, meaning the other two had been built to make the office. These new walls were half-glazed, and the Blade was aware that any customer entering the showroom would see him. He vowed to be quick.

"Mr Bowie?"

"The seated man put his newspaper down and stood up expecting to shake the newcomer's hand. As he did so, the Blade with a dexterity that defied his size and shape, produced his knife from his pocket, activated the switchblade and drove the blade firmly into the heart of Mr Cameron Bowie. Bowie uttered a short and quiet scream before collapsing into his chair. The Blade closed his knife, returned it to his pocket and turned Mr Bowie's chair around so it faced the back wall. Anyone entering and looking through the glass wouldn't see the body. The Blade calculated this would buy him some time.

He quietly opened the office door, saw the two sales guys were still deeply engrossed in their game, closed the door and as slowly as his racing heart would allow, he made his way outside. As he did so he congratulated himself on a perfect job and headed back to the car.

As he exited the glass doors of the showroom and headed for the kerb, he realised the car wasn't there. For a second his heart stopped. He looked around but couldn't see the Granada anywhere. As panic set in and the realisation that he needed to get away from here right now, he heard a voice call.

"We're over here." It was Frankie.

With an incredulous look on his face, the Blade saw the car and his colleagues at the petrol pumps. Bert was pumping petrol! The Blade couldn't believe what he was seeing. He'd just killed a man no more than 75 yards from where he stood and his getaway car was being refuelled.

Anger didn't describe his mood. He ran to the car, pulled the petrol pump nozzle from Bert and replaced it.

"Get the hell in the car." Frankie was standing beside the pump and on hearing the Blade's instructions said, "I'll just go and pay."

Before the Blade could stop him, Frankie was off. The Blade got into the back of the car. He was seething and mentally cutting these imbeciles into little pieces when they got back to Eddie's place. Things couldn't get worse, but then they did. The Blade saw Frankie leave the pay station holding a bag of sweets. Instead of returning to the car, he had stopped to open his bag of sweets. With no sign of urgency, he ambled back to the car, got into the driver's seat and offered his two colleagues a sweet.

The Blade exploded. He smashed his open hand into Frankie's hand scattering the sweets inside the car. "You bloody moron, you bought bloody jelly babies. Idiot!" The Blade was fuming. "Just get us out of here now!" he screamed at Frankie.

As Frankie drove off the forecourt the Blade had a thought. Maybe these idiots had done him a favour. If anybody was looking for suspicious characters to tie to the murder, they'd certainly discount this pair and whoever heard of putting petrol in a getaway car as the job's taking place, never mind buying jelly babies.

Owing to his pent-up anger and high adrenaline level, the Blade suddenly burst into uncontrollable laughter. Bert and Frankie, knowing nothing, joined in and the three made their escape laughing with the Blade saying over and over again, "No bugger would believe it."

***

The trio arrived back at Eddie's office without incident. As the Blade left the car and entered the office, both Frankie and Bert were climbing all over the interior of the car rescuing jelly babies.

Eddie was keen to learn if the operation had been a success.

"Yes, but no thanks to Bill and bloody Ben out there." The Blade went on to explain that the pair decided the car needed petrol and to top it off Frankie bought sweeties before they drove off.

"I tell you what Eddie," the Blade was laughing as he told the tale, "those two are priceless, but they're a menace."

The tears welled up in Eddie's eyes and his over-large stomach hurt from laughing.

Bert and Frankie strolled up to the office having recovered most of the jelly babies. They entered the smoky atmosphere without a care in the world. These two emaciated five-foot-nothing, one-hundred-and-fifty-pound idiots acted as though they didn't realise they were now accessories in a murder, nor how close they had been to blowing the whole thing.

"Boss. We put petrol in the motor, I got a receipt. It's six quid." Bert offered the receipt obviously expecting to be reimbursed. Frankie was looking for the black jelly babies and, finding he'd already eaten them, offered the packet to Eddie.

"Want a sweetie boss, the black ones are finished."

Eddie looked across to the Blade. Both men were incredulous but couldn't help another bout of raucous laughter. The centre of the amusement looked at one another and they too started laughing without knowing why.

Eddie resolved to get rid of his two long-standing self-employed staff members but was relieved at the Blade's reaction. It could have been a lot worse.

***

Tuesday the 17th of March dawned grey and unfriendly. Eddie was in his office early to receive his call from the Voice. He'd received his coded message as a reminder. He opened his phone and stared at it. The text message simply read O (for office), 09 (for nine o'clock in the morning), and (T for Tuesday.)

That was it. Nine o'clock Tuesday morning.

As Eddie waited, he again thought who the Voice might be but couldn't come close to working it out.

At 09.00 exactly Eddie's burner phone shrilled. He answered on the first ring.

"Good. On time as always Eddie, I like that. Did you take care of the other business yesterday? I haven't heard anything on the news."

"The job's done. No sweat."

"Good." There was a pause as the Voice seemed to consider Eddie's reply. "Yes, very good."

Eddie remained silent in anticipation the Voice would explain the paper with the cars written on it.

"You stole a BMW a few weeks ago. That was good work and good work should be rewarded. The Beemer was a test as is the sheet of paper you received yesterday. I want you to steal these three models. You have a week. Keep them covered in your yard, and I'll call next Monday the 23rd and tell you where to take them. Can you do this?"

"Yes, piece of cake."

"Good. Now if you perform well, you'll receive a payment of thirty thousand pounds. That's ten thousand pounds a car. If you perform, I'll make you my main car man and you'll be stealing up to six cars a week. That's sixty thousand a week."

Eddie could count and was pleased to be becoming more indispensable to the Voice. This gave him more courage.

"I'm flattered and I won't let you down, but can I ask you something?"

Eddie felt the tension coming from his phone, but he ploughed on. "Why did you want Cameron Bowie murdered in such a public way?"

There was a long silence followed by a long sigh. "All right, just this once. Cameron Bowie and I worked together. He was my old car man just as you are my new car man if you perform this week. Unfortunately, he got greedy and set up deals behind my back. My contacts didn't like it, especially as he was using our people to split the vehicles down and ship them. The more public killing was a warning to others. If you step out of line, you're dead." The Voice stopped talking before starting again.

"Do you get the message, Eddie?"

Eddie was sweating knowing it was his predecessor the Blade had dispatched. "Yes sir, I get it."

"Very good. Now get out and find those cars. We have customers waiting."

The Voice failed to inform Eddie that although his payday of ten thousand a car was generous, he, himself, would make thirty thousand a car now he didn't have to split the total proceeds with his ex and now dead partner.

Eddie knew he couldn't trust his staff to steal the cars, but they could drive him around until he found what he was looking for. He knew where such vehicles could be found. He and his staff driving the same rusted Ford Granada they had used in the killing of Eddie's predecessor, cruised Pall Mall and the streets surrounding it. They got lucky. Eddie decided to start straight away and so on the same day, he spotted the correct model and colour Jaguar being valet parked by a bellhop from one of the vast hotels fronting Pall Mall.

Eddie took Frankie and Bert out to try to educate them into the big time but all they did was let their jaws drop at the sheer wealth in this part of London.

"Did you see that, Frankie?"

"Er, no boss."

Eddie wasn't in a forgiving mood and laid into Frankie, explaining he wasn't along for the ride but to spot cars. He could see neither of his employees understood. Again, Eddie determined to get rid of them.

Sitting in the back being chauffeur driven, Eddie told Frankie to pull up outside the main hotel entrance, much to the annoyance of the doorman.

Acting as though they were eccentric millionaires and with Frankie using his refined voice character, Eddie told the doorman to valet park the car. The doorman knew they occasionally got oddball clients and against his better judgement rang for the valet parking porter.

Frankie still acting dropped the keys into the young porter's hand. "Make sure you don't scratch it. It's a rare model."

Eddie laughed inwardly at Frankie attempt at class especially dressed as he was in an old, stained t-shirt and holes in his tennis shoes. As soon as the car was coaxed away with a stream of blue smoke exiting the exhaust pipe, Eddie slapped his forehead with the palm of his hand.

"Oh! No, I've left my papers in the car." This was said for the doorman's benefit and turning to the doorman, Eddie asked, "How do I get to the garage; I need my papers?"

The doorman, relieved that the trio wasn't making any effort to enter the hotel, was only too pleased to direct them to a service stair that led to the garage. Once in the garage, Eddie spotted the Jaguar. He knew this model was difficult to open but seeing his own car parked, he opened the boot, selected a tool from an old briefcase and had the Jag opened in less than a minute.

"Right, you two go back up. Tell the valet guy you need the car, and you'll collect it yourself from the car park. Here's twenty quid. He should give you a ticket to operate the barrier so you can get out." Eddie once more looked at the blank expressions on the faces of his staff. He made a decision.

"On second thoughts, you two wait in the Granada. I'll be back in ten minutes."

Exactly eleven minutes later Eddie appeared with the ticket. He handed it to Frankie. "Now Frankie, just drive out. Put this in the slot by the barrier and the barrier will lift, I'll be right behind you in the Jag. Have you got it?"

It was clear Frankie understood but continually looked at the Jag. Eddie knew he was wondering how you could get two cars out with only one ticket.

"Don't worry Franke. Just get the Granada out of here and back to the yard." Eddie thought sometimes too much information was dangerous especially when dealing with adult children.

As the barrier opened and the rusted Granada exited the car park Eddie raced behind in order to clear the barrier before it came down.

Just over an hour later, all three were in Eddie's yard. The Jaguar was under a dust cover parked at the rear of the yard. On his drive back Eddie was pleased to note the mileage was only 3777. The Voice would be pleased.

The crack team of car hijackers performed miracles during the rest of the week. They heisted an Audi Q8 on Wednesday and a Land Rover Discovery with exactly the right specification on Friday. By Friday the 20th of March, all three cars were ready.

Eddie seated at his desk thought with pleasure that apart from a few close calls Frankie and Bert had worked well. He considered keeping them on. After all, they were cheap.

He was pleased with his week. He'd taken care of the murder of Cameron Bowie and had his longest conversation with the Voice. He'd stolen the three cars to order and had received his coded message telling him to be in his office at ten on Monday morning. The three cars would give him a nice little cash injection and he seemed to be finding favour with the Voice. The thought of being the main car man excited him. He sat dreaming of the money he'd receive month on month. He closed his eyes for a few seconds and visualised spending the money he'd earn working for the Voice.

He shook himself out of his reveries and locked up. A peaceful weekend called him. Monday was another day.

Chapter Six

Steve's team had done well while he was away. It was just after five p.m. on Friday the 20th of March and DI Peter Jones had the team together in Steve's office. He wanted to debrief them to make sure none of them had missed anything on the cases assigned to them.

After a good-natured discussion and an acknowledgement that they hadn't been overworked in the DCI's absence, Peter had the last word.

"Well done everyone. Good job. Now, remember, the boss is back on Monday so don't be late."

DS Matt Conway spoke up. "Maybe we'll get something decent to work on. Have you noticed how the DCI seems to attract difficult cases?"

"Sure, it's just coincidence but I'll bet you, after a week off he'll be keen to get his teeth into something." Peter Jones voiced what everyone was thinking.

As they left, each detective was relishing having the boss back. Somehow it wasn't the same without him.

***

Saturday and Sunday in the Burt household were a bit chaotic. Rosie hadn't settled into a sleep pattern yet and Alison, despite hiring a locum, had promised to look over a few patients' notes over the weekend. Her stand-in didn't feel comfortable with his diagnosis and wanted Alison's opinion. To cap it all off, Steve was on baby feeding and cooking duties. He struggled manfully with both but conceded Alison was better than him.

Sunday evening saw the couple settled on their sofa curled up together watching a repeat of a repeat on television. Alison reached for the remote and switched the programme off. Still folded into her husband's arms she looked at him with a serious expression on her face.

"Steve, you will be careful when you go back, won't you?"

The DCI unwound himself from his wife in order to look at her.

"What do you mean? I'm always careful."

"Yes, I know, but I also know you sometimes get yourself into dangerous positions." Alison sat further back from her husband. "You see, I've been reading this article in the *BMA Journal*. It was about men in dangerous jobs. This study from the States said that such men, presented with more responsibilities in their domestic lives, like a baby, are less likely to be so positive in their jobs. It found that fatalities among such people increased fourfold. It said given a situation where being positive and sure in their own abilities was the correct decision, sometimes these men held back a few extra seconds thinking about their new situation and this delay put them in more danger. This led in some cases to them being killed or injured due to the delay in their actions."

"I can see that, but I don't get myself into dangerous situations any more. Not after this doctor I know got herself shot during one of my cases." Steve was referring to a previous case that ended with Alison being seriously injured.

Alison Burt leant forward and lightly punched her husband on the arm. With a big grin, she looked straight at him. "Yes, that's what you say now." She paused and her facial expression changed to her most serious look. "You do know what I'm saying, darling. Tomorrow will be your first day as a DCI with a baby."

Steve shuffled up the sofa and cradled his wife in his arms. He stroked her hair. "Yes, I know what you mean, and I promise to remember it."

If the DCI knew what Monday the 23rd of March would bring, he might have phrased it better.

***

Monday the 23rd of March dawned promising some fine weather. The DCI arrived at his office early and was surprised to see his team were already there. After being congratulated on his new arrival and acknowledging the welcome back he settled down behind his desk with a large coffee provided by Poppy.

Steve called everyone into his inner office for a debrief and had to listen to their mild complaints about the cases they'd been given over the past week, just as the Commander had thought.

"Everything's tied up Steve," DI Peter Jones as Steve's official number two said, "Only the usual paperwork to organise."

"Good. Well done, everyone. You carry on and I'll look at what's here." Steve pointed to a pile of internal envelopes on his desk.

By 09.20 a.m., the DCI had cleared the envelopes and was sitting looking at a form he had to complete. He called out to DC Mary Dougan to come in. As she closed the internal office door behind her, Mary wondered what was going on.

Steve laughed. "Don't look so apprehensive. You're not in any trouble. It's just that HR needs your six-monthly progress report and appraisal."

The detective constable immediately looked relieved and relaxed. She sat in front of her boss' desk.

"So, Mary, you've been with us six months. Any thoughts or comments?"

"No sir. It's been great. I've really enjoyed it but I'm hoping for more exposure to the really difficult cases you usually work on."

Steve opened Mary's file. He knew she was a graduate entrant and bright. He liked her dress code of always wearing a dark coloured trouser suit and styling her hair in a ponytail. The DCI thought she looked like a poster girl for exactly what she was: the public face of policing. She was pretty enough and wore very little make-up. Her sophisticated vocal tones hid her knowledge of and occasional use of police jargon and street expletives. Steve thought his newest DC had real potential.

"I know I was designated your mentor and that the last six months haven't been very exciting caseload wise, but I'm reporting that you have settled in well and have shown good initiative when it was called for."

Mary said nothing but nodded. She knew this was a fair assessment but not the glowing report she had hoped for. She also knew the right cases hadn't been there to be worked but vowed to put herself forward when the next big case broke.

Steve talked to his DC for a further ten minutes promising to work more closely with her and encouraging her to carry on.

As Mary was leaving Steve's phone rang. It was the Commander. "Welcome back; I need you here at ten." The line disconnected. As Steve returned the receiver to its cradle, he thought Alfie had been unnecessarily sharp.

***

While the DCI had been interviewing his colleague, Eddie Randall answered his burner phone on the first ring. He knew it would be the Voice.

"Did you get the cars?"

"Yes. It was easy enough. I've got a beau—"

"I don't need selling to. Just the facts."

Eddie could detect a tension from the Voice despite the electronic distortion.

"Yes. I have the cars."

"Good. Take them to the workshop behind Crystal Motors on Mile End Road. Take them one at a time starting with the Jag. Have it there at eleven o'clock today. Go through the petrol station and around the back of the showroom and ask for Rory McClean. He'll tell you when he needs the other two delivered. Do you understand?"

Eddie didn't understand and said so. "We did that guy in last Friday in his showroom on your orders. The cops will be all over the shop and you expect me to drive a stolen motor into a crime scene full of police. Are you mad!" Eddie was panicking and visualised his payday disappearing or himself in handcuffs.

The Voice was ominously silent. "Eddie, I do not like explaining my orders. This is the last time and only as you are new, but never again. Do you understand? I expect total compliance." The Voice paused as though expecting Eddie to confirm he understood but Eddie was taken aback by the Voice's statement and said nothing.

"Firstly, and as I explained already, the death of Cameron Bowie was a warning and therefore needed to be public. Secondly, the police at the scene are homicide detectives, not car crime boys. They won't know one stolen car from another and certainly won't have been briefed to look out for our cars. Thirdly, they will only be interested in the showroom. The workshop behind is a separate and legitimate business. All that will happen is the staff of the workshop will be interviewed as potential witnesses but none of them can tell the police anything. Lastly, the enquiry will be winding down and I doubt if anyone will be there except a uniform guarding the door. By tomorrow the murder will be filed away. If you've done your job right then by the end of the week the file will be archived." An electronic sigh was next. "Now do you understand?"

Eddie was amazed at the logic of the Voice. He surmised he had to be a copper to know these things but kept that thought to himself.

"Yes, I understand." Eddie thought he might try for more information. "But how do you know all this?"

"Eddie, you didn't listen. Never question my instructions nor ask unnecessary questions. Now move on and get the Jag delivered this morning."

The line disconnected leaving Eddie with an earful of static.

***

At exactly ten a.m., the DCI entered the office of Commander Alfie Brooks. The big man was resplendent in his uniform, as always, standing by his office's floor to ceiling window apparently just staring at the view. As Steve walked in Alfie turned, waved and called to his gatekeeper-cum-secretary. "Three coffees, please, Hilda."

He pointed to his conference table inviting Steve to sit down.

"How's the family?"

Steve explained at some length his new domestic situation. He knew he sounded overexcited and gave Alfie too much detail, but he was a proud father and happy with his life.

"It'll take some getting used to, but Alison wants me out from under her feet. She's really great with Rosie and well organised so I'm better here."

The gatekeeper arrived with the coffee accompanied by a uniformed female inspector. From his chair, Steve summed up the new arrival. She was short for a police officer standing no more than five foot five inches. He put her age at the late fifties. She was on the tubby side and her uniform jacket was probably two sizes too big for her. Ungallantly, Steve thought she may have ambitions to fill it. Her uniform skirt was longer than regulation leading Steve to further conclude this part of her uniform might also be oversized. What the DCI could see of her legs were covered in black nylon, her flat black regulation shoes were scuffed, and her ankles were non-existent. She wasn't wearing a cap, but her short old-fashioned greying mop looked unruly enough to complete the picture of a very untidy police inspector.

"Steve. This is Inspector May Dunlop. She's head of the Child Protection Unit."

The DCI rose and shook the Inspector's hand. "Good to meet you."

May Dunlop just smiled. Despite her not too promising appearance, Steve felt a warmth being emitted by this lady. He couldn't explain it, but she had a friendly aura surrounding her. The DCI took an instant liking to this odd-looking officer.

"May called me last week with a problem and as I knew you were back today, I thought I'd like her to tell you directly."

Steve knew Alfie well enough not to take anything at face value. Whatever the reason Inspector May Dunlop thought she was here for, it wasn't what she thought.

The Inspector had three thin buff-coloured files in front of her. She started talking without reference to any of them.

"Mr Burt, my unit—"

"Please, Steve."

May assumed a 'well I should think so' pose but tried to hide it. "Steve. My unit usually deals with domestic situations where minors are involved. You know, kids are left alone while their parents disappear to the pub, that sort of thing. We work mainly with council officials, Social Services mostly. We've been going for ten years now and our involvement actually works. We're able to steer the social workers towards solutions they've never dreamt of." May paused and took on a pensive look. "Sometimes we get cases we can't handle, and I think this could be one of them." May tapped the files and spoke directly at the DCI.

"Three weeks ago, a kid we had an interest in went missing. His name was Billy Daley. He's ten years old. His mother contacted us as she knew us as the police and like all of them, they think we do everything."

May smiled a sad smile. "She was in a panic. Billy hadn't come home from school. Believe it or not, that was it. She hadn't called the school, neighbours, nothing. She waited until ten at night and rang her liaison officer who is one of my WPCs." May shook her head. "Unbelievable." She was talking to herself and quickly returned to her narrative.

"We checked the next morning. Seems Billy left with his mates to walk the half-mile home with two friends. One peeled off onto a side street where he lives and the other walked with Billy to the end of his road, but Billy never got home. He just disappeared."

The Inspector stopped talking but was still looking at Steve.

"Interesting," was his only comment.

"Then two weeks ago we had almost the same thing. Different school but an eight-year-old boy called Frank Jackson left school on his bike to cycle a mile to his house. Young Frank has been on our books almost since he was born. His homelife is shot and he's already been warned over petty stealing especially from his corner shop, cigarettes mainly. He didn't make it home and believe it or not, it was the school who contacted us to say he wasn't at school the next day. His mother hadn't missed him."

Again, May Dunlop looked enquiringly at the DCI who returned her stare but said nothing. As a new father, he was finding this sort of story disturbing, not wanting to believe some parents didn't care for their children. He could never imagine treating Rosie like this.

"Then, last week one of my caseworkers visited a Miss Vivien Strachan. She's on our books and has a son called William. She was raped when she was fifteen and William is the result. He's seven years old now and not too bright, neither is his mother. We wanted to see William and were told he was missing. Vivien admitted he hadn't come home from school the day before. We followed up and the school confirmed he'd been present and that he usually walked to and from school. It's only about a quarter of a mile. The school said he left with a friend. The friend was in class the next day, but William didn't turn up."

After a brief pause, May carried on with a pleading look on her face directed at the DCI.

"Steve, I'm concerned about what's happened to these three kids. We're not equipped to investigate this sort of thing, but you could be. We all know Missing Persons won't be able to handle this. Another kid might have vanished as we sit here. Somebody needs to look into this."

As the Inspector looked pleadingly at Steve, the Commander spoke up. "As I said May, it's a missing persons case. I don't really see how we can help."

May Dunlop spoke up addressing the Commander like an equal. "Look, Alfie Brooks, over the years I haven't asked you for one favour, despite your journey up the greasy pole. Don't give me Missing Persons, something's wrong here. Three weeks, three young boys from dysfunctional homes vanish and you say, '*Missing Persons*'!" May was beginning to raise her voice. "I don't think so and I bloody well know neither do you!"

Silence followed and Alfie looking slightly shell-shocked looked at Steve. From his body language, it was obvious he didn't want to take this case. "What do you think, Steve?"

The DCI was curious about the story. As May had said, three boys in three weeks can't just vanish. Having listened to the story he felt guilty that young children could just disappear without a parent causing more fuss. His new responsibility as a father was already weighing on his judgement but he could tell the Commander didn't want to touch it. However, Steve was intrigued and wanted to look into it. He resolved to try to play it smart.

"Well, Inspector."

"May, please."

"Well, May, the Commander's right. It's either Missing Persons or Social Services. I must say combining the police and social services is something new to me." Steve thought he was playing it smart. "But unless a body turns up, I'm not sure what we can offer. At the moment it's a Missing Persons case." Steve stole a quick glance at Alfie who was nodding and smiling in agreement. The DCI thought, *So far so good.*

But as he carried on, he saw concern appear on the Commander's features once he realised Steve wasn't finished. "However, the fact it's been three in three weeks might suggest a pattern. It can't be a kidnapping for ransom. You say the families are poor. So, unless these three boys have just taken themselves off somewhere, what are we looking at?"

Steve saw Alfie sit upright in his chair. He didn't look happy. The DCI pressed on. "It has to be some kind of abduction." The DCI was thinking and despite his plan to back Alfie into a corner and gently persuade him to take the case on, he found himself seeking answers. He was almost talking to himself. Lost in his own analysis of what he'd been told. "If it's abduction, why? And what happens if there is another one this week? Are we looking at a serial abductor and if so why kids from poor homes?"

Steve forgot about his plan with Alfie. "Sir, I think we should look into this. It seems there are too many links to a serial abductor and that usually leads to bodies. If we can get to the bottom of it before it goes too far, we'll save young lives."

May thumped the table. "Bravo DCI Burt, everything I've heard about you is true." She stared at the Commander, who gave a resigned shrug.

"Yes, May, I dare say everything you've heard is true, but you haven't heard how he gives me a real pain in the bum by looking for awkward cases and I dare say this will be one of them." Alfie sighed. It was two against one and he didn't feel like an argument. "Right, pass over your files and contacts but remember May, it's now our case. I don't want you interfering. Clear?"

Inspector May Dunlop was gushing as she stood and slid her three thin files over the table in Steve's direction. "You know me, Alfie."

Smiling a warm smile, the Commander replied. "Yes, I do, that's the problem."

Inspector May Dunlop was happy as she waddled rather than walked out of the Commander's office, telling Steve she'd get all available information to him, and she'd keep in touch.

The DCI was about to leave when Alfie Brooks called him back, shouted for two more coffees and said, "We're not finished yet. You may regret having been taken in by May Dunlop but don't worry about it, better men than we have suffered. She's nothing to look at but she's a tiger if she thinks she can make a difference to her clients' lives. Just watch out."

As the coffee was served, Alfie walked to his desk and returned holding what was obviously a murder file. The DCI sat up expectantly.

Alfie sat down and patted the file. "There was a murder last Friday, the 20th, at a car showroom in the Mile End Road." Alfie sipped his coffee. "Nothing special, the owner was knifed in his office and just left sitting in his chair. The murder squad DI who had the case put it down to a falling out among competitors or a mini turf war over car sales. He went through the motions but with no forensics or witnesses he's filed it as active but low priority."

Steve raised his left eyebrow. "But you think there's more to it?"

"Strangely, no I don't, but someone else does." Alfie was enjoying dragging his story out. "A railway work party discovered a body on an embankment beside the main line into Victoria Station a week or so ago. Nothing strange except the body was bound in an old blanket and tied with plastic ties. You know the sort you get in garden centres?"

Steve nodded.

"Right. Well, the pathologist who did the post-mortem on our railway body also posted the car dealer Saturday morning just past. She highlighted that both bodies had been stabbed and cut, with what seemed to be the same blade. She says it could be a stiletto blade and very distinctive. The knife has a double-edged blade and tapers to a point. It's about six inches long so a pretty fearsome weapon."

"Is the pathologist linking the two bodies?"

"No. There's no forensics to connect them and she says the first victim from the embankment was a bit rough. Cheap clothes, chipped nails but strangely, well fed, so not a down and out. The only connection is it could have been the same knife and that means…"

"The same killer." Steve finished Alfie's sentence.

"Exactly. Stilettos like this are rare these days. They were common enough in the seventies but not now."

"OK. I see the file. Do you want me to take a look?"

"Yes, but tread softly. This is hot off the press and the DI from the murder squad doesn't know it could be a multiple murder case. I'll bring it up at the case review meeting later this week, but I want you to make a start now. I've a horrible feeling about these deaths. Don't know why, just a gut thing."

The DCI stood and laughed a short laugh. "The famous Brooks' gut. It's been years since I've heard that! But I seem to remember it was never too far off."

Both men walked to the office door, Steve promised to keep his senior officer apprised of progress in both cases and left to return to the eighth floor and his own offices.

Chapter Seven

In a remote part of Yorkshire near Wetherby, the three armed services had recently built what appeared to be a pre-recruitment selection centre. Its purpose was to test applicants both male and female for their suitability to join one of the branches of the military. It had been built in response to the high cost of accepting unvetted recruits who were either not physically or mentally suited to service life and who were dropping out in alarming numbers during their basic training.

Montgomery Barracks had apparently been established as a solution to this problem. Its purpose was to test all applicants in an attempt to slow down the attrition rate among volunteers. To call the scattered collection of precast concrete buildings a barracks was a stretch, nothing that had been built looked permanent. The whole area covered about 25 acres and was surrounded by a seven-foot-high mesh fence. The metal poles that supported the fence had been bent at 45 degrees at their top and fixed in such a way that the bent tops faced out. Barbed wire had been strung between the outwards facing ends to make climbing over the fence dangerous and difficult.

To the casual observer, everything about Montgomery Barracks was military. Anyone looking at it would see a security barrier manned by uniformed and armed troops. The guardhouse looked solid enough and a large sign saying: MONTGOMERY BARRACKS PRE-SELECTION SCHOOL was emblazoned on the roof facing the B-class road that ran past the camp. In the centre was a large concrete square where applicants for the Army, Navy and Air Force could regularly be seen marching and being shouted at by their instructors. Personnel in the uniforms of all three services could be seen walking together inside the camp and usually with a purpose. Security lights were evident around the perimeter and several army trucks and Land Rovers were neatly parked outside what looked like a temporary wooden structure that clearly acted as the base's MT section.

To the casual observer, everything was military and normal.

However, to the more experienced observer, nothing about Montgomery Barracks looked right. There were four long narrow buildings; three that were clearly the sleeping quarters for the would-be recruits and the fourth serving as an indoor firing range. There was a square building located in the centre of the camp that looked like an education block together with a small rectangular structure that had the word NAAFI stencilled on an outside wall. The only other normal structure was located behind the guard room and appeared to house the administration unit together with staff accommodations and an officers mess.

Apart from these obvious buildings, found on every military base throughout the world, it was curious that all the other buildings within the camp were small structures about 3 metres square and 2 metres high with no windows or doors. There were 22 such buildings spread throughout the base plus a slightly larger version situated in the far corner of the camp. This building had no windows, but a heavy metal door operated by a security keypad and fingerprint recognition locks.

On this dank late Monday morning in March, an officer wearing an ill-fitting RAF uniform that clearly wasn't made for him but showing the rank of a Group Captain walked to the far corner building and using his forefinger keyed in an eight-digit code then pressed his thumb on the wall-mounted scanner. On a separate keypad, he keyed in the day and the month: 23/03. After five seconds the steel door clicked open. There was an immediate pull of air from the outside that almost caused the Group Captain to stagger forward. Positively charged airlocks weren't common in military training establishments.

The Group Captain knew Montgomery Barracks was a front for more serious and dangerous work being carried out below this camp. He knew its secrets.

***

The DCI returned to his office as the Group Captain was entering the airlock at Montgomery Barracks. To his surprise, he was met by the sight of Inspector May Dunlop sitting on the edge of a desk in the outer office chatting to his entire team. Under the more intense fluorescent lighting of the office, Steve noticed the number of stains evident on her jacket, skirt and tie. He concluded this was probably the untidiest police officer he had ever worked with. The image was completed by the scuff marks on her flat shoes. The DCI surmised they had not been polished since they were new.

"May, I thought you'd left?"

"Yes well, I just wanted to fully brief you on the case." She looked conspiratorially at Steve. "You know how these things get sanitised." May nodded towards Poppy. "I was just telling young Poppy there that once you write up a file note it loses in translation. You can't write what your gut is telling you."

"Yes, we all know that Inspector, but we have work to do. I promised to keep you apprised of developments." Steve liked May but remembered Alfie's warning. As he walked into his office, May Dunlop followed.

"Look, Steve. I know the old fox upstairs has warned you off me, probably said I'd interfere." Steve opened his mouth to reply but May cut him off. "Don't bother to deny it. I've known Alfie since we were constables together. He's a kind and generous man but doesn't allow personal feelings get in the way of the job." To Steve's surprise, May sat down and started to tell Steve about her history with the Commander.

"I was at his wedding you know. I've seen his kids grow up and I get a Christmas card every year. Alfie's a good cop but as I said, I'd never ask him for a favour unless I had to." She appeared to pull herself out of her daydream. "This is the first time in a long time I've asked for his help. You saw how reluctant he was but now you have the case I want to help. My gut tells me this isn't just a missing person's case. It's a lot more."

The DCI had reached the same conclusion and understood why the Inspector wanted to help. He called his team into his office and walked to the large whiteboard attached to one wall.

Once everyone was in and seated Steve started. "For those of you who don't know, this is Inspector May Dunlop. Inspector Dunlop heads up a community project and deals with various council social services departments. She's brought us a missing persons case, although we think it might be the abduction of young vulnerable children. Why? We don't know. That's why we have the case so let's get to it." Steve was wise enough to let May introduce the victims as only someone with her background could.

She stood up, approached the whiteboard and picked up a marker pen. "The first boy to go missing was Billy Daley, aged ten years. He walked out of his school with two mates and didn't make it home." She wrote this information on the board.

"The second boy is Frank Jackson, aged eight years. Left his school on his bike to cycle the mile to his home but never arrived." Again, she added this to the board.

"The last one so far is William Strachan, aged seven years. Only lived a quarter of a mile from his school. He left as usual but never made it home." May wrote this last piece of information on the board and returned to her seat.

Steve continued.

"Right, that's the bare bones. We need to dig into the backgrounds of these kids. Peter, I want you to lead this. Matt, you work with Peter. May tells me all three kids come from broken or dysfunctional homes. Get backgrounds on the mothers, any boyfriends, drugs, alcohol, prostitution. You know the thing, speak to the school, get the opinions of their teachers. Interview their friends and try to get to know their secrets. Got it?"

DI Peter Jones as Steve's number two acknowledged he understood.

The DCI continued. "All kids have dreams and stories to tell. See if these three did and have they acted on them. Have they run off to Scotland, for example? At the moment I'm happy to call this an abduction only because it's been three weeks since the first boy went missing and nothing has been heard since. May has a theory that these boys, all from rough homes, are being targeted and so far it's been one a week. We may be looking at a fourth by the end of the week."

Steve looked at his colleagues. They were all looking very serious. "Poppy, you have the files from May. Check CCTV around the schools and go as far as the addresses we have for the boys. We might get something. Peter, let's hope this doesn't develop into a serial murder case, but you'd better check with the collator. You know, unidentified kids found dead and still waiting to be identified but start by keeping it local. I really don't think these kids have wandered far and I pray to God, we find them. Every day we don't puts them more at risk."

The DCI stopped again but had yet another thought. "Poppy, get a map of the whole area around the three schools. Better send a circular to all primary schools within a ten-mile radius warning them that kids are going missing but keep it low key. We don't want a panic but say they should look out for any odd characters hanging around the school gates."

Steve thanked May who wasn't keen to leave. She was pleased with the DCI's enthusiasm for the cases and wanted to be part of the enquiry. However, Steve was firm with the Inspector and thanked her for her input and escorted her out of the office. Without being asked Poppy left and returned with coffee for everyone.

DI Peter Jones and DS Matt Conway retreated to a corner to discuss strategy. This would be Peter's first big solo case and neither man had ever dealt with either missing persons or abduction cases before.

The DCI called everyone to order again. "Right. We also have a double homicide on our plate." Pointing to DC Mary Dougan, Steve said, "Mary, you and I will work this one, but everybody must listen in. As always, we share ideas on all our current cases, so you all need to be briefed."

The DCI stood in front of the whiteboard and leaving the notes May had made on one side, he drew a vertical line to keep both sets of notes separate.

He wrote as he spoke. "The first victim is one Vincent McGuire, low life and friend to people better than him. He has convictions for GBH, theft, pimping and armed robbery; a totally unsavoury character. His body was found by some rail track maintenance workers on a railway embankment about three miles outside Victoria Station. That was a couple of weeks ago. His throat had been cut and the body wrapped in an old blanket. The case was given to the murder squad, but they've come up empty. There's no forensics and they couldn't find a likely motive. It was filed as an open case but a couple of wet behind the ears DCs were left with the case. At the time the word was it was likely gang-related and a one-off."

Steve played with his marker pen as he gathered his thoughts. "Poppy, you've probably got the file by now. Process it as usual but use the programme Andy Miller left."

Andy Miller had been Steve's admin officer and a genius with software. He had helped the DCI solve several high-profile cases by using his vast brain to look at problems from different standpoints. He was now a Detective Sergeant with the National Crime Agency but had left behind a legacy of outstanding crime-solving tools.

"Right you are, boss."

"Good. Now, the pathologist who performed the post-mortem on our friend McGuire also performed the post on a second victim."

The DCI started to write on the board as he spoke. "The second victim is a Cameron Bowie, said to be mid-fifties. Killed between two and four on Friday afternoon in his office in his showroom. He ran a successful car dealership from the showroom on Mile End Road called Crystal Motors." Steve turned to face his team. "Seems he dealt in vintage and classic cars. Looks like he was successful, but we'd better check out his finances. Poppy, you know the thing, company accounts, banks and credit cards, the works."

Poppy raised her head from her notebook and smiled at her boss. "Got it." She secretly liked trawling through other peoples' private financial dealings but knew she'd need help if anything other than a cursory glance was required.

Steve continued. "Mr Bowie was knifed. According to the pathologist, a straight thrust into his heart. There were two staff members in the showroom but neither apparently saw anything. It was the pathologist who noticed a similarity with the McGuire killing. She's certain the same knife was used in both killings or at least two very similar and distinctive blades. She reckons a flick knife was used with a long narrow double-sided blade that has a sharp point. She says she used to see a lot of flick knife wounds early on her career and swears that's the style of knife our killer used."

"But we've nothing connecting these murders?" DC Mary Dougan was writing in her notebook and asked the question as she wrote.

"No Mary, nothing except the pathologist's instinct. Both men were complete opposites. One an out and out villain, the other a law-abiding businessman, but that'll be part of our enquiry. Trying to tie them together." The DCI carried on not wishing to miss his current train of thought.

"Poppy, the murder squad don't know we have the second case yet. They started their investigation on Saturday, so you'll have to wait until the Commander does his thing and officially releases the case to us but like I said, the file should be in your in-tray. OK?"

"Yes, that's fine."

"Good, but we can make a start. Get onto the traffic camera unit. See if they have any CCTV around the showroom for last Friday afternoon, that's when the killing took place. We might get lucky. Mary, we'll visit the second scene today. I don't suppose we'll learn very much but we have to start somewhere."

"Right, I'll call up a pool car and I'll drive." The DC suddenly seemed very self-assured.

The DCI drew the meeting to a close. "Right. Peter and Matt, you've got the abduction cases. Keep me posted every step and avoid Inspector May Dunlop. She means well but might get in the way. I'd start with the schools. Poppy can help by collating everything we know and everything you learn. There might just be a thread linking these kids and you need to find it. The best way is to get your notes to Poppy regularly. Got it?"

"Yes, Steve. No problem."

"And Mary, we have the two murders.. Get copies of the files, such as they are, from Poppy. We'll get started in an hour."

The detectives left the DCI's office in a state of nervous excitement. This was the most activity they'd had in weeks and for the team, it was their first real taste of seeing DCI Burt in action. Everyone liked what they saw of their boss.

As Steve found a few quiet moments to contemplate the new cases he realised he was a happy man. The excitement of starting new cases always gave him an adrenaline rush second to none. The only thing better was when the cases were solved. He openly smiled and agreed with himself that he really liked his job.

Just as he was coming out of his daydream, Poppy appeared with an internal envelope marked URGENT. "It's just been delivered from the

Commissioner's office." She smiled sweetly and shrugged as if saying, *I don't know what's in it.*

Steve reluctantly opened it and fell back in his chair. There were several pieces of paper and a letter on the House of Commons headed notepaper. As the DCI initially scanned the contents and re-read the information in detail, he realised he'd been ordered to attend a meeting of the Parliamentary Committee on Policing and was to give evidence to the Committee. It was signed by the Committee Chair, one Malcolm Fielding. Worse still he was ordered to attend the next day, Tuesday the 24th of March at 11.00. He noted that inside the envelope was a House of Commons security pass, a new Metropolitan Police Force security pass showing the highest level of access to all parts of New Scotland Yard and a handwritten note from the Commissioner herself.

The DCI had only met the Commissioner once and then only to be introduced. The note apologised for the short notice, said she relied on his total discretion when answering the Committee's questions and wished him good luck. She looked forward to hearing good reports of his performance.

The DCI's first instinct was to call Commander Alfie Brooks but realised it was the Commissioner herself who had ordered him to sit in front of this Committee. Running to Alfie to explain he had just taken on two difficult cases would make no difference. Reluctantly, he put everything back in the envelope and placed it in the top drawer of his desk.

***

Just after 11.33 on Monday the 23rd of March and as DCI Burt was completing his briefing and receiving his orders to attend the House of Commons, Eddie Randall drove the stolen Jaguar up to the large roller shutter door that gave access to the garage behind Crystal Motors. The door was closed but Eddie spotted a pedestrian door that had been built into the roller door. As he exited the Jaguar his two faithful servants in the guise of Bert and Frankie drove up behind him in what they told everyone was their company car. It was the old, rusted Ford Granada they'd used to drive the Blade last Friday. Eddie had told them to meet him at the workshop in order to give him a lift back to his office.

"You two stay here, don't move! Do you understand?"

Frankie was in a lippy mood this Monday. "We're not daft you know. You tell us not to move but you know that's impossible. We have to breathe and that's moving." He looked at his sidekick. "Ain't that right, Bert?"

Bert, the man of few words, nodded. "Yeah, I suppose so, Frankie."

"So, don't tell us to do impossible things, boss."

Eddie rolled his eyes in despair. He would have to get rid of this pair. "OK. Just wait there until I'm finished. Is that OK with you?"

"That's fine, boss. We just don't want you to think we can't obey orders, but you can't give us impossible orders, that's all."

Eddie, shaking his head in disbelief marched off in the direction of the small door.

As he entered the workshop, Eddie was surprised at how clean everything looked. There were no oil stains on the floor and no old used bits of cars scattered around the edges of the large building. In one corner off to the side of the roller shutter door was a small office and Eddie heard voices in what sounded like good-natured banter.

As he knocked on the office door, Eddie simultaneously turned the handle and pushed the door open. He was greeted by four men, all dressed in crisp clean white overalls sitting at a table playing cards.

The man at the head of the table who, from his appearance, seemed to be the oldest of the bunch looked up and spoke. "You must be our Jaguar?"

Eddie had expected a warmer welcome but conceded he didn't really know what he was getting into. He decided to be seen as no pushover. "If you mean am I the one who nicked the Jag and am delivering it to you, yes, if you're Rory McClean then I'm the Jaguar."

The older man Eddie assumed was in charge stood up and walked around the table. Eddie noticed he walked with a limp, but his bulk was impressive. He stood a good head taller than Eddie, was bald on top of his head although his hair above his ears had been left long and the most noticeable thing about Rory McClean was his beer belly. His overalls only just met at his stomach.

"So, you're the new car thief?" Rory McClean wasn't unfriendly but something about this large unsmiling man scared Eddie.

"Well not exactly, I get a list of motors that you want, and I find them and deliver them." Eddie looked out the office window to the pristine workshop. "What exactly do you do with the cars?"

"Well, well, you are a nosey parker and no mistake. Unless you're also a choirboy what the hell do you think we do with them?"

Eddie stood his ground. "Well, if I knew, I wouldn't ask. Would I?"

The big man looked annoyed but humoured the newcomer. "Look, we get told what cars to expect and when to expect them. We get told which ones to ship untouched and which ones we to break down into their parts and then ship the parts. Everything goes to St. Petersburg in Russia. For your information, we've never met the guy who gives us our orders. We only do as we're told. The last guy to try and double-cross our man finished up dead last Friday. It was just upstairs as a matter of fact." Rory McClean stared at his delivery driver. "So, it's not wise to ask questions, just obey your orders and take the money. That's all any of us are doing. Understand?"

Eddie understood but still had questions. He decided this was not the time to seek too many answers. "Yeah! I understand." This was said as casually as Eddie could manage. "Where do you want the Jag?"

"Follow me. This is the easy one, it's being shipped whole. That's why we needed it first."

Rory pulled on the heavy chains that opened the roller shutter door.

"Bring it in here. We need to remove all the trackers."

Eddie almost fainted. He hadn't thought about trackers. He knew it was the insurance companies who insisted most luxury and expensive cars have them fitted and seemed to remember it was the insurers and not the police who initially monitored them. He asked Rory as the pair walked outside.

"The insurers do first-line monitoring and when a car is reported stolen, they activate the tracker and inform the police. It's great in theory but in reality, either the owner doesn't miss his car for days or the insurer's GPS doesn't function. Even if it does, it takes the cops a couple of days to process the paperwork before they come looking. Usually, you're safe for at least 72 hours by which time we've stripped the trackers out, even the cunningly hidden ones, and the car is on its way out of the country." Rory placed his massive arm around Eddie's shoulder. "But take my advice, only lift a car the same day you bring it here, less risk."

Eddie could see the sense of this and regretted stealing the other cars so early. He'd just have to get them out of his yard as soon as he could. Just in case!

"Nice car. I like these electric Jags but what's that?" Rory was pointing at the rusted Granada. Eddie misunderstood. "They're my associates, they help out from time to time."

Rory didn't correct Eddie's mistake. He simply refocused on the two poorly dressed and obviously anorexic characters standing beside the rust heap. They saw they were under scrutiny, so they smiled and waved at the big man. Rory thought the smiles improved nothing. He dismissed Frankie and Bert from his thoughts. Turning to Eddie he said, "Right, drive it in."

Once the car was inside the roller door was closed. The three remaining white-suited mechanics emerged from the office and without being instructed started to scan the Jaguar using some form of handheld scanning device. Eddie surmised they were hunting for the trackers.

"Now, you'd better bring the Audi Q8 over this afternoon. Get here around three o'clock. The Land Rover can wait until tomorrow. Have it here about the same time. Both cars are for stripping, so we've got a bit of work to do."

Eddie stood staring at the team working on the Jag. Rory looked to where Eddie was staring and turned back to Eddie. "OK, you can go now, be back here around three. Got it?"

Eddie returned to his clapped-out Granada and his two inept employees. From his rear seat, he instructed his team to return him to his office. He had some thinking to do.

Chapter Eight

The DCI and his assistant, DC Mary Dougan, arrived at the showroom of Crystal Motors in Mile End Road just in time to see a very old, rusted Ford Granada exit from the far side of the filling station. It wasn't so much the fact the car was an obvious MOT failure that caught the attention of the two detectives but the way it was being driven. The noise of tyres screaming as drivers applied emergency brakes and the sounding of horns as the driver of the Granada totally ignored other cars and simply drove across the two lanes of traffic and serenely turned west as though it was the only car on the road.

Steve caught sight of the passenger who from a distance looked like a schoolboy except for the heavy black stubble evident on his face. The driver appeared to look the same but might have been smaller as he was obviously not tall enough to look over the steering wheel. He appeared to be seeing the road through the wheel. There was a figure in the back, but the DCI couldn't see clearly enough to have any idea of who it might be. His overriding thought was how this car of choice of London gangsters in the mid-eighties had fallen out of favour if what he had just seen was a current example.

The DCI and Mary stood in front of the showroom with its bifold doors allowing easy access and exit for cars both into and out of the showroom. They noted a high stone wall ran from the front right-hand corner of the showroom all the way to the edge of the pavement. There was a gap of about ten feet from the left edge of the showroom before the filling station buildings started. The filling station was like most seen around the country The forecourt appeared to continue beyond the petrol pumps to provide an exit for cars where it merged with a road coming uphill from behind the filling station. Steve noted this was the road the old Granada had driven up.

There was police blue and white tape strung across the bifold doors and a uniformed officer stood guard outside. As the detectives approached, they produced their warrant cards, and the constable opened the right-hand section of the door and lifted the tape so as to allow the two CID officers entry to the showroom.

"Hang on a minute sir, I'll be right back." Without waiting for a response, DC Mary Dougan walked briskly away from her boss who simply shrugged and wondered what his DC was up to. On entering the showroom, Steve was hit by the smell of polish. He observed the floor was covered in highly-polished vinyl tiles and the six cars he counted were gleaming under the florescent lights. He stood for a few minutes taking in the atmosphere of the place. He saw a white-suited scene-of-crime officer working away in an office located on the right side of the back wall. He was also surprised to see two civilians sitting at separate desks at the rear of the premises. He casually walked up to them. They were both reasonably well dressed and seemed to be in their late twenties.

"And who might you two be?"

The one nearest the DCI stood and offered his hand. "I'm Fredrick and this is Simon, we work here. The policeman who came on Friday told us to be here today to answer questions, but we've not seen him so far." Fredrick paused, gathering his courage in the face of authority. "Maybe you know what's happening?"

This explained their presence at a crime scene but also told Steve the detective in charge on Friday was sloppy and inefficient. It was not accepted procedure to ask potential suspects to come back to the crime scene to answer questions.

"Wait here." The DCI left the two car salesmen to stare at his back. The damage to the crime scene had been done so Steve thought these two could wait.

As he entered the office to meet the white-suited figure, Mary arrived clutching old VCR tapes. "I noticed there were CCTV cameras around the filling station forecourt. They only have an old black-and-white VCR system, but I've got the ones from last Friday. I thought we might get something from them." She beamed at the DCI.

"Well done, Mary, we might find something useful." Steve was pleased with Mary's initiative but again wondered why the murder squad hadn't already collected these tapes.

The scene-of-crime technician saw the pair through the glass panels in the wall and the door. He waved them in, meaning he was finished. Steve recognised him even under his white hood and mask but didn't know his name. The white suit pulled back his hood and removed his mask. He also pulled down on the zip of his suit stretching himself as he did so. "I'm getting too old to be scratching around on my hands and knees at these crime scenes." This was said with a smile.

"Find anything?"

"Not a thing. Whoever killed the victim was a professional. He must have been in and out. Didn't even leave a whiff of aftershave. The whole place is polished to within an inch of its life so if there was anything, we'd have found it. Sorry Mr Burt, but we've nothing for you except a drop of blood on the floor right where you're standing. My guess is it's from the knife and the killer must have let a drop drip off the blade as he put his knife away. I'm pretty sure we'll find it belongs to the victim."

The DCI sighed not from fatigue but from frustration. He knew most murder cases were solved by a combination of good police work and sound forensic evidence. With no forensics, it would be doubly difficult to solve this case. He thanked the technician. "Let me have your report as soon as, even if it says nothing."

Both men smiled and the scene-of-crime officer lifted his large metal case that contained the items he used at each scene and left.

"Well Mary, any ideas?"

"I've read the file such as it is. Poppy sent it to my phone. What I don't get is how could our killer just walk in, stab the victim and walk out again without being seen. The report said these two lads outside were here all day." Mary was enjoying the puzzle. "You don't think they're involved, do you?"

"Probably not but let's go and ask them."

The detectives pulled up a chair each and sat facing the two salesmen. Mary produced her notebook ready to record what was said.

"Tell us about your boss." Steve knew from experience this type of unexpected question often confused guilty parties who had their answers ready for the standard police questions.

The one called Simon spoke. He looked nervous but the DCI put it down to inexperience in dealing with the police. "Not much to tell. He was hardly ever here. He didn't work us hard and left us to get on with things. The money's not bad and he was generous with commissions when we sold a car."

Steve switched his gaze to the other salesman who appeared equally nervous. "Yeah! Well, it's like Simon says. He only came in for the afternoons. Sometimes he'd have meetings in his office but usually he just read the newspaper."

Mary looked at Steve who nodded. "How many cars do you sell a week?" The DC was curious that the showroom appeared to need a staff of two.

"Not many." answered Fredrick. "More like how many a month."

"OK. How many a month?"

Simon chipped in. "Say about one, maybe two in a good month."

"That's not many. How much does the average car sell for?"

"That depends," Fredrick spoke up again. "If it was a real punter just off the street then say around fifteen grand. If it was one of Mr Bowie's contacts, we'd have no idea. The boss would just tell us to move a certain car outside ready for someone to collect it."

Steve had been listening and calculating. "So how did Cameron Bowie make his money?"

The pair of salesmen looked at each other and the DCI saw fear pass between them. They both tried to answer together but Simon won. "We don't know. We don't know anything about the business. We just looked after the showroom. Anything the governor did was nothing to do with us."

Steve smiled. He sensed there was more to tell. He changed tack. "What did you see last Friday when your boss was being murdered."

"Nothing, we were busy doing paperwork." Simon lied.

Steve noticed both men were beginning to sweat.

"I don't believe you. You admit you sell a car a month. That doesn't sound like a lot of paperwork to me." Turning to Mary. "What do you think, Constable?"

"No sir, I don't think they were here, or they know who killed their boss."

"No! No! For Christ's sake, we had nothing to do with the murder. We were playing a game on our mobiles." Fredrick was panicking.

"There's nothing to do on a Friday so we always play games. Anybody could have walked in, and we'd not see them unless they coughed or something. Please! You have to believe us."

Mary had achieved what Steve wanted. He returned to his other line of questioning. This was a tactic designed to keep suspects from becoming too comfortable with the line of questioning.

"OK. Say we believe you, but what about the other things you get up to." Mary had also opened this door. "It doesn't take two of you to sit here all day and sell a car a month so what else happens?"

Both salesmen were now visibly distressed.

"Nothing!" Fredrick was almost in tears and had raised his voice to try and cover his fear. "We don't know anything of the governor's other business."

The DCI locked eyes with Fredrick. "Now, we can either look at a conspiracy to murder charge or you can tell us the truth about your boss' other business interests."

It was Simon's turn to speak up. "Listen, we really don't know anything. All we did was help out on a few occasions, that's all."

"Help out how?"

"Just help out, do the odd bit of driving, nothing serious."

Steve knew these two had more to say and felt they were involved somehow. If not with the murder, then with some other criminal activity. Having listened to them he felt they could potentially be flight risks, but he wasn't ready to continue the interrogation until he knew more about the victim.

"Constable, call up a car; our two friends are going to help us with our enquiries back at the Yard."

"You can't arrest us!" Simon was almost screaming. "We've done nothing wrong!"

"I'm not arresting you, you're just helping us, but if you prefer, I *can* arrest you." Steve looked sternly at both men. "Oh, and by the way, I think you have both been involved in something really wrong and the sooner you tell me the better for all concerned."

A patrol car arrived ten minutes after Mary placed the call. "Go with them Mary, see they're settled. We'll give them a grilling once we know more about our Mr Cameron Bowie. I'll follow in the pool car and hand in your CCTV tapes to Technical Support."

***

The Voice was having lunch at his desk just as DC Mary Dougan was escorting the two salesmen to Scotland Yard and the DCI had set off after them driving the pool car.

Mondays were always hectic, and he tried to clear his in-tray by mid-afternoon. His office was large and steeped in tradition. The walls were clad in oak panels and a particularly fine open fireplace completed the picture of understated opulence and comfort. The fine Indian carpet added to this picture as did the large leather-covered Chesterfield style sofas. This particular Monday he didn't have any outside engagements and was happy to be seen to be working hard. He liked to portray himself as a hard-working self-made man and held himself up as an example of what hard work, street cunning and determination to succeed could achieve. He knew his secretary and most of his staff loved him for what he contributed to their lives and was sure he could probably bed a couple of the better-looking women if he put his mind to it.

He also knew the other side of himself. The side he kept secret even from his nearest and dearest. The side that was anonymous to the outside world. The harsh, brutal side steeped in corruption and illegal dealings, that gave him a feeling of power. The side that had over the years made him very wealthy, but it was also the side that worried him most, especially since he'd been sucked into working with the Russian.

As he finished his lunch, his burner phone started to vibrate in his jacket pocket. The Voice instantly knew this was trouble. Only Vlad his Russian contact had the number. He knew it wouldn't be another order for stolen cars as he'd not completed the last order. It had to be something else.

With a fear he hadn't experienced for a while, the Voice answered. "Hello."

"It's me; be in the coffee shop in ten minutes."

"What! You're in London?"

"Yes, ten minutes." The line disconnected.

The Voice had met the Russian a few times at the Costa coffee house just round the corner from his office. Such meetings had never been friendly, but Vlad always made them profitable, so it was with a mixture of fear and anticipation that the Voice left his office to walk the few minutes it took to get to the coffee house.

The Voice spotted Vlad at a corner table. The place was busy with lunchtime customers, but Vlad's table had been set into a corner alcove and was reasonably quiet, despite the number of people milling around.

Vlad had ordered coffee but neither man seemed keen to drink. "We have a situation, and you need to perform a few tricks for us." Vlad didn't believe in long-winded introductions.

The Voice knew how Vlad worked and was suspicious of this innocent introduction. "What kind of tricks and what situation?"

Vlad sighed as though indicating he didn't have time for questions. He looked around the coffee house and, seeing nothing that made him suspicious, he sat back and relaxed.

"OK, I suppose you'll work it out eventually." Vlad had decided to tell all.

"I represent a faction within Russia that is anti the current president. In fact, we tried removing him before but failed. Anyway, my colleagues don't like how he is starving the country and only favouring his friends. One of his friends is the largest arms dealer in Russia, a man called Koptic. Koptic is greedy and uneducated, but he promises our president more and better weapons all the time. Trouble is, he doesn't know how to develop new weapon systems. He can only slightly improve existing ones." Vlad paused to see if the Voice was following him.

"A year ago, Koptic was forced into a corner by my colleagues to say he had a new weapons system under development. Of course, he didn't but he had to look good in front of the Russian Weapons Committee. We were happy he'd got himself into an impossible position especially when he declared his new weapon would be ready for testing in eighteen months. You see in Russia if you make promises and don't keep them, you tend to disappear. We knew Koptic was history as soon as he failed to demonstrate his new revolutionary weapon. What we didn't bargain for was that if you are a friend of the president, you are sheltered from the worst that can happen. Our President always saves face. The government gave Koptic unlimited funds to make some kind of weapon happen."

The Voice was intrigued by the story so far but couldn't see how he fitted in. Vlad reluctantly took a sip of his coffee.

"We've been spying on Koptic since he made his announcement. We knew he wasn't educated but that doesn't mean he's not smart. We discovered he's done a deal with your government for a joint venture for a new weapons delivery system. He fronted the deal on behalf of the Kremlin and is using Russian state money to pay for most of the research and development although the UK scientists and weapons engineers are doing all the work. His plan is to claim this weapons system was his work.

Unfortunately, the UK think it's a genuine joint venture with the Russian Government and we're sure Koptic will never allow your government to have the weapon. We don't know how but we're certain he'll find a way to steal everything claiming it's all his work. Of course, even if both governments had the weapon and word ever got out that our two countries were jointly developing weapons systems, all hell would break out and the Americans would go crazy."

The Voice still couldn't see where he fitted in. "This is all very interesting Vlad, but what has it to do with me?"

Vlad took another sip of his now cold coffee. "There's an old nuclear underground bunker in Yorkshire, near Wetherby. Your military has converted it into a research base for the development of this new weapons system. They've built a training camp of some sort above the bunker as a front to cover up the comings and goings of the various engineers and scientists. We have a man on the inside who occasionally gets information to us but it's not easy for him."

The Voice was now worried. "Hang on, are you saying there's a Russian spy in one of our top-secret weapons establishments?"

"Yes, but it's complicated. Remember, your government thinks it is working with my government, so our spy is technically not a spy except he's working for us, not our government."

"I don't see the distinction; a spy is a spy."

"Yes, you're probably right, but you see we want the weapon and to deprive Koptic of his moment of glory. We want to show Koptic up as a fraudster. If we had this weapon then we could overthrow the dictator and his corrupt friends. The only way we'll get it is to steal it."

The Voice wasn't sure what he was being asked but he knew he had to refuse to have any part of it. "You're mad, that place will be on 24-hour lockdown, seven days a week. You can't just walk out with a weapon under your arm."

Vlad smiled. "You see, now you know where you come in. We need you to be our inside man's handler. He must have a way of getting information to you. When he says the weapon is ready you need a plan to remove it and send it to us with one of the stolen cars."

The Voice was incredulous. "It's impossible. I don't know your spy, and I don't even know how big or heavy this supposed weapon is." The Voice was sweating. "It's impossible, there's no way it can be done especially if it's underground with the military on top."

"My dear friend, knowing your fondness for money we know you'll find a way. We know the weapon is for battlefield use so it must be light enough and small enough for a soldier to carry. We don't know enough yet, but we do know it's a chemical weapon."

"Stop right there! Chemical weapons are banned under an international treaty; the UK would never get involved with them. Your spy is way off; it's not possible."

Vlad was still smiling and sat back further in his chair. "There are many things in this world that are not allowed but they get done anyway. One of the scientists at Wetherby is from Porton Down, your chemical weapons research establishment. Now he's not part of the development team unless chemicals are involved, is he?"

The Voice sat back staring at the Russian. He slowly gathered his thoughts. Silence hung in the air between the two men until the Voice spoke.

"All right. There's a secret battlefield chemical weapon being developed in an underground bunker near Wetherby in Yorkshire. The UK Government believe it is a joint venture with Russia but in reality, it's this Koptic fellow who's spending Russian money illegally to save his and the president's reputation. You have a spy inside the establishment, and you want me to liaise secretly with him and pass on to you any information I get. Then, once the weapon is developed you want me to arrange to steal it, and ship it to Russia with one of the cars I'm stealing for you every week."

The Voice spread his arms wide as he sarcastically addressed the Russian. "Anything else you want me to do. Maybe steal a ballistic rocket or two or a couple of Challenger tanks?! They're always useful when you're overthrowing a government. You are mad; I want no part of this." The Voice stood to leave but was prevented from standing by Vlad's large fist on his arm.

"My friend remember we have the pictures of your little indiscretion so you will do this and do it well. Your fee will be twenty-five million dollars, and this will be the last thing we will ask of you. The photographs and the negatives will be returned."

Vlad sat staring at the Voice who was half in and half out of his seat. He sat down and realised he had no choice. The pictures of him with a prostitute would be devastating for his career plus his darker side liked the sound of twenty-five million dollars.

"All right. What can you give me?"

Vlad produced a brown A4 envelope from the chair next to his.

"In there are the details of our man on the inside. There's a burner phone and only he will call you on it. Security is tight and there are no phones inside the bunker and no signal for mobiles underground. Our man has a mobile hidden above ground somewhere in the training camp, but he isn't allowed above ground very often. I can tell you he's an engineer tradesman and believes in our cause, so treat him with respect. He'll call you when he can."

"Also," Vlad tapped the envelope, "you'll see how to keep in touch through a newspaper, called *The Yorkshire Evening Post*. Personal adverts are still a good way of communicating. They're allowed newspapers but no phones. We've already posted a message giving him your new mobile number."

"You've thought of everything." The Voice was deflated wondering how he could pull this off and get his money.

"Yes, everything except how to get the weapon." The Russian stood and shook the Voice's hand.

"Good luck and keep me up to date. I'm in London now until you've succeeded."

The Voice sat down again as the Russian left. He contemplated his situation. Since meeting Vlad he'd become an international car thief and now a handler for a Russian spy and soon to be an international dealer in stolen chemical weapons. He needed to do some serious thinking. The thought of twenty-five million dollars would certainly help him find solutions.

Chapter Nine

The DCI arrived at his office to find Poppy working at her computer in splendid isolation. It was one of the few times Steve could remember such an air of calm within his offices.

"Where is everyone?"

Poppy looked up from her keyboard. "Well. The DI and DS Conway are out chasing up the abduction cases and I thought you and Mary were out at Mile End Road on the murders." She impishly opened her arms and shrugged her shoulders before carrying on. "I got the map you asked for. It's in your office. All I've done so far is mark the three schools with a red dot and the kids' addresses with a blue dot. It's on your wall."

The DCI was pleased that Poppy was developing into a good admin officer, using her initiative when it mattered. Steve handed the VCR tapes to his admin assistant. "See if Tech Support can make anything of these. They're a bit old and bashed but you never know. It'll give your uncle a challenge." Steve looked knowingly at Poppy.

She put the tapes to one side of her desk. "Right, I've asked UNCLE TERRY…" Poppy emphasised her family connection to Inspector Terry Harvey, Head of the Technical Support Unit and a friend of Steve's "…to get the CCTV from around the schools for the abduction cases and the same for the area around the car showroom on Mile End Road for your murder. He's going to look at the images for the three weeks between the first and third kid going missing. He says there are a few cameras so we might get something. He has identified the cameras around the car showroom, so he's called up the images for the day of the murder and two days before." Poppy picked up the VCR tapes and stood up. "But he says you owe him big time and you can use the viewing suite when you're ready."

Steve knew Terry Harvey had access to all the latest technology and had somehow persuaded the powers that be that he needed a cinema-style viewing room to better review CCTV footage.

"I'll always owe Terry and tell him I'll use the viewing room probably later today."

"Will do." Poppy skipped out on her way to deliver the tapes to her uncle.

Before she was out the door the DCI remembered he'd asked for a financial check on both his murder victim, Cameron Bowie and his company, Crystal Motors.

"Poppy. Before you go, did you get those financial checks?"

Poppy returned to her desk and lifted a folder. As she handed it to her boss, she looked puzzled. "Yes. They're in there but I don't understand them. The personal stuff for Cameron Bowie is a bit weird. He was getting money regularly from an overseas account somewhere I've never heard of and then transferring it straight back to another overseas account in Gibraltar. He lived out of his business with even his weekly shopping being paid for on his company credit card. His main spending was at a golf club, again all on his company credit card, but he paid the balance off each month using his company bank account by the look of it from his credit card statements. I couldn't see anything else suspicious except the money going into and out of his personal account. I'm waiting for Companies House to get back to me with the business accounts, but I did a Land Registry search and guess what…? The showroom wasn't owned by your man. An offshore business listing nominee director owns it. It's called Maple Leaf Inc registered in Delaware USA."

Steve scratched his chin. "Interesting."

"Yes, it is." Poppy carried on, "So, I did another search of properties around the showroom, and it seems the same offshore people also own a building directly behind the showroom."

"Really! Good work, Poppy. Anything else?"

Before Poppy could reply, DC Mary Dougan arrived carrying three cups of coffee. "The two spivs are downstairs sir. I've put them in separate interview rooms and a uniform is looking after them." Mary realised she'd interrupted something but carried on, "I thought we'd have a coffee before we started interviewing."

Steve smiled inwardly. He had two young, female and very bright detective constables making his life easier, but he felt somehow, he was acting in the role of trainer instead of lead detective.

"If there's nothing else boss, I'll get these tapes over to Tech and let you know when the other financial stuff comes in." Poppy set off again but with her coffee. As she left, she thanked Mary for the drink.

The two detectives settled into Steve's inner office. "I've just learnt that our victim was receiving regular cash payments into his personal bank account from an overseas account, and he didn't own the showroom, an offshore business does. Plus, the same company apparently also own the building behind the showroom."

"Mm. Interesting. Do you think it's mob-related and the killing being so public was a warning?"

"Maybe but what mob connection could a second-hand car dealer have?" Steve was thinking out loud for Mary's benefit. "We need to find out what the other building is used for."

"As you say, we can easily find out, but the money sounds suspicious and the building behind the showroom being owned by the same secretive company can't be a coincidence." The DCI realised his detective constable was no dummy.

"You're right, I don't believe in coincidences." Steve drank his coffee. "Poppy's getting more details about Crystal Motors. Once we have that, things should be clearer."

Steve gulped the last of his coffee and threw the empty cup into his wastebasket. He stood up as he spoke. "Let's go and see what our two friends downstairs have to say for themselves."

The detectives descended into the interview suite below New Scotland Yard. It was a modern facility comprising six identical interview rooms each with a viewing room attached, where other officers could watch interviews as they took place through a one-way window.

They decided to talk to Simon first on the grounds that Mary thought he was the weaker of the two. They entered interview room two. Simon was lounging back in his wooden chair and sitting at a table that, like all tables within the six interview rooms, was screwed to the floor. A black metal box was at the end of the table. This was the twin recording machine used during interviews under caution. Steve and Mary took chairs opposite Simon and the uniformed officer remained by the door.

Steve began. "Is your name Simon West?"

"Yes, but what am I doing here?"

"All in good time. You are employed as a used car salesman at Crystal Motors located on Mile End Road?"

"Yes, but you know that already. Look, I've got places to be."

"Don't we all, Simon." Part of the DCI's interview technique was to get his suspect angry at the futility of his initial questions.

"How much do you earn as a car salesman, Simon?"

"That's none of your bloody business."

"Humour me. Is it a grand a week, five hundred a week or are you paid only on commission?"

Simon was looking nervous but somehow strong. Maybe Mary had read him wrongly.

Simon leant into the table. "Look, I'm paid cash in hand. Right, I know it's not legal but Cameron preferred it that way so you see I can't tell you anything or I'll incriminate myself, won't I?"

"I'm not the Revenue Simon, I don't care about your under-the-counter financial arrangements. I only want to catch the person who killed your boss."

Steve thought the payment arrangements used by the victim were interesting and painted a picture of someone who lived on the edge. Maybe Mary was right and there was a mob connection.

"So how much cash in hand did your boss pay you?"

"So, you're not going to report me to the taxman?"

"No, but I will if you don't tell me what I want to know. So again, how much did you get from your boss?" Steve needed to know to gauge the sums involved and to judge if Crystal Motors was legitimate.

"It varied," a relieved Simon started. "But say around a grand a week." Steve thought this was too much for just sitting in a car showroom all week and selling a car a month.

"That's a lot for doing nothing. Maybe you can see why I don't believe you're an innocent bystander. Now, tell me what you really did." Steve stared hard at his suspect. He noticed Mary was taking notes.

"I can't. If I cough, you'll charge me, and I'll go to prison. But honestly Inspector, Freddy and I didn't do much."

"Just tell me or I'll charge you as an accessory to murder and whatever you've done will seem lightweight compared to a murder charge."

Simon was visibly shaken. He could see no way out, so he tried to be a hard man and bluff it out.

"We're not murderers like we said." Little drops of sweat were forming on his top lip. "But if I tell you what we did I need a deal. You have to tell me you won't charge us over what we did for Mr Bowie."

Steve was inwardly pleased. He knew he had his man but realised he needed to tread carefully.

"We don't do deals, Simon, but if your crimes are low grade enough, we might not charge you. However, if they are serious enough to warrant charging you, I'll talk to the CPS, tell them how cooperative you've been and I'm sure they won't press for a long sentence."

Simon sat back in his chair obviously pondering his options. His next statement threw the DCI off balance.

"OK but I want to talk with Freddy. We're mates and are in this together. I want to speak with him first and I don't want you lot listening in."

The DCI knew this wasn't procedure but could see Simon was serious. He agreed and Simon was escorted to the interview room housing Fredrick Poole. Steve and Mary sat waiting.

"What do you think sir? Think he knows anything?"

"Well Mary, I'm sure he knows something, and Cameron Bowie wasn't paying them a grand a week just to sit in a shitty little car showroom. So yes, I think they both know something. I just don't know what."

The detectives chatted for around ten minutes. As Steve consulted his watch and noted it was 2.44 p.m., the door opened, and a uniformed officer said the pair would like to speak to the detectives together. Steve and Mary left interview room two and settled into interview room five.

"Before we start, boys, I'm going to tape this conversation."

Mary switched the twin tape machine on, recorded the time and date and stated that she and the DCI were present. "For the tape please, lads, say your names, starting with you." Steve pointed to Simon.

"Simon West."

"Fredrick Poole."

"Right. One of you, tell us in your own words what you did for the late Cameron Bowie and what you know about his business."

Both car salesmen looked at each other. Fredrick gave a nod to Simon who started talking.

"We don't know much but we heard things. We started working for Mr Bowie more or less together. That was about two years ago. We were told to keep the place tidy, to keep the showroom open at the advertised hours and not to be too concerned about selling any motors. If a punter came in and we could sell him a car, then all well and good but if we never sold a car we shouldn't worry." Simon stopped to assess the effect his story was having on the two officers.

"Go on." Steve was hooked and had no idea what was coming.

"We'd been there a few months when a bloke turned up. I think he was Russian. He spent a long time with the boss and after he'd gone Freddy and I were called into the office. Mr Bowie said he wanted us to steal a car and the gent who'd just left was very particular about what we stole. I think it was a series 7 BMW, but it had to be nearly new and a dark colour."

Steve interrupted. He would get all the details later. For now, he just wanted the bare facts. "We'll go into the details later; we only need to know what you did and what Crystal Motors did."

"Yeah, I'm getting to that. So, we stole the Beemer, then another one and then a Jag. Next thing we're told that a workshop's being installed behind us and every car we steal should be delivered straight there."

"OK. So, you stole cars to order, and Crystal Motors had a chop shop behind the showroom. Is that correct?"

"Yeah. More or less, except it wasn't really a chop shop. Some cars were being shipped as they came in and some were chopped for spares. All the cars went to Russia. A guy called Rory McClean is in charge of the workshop. He's pretty evil and not someone you'd cross." Simon became more relaxed the further he got into his story. The DCI wanted him to speed up and told him so.

"Things went on fine for a year. We stole the cars and Rory shipped them to Russia. We got paid cash in hand and everybody was happy. Then, about six months ago another Russian turned up. We heard raised voices coming from the office. You know, shouting and swearing, and after this second Russian left, the boss was shaking. Eventually, he told us the operation was going to be run by a different group of people and that we wouldn't be nicking cars any more. He said we'd be OK because he'd still pay us as before but all we had to do was look after the showroom."

Steve interrupted. "So, who was this second Russian?"

Freddy Poole had been sitting in silence but decided to contribute to the narrative.

"We don't know but it looked like the boss was in over his head. We saw cars arriving every day. Great articulated container lorries were arriving at the workshop almost on the hour. Cars were being put in them and being driven off. It was car theft on an industrial scale."

"So, what happened?"

Simon took up the story again. "It was obvious that this was now a big-time operation and about four weeks ago the first Russian turned up. He wasn't happy and we heard Mr Bowie shouting that he had no choice and the Russian shouting back that he should have said something, and that Mr Bowie wasn't unhappy about the extra money he was making."

"What do you think that was all about?"

Simon and Freddy looked at each other. This time Simon nodded to Freddy.

"We're not sure but we think the second Russian took over the car ring and the first Russian wasn't too pleased. Like we said, the operation became industrial-sized and then suddenly the cars stopped arriving for a week or so and then only a few started turning up at a time. We think Mr Bowie was dealing with the second Russian and his first guy didn't like it. We think the first Russian killed him because he went to work with a competitor."

"Mm. Very clever of you. Who was the first Russian?"

"We don't know. We never really met him, but we saw him hanging around the workshop last week talking to Rory McClean. He might know."

Steve looked at Mary who shrugged and asked. "Last Friday, the day Cameron Bowie was murdered. What did you see? Did anything out of the ordinary happen last week?"

The DCI thought this was a good question.

"No, not really," Freddy answered.

"There were just those two weirdos. Remember, the two idiots? One of them was talking in a funny voice and you told him you'd sell him a car for thirty grand."

"Ah! Yes, but they were harmless," Freddy said, recalling the pair. "They looked like tramps and a good gust of wind would blow them over they were so thin. I can't see them killing Mr Bowie. One of them came back to ask when Mr Bowie would be in, and I told him the boss only worked afternoons."

Mary sat up. "Let me get this straight. What day were these blokes in the showroom?"

Freddy answered straight away. "Thursday last week."

"The day before Mr Bowie was killed?"

"Yes, I suppose so."

Mary wrote a note in her notebook.

The DCI knew they had uncovered something useful. He asked, "You're sure they asked for Mr Bowie by name?"

"Yes. The one with the funny put-on posh voice said he'd heard if he spoke to the boss directly, he'd get a good deal on a car."

Steve pressed on. "And you hadn't seen them before?"

"Never."

Steve nodded to Mary to formally finish the tape. As neither man had asked for a solicitor, she removed and kept both tapes. The detectives left the salesmen, telling them they would be charged with car theft, and they'd have to make formal statements later in the day. Steve told them they'd be officially cautioned, charged and released on police bail. Both men looked worried as the detectives left.

Steve and Mary were silent as they climbed the stairs to the ground floor of New Scotland Yard and were equally quiet as they shared the lift to the eighth floor and back to the DCI's office.

"Well, Detective Constable Dougan. What do you make of that?"

They were in Steve's inner office. Steve was behind his desk while Mary Dougan stood and started to pace around.

"I'm not sure. Those two think their boss was murdered by some Russian connection. We don't know who they are, but we can pick any one from two. The information about the carjacking ring is significant and the fact the showroom and the building behind are owned by the same offshore company isn't a coincidence." Mary walked and talked. Steve sat back.

"The description of the two characters visiting the showroom might mean something. It's just possible they were casing the place and planning the killing. I think we need to find these Russians and find out who really owns the buildings. Also, we need to involve Customs and Excise. Try and get a handle on where the lorries with the stolen cars left from and where they were going."

The DCI leant forward. "Good points but let's see. First, I don't think the Russians would have carried out the killing themselves and if the pathologist is right, what's the connection to the body on the embankment? We need to know more about the first victim."

Mary made a note in her notebook.

Steve carried on. "Second, why did the second Russian get involved. According to our salesmen, the operation went from a few stolen cars a week to a full-blown commercial operation." Steve was stroking his chin. "Was it a takeover and is this thing mob-related after all?" The DCI waited for Mary to respond but she remained silent.

"Then we've got the two so-called tramps. If you're right and they were casing the place, are they our murderers?"

Steve gave a deep sigh and Mary sat down. "Look into the first victim in detail. I think he was called Vince McGuire, from memory."

Mary flicked through the pages of her notebook and confirmed the DCI's memory was still sharp.

"Look into his known associates. See if there's any link back to our second victim. We need to talk to the workshop boss." Steve held out his hand asking for the name. Mary again flicked through her notebook.

"Rory McClean."

"Right. This Rory apparently knows the second Russian, at least, according to our car salesmen. We need to interview Mr McClean tomorrow. Poppy's getting details on Crystal Motors accounts and ownership of the buildings. That might tell us something."

Steve looked at his watch. It was 5.26 p.m. He stood up from behind his desk as Poppy returned. Speaking directly to Mary and in a softly spoken voice, Steve said, "Write up your notes and get Poppy to transpose the interview tape with the two lads. We'll start again tomorrow at nine. I've got an appointment at eleven tomorrow morning, so you'll be running solo most of tomorrow."

"No problem. What do you want to do about the mechanic, this Rory McClean?"

"He can wait till later tomorrow once I get back."

DC Mary Dougan nodded and smiled. She liked working with Steve.

Poppy was tidying her desk as Steve walked past. "Poppy. Tell Tech we'll look at the CCTV tomorrow morning and get hold of Peter Jones. I want him and Matt Conway here tomorrow before nine for a debrief." The admin assistant nodded.

"Have you got anything yet from Companies House on the accounts for Crystal Motors?"

"Yes, and the stuff from Delaware on the Maple Leaf business. To be honest Steve, I'm out of my depth. We need an expert and I know you know one." Poppy grinned. She was referring to Steve's ex-colleague, Twiggy but better known these days as Miss Rough.

Steve laughed. "I'll call her tomorrow, but you'd better get all the financial stuff into one folder."

"Will do."

The DCI left his two youngest members of staff behind as he said goodnight and set off home for some quality time with his wife and baby daughter.

Chapter Ten

The man in the RAF Group Captain's uniform, having passed through the security checks at Montgomery Barracks, descended into the vast harshly lit concrete bunker that was now known as Station K.

The RAF Group Captain was, in fact, Professor Karl Symonds. He was head of the Practical Physics Department at Imperial College London. Karl was a genius at finding elegant and practical solutions that turned theory into practice. He was often called upon by weapons manufacturers to assist in the design and development of all kinds of weird and wonderful ideas most of which were never fully developed, but those that were usually managed to change modern warfare in some way or another.

The Professor stood erect and didn't look his seventy-plus years. His grey hair was longer than military regulation would allow, and the half-moon spectacles perched on the end of his nose gave him the academic look he sought. He always walked with his hands behind his back and possessed a knack for immediately empathising with people he met for the first time.

Karl had been seconded to Station K as its head. He was leading a team of scientists, engineers and military personnel all of whom were dedicated to making their new weapons system work. The Professor had been off-site for several weeks attending meetings and seeing his own medical doctor about a potential problem with his heart. As the head of the unit, he took the opportunity to walk round and visit each section in turn. In this way, he was able to reacquaint himself with his team's issues before chairing the project development meeting planned for later in the day. Karl knew this Monday would be busy.

He admired his colleagues' dedication especially as the terms and conditions applicable to working at Station K were particularly onerous. It was a male-only environment although Karl had lobbied for the best brains, and knew several eminent ladies, however the decision had been taken to employ only men. Each man, having signed the official secrets act, had additionally agreed to spend up to four consecutive months locked away in this underground bunker. Given the ultra-top-secret nature of the project, there were no landline telephones installed except for one that was locked away in the Professor's desk drawer and even this needed a secret code to gain access to an outside line. No mobile phones were allowed, there were no photocopying facilities and regular sweeps were made to ensure no listening devices had been installed. Overall, the people who worked at Station K were completely cut off from normal contact with the outside world. Even their food was stockpiled in large freezers and tinned food had become part of their normal diet.

When the military had refurbished the fall-out bunker, they had planned for its new function. Individual bedrooms were built to accommodate up to a hundred personnel. A restaurant and kitchen had been installed together with a TV room, a cinema room and a lounge area where off duty scientists and military personnel could unwind. There was no alcohol within the walls of Station K and smoking was completely banned. The builders had tried to make living such a spartan existing more bearable by installing air exchange units that were thermostatically controlled, meaning in the majority of areas underground, the air was always fresh, and the temperature was maintained at a steady 20 degrees centigrade. The odd-shaped windowless structures above ground housed the air exchange units.

Karl Symonds looked in first on the microbiology laboratory. This was the coldest place in the complex. Whilst the main areas were kept at 20 degrees centigrade, this laboratory was always at a constant 10 degrees centigrade and the large walk-in freezers were set to minus 30 degrees centigrade. This was the domain of Dr Perry Hughes PhD. Dr Hughes was the senior biologist at Porton Down and had developed the nerve agent currently being experimented with as part of a battlefield weapon. Karl Symonds didn't like biological weapons but admired Perry Hughes' skill and ability as someone who understood such things.

After a cursory greeting and being confined to the safer white zone outside the main laboratory, Karl reminded his colleague about the project development meeting and left the cold laboratory and continued his tour. He found most people in good form and was excited to learn about the individual progress in the various departments whilst he'd been away.

He eventually finished up in the machine room. This was the Professor's best-kept secret. It was a place where practical things happened. Where men worked with their hands and their brains. It took Karl Symonds away from theoretical problems to real engineering problems where the solution could be seen and handled. This was an engineering workshop that would not have looked out of place in any major industrial company.

The man in charge was Staff Sergeant Bobby Tay. Bobby was a career soldier and a member of the Royal Engineers. Bobby's skill lay in metal turning and finishing and he had proven to be an invaluable member of the team. Not only could he produce metal components to the finest tolerances, but he would suggest design changes to certain components that would lead to simpler manufacture later on.

Bobby was at a desk sketching something on a piece of A4 paper. Karl saw a face he didn't recognise sitting at another desk typing into one of the site's secure computers. All computers at Station K were slave units linked to a central processor and were thus shielded from the internet and social media sites. They could only process internal data. The main processor had so many levels of security and encryption the boffins estimated it would take a hacker more than 1000 years to crack it if they could find a way in in the first place.

The unknown man was wearing the uniform of a corporal in the Royal Air Force and was introduced to the Professor as Corporal Edward Hicks. He was a specialist in devising secure records and had only been at Station K for three weeks.

Karl welcomed the new member of staff, told Bobby to keep up the good work and retreated to his office.

After removing his poorly-tailored uniform jacket the Professor sat behind his desk. He was feeling his age and sat back closing his eyes. He reflected on his doctor's advice to slow down and retire to a peaceful haven in the country. Karl smiled remembering the conversation. Of course, the doctor had no idea how important the Professor was to national security nor that his advice could not possibly be taken.

Karl thought of the various stages the project still had to find resolutions for. He opened his eyes, sighed and told himself he would take the doctor's advice once the project was finished.

The meeting underground took place in the only conference room that had been built. There were several large flat-screen TV monitors on the wall at one end of the large conference table, and seating for up to fourteen people, plus the chairperson who sat at the head of the table under the TV monitors. This was usually Professor Karl Symonds.

Only department heads usually attended the project development meeting although if a particularly difficult problem was being discussed more junior scientists with more detailed knowledge would be invited.

There were eight people seated around the table. Each was eminent in their own field. They were experts in biological weapons, biological nerve agents, molecular science, materials engineering, propulsion systems and of course security. One small man with balding hair and 1940s style round glasses was sitting in the last chair down the table on Karl Symonds left. He looked out of place and was being ignored by these eminent scientists as they talked among themselves before Karl called the meeting to order.

"Gentlemen, it's good to be back. I hope you all got your work done despite my absence so let's get on with it. But first I'd like to introduce Mr Hector Forsyth. Hector joins us from the Ministry of Defence and is an accountant among other things." Karl let the end of this last remark hang in the air. "It seems we are to be audited and Hector here is the man who'll be doing it but don't expect to be asked for your financial details."

Everyone around the table looked suspicious but said nothing. As good manners dictated everyone said hello to the accountant who raised his hand to ask a question.

"I'm sorry, Professor, I know your work here is top secret but if you could fill me in a little, I'd have more idea of what I'm supposed to do. Otherwise, I might just get under everyone's feet.

Karl thought for a second. "Yes, I see. I know you've been vetted and are one of us although from a different discipline. I suppose there's no objection to reading you into the programme." Karl looked around the table. "Any objections?"

Everyone shook their heads.

"Now then, Mr Forsyth. It goes without saying that everything you hear from now on is super confidential and passing on anything you hear is punishable by a long prison sentence or worse."

"I understand, Professor."

"Good. I'm sure you know as well or better than I do how this project started. It is in my opinion this is an unholy alliance I never thought I would see. We are being funded by Russian money and working on a weapon that could be used against the nations in the West." Karl was sweating and wiped his brow with his handkerchief while taking a sip of water. "But that's for another day and another debate."

Hector Forsyth nodded as Karl started his tale.

"As you know chemical and biological weapons are banned under international treaty. But like all these things, those countries with the skills and the resources have carried on experimenting. Modern warfare is changing. The last two or three major conflicts have all been the same. The big powers thought smart laser-guided bombs were the weapons of the future. Fire them from an aircraft or a drone, miles away, and nobody is at risk. However, this form of warfare has been shown to be flawed.

All that happened was we destroyed a load of buildings and infrastructure such as roads, airports and so on but the enemy troops were still in place. Our infantry still has to go in and clean out the enemy's infantry and with all the destruction to buildings it's very dangerous and casualties are high. Also, once the target has been taken, we spend a fortune rebuilding it, having just knocked the hell out of it with our smart bombs." The Professor paused to sip more water. "Do you follow this, Hector?"

"Yes, yes I do. Please continue."

"You see, we were tasked many years ago with finding a way of hurting the enemy without destroying the buildings. It seemed more like science fiction, until now. Previously things like mustard gas in World War One had the advantage of putting enemy soldiers out of commission but if the wind changed it did the same to our troops. Also, in World War One, we rarely fought through towns so there was no physical damage from shelling and the like. The opposite as I've explained is true today so a general gas released over a town might wipe out its defenders and preserve the buildings, but our troops would have no protection when they entered, and the gas could still blow back."

Professor Symonds took another sip of water. A few scientists seated around the table showed signs of impatience with their leader but said nothing.

Karl continued. "Porton Down developed a slow-release compound that could overpower humans without killing them. The smallest drop either inhaled or dropped onto the skin can knock any human out for up to 48 hours. We saw the potential as a weapon. Something you can send into a fight zone that disabled all humans inside but didn't kill them; plus, if it was launched successfully, there would be no collateral damage." The Professor eyed the accountant.

"That's where we come in. Our mission is to devise a non-explosive means of delivering the chemical in such a way as to infect the enemy without them realising it and that my dear Hector is why we are here."

Hector was stunned. He knew about the connection with Russia after all, that's mainly why he was here, but the thought of chemical weapons disgusted him.

"So, what about our troops? You say you are developing a battlefield system meaning our soldiers are in contact with this liquid before they fire it."

"Good point and Dr Hughes from Porton has the answer." Karl opened his hand toward the Porton Down scientist, inviting him to answer.

"Mr Forsyth, I'm Perry Hughes from Porton Down." Both men nodded to each other. "As we developed Reagent 101, we also worked on an antidote. We have developed a simple pill that our troops take an hour before preparing to fire the weapon. If they take the same pill every twelve hours, Reagent 101 will have no effect on them whatsoever." Dr Hughes sat back looking pleased with himself.

Karl wanted to move on. "We have the material in Reagent 101, but we still need a lightweight delivery system. Our engineers have devised a very clever solution and it is that we are presently engaged on making happen."

"Can I ask what it is?" Hector Hughes paused seeing reluctance in the face of the Professor. He rapidly followed on, "Even if only in outline."

Karl clearly relented. "Imagine a normal shell. The things you see in all the war films. Well, suppose we used a regular handheld anti-tank weapon and re-engineered it to fire one of our R101 shells. The beauty is the round could be fired on a flat trajectory, be laser-guided and land on the ground untouched especially as there would be no explosive in the head. To the enemy, it would simply be an unexploded round. We're working to engineer a shell head connected to an onboard battery. It's a bit complicated as you might expect, but simply, we intend to place a rubberised cartridge of Reagent 101 inside a small door built into the side of the shell just above the firing charge. This part of the shell will also house the battery and the switch. Once it lands the impact will trigger the switch that will activate the onboard systems. Small vents built into the nose of the shell will open and jaws around the rubber cartridge will squeeze every fifteen seconds, sending R101 into the atmosphere. As the soldier who fires the weapon can direct the shell to the most heavily defended places, we estimate two shells could take out at least one infantry company." All eyes were on the man from the Ministry.

Hector had heard it but couldn't get his head around it. He tried to play everything back in an effort to better understand. Silence descended as Hector Forsyth grappled with what he's just heard.

"Let me understand this. You have a substance called Reagent 101 that if touched or comes into contact with humans in any way puts them into a coma?"

"Yes. Effectively sending them to sleep and therefore useless as fighters for up to 48 hours."

Karl continued to supply the information.

"You're developing a weapons delivery system to launch this R101 at the enemy using a lightweight battlefield antitank weapon?"

"Yes again. We haven't refined the propellant yet. We need a range of up to a mile and it may be simply re-engineering the existing weapon won't work but broadly speaking, yes. Once we've ironed out the systems the chemical will be fired by soldiers in the field using an anti-tank style laser-guided delivery system."

"And you say that R101 in gas form will be contained in a rubberised cartridge and will be introduced to your new shell through a side flap?"

"Spot on Mr Forsyth. The troops will have R101 in rubberised cartridges. Instead of loading a rifle during a battle, they'll simply load R101 into the shell and fire it from an anti-tank device."

"How big is the shell?"

"At the moment it is thirty centimetres high and eight centimetres in diameter."

"You say each shell is laser-guided and has moving parts so when it lands the impact will trigger the innards of the thing to start. What happens if a soldier drops the shell as he's loading it into his weapon?"

"Good point. The shell remains inert until it's loaded, and the anti-tank device is switched on. It's the combination of the shell inside the weapon and an external switch that effectively sends a small current to activate the onboard systems. So, you see, it's impossible to spread R101 by accident."

"And you have an antidote in pill form?"

"Yes. Our troops will be fully protected."

"You're sure a complicated shell with its side door loading and veins that pop open when it lands and rubber cartridges that get squeezed to release the gas will be robust enough to be a viable battlefield weapon?"

"Once we have perfected everything, then yes, Mr Forsyth. We will give this country the weapon the world has been looking for. A way to wage war with no casualties. Once R101 has been launched we simply wait a few hours and walk into our objective with no resistance, and nobody has died. It could be the end of war altogether."

Hector Forsyth was impressed but sceptical. However, he didn't voice his scepticism. He simply said he was impressed and looked forward to working with the team. He didn't reveal the real reason for his secondment to Station K.

The meeting went on to discuss various aspects of the project. Everyone admitted to making progress but engineering the shell casing from a new metal was proving difficult. The engineer in charge said he was working on a new approach and hoped to be able to report at the next meeting.

After a few hours of intense debate, the Professor called the meeting closed. Everyone was pleased to get back to their various tasks, but Hector Forsyth remained seated.

Once everyone had gone and the door was closed, Hector spoke up. "Well, I think that went OK."

"Yes, I agree. I'm sure they believed your cover story and asking those questions made it all sound logical." The Professor sat back and steepled his fingers in front of his face. "What do you plan to do?"

"I'm not sure yet. You know my brief from MI6, it's the money thing and the Russians. Whatever happens, we cannot allow them access to either the chemical or the weapons system. We're taking their money, but we already know the source of the funds is unofficial. It's the old saying of 'keep your enemies close'. When we got the approach from this character Koptic, we went along with it as a way of keeping an eye on what the Russians were up to. We don't want their money and equally, we can't allow them access to anything you're doing here. There's something afoot in the Ural Mountains and we need to know what it is. Koptic could be the key." The man called Hector Forsyth sat back. "I suppose it's a wait-and-see game but the nearer you get to field trials the nearer Koptic will expect something from us."

Karl Symonds stood and shook his head. "I'm glad I'm only a simple scientist. I'm happy to leave all the cloak-and-dagger stuff to you and MI6."

Both men left the room and headed for the canteen.

**

The Voice was in his office even though it was after seven o'clock. Mondays were always long and working late bolstered his hard-working man of the people image. In reality, he had spent the past few hours grappling with the problem the Russian had set him. He knew he could do nothing until the spy inside the station in Yorkshire contacted him, but he also needed a plan. How could he steal a new secret weapon from a highly protected army camp?

As was his usual practice, he was sipping a very expensive 25-year-old single malt when one of his burner phones vibrated. This was his own working phone, so he had no fears in answering it.

"Yes?"

"It's Blackstone. We have a problem."

The Voice was annoyed. He wondered why people only brought him problems and bad news. "I don't pay you to bring me problems. I pay you to make problems disappear."

"That's as may be, but your love of decisive action has backfired. Killing that car dealer was a big mistake."

The Voice thought back. It was Vlad who told him to have Cameron Bowie killed and to make sure it was public.

"What do you mean? You told me it would be investigated by a second-rate murder team and filed as unsolved. You said no one would think twice about holding a proper investigation." The Voice raised his undistorted voice. "So, what's gone wrong?"

"Some interfering pathologist, that's what. You used the same killer to get rid of the first victim as you have with the car bloke. The pathologist noticed the similarities and marked them as related."

"So?"

"So!" The man called Blackstone was incredulous. "So! You say *so*! Related murders aren't filed away as unsolved, nor are they given to normal overworked murder detectives. Cases like this are given to heavyweights and you've pulled yourself the heaviest of them all, Detective Chief Inspector Steve Burt and his Special Resolutions Unit."

"Listen. I pay you well to take care of things. Just deal with it."

"How?" Blackstone was screaming into his phone.

"It's your problem. Just calm down."

Blackstone breathed heavily. "I am calm. This DCI has a reputation of being like a dog with a bone. Whoever killed your car dealer and your latest find's sidekick had better get out of town because they are as good as behind bars."

The Voice sneered. "Not necessarily, they don't know who I am so if this ace detective picks the whole crew up, I'm clean, but I do agree it's a distraction. Do what you can. You know the sort of thing, run

108

interference on the investigation. You've done it before. If this Burt guy gets too close, we'll have to think of a more permanent fix."

"Yeah. I suppose so, but I want no part in killing any policeman especially a senior one like Burt. He has one of the highest profiles in the Met. Go near him and the whole of the Met would be on the case. I'll run what interference I can but if I were you, I'd give your man the heads up and at least warn him."

"Yes, except he's still stealing cars for me, but I'll think about it. Now listen, I'm glad you've called." The Voice was concerned about the murders being connected but felt he was safe. However, Blackstone might be able to help with his spy problem. If he did, the Voice surmised he could have Eddie do away with him to preserve the Voice's anonymity.

"I have a problem up in Yorkshire that needs dealing with. There's not a lot to do just now but we need to meet up to discuss it. I'll call you and don't panic over the killings, we're safe."

The Voice hung up and lifted the crystal glass containing his whisky. As he sipped, he wondered if it might be time to get out of this business of taking orders from Vlad. If Eddie Randall was close to being arrested for the killings, then maybe he should take care of the Russian before he was arrested, especially if Blackstone could interfere with the murder investigation and buy Eddie some time.

The whisky was tasting better and doing its job of reaching the Voice's darker side.

***

The Voice was preparing to leave his office as Steve Burt was laying his daughter, Rosie, into her cot. He stood looking at the little pink bundle and marvelled at what life had given him. Not only a lovely and healthy daughter but a beautiful, intelligent wife. He continued to stare into the cot and sighed. Life couldn't be any better.

As he returned to the living room of their apartment Steve's mobile rang. He glanced at the clock on the wall. It was 8.17 p.m. Slightly annoyed at being called at this time, he noticed the caller ID. It was Major Robert Hope, Steve's old commanding officer from his days in the Army.

The DCI had met Bob at a recent reunion and knew he was worried about his son who had apparently gone missing. Steve's wife Alison rolled her eyes and silently mouthed at him, "It had better not be work."

Steve shook his head as he accepted the call. "Hi, Bob. How are you doing?"

"Steve I'm really sorry to bother you but we still haven't heard from our son, Alex. It's been another week. His mother and I are quite frantic. I've pestered the MOD but am getting nowhere. I've reported him missing to the police but they're not doing anything. You're our last hope, Steve. Can you please look into this and find our boy?"

Steve could tell the ex-Major was close to tears. At the reunion Bob had told Steve that his son, Captain Alex Hope, had been commissioned into the Royal Military Police and was now working undercover on some secret operation. Steve had learnt he'd been out of contact with his parents for seven weeks at the time of the reunion and with another week gone it was now eight weeks. The DCI didn't know much about RMP covert operations, but this seemed a long time without contact. Usually, a liaison officer would be in regular contact with an officer's family when he was on such an operation. Silence wasn't normal.

"You've heard nothing at all?" It was a silly response, but Steve couldn't think what to say to his old friend.

"Not a thing, Steve. We both know even from our days this is unusual. Something's wrong. I just feel it. I'm begging for your help."

Steve heard himself reply. "I'll look into it tomorrow, Bob. Can you send me Alex's details by email? You know the thing, service number, age and a picture if you have one. I can't promise but I'll see what I can do and get back to you."

Relief flooded over the mobile connection. The Major was overwhelmed and was almost crying.

"Thanks, Steve. I'll get everything to you right now."

"Address it to Detective Constable Amelia Cooper. She's my admin assistant."

"Will do and God bless you, Steve."

An embarrassed DCI broke the connection and wondered what he had just committed himself to. If he knew what was ahead of him, he might not have enjoyed the sound night's sleep he did.

Chapter Eleven

Steve's wife insisted he wear his best suit. Over breakfast, she told him she'd laid out his suit together with a new white shirt and she had polished up his newest black shoes.

"I'm not having you go in front of that Parliamentary Committee today looking like a scruff. Just for once, you'll look like a senior police officer," she gently chided him as she fed their daughter and watched her husband retreat back to their bedroom to change into his best clothes.

Tuesday the 24th of March had dawned bright enough for Steve to walk to his office. He enjoyed the walk, and it gave him time to consider his day ahead. He was worried about the late-night call from Robert Hope. As he walked, he considered he'd perhaps promised more than he could deliver. He had no particular pull with the MOD, nor did he know anyone who might help. As he rounded a corner, he had to take avoiding action as a youth on an electric scooter drove toward him. At that moment, his mind cleared, and he saw a way to help his old commander.

As his walk progressed, Steve thought about the day ahead. He'd meet with DI Peter Jones first and bring himself up to speed on the children's abduction cases. He'd then go over what they'd gleaned about the two murders, and he'd have Mary Dougan talk to the pathologist who had started the whole murder enquiry off. He took a deep breath as he walked, thinking about the CCTV footage plus the VCR tapes Mary had secured from the filling station, and to his horror, he also had to go to Parliament and meet some committee.

The DCI was deep in thought and surprised himself by talking out loud as he walked. "All that before lunch. I wonder what the afternoon will bring?" He arrived at the office at exactly 08.14 a.m.

The place was quiet, and he thought he was the first to arrive but as he settled behind his desk Peter Jones peered around his office door minus his jacket and with his sleeves rolled up. Clearly, he'd been in for a while.

"Morning Steve; coffee?" The DI held up a cardboard cup.

"You need to ask?"

Peter put the coffee down and sat in front of the DCI. He looked over his shoulder at the map on the far wall. "That map is a good idea. I see Poppy's marked the schools and the kids' addresses. Matt's marked the location of all the CCTV cameras around the schools and the home addresses. The problem is a lot of them have fixed views. They only look at the school gates and road junctions so unless our abductor has been standing at the same place for days, we're unlikely to spot him if he's on foot." The DI sipped his coffee. "It's the same with a car, but we might get lucky. Terry Harvey's letting us use his viewing suite and Matt's there now trawling through three weeks' worth."

"Good. How did it go yesterday?"

"Not well. I just don't get it, Steve. Three kids have just vanished. We started with the first one. We spoke to his teacher, the headmistress, the caretaker and the lollypop lady. We drew a blank with them all. We tried to catch as many parents as we could when they were dropping off their kids but none of them saw anything suspicious except one said she thought she'd seen a red van parked up outside the school a few times but didn't know the make. We interviewed the mother. What a mess she was in but couldn't help. It seems the young lad Billy Daley has just vanished. We did a house to house around his estate but again nothing."

"What's your best guess?"

"I'm sorry Steve but I don't have one. I've got uniform out at all three home addresses doing house to house and I've got warrants to search the houses. They may have been done away with and hidden in the houses." Peter finished his coffee. "But to be honest, I'd be surprised. Having met the mothers, they looked a poor excuse for womanhood. They could be sisters. They're all small, undernourished, need a good wash, chain smoke and I'm sure they're all on some form of illegal substance. You should see how they live. It's real squalor. If these kids have run off, I wouldn't blame them."

"How about the second and third?"

"Just the same. We interviewed the mothers. Like I said they're all the same and no help. The other two schools were the same. No one saw anything, no one knows anything, and no one seemed surprised these three kids might have run off."

The DI noted his boss seemed to be lost in thought. Steve was staring ahead as he often did when an idea was forming in his head. He sat forward, obviously wrestling with something.

"Something you said, Peter. It's triggered a thought, but I can't get it out."

Steve often had ideas that refused to immediately surface. He knew he would agonise over the disappearing thought until it surfaced.

"Sorry Peter, whatever it was has gone." Steve gulped the last of his lukewarm coffee down and expertly threw it into his waste basket.

Peter Jones stood up. "Once we've finished the CCTV, we're planning another sweep of the areas around the kids' houses. I've got uniforms lining up. No one likes kids going missing. We'll search the houses but unless we get lucky, we're stuck."

"Yeah, sorry to land this one on you Peter. Do your best and remember, May Dunlop will be looking for a progress report later."

"Oh no, something to look forward to." As he was leaving Peter stopped and turned to Steve. "I just hope none of these three turn up dead."

Poppy and Mary seemed to arrive at the same time. They were giggling like a couple of schoolgirls at something. DC Mary Dougan was a believer in power dressing and was wearing her usual tailored trouser suit, white blouse and black shoes with small heels. The DCI had to admit she looked good. Poppy on the other hand was wearing a pale blue tight and very revealing dress that made her look young and a bit flirty. The DCI wasn't sure about Metropolitan Police guidance on dress code for a junior officer, but he felt sure Poppy's attire probably breached the code. She seemed to have an ever-extensive wardrobe of similar style dresses and the DCI wondered if there was a rich boyfriend on the scene.

Both detectives entered Steve's office and presented him with his second coffee of the day.

"I've got all the reports from Peter to tie up and Mary's going to let me have her notes from yesterday. The post-mortem reports on the murder victims are on the system but haven't thrown anything up. The two lots of CCTV are with Tech Services and I've sent all the financial stuff over to Financial Crimes." Poppy was smiling sweetly. Despite appearances, Poppy worked very hard. "I think we're getting up to date."

Poppy was standing and clearly keen to be at her desk. "Oh, and Miss Rough from Financial says she'll pop in this afternoon once she's examined our file and there's an e-mail from someone called Robert Hope."

The DCI nodded. Poppy left but Mary stayed and sat down in the chair recently vacated by Peter Jones.

"What have we got on the case then, DC Dougan?" The DCI was smiling but he could see his DC wasn't too sure about his use of her formal title.

"Well, I've written up all the notes and Poppy has the tapes from our interview of the two car salesmen to transcribe. The pair have been charged and released on police bail as you said, but here's the thing. After you'd gone yesterday, I got a call from central. The processing desk sergeant wasn't happy with one of the forms, so Poppy and I went over. Our two guys were locked up, but we had to get them into an interview room to keep everything correct. We started asking them formally for their addresses and so on just for the form." Mary looked a bit contrite. "I missed something on the form." She shrugged as though to say it has been corrected.

"Anyway, during this interview, the pair start to talk again about the Russian. I didn't want to call you in, and Poppy was able to sit in as the second officer, so I knew we were by the book."

Mary looked expectantly at her boss, hoping for an acknowledgement. She didn't get it so carried on.

"Anyway. They had a disagreement about which Russian was the one who might have ordered Cameron Bowie's killing. They'd obviously put their thoughts together. It seems the first Russian had visited the showroom before. They think Bowie was working for this first guy and his name was Vladimir. Then a few months ago a second Russian turned up and it was after this visit that a load more stolen cars started to arrive, and remember, the sales guys were told they didn't have to nick any more cars."

"Yes. I've got that. Carry on."

"Well, the first Russian, this guy Vladimir, turned up not long ago and had a stand-up row with Cameron Bowie but this time our pair admitted they'd heard more than they told us yesterday." Mary paused for effect.

"Go on." The DCI was interested.

"They heard things like, 'You are using our facilities to line your own pocket!' and, 'Dimitri is a member of the mob. He'll cut your balls off if you cross him!'. But more interestingly they heard this Vladimir say, 'I'll kill you myself you two-timing rat'."

Steve sat back looking at his detective constable. "What do you make of it?"

Mary had realised her boss was looking very smart today but decided to say nothing. "The two boys think that their boss Bowie was tied up with Vladimir but there's someone else below the Russian who keeps a low profile but organises all Vladimir's dirty work. They think the second Russian moved in and tried to take over Vladimir's empire and Bowie went along with it while still working for the first Russian. When Vladimir got to hear about it he had Cameron Bowie murdered to make a point to any of his other associates who might be lured away by this Dimitri."

"I see." Steve was stroking his chin. "You now think there is a turf war going on in London between two Russian gangs involving shipping stolen cars to Russia and that Bowie was killed as an example to others?"

"That's about it."

"Sounds feasible. Look, Mary, get this new tape to Poppy. We need it transcribed, and I need you to go and see the pathologist who posted both bodies. Try and find out what's not in her report. Do that this morning. I'll look in on the CCTV suite but I've to be somewhere at eleven this morning. After you've spoken to the pathologist get back here and try and view some CCTV. Also, get onto the collator. See if there are any links to Russian gang activity. We'll go back to Mile End this afternoon and interview the foreman at the workshop behind the showroom. See what he knows. Remember one of the sales guys said the second Russian had spent some time with Rory McClean. Chances are he knows who this Russian is."

"Right. See you here about two?"

"Yeah. I should be back by then."

Mary Dougan left to talk to Poppy.

On his mental to-do list, Steve came to Robert Hope's son. On his walk in, he'd decided to try and get in touch with Sir Patrick Bond and elicit his help with an introduction to the MOD. Sir Patrick was Head of MI6 and he and Steve had crossed paths a few times over the years. Sir Patrick had always been approachable and had even suggested at one point the DCI might become an agent.

Steve had Sir Patrick's private mobile already in his phone's memory. He speed-dialled it and Sir Patrick lazily answered on the third ring.

"Yes?"

"Sir Patrick. It's Steve Burt."

"I have caller ID. I know it's you and I'm very busy."

Steve had expected a warmer welcome. He hadn't spoken to Patrick Bond for several months.

"We're all busy and I wouldn't have called unless it was urgent."

"Sorry, Steve. I've got a bit on just now and every time you call its usually means trouble, but I was a bit sharp. I apologise." Steve heard Sir Patrick shuffling papers. "Now. What can I do for you?"

"I need an introduction to someone at the MOD. Doesn't have to be top brass. Just a colonel or something similar." Steve laughed so Sir Patrick would understand.

"Just like that?" Sir Patrick wanted to know more.

"Yes. I know you have contacts all over. I just need to talk to someone about a missing RMP officer."

Even over the airwaves, the DCI could detect a change in Sir Patrick. There was silence for longer than was necessary.

"What about a missing officer?" Sir Patrick's tone was slow and deliberate. It was also full of suspicion.

Steve had picked up on the vibrations and knew something wasn't right. Despite regarding Sir Patrick Bond as a friend, Steve also knew he was head of the UK's international spy network and as such had a ruthless streak to him. The DCI decided to be careful and not give too much away.

"I served under his father when I was in the Army. His son's off somewhere and his father simply wants to know he's all right."

"Mm. What's the name of this missing son?"

116

"Look, Patrick. I don't need to bother you with the details. I only need a name and a phone number of a pen pusher within the MOD."

"Afraid it's not that simple Steve. What's the boy's name?" Suspicion rested in the air. The DCI saw no harm in giving out Bob's son's name.

"It's Captain Alex Hope RMP."

The response wasn't what Steve had expected from a Knight of the Realm. "Shit!"

Steve waited until Sir Patrick had recovered his composure. He waited in silence, but it was obvious the Head of MI6 wasn't happy with this conversation.

After what seemed like minutes Sir Patrick was back. "Look, Steve, we'd better meet. Be in my office this afternoon at four o'clock and do not discuss this or tell anyone, including your Commissioner, that we are meeting. Till four." The line went dead.

Steve sat back and blew out his cheeks. He wondered what that had all been about and tried to play different scenarios in his head. After five minutes he gave up and looked at his watch. It was 09.22. He headed for the viewing suite in Technical Support to see how Peter Jones and Matt Conway were getting on viewing CCTV images from around the missing boys' schools and homes.

***

09:22 hours in any military establishment, was just like 09.22 a.m. anywhere. This Tuesday morning was also just like every other Tuesday below ground at Station K. The scientists and engineers were working on their specific part of the project while the senior people held their daily briefing.

An engineer from the army's Shrivenham College was describing his latest idea for the internal cavity of the shell. "I'll get it drawn up and give it to Staff Sergeant Tay to knock up. He should only need a few days and then we'll see." The Shrivenham engineer rubbed his hands in excitement. He found this whole experience of working underground one big adventure.

After listening to his senior staff, Professor Karl Symonds closed the meeting. He noticed the man from the MOD was missing.

The Shrivenham man called in on the workshop to find Army Staff Sergeant Bobby Tay and RAF Corporal Edward Hicks sitting at their desks reading. Although members of staff assigned to Station K were not allowed to leave except in cases of dire need, the Professor had agreed with his head of security that military personnel could visit the NAAFI store above ground within Montgomery Barracks. The Head of Security had undertaken a risk analysis and concluded that provided anyone who ventured above ground was put through the body scanners attached to the above and below ground airlocks on their way out and back, then there was no real security risk.

The two military men had only recently returned having bought a couple of new novels.

"Ah! Bobby. Can you and the corporal come with me to the drawing office? I have a new project for you."

The Shrivenham officer left whilst Bobby and Edward stood and followed. Bobby didn't like officers and especially officers who thought they knew more than him. He looked at the corporal and rolled his eyes.

The drawing office was almost next to the workshop but had the highest level of security. Because engineering blueprints could be easily copied, they were treated as though they were gold. As the record keeper Corporal Edward Hicks was responsible for collecting and returning all documents, including blueprints, back to the safe in the drawing office. A strict record was maintained, and each document had a unique bar code reference that could be tracked anywhere within Station K when it was passed through any of the forty fixed scanners.

The drawing office was like most seen in the industry. Because of the uniqueness of their work the military draughtsmen preferred the old-style large drawing board that required a pencil upon the drawing paper. They had access to CAD systems and although they used them, they often found them slow due in part to everything being on one mainframe. Slave terminals were never as fast.

The six draughtsmen who worked here also liked to see their designs forming on paper. It was easier for some of them to visualise a component as it developed and how it interacted with another part if it was drawn by them.

"Right Corporal, there is your signed authority form." The Shrivenham officer handed Edward a pink piece of paper. Edward Hicks then took the paper and scanned it into a reader that authorised the signature and imprinted a code onto the pink paper. He then walked to a safe that was built into the wall of the office but was surrounded and enclosed by thick armour proof glass. The pink form was again scanned as was Edward's cornea, as proof it was he who wished to open the heavy glass door, and then the safe. Whilst this was going on, Staff Sergeant Bobby Tay was not allowed inside the secure area. He and the officer waited for Edward to complete his task of gaining entry and retrieving the exact blueprint the pink form authorised him to remove.

Once everything was locked, Corporal Edward Hicks returned to the outside office, placed the pink sheet of paper inside a clear plastic wallet and stapled it to the blueprint. He handed everything to the army officer.

All three men returned to the workshop where the drawing of the latest component was described and discussed with Bobby Tay.

"You don't make it easy sir. This looks impossible. I'm not sure I can maintain the internal integrity of the metal if I make the walls so thin."

"I know what you mean but I've had a word with the manufacturer, and they say just because it's light, doesn't mean it's not strong."

The army officer from Shrivenham Engineering College laughed out loud at his own joke. Bobby thought he sounded like a horse.

"Seriously. The tensile strength will hold up but remember we only have a small amount of the material. It's very experimental and not scaled up for mass production yet."

Bobby nodded. "Yes sir. I see what you want. Give me a couple of days and we'll see what we can do."

"Splendid. I'll be off and leave you to get on with it." The officer turned to Corporal Hicks. "Remember Corporal, the blueprint has to go back tonight. I'll give you another pink slip tomorrow so you can get the drawing out again." He walked to the door. "If you need anything just let me know."

With that, the Royal Engineers officer was gone.

119

Bobby Tay took the drawing and started taking measurements before withdrawing a slug of the experimental metal and commencing the milling process that would result in a beautifully turned component that met each requirement of the drawing.

Staff Sergeant Bobby Tay mused he could do his part but wondered if this would be the last time he'd work on such a component.

***

The Voice received a call from the spy inside Station K at exactly 08.49 a.m., although he didn't know what the place was called or exactly what it was. The caller simply said: "It's in play. Be ready in four weeks from now. Got it? Four weeks from Tuesday 24th of March. Next time I call we're on. Use the adverts in the newspaper when you have something to tell me. Simple code. The product is mobile and weighs around five kilos loaded so transportation won't be a problem."

The line went dead, and the Voice panicked; he was afraid and needed help. He also needed a plan.

Chapter Twelve

After Mary had left, the DCI visited the viewing suite located in the vast area called Technical Support. He found Peter Jones, Matt Conway and the head of the unit, Inspector Terry Harvey, studiously looking at frame after frame of slightly grainy images on a vast television screen. The three were sitting in cinema-style seats and apart from the lack of sound and popcorn they could have been in an upmarket West End theatre.

As the DCI approached all three waved to acknowledge they'd seen him, but Terry Harvey rose and signalled Steve to join him outside the suite.

"We've got a problem or rather, you've got a problem."

Steve knew Terry well and knew he was being serious. "What kind of a problem?"

"One in a superintendent's uniform called Blackstone."

"Never heard of him. Who is he?"

"He's a bit cloak-and-dagger. Says he's head of a special serious crimes undercover unit."

"So?"

"He says your CCTV tapes of the Mile End crime scene are off-limits and cannot be viewed by the likes of us."

The DCI's jaw fell. "You're joking!"

"Afraid not. He told me the area was part of a sensitive operation that had nothing to do with any murder case and those tapes contain sensitive information pertinent to his project. In short, we can't have them."

Steve stood staring at Terry almost lost for words. "Where does this guy live?"

"Don't know but I imagine above the tenth floor."

"Thanks, Terry, I'll deal with this." Steve made to leave the Head of Tech Support when he turned round. Remembering how Terry had conjured up solutions to problems in the past, Steve looked at his friend and raised an eyebrow. "I don't suppose…?"

Inspector Terry Harvey was grinning. "Well, those cameras are linked into the Metropolitan Police Camera unit, and it just so happens I have a new piece of software I need to get my people trained on that might just be able to access certain cameras' individual outputs."

Steve remembered Terry was a gifted manipulator of the rules. Both men looked at each other and an air of conspiracy passed between them.

"How soon?" The DCI knew not to push it.

"If it works and we don't get caught we might have something by close of play today but no promises. It might not work."

"Terry, you're a star. See what you can do. I'm out now for the rest of the morning and am a bit busy this afternoon so maybe we can see if you get anything first thing tomorrow?"

"Yeah, that'll work. See you then oh, and by the way, nice suit!"

The DCI headed back to his office determined to discover who Superintendent Blackstone was and why he thought he could interfere in this murder case.

***

In his office, the DCI called his boss, Commander Alfie Brooks. Alfie answered on the first ring.

"Got a minute, sir?"

"Yes, if it's important but are you not supposed to be over in Parliament about now?"

"I've got a few minutes. Can I come up?"

"Yes of course but you'd better not be late for that committee." Alfie cut the call.

The DCI went straight to the twelfth floor where Commander Brooks' office was located. Alfie had a fearsome secretary who acted as his gate guard. Rumour had it that many officers had tried to see the Commander without an appointment and had regretted their encounter with this lady.

On this occasion, Steve was ushered straight in. Alfie was in civilian clothes today. Steve thought the Commander out of uniform resembled an old farmer or a retired bank manager.

"What's on your mind?" Alfie was seated in one of two comfortable armchairs located away from his grand desk. Steve was seated in the other.

"Ever heard of a Superintendent Blackstone?"

Alfie looked puzzled and screwed up his face in concentration. "There's a Blackstone runs a specialised surveillance unit. Is that him?"

"Sounds likely. He's denied us access to some CCTV footage. Any thoughts."

"No, none at all. What case is it?"

"The Mile End Murder."

"Strange. I can't think why CCTV around the Mile End Road would be a problem." The Commander sat more upright in his chair. "You're not asking for any footage from secret surveillance cameras his unit might have set up?"

"No, just the traffic cameras."

"Leave it with me. I'll ask around quietly. I presume you've found other ways of viewing the footage." Alfie Brooks was smiling and looking at his watch.

Steve took the hint and stood. He looked directly at the older man. "I couldn't possibly comment, sir."

DCI Burt left to attend his interview by the Parliamentary Select Committee on Policing. This was a distraction he could do without given the workload he had and now an afternoon meeting with the Head of MI6 and a mysterious superintendent to contend with.

***

The DCI arrived at the correct meeting room to find two other officers present. Both were in uniform and wore the rank badges of superintendents. One was a female officer and based on the medals she was showing, she'd been a police officer for quite a few years. As they introduced themselves Steve wondered if one of them might be Blackstone. Neither was.

The committee filed in as the three officers took their seats at a table facing into a horseshoe-shaped table arrangement. Steve sat on the left of one of the superintendents. There were only five members on this committee, three men and two ladies. As he'd been briefed in his instructions to attend, the DCI knew the committee chairman was one Malcolm Freeman. From the seating arrangements, he assumed the well-dressed, rather portly man sitting at the top of the horseshow was the chairman. The two ladies sat on either side of Mr Freeman and the remaining two men sat next to the women.

There was a general air of getting organised as a bailiff placed name cards in front of each committee member to identify them for the three officers. He then approached the table and having asked each their name, he put similar name cards in front of them. Steve thought now everyone knew who they were. He found the whole exercise a bit out of date but tried not to smile. Everything seemed very serious.

Malcolm Freeman as the chairman opened the meeting by introducing his committee colleagues and thanking the three busy and dedicated officers for sparing the time to attend his committee. He explained this was an informal gathering designed to allow the committee members to better understand the concerns of more hands-on senior officers rather than the usual career officers who were more political than the police. Steve noticed the members of the committee smiled and nodded at this statement.

"Let's get to it, shall we?" The DCI warmed to the chairman. He seemed to be friendly enough and appeared to want to hear from the three officers. "Our style is more informal than most Parliamentary committees, but we do seek answers."

The chairman started off by asking the female superintendent to give an account of her many years' service in the Met. Similar questions were put to the other two officers and Steve found himself happily explaining his career to date.

The other members of the committee ferreted away at topics like budgets, manpower, resources. The list went on. The DCI got off lightly as being the only CID officer and the most junior present he wasn't expected to have responsibility for funding or expenditure. The few questions that came his way he easily answered until he was put on the

124

spot at the end of the ninety-minute grilling each officer had sat through. The question came from Malcolm Freeman himself.

"Mr Burt, as a CID officer with a long history of successfully solving serious crimes such as murder, what is the one thing you would change within the Metropolitan Police?"

Steve knew this was a difficult question. So far, his answers had been neutral and knew that no one on the twelfth floor back at the Yard could object to any of his statements. But this was a different question. This would go on the record and if he got it wrong, there could be consequences.

The DCI thought hard. "Well, sir…" he dragged out his answer, "I suppose I'd be more selective with our graduate entry scheme." This seemed a good neutral response until Malcolm Freeman spoke again.

"In what way would you be more selective? We've been told by various officers sitting where you are that recruiting graduates has been a good thing for the Force."

Steve was getting in deep and decided in for a penny, etc. "I agree but what I mean is we sometimes get entrants who simply don't have the basic cunning to be front-line police officers. A degree in geography doesn't mean the degree is any good on the streets. We have very young, wet behind the ears graduates, being promoted into CID as sergeants after only three years in the job while we have qualified experienced CID officers with ten years' experience, but no degree stuck as detective constables. We need to vet applicants better to make sure they are mentally suited for the job and extend their training periods."

Steve realised he'd maybe said too much.

Malcolm Freeman had made notes all through the DCI's rant. "Interesting, Mr Burt."

The chairman smiled benignly at his audience as he gathered up his papers and called the meeting to an end.

"There are tea and biscuits in the anteroom. I'll join you in a minute." Malcolm made a performance of being seen to be busy. As he exited through a door at the rear of the room, he called over to Steve. "Mr Burt? If you have a few minutes, I'd appreciate a chat over our tea. I'll only be five minutes, I promise." Malcolm waved and was gone.

Steve was on his second cup of tea although he'd have preferred coffee and was talking to a member of the committee called Sarah Wilson. She was MP for a Manchester constituency and clearly knew nothing about policing. Malcolm Freeman rushed in. He seemed to be a man in a hurry. A real go-getter. Steve was impressed by the chairman who singled him out as soon as he entered the room.

Malcolm arrived with hand outstretched. "Mr Burt, nice to meet you at last." Both men shook hands and Malcolm expertly guided the DCI away from the Manchester MP.

"Please, it's Steve."

"And it's Malcolm."

Steve was always suspicious of such gushing introductions but felt this was just how this man was.

"Your views on Graduate Entry were very enlightening. We've heard similar points raised but the people on the twelfth floor of your building think it makes them look good and of course you're right. It's the poor passed over men and women with experience that suffer, plus they end up carrying over-promoted colleagues." Malcolm seemed passionate about this, but Steve thought he was probably passionate about everything he became involved in.

"Good to know it's not just me."

"No. No, but you're the figurehead. Your name comes up a lot as an officer with the best clear up record in the Met. Plus, your reputation is of someone who gets the job done regardless of all the red tape we politicians place in your way." The committee chairman smiled at the DCI.

"Look, Steve. I've long felt the graduate entry scheme needed overhauling but there's no willingness from within. I could do with your help." Malcolm stared at Steve trying to gauge his reaction. "I could set up a subcommittee to look into this. If you would agree to serve on the committee, I really think we could make something happen and open up opportunities for long-serving good quality officers who don't have a degree. What do you say?"

Steve thought back to his conversation with Matt Conway and how Matt really resented being older than Peter Jones and still only a sergeant despite having passed his inspector's exams. Steve remembered Matt's comments about fast-track graduates.

"Malcolm, I'd love to help but to be honest, I'm not a committee man and I've got a horrible workload at the moment."

Malcolm put his teacup down and placed his hand on Steve's shoulder. "Don't decide now." He paused. "Look, we're having a drinks party here at the house next week. Nothing grand, just an excuse for we MPs to load up on taxpayer's booze on the pretext of promoting Parliament." He laughed at his own joke. "Come as my guest. I'll leave a card for you with the Sergeant at Arms. That'll see you in. It's six-thirty next Tuesday night. I'll see you there and we can chat some more."

Malcolm looked at his watch. "Must dash. More meetings and paperwork. See you next week."

Steve was left standing feeling a whirlwind had just passed through. He hadn't agreed to attend the bash but knew he was expected and that he'd be going. The DCI suspected no one turned down Malcolm Freeman.

***

The DCI arrived in his office at one fifteen. Peter Jones and Matt Conway were out following up on the abductions. Poppy was working away at her desk and Mary Dougan was writing up what looked like notes.

Steve felt exhausted but seeing the map of the abduction sites on his wall stirred something inside his brain. He tried to recall the conversation with Peter Jones. Something Peter had said had triggered a thought that remained stuck at the back of his brain. He sat, eyes closed, trying to force whatever he was thinking out into the open. After a few minutes, he gave up and called Mary into his office.

"How did you do with the pathologist and the collator?"

"The pathologist tried to help but she didn't have a lot, no forensics whatsoever. As she said, not even a hair. All she had was the similarities to both bodies. The knife is the only link, and she did say even that was tenuous at best. The second killing was professional given the precise nature of the wound. The CSIs found a blood drop near the second victim and the pathologist hoped it might have been from the killer, but no such luck. It belonged to the victim. She thinks the killer may have either wiped the blade or the blood dropped from it as he closed the flick knife up. If he did and we find the knife she'll be able to get a match." Mary sat down. "But that's all we have."

"Mm. It's not much." The DCI stared at the far wall and his eyes were once again drawn to the abduction map. He stared at it for a while, but nothing came back to him. He returned his attention back to his detective constable.

"What about the collator?"

Marry giggled. "What about the collator? He's a randy old man. You might have warned me."

She continued to giggle.

"Sorry Mary, but I didn't know. What happened?" Steve was smiling as Mary continued.

"Nothing happened but it could have. All his records are computerised, but he insisted on showing me his archived files. They're kept in a separate storeroom. As soon as we were in there, he started making comments about my hair and my clothes. Asked if I was married or had a boyfriend. When I said no, he asked me on a date. I tell you sir if I hadn't escaped, I'd be the next Mrs Collator. He said he'd been married four times and was looking for number five."

"Do you want to report it?"

"Good God no! He's harmless and once we were outside in his main office, he was the perfect gent. I think he's just lonely." Mary looked oddly at her boss. She arched her left eyebrow. "But two can play that game. A bit of flirting and it's amazing how cooperative certain gentlemen can be."

Steve knew exactly what she meant but was surprised. He had Mary Dougan marked down as a bit strait-laced. This admission moved her up a few notches in Steve's opinion.

Mary carried on. "Several Russian gangs are trying to get established in London. The biggest has direct links to the Government in Russia. They're mainly into drugs and prostitution and are by far the most established. One of the late comers is an anti-Government gang. They seem to be intent on destabilising the Russian Government and any organisation that supports them. Seems it's run by a guy called Vladimir

Skoysky. They're pretty small time and are into carjacking among other things. The Collator said they were well-financed and have been linked to a couple of shootings, but nothing sticks."

Steve interrupted. "Any suggestions their carjacking could be linked to our Mile End murder?"

"No, but I'd bet this Vladimir is the one those two car salesmen spoke about. I'd say he could be the first Russian our victim was working for."

"Yes. You could be right. Anything else?"

"There are other mobs but mostly small time, so I got the collator to print out any names he had of Russian gang members on file. Nothing stood out except one. A Dimitri Grochic, he's the enforcer for another new Russian mob." Mary looked expectantly at her boss who sensed she had something to say.

"Go on."

"Well. It's only a theory but what if our victim Bowie was set up by the other Russian mob, this bloke Vladimir, to chop cars? Suppose the operation was small-time, low-key, with our salesmen stealing the cars. Then the mob got greedy and upped the ante. Say they brought in more professional car thieves and started to process more cars. Then say our other gang — that's this Dimitri — push their way in. Remember the sales guys said that after the second Russian visited, the throughput of stolen cars became industrial. Vladimir had set the operation up, but Dimitri wanted to take it over."

Steve thought Mary was onto something. "Go on."

"Well. Vladimir wouldn't be happy as you can imagine. Suppose he confronts Bowie. Remember what the two lads told me they'd overheard the last time Vladimir was at the showroom. Say Bowie was in over his head and the first Russian, that's Vladimir, has him killed publicly, making a statement to the other gangs, including Dimitri."

"So, you think this Vladimir is our man for the killing?"

"I think he might have ordered it. According to my lecherous collator, the mob Vladimir is associated with tend to hire in their muscle. Maybe a local hoodlum was contracted to do it."

The DCI sat back. "Interesting; well done, Mary. I don't suppose you got an address for either of these Russians?"

"No. Sorry Steve." Mary ventured to use the DCI's Christian name. She had used it before, and he had told her to use it when there was no one else about. The DCI also noticed and took it as a sign of growing confidence in his DC.

Steve stood up. "Let's get over to Mile End and see what Mr Rory McClean has to say. At least we have a couple of Russian names to throw at him."

***

The Voice was at his desk finishing his sandwich and trying to relax just as the DCI and Mary Dougan were exiting the car park from New Scotland Yard.

The Voice had enjoyed his morning but needed to find a plan to steal the weapon the Russian was going to pay twenty-five million dollars for. He had four weeks but nowhere to start. As he crumpled up the paper his sandwich had been wrapped in, one of his seemingly growing number of burner phones vibrated. He saw it was Vlad. He let it ring longer than usual before answering.

"Yes?"

"We need three Audi A8s all in dark colours, all less than five thousand miles and have them at the workshop by the end of the week. Got it?"

The Voice was taken aback. "The police are all over that place. It would be suicide to take stolen cars anywhere near the workshop."

A long sigh came from the other end of the phone. "You can take care of the police. We didn't bump off Cameron Bowie just to stop. We have buyers for these cars. Get them there by Friday."

The Voice knew he was beaten and agreed. He carried on. "I've heard from your man."

"Good. Deal with him. Only tell me where you'll get the weapon and when. I'll give you instructions on where to deliver it." Vlad hung up.

Chapter Thirteen

As Mary drove the pool car towards Mile End Road, the DCI sat contemplating his caseload. He couldn't see a clear way forward with either the double murder or the abductions, although he was convinced he had something in his subconscious that might shed some light on the case. If he could only bring his thoughts to the surface!

His upcoming meeting with the Head of MI6 was a concern. All he wanted was to help his old company commander gain some peace and prove his son was alive and well but Sir Patrick's response didn't sit well with the DCI.

Then there was Superintendent Blackstone. Why was he being awkward about the CCTV tapes? Steve knew they were only national road safety fixed cameras and couldn't possibly have anything to do with a sophisticated surveillance operation. So why object to handing over the images?

The journey passed quickly and the two detectives drove to the rear of Crystal Motors showroom and parked up. The large roller shutter door was down but the pedestrian door attached to the large door was ajar.

Steve and Mary approached and, without knocking or announcing their arrival, simply walked in. A Land Rover was sitting on a hoist but there was no one working on it. The DCI consulted his watch. It was 2.33 p.m. Steve spotted the office and saw figures sitting inside. He nodded to Mary who followed him as he pushed open the door to reveal three men in white overalls sitting, smoking and drinking tea.

Without any preamble, the DCI opened up. "Which one of you is Rory McClean?"

The oldest of the three put down his tea and looked at the newcomer and his attractive companion. "Who wants to know?"

"I do. Are you McClean?"

"Might be. Might not be but I'd rather admit who I am to your associate. Don't you need to know who I am, darlin'?"

Mary ignored him.

"Just tell me if you're McClean and we can get on. If you don't want to say who you are we'll have to arrest all three of you and have our conversation at the local nick."

"You, cops?"

Steve knew the type of individual he had in front of him. "Did you see that Detective Constable Dougal?" Quick as a flash he worked it out. The DCI paused as he produced his warrant card.

"DCI Burt. This is DC Dougan." Steve nodded towards Mary. "Now. You are…?"

"OK. I'm Rory McClean. What of it?"

"Well, Mr McClean, we understand you run this chop shop."

"Just a minute copper, this ain't no chop shop. We do auto repairs, that's all."

"Repairs on stolen cars I hear."

"Sorry copper, you got it all wrong. You can't prove anything. This is a legitimate business but I'm just the foreman. See, me and the lads just follow orders. You'd have to talk to the owner."

"I'd like that. Who is he and where will I find him?"

"That's difficult. See, he travels a lot and I'm not sure of his name."

The DCI was happy the way the interview was developing. He knew that if he led a suspect to think he had the upper hand then Steve usually got on top of the interview.

"But he pays you?"

Rory McClean wasn't sure where these questions were leading but was confident he could handle this policeman.

"Of course, he pays us." He looked at his two colleagues and all three started to laugh. "We don't do this for fun."

"What else does he pay you to do? I'm talking about the Russian."

All three men in white overalls instantly stopped laughing. Their expressions changed and Steve sensed fear in the room.

"No idea what you're talking about."

"Did he pay you to kill Cameron Bowie?"

McClean turned red. "What!" He stood up. He was a big man but would be no match for the DCI should he try force. As soon as he stood up, he immediately sat down again. "You think any of us done a murder? You're mad, mate. You can't pin that on us."

"But maybe I can unless you cooperate." Steve sat down on a spare chair. He was deliberately talking softly in order to appear reasonable.

"Look. We don't know nothing about murder. Like I said, we're an auto repair business and do what we're told. That's all."

"You had a Russian visit you last week. Who was it?"

Rory McClean didn't answer straight away. Steve took this as a good sign. McClean was thinking about his answer.

"How do you know that?"

"Information. So, he was here. Who is he?"

Rory McClean again paused, still thinking. He concluded it wouldn't do any harm to admit what this copper already knew.

"He's the boss. His name is Dimitri Grochic."

Steve thought he'd turn the screw. "Interesting but you're lying. You see we know this building and the showroom are owned by a company called Maple Leaf Inc based in the States." Steve waited for a response but decided to lie before Rory could think of an answer. "They've never heard of a Russian called Dimitri."

It was clear Rory McClean had reached the extent of his brain power. Steve moved in when Rory didn't answer.

"You see Mr McClean. We know you chop up stolen cars here and you do it for a Russian mob based in London. My bet is you ship them to Russia. You were here when the person I think was your boss, that's Cameron Bowie, was murdered, so naturally, we have to look at you as a suspect." Steve paused seeing a deflated Rory McClean in front of him.

"A charge of receiving and chopping stolen cars is nothing compared to a murder charge. This is your one chance to help yourself. Tell us what you know and satisfy us you and your buddies here…" Steve swept his arm around the room indicating the other two white-suited and so far, silent mechanics … "are not killers." Steve paused and lied. "We're not interested in a car thieving ring. We're only interested in finding the murderer."

The DCI sat back in his uncomfortable chair and was glad to see Mary standing by the door taking notes. Rory McClean was silent for several minutes. There was tension in the atmosphere as Rory finally spoke. Steve was always surprised how, in certain suspects, arrogance quickly gave way to compliance especially when faced with a choice of charges.

"All right but we aren't killers."

Steve nodded.

"We was recruited by old man Bowie to do as you say. Sort out high-end stolen motors. He was in a deal with a Russian. The Russian had contacts back home and ordered cars stolen to order to mainly ship to Russia through Felixstowe. The two young plonkers of sales guys stole the cars, we sorted out the trackers and a lorry would arrive to ship the cars, purely small time. That's how it started."

Steve saw Mary writing in her notebook. He crossed his arms and settled in his chair.

"We was doing about a car a week and then it went up to three. We was going along nicely. Then the plonkers upstairs stopped nicking the cars and some other lot started delivering cars but still never more than three a week. Old Man Bowie said the Russian had recruited a new partner. Somebody who had contacts and could help keep the coppers out of our hair." Rory looked nervous as he told his tale. It was clearly a strain on his memory banks.

"Then this other Russian turned up. Said he was taking over and unless old man Bowie agreed he'd be hurt really bad as well as his family and us." Rory was shuddering at the thought.

Steve remained silent as Rory carried on. "This other Ruskie wanted the operation expanded. He wanted more cars processed but Cameron Bowie said we had to look after the first Russian 'cause he was our main sponsor like."

Steve interrupted. "What does that mean?" He asked the question, but he knew from Poppy's research that Maple Leaf Inc of Delaware USA owned the buildings, not Cameron Bowie.

Rory was trying to be helpful. "I don't know really. I know the first Russian had been working with the old man for a while. I think maybe he paid the bills for this place but all I know was that Bowie told us to do the normal three cars a week and not to mention that we was doing other motors."

The DCI tried to rationalise this but failed. "Carry on."

"Well, that's it, except the second Russian, the one called Dimitri started coming down here. He'd have a smoke and a cup of tea. He got really friendly like and kept asking questions."

"What kind of questions?" Steve unfolded his arms and sat up.

"You know, just questions. Things like, did we know the people who used to deliver the cars and how often did the first Ruskie— that's the one called Vladimir, come to the workshop."

"And what did you tell him?"

"That we didn't know the guy who delivered the motors, but I tell you what, he employed a couple of right Herberts. I don't think it was an organised operation by the look of these two. They looked like they needed a good feed." Rory paused to think. "I told him this Vladimir really hadn't been to the workshop. He did most of his talking upstairs in the showroom."

Rory McClean looked washed out with the effort of telling his story.

Steve looked at Mary and nodded. She understood his meaning and left the office clutching her mobile phone.

The DCI wanted to make sure he understood. "You're saying Cameron Bowie worked for the Russian you know as Vladimir. He had his two sales guys steal the odd car and then the Russian introduced another team to supply three stolen cars a week. Is that right?"

Rory confirmed by weakly nodding his head.

"Then a second Russian called Dimitri turned up and you were knocking out more than three cars a week for him plus the three a week for Vladimir?"

"Yes. This Dimitri would often have ten cars a week, but Mr Bowie told us not to say anything especially if this Vladimir ever came down."

"And your boss said Vladimir had a new partner who would help to keep the police off your backs?"

"That's what he said."

The DCI was puzzling over this new information. "Do you know Vladimir's last name?"

"No."

"If you didn't kill Cameron Bowie, who do you think did?"

Rory McClean stared into the distance. He'd recovered some of his composure, but his earlier arrogance had gone.

"Stands to reason it was the Russians. The way I saw it Mr Bowie had a good thing going with the first one. He called him his main sponsor. I reckon this Vladimir was paying for this place and the showroom and he was cutting Bowie in for a share of the takings. I think the second guy, this Dimitri, is part of a rival gang and wanted in on Mr Bowie's action. He threatened his way in, but Mr Bowie didn't tell Vladimir. If Vladimir was paying for this…" He waved his arms around. "Then he'd be pretty cheesed off. Maybe he killed the boss as an example or maybe the boss told Dimitri he wasn't doing any more cars. I really don't know." Rory sat forward in his chair, apparently exhausted and rested his head in his hands.

Detective Constable Mary Dougal re-entered and nodded to her boss.

Steve stood up. "Right, you three, there are three police cars outside. They will take you to Police Central Booking where you will be interviewed by an officer from the Auto Crime Unit. DC Dougan here will accompany you and ensure you are properly processed."

All three men in white overalls stood. Rory McClean was about to say something but a fierce stare from the DCI dissuaded him. Mary ushered the three out to the waiting cars. Steve followed.

"You go with them and call the Auto Crime Unit on your way. Make sure they meet you at Central and let them take this over but have Poppy forward them your notes as soon as she can. You can tell them it's a gift from us. Also, have Poppy include the files on the two car salesmen, they may as well handle both cases, the car stealing and the car chopping." Both detectives had made their way outside.

"Oh! You'd better contact Customs and Excise. They may want to know about an illegal car shipping ring." Steve headed away from Mary but stopped and turned. "I'll take the car. I've to be somewhere at four." Steve looked at his watch. It was three twenty-four. He calculated he had just enough time to get to MI6 Headquarters. He carried on. "It's unlikely I'll get back tonight so when you're done with this, get back and write up your notes and make sure Poppy updates the file. We'll look at the CCTV tomorrow morning first thing if Terry Harvey has worked his magic. There's nothing these guys have given us that helps our case except another theory."

"What's that?"

"That the first Russian, Vladimir, killed or had Cameron Bowie killed because he was using the equipment here for his own gain and as a warning to the second Russian, Dimitri, to keep out of his business. That's why the killing was so public."

The DCI left for his next encounter with Sir Patrick Bond, the country's top spy.

Chapter Fourteen

As the DCI drove towards central London, his mobile sounded. Luckily, this pool car had a hands-free facility already paired to most Metropolitan Police mobile devices so Steve could take the call.

"Yes?"

"I suppose you're out catching bad guys and that's why you're not in your office to meet me?"

Steve recognised the voice as belonging to Florance Rough. Florance, also known previously as Twiggy due to her enormous size, had worked for Steve when his Special Resources Unit was first set up. She'd moved on and was now a successful civil servant attached to the Met's Financial Crimes Unit and Steve's go-to person when anything financial appeared in any of his cases.

"I'm sorry Twiggy, Poppy said you'd call in this afternoon, but it's been a long day and it's not over yet."

Twiggy was sympathetic. She knew how hard-working her old boss was but pretended not to care.

"Yeah, right; I bet you're in a restaurant somewhere finishing a late lunch."

Steve would normally have enjoyed a bit of banter with Twiggy, but his mind was on what was to come, and he was still wrestling with whatever was stuck in his head involving the child abductions.

"I wish! Listen, Twiggy, can we do it tomorrow, say mid-morning? I should be free then."

Twiggy picked up the vibrations coming from the DCI and knew when to pull back. "That's fine, Steve. Look, get sorted and call me. OK?"

"Good idea. Thanks, Flo, I'll call you tomorrow."

Florance Rough hung up. Her old boss had used her Christian name at the end. He only did this when he had something serious on his mind. For some reason she became concerned for him.

MI6 Headquarters building on the banks of the Thames was a grand construction. As the DCI stepped through the revolving door he was greeted by a splash of ornate fittings and an air of corporate London. Before being allowed beyond the threshold he was required to empty his pockets and then pass through a full-body scanner. His pocket's contents were x-rayed and returned to him. He was guided by a roped off cordon to a secure looking desk behind which was a bank of CCTV monitors. A man in uniform was sitting in front of the monitors studying them. He was seated behind the guard who was obviously the receptionist. Steve saw himself approach the desk on one of the monitors. The guard asked for his ID and after scrutinising Steve's warrant card, had him fill in a visitor's form. With formalities completed and a recognition that he was there by appointment to see Sir Patrick, he was quickly given a security badge to hang round his neck and escorted by another security guard to Sir Patrick's office.

The DCI was ushered into a large outer office with three desks, each manned by efficient-looking girls. One of them, dressed in sensible shoes and a tweed suit, rose and approached the DCI.

"Mr Burt?" Without waiting for a reply, the lady turned away from Steve obviously expecting him to follow her. Over her shoulder she said, "Sir Patrick is expecting you."

Steve walked into Sir Patrick Bond's inner sanctum. His first impression was that it was a large office but not well furnished. Functional came to mind as the DCI looked around. In the centre of the room was a walnut dining table seated for ten people but obviously now used as a meeting table. Seated beside Sir Patrick was a full colonel in Army uniform and a lady dressed in severe civilian clothes.

Sir Patrick rose and with the slightest of smiles approached Steve, shook his hand and asked him to sit opposite the lady. The colonel was sitting next to her, and Sir Patrick sat at the head of the table. All four were seated at one end of the large piece of furniture.

Steve spotted coffee was on the table and, as Sir Patrick saw him looking and remembering his fondness for coffee, he said, "Help yourself to coffee, Steve, before we get started."

Sir Patrick introduced the lady first. "This is Dame Helen Goodbody. She is Chair of the Experimental Research Facility at Finsham in Yorkshire." Sir Patrick carried on. "This is Colonel Colin Lockhart; he's Military Intelligence." Both strangers acknowledged Steve's presence, but it wasn't exactly a warm welcome.

"DCI Burt. You called me this morning enquiring as to the whereabouts of a Captain Alex Hope of the Royal Military Police. Is that correct?"

Steve was taken aback. Patrick Bond was a friend yet here he was being unusually formal and not very friendly. Steve decided to play it formally.

"No sir, that is not quite correct. I asked if you could suggest a senior officer within the MOD that I could talk to regarding the apparent disappearance of Captain Hope."

"Quite so. Better to be correct."

The colonel spoke up. "What is your connection to the captain?" His voice was full of authority and his well-tailored uniform didn't hide his physique. This man in his early fifties obviously worked out.

"I have no connection other than he is the son of my former Company Commander."

"I see, and Major Hope is concerned something has happened to his son and has asked you to help?"

"Yes sir. Nothing more sinister than that."

The colonel exchanged glances with Sir Patrick and Dame Helen. Steve noticed they each gave a slight nod.

The colonel took the lead. "Mr Burt, what you hear here today must go no further. Not even your Commissioner at the Met has been read into what you are about to learn. You are governed by the Official Secrets Act and must not divulge anything to anyone. Is that clear?"

Steve wondered what he'd walked into and didn't like being here.

"Yes, sir."

The colonel visibly relaxed as did Dame Helen.

"Patrick here tells me he knows you well. May I call you Steve?" Without waiting for confirmation, the colonel carried on.

"We have been developing in secret a new version of a biological battlefield weapon. I don't need to bother you with the details, but it will revolutionise warfare as we know it. The funding for such a weapon has been difficult. The government can't be seen to be funding research into what are technically banned weapons systems. A few months ago, one of Sir Patrick's agents was approached by a Russian arms dealer called Koptic. He claimed to be connected to the Russian government and was looking to purchase a new, weapons' systems that he could offer to his country as his own invention. The agent passed this on and without going into the whys and wherefores a group of interested parties met with Koptic and let him know we had a new weapon in the pipeline, but we needed funds to complete the research. Are you following this, Steve?"

The DCI was fascinated. "Yes, please go on."

"We might have led Koptic to believe if he funded the remainder of the project, we would allow him access to the weapon. It's more complicated than that of course but we needed the money and we needed to keep Koptic in our camp as a way of keeping tabs on military thinking coming out of the Kremlin. Sir Patrick here has designs on turning Koptic and getting him to work for us." The colonel smiled at Sir Patrick, who sat straight-faced.

"Of course, we'd no intention of giving our prototype to Koptic. Please don't try to moralise our actions. In the world of international politics and spying dirty underhand deals are done every day. We took the Russian's money because we needed it. We didn't sign a contract and as far as we know, apart from us four and Koptic, no one knows of our deal. Or at least, that's what we thought."

Steve looked surprised. The colonel paused and nodded towards Dame Helen.

As she started to speak, Steve got an impression of a headmistress addressing her school. "Although unofficial, my unit works closely with Military Intelligence and the security services. It came to our attention that someone was going around asking questions concerning our other facility at Wetherby also in Yorkshire. One of our technicians was having a rather jolly night out and had drunk too much. Suffice to say the people who were buying him drinks were not his friends and he finished up in a compromising position involving sex-trade workers. His new friends told him they had pictures and unless he talked to them about his work and the Wetherby facility, they'd publish the photographs."

Steve was enjoying the story but interrupted. "Did this technician know anything secret?"

"My dear Inspector, everyone who works for me has their head stuffed full of secrets, so yes, he had a lot to tell. Fortunately, he's single and reported the incident to our security people who, in turn, reported it to me. I, in turn, reported it to Sir Patrick."

Sir Patrick Bond cleared his throat ready to continue the narrative.

"We knew about Koptic and thought he was covering his bases and not trusting us, but we were wrong. One of my agents unearthed a Russian operating out of London called Vladimir Skoysky. We were able to trace his movements and place him in the pub when Helen's technician was having a good time. We did a bit more digging, and it seems our Vladimir is part of an anti-Russian Government movement determined to overthrow the lot in power just now in Russia. We've had him under surveillance, tapped his phone and bugged his office and home. He's been talking to someone using a burner phone. We don't know who, but we heard him refer to the Wetherby place and the need to steal the prototype weapon as soon as it's finished." Sir Patrick stopped and nodded to the colonel.

"Weeks before, from the surveillance devices, we'd heard conversations concerning a man who was sympathetic and had been placed inside the Wetherby station. It's called Station K by the way." The colonel paused and smiled. "Once we knew this other faction had nothing to do with Koptic and in fact were plotting against him we took action. That's where your Captain Alex Hope comes in. He volunteered for hazardous duty and is now working undercover in Station K. He's tasked with unearthing this spy that Vladimir has inside Station K."

The colonel sat back.

Sir Patrick took over. "In addition to your Captain Hope, I've now got a man inside posing as an MOD auditor. The only person who knows about my man is the Head of Station, one Professor Karl Symonds, but he knows nothing of Captain Hope."

Silence descended. It was obvious the storytelling was over. Steve needed to know more.

"If I'm understanding this, you've got a secret research centre called Station K where you're developing an illegal biological weapon that the

Russians are paying for but they're not going to get. You know there's an anti-Russian spy within Station K who is intent on stealing this illegal weapon once it's finished and you've got an MI6 agent posing as an auditor presumably trying to identify this spy. Then just to be sure, you've planted Captain Alex Hope to also try and unearth the spy and he's been at it for weeks." Steve paused and looked at the three faces focused on him. "Is that about it?"

Sir Patrick leant forward. "More or less. As we said, it's complicated but we need that weapon developed and this way we get it. What we don't need are rival gangs getting in each other's way and one gang stealing the thing and using it to overthrow their own Government. You wanted to know where Captain Hope is, well, now you know. I suppose you can at least tell his father you have it on the highest authority his son is safe."

"Why can't Captain Hope phone his father?"

Dame Helen looked up. "Station K is in a refurbished nuclear fallout bunker. It's underground, the walls and roof are reinforced concrete plus security is tight. No phones are allowed; no copying facilities are available and people who work there agree to spend up to three months underground with only limited outside contact."

"Wow! That's tough." Steve couldn't begin to visualise what it must be like.

The colonel cleared his throat. "So, you see Steve, a lot is riding on this. We have to unmask this spy before he gets a chance to steal the weapon. We can't tighten security any more. It's already watertight but our friendly Russian must think he can circumvent it and get the weapon out. Your friend's son is a very brave man and is an integral part of finding this spy before the weapon is ready. You do see that don't you?"

The colonel had spoken in a low almost pleading voice.

Steve had to agree this was important work that young Alex Hope was involved in.

"Yes sir, I do see that." For something to say, Steve carried on. "Thank you for briefing me on this. It helps to have the full picture."

Smiles and light laughter all round. A relieved air suddenly appeared until the DCI picked up on something. "Can I have Vladimir Skoysky's address?"

143

Sir Patrick almost choked. With great difficulty, he controlled his breathing. "Haven't you been listening? This is all highly confidential. We can't have you visiting the people in play. We can't alert them to the fact we're on to them. Don't you see that, man?"

"Yes. Of course, I do but I believe Vladimir Skoysky is involved in a murder case I'm investigating. I need to interview him as a policeman, not part of this plan, to either arrest him or eliminate him."

The colonel spoke next. "Steve." He was clearly appealing to Steve's sensible side. "You know we can't allow that. We can't chance this person being spooked. We need to round up his operation. It's a matter of national security. If Vladimir Skoysky is involved in your murder, then once we've dealt with him, I promise you we'll let you have him."

The DCI knew he wouldn't win against such tough odds and the colonel was right. If he focused on Vladimir now, he might tip his hand and alert him. Steve also told himself it may not even be the same Vladimir. There could be hundreds in London.

"OK. I agree. I can see the problem, but I insist on interviewing him as soon as your operation is completed."

The smiles all round had returned, but the DCI knew he would be looking up a Vladimir Skoysky sooner than these three imagined. It was too much of a coincidence to let pass. There may be more than one Russian with that name in London, but Steve needed to know.

As Steve drove home, he wondered what he would tell his old boss. At least he had news and it was better than Bob and his wife had hoped for. Captain Alex Hope was alive and well and serving his country.

Chapter Fifteen

Wednesday the 25th of March started like most days for Steve. He looked forward to holding his daughter while he fed her, and his wife made breakfast. He'd explained as much as he could about the events of yesterday especially his time in front of the Parliamentary Committee. He avoided any reference to his visit to MI6.

"What was Malcolm Freeman like? I've seen him on TV. He always looks self-assured and is never lost for something to say on any topic. One interviewer even suggested he'd be in the government at the next reshuffle." Alison was a keen follower of current affairs, unlike her husband.

"He seems fairly decent but a bit of a go-getter. He's invited me to a drinks party at the Commons next Tuesday. He wants me on one of his subcommittees, but I said no. I think he feels a few drinks might make me change my mind."

"You're not committee material, my darling, better just have soft drinks." She smiled as she took their daughter and kissed him lightly on the lips.

Five minutes later, Steve was behind the wheel of the pool car and was heading for his office in New Scotland Yard. He went through his workload as he drove.

First the double murder. Perhaps they would have some CCTV to examine plus the VCR tapes Mary had acquired from the filling station. Steve hoped they might see something but wasn't hopeful. They'd closed down the carjacking ring but that didn't help his case. As he drove, he wondered about the first murder victim. They hadn't really looked at him closely, and he decided to rectify this.

Then there were the abductions. He'd meet with Peter Jones and Matt Conway this morning and try and understand the case better. His mind wandered to how Superintendent Blackstone fitted in and made a mental note to follow this up with Commander Alfie Brooks.

Steve arrived at the garage at the Yard in what seemed no time. He exited the car and suddenly remembered he had to call Robert Hope and give him the good news about his son.

When he arrived at his office, Steve was surprised by how empty it was. He noticed on his desk a handwritten note from Poppy. "IN VIEWING SUITE".

Steve looked at his watch. It was 08.44. He walked to the viewing suite located inside the Technical Support area. He remembered being amazed the first time the head of the unit, Inspector Terry Harvey, had shown him around this facility. It was cinema standard and seemed to have a load of technical wizardry that went well beyond Steve's understanding. The most surprising thing was how Terry had found the budget and persuaded someone senior to agree to create the thing.

The DCI entered to find Mary and Poppy sitting in the large viewing chairs in the front row and Peter Jones and Matt Conway sitting behind them. Terry Harvey was sitting off to one side with a remote-control device in his hand while off to the other side a technician was seated in front of a bank of computers, typing away.

"What's going on?"

Peter Jones as the senior officer present spoke first. "Sorry boss, Mary thought we'd enjoy a few minutes of humour. Some of the antics on these CCTV images are very funny. We've only been here a few minutes."

Normally the DCI would take a dim view of what looked like playtime, but he knew his team rarely skived off. He decided to say nothing and embrace a few minutes of recreation.

Terry Harvey stood and told everyone they'd succeeded in acquiring the CCTV footage from the four cameras situated around Crystal Motors. He told Steve they'd played them through last night and had spliced together different frames to make an amusing five-minute film of events around the car showroom. "Do you want to see it, sir?" This was directed at Steve.

"Not yet; can we look at the images starting a few days before the murder?" Steve didn't ask at this time how Terry had got hold of these disks.

"Right." Addressing the technician in the corner Terry instructed, "Load up camera one from Friday the 20th."

Instantly, images appeared on the oversized TV screen mounted on the wall. There was a date and time stamp in the bottom left-hand corner. They were witnessing the comings and goings on Thursday the 19th of March at 07.10.

Terry pressed some buttons on his remote and the picture fast-forwarded but due to new technology the speed of looking forward was enhanced but the images did not speed up. Everything that was happening was visible only not in real-time.

"I'll take it back to normal speed from say eleven o'clock and speed up the drive, so it won't take hours. Something is coming up we've already looked at."

As Terry manipulated the images and the clock rolled forward, he paused the frame. It showed two badly dressed and poor-looking individuals, dressed in black, pacing about outside the showroom. "I'm guessing these are not the usual clients for vintage cars. As I run it forward it's clear they haven't a clue."

Terry ran the images forward and Steve had to admit it looked like something from a silent comedy. The pair walked one way, then the other, then round in circles clearly trying to work out what they needed to do. Eventually, the pair entered the showroom.

"Stop it there, Terry." Turning to Mary, he said, "Didn't one of our car salesmen say there were a couple of oddballs in the showroom?"

Mary was impressed by her boss's recall. "Yes, you're right. He said one of them tried speaking in a posh voice and they were looking for Cameron Bowie."

Steve started to stroke his chin. This was a sure sign he was thinking. Everyone recognised the signs and remained silent. Eventually, the DCI returned from his thinking.

"Does anyone recognise these two?"

No one did but Terry Harvey stepped forward. He had a glint in his eye and a silly smirk on his face. "As you know we have a lot of experimental technology here." He looked conspiratorially at Steve. "One of the things we're trying is facial recognition protocols linked to the National Crime Database. In other words, we can take an image like our two friends there and scan their image against the big database. If they have a record, and our image is good enough for six points of clarity, then we can say who they probably are." Terry opened his arms. "No applause please."

The DCI was amazed that such a thing was possible. "So, you can give us their names?"

"If the image is good enough and if they are on the national database, yes."

"Terry. You're a marvel. How soon can you do it?"

Terry made a show of annoyance, but everyone knew he was acting. "Always in a hurry you lot. Let's finish with the CCTV and then we'll make a start. I've no idea how long it'll take but we'll crack on."

Peter Jones and Matt Conway left to carry on with the abduction case although they admitted they were stumped. It was agreed to hold a case review over lunch. Poppy left to return to the office and Mary and Steve settled down to watch the CCTV footage.

***

Eddie Randall had received a coded message on his phone telling him to be in his office at 12 noon, today, the 25th of March.

He hadn't heard from the Voice for a few days and was surprised to receive this message. Eddie had done well financially from working for the Voice and liked the money. He also liked the fact that the Voice was able to keep the police off Eddie's back. He daydreamed as he surveyed his car empire. Through the not too clean window of his portacabin office, he saw his stock of fine used vehicles. Some stolen and now with false plates, some MOT failures that now had a year's MOT and some top of the range slightly rusted executive motors fit for any chief executive. He looked at the mud-covered yard and admitted he may have to resurface this unless he could take over the Crystal Cars premises in Mile End now that the proprietor was no longer with them.

He saw his two faithful retainers washing some of his stock. He was in two minds about Bert and Frankie. He admitted they weren't bright and couldn't punch their way out of a paper bag, but they were cheap and usually did as they were told. Eddie thought he'd give them one last

148

chance. He'd test them on the next order from the Voice for knocked off cars.

Eddie Randall sat back in his cheap executive chair and lit a cigarette. He drew deeply and considered how good his present life was.

***

In the viewing room, the images from the other cameras were examined. Camera 3 looked along Mile End Road and was sighted 500 yards before the filling station and Crystal Motors was being shown on the TV screen and had been speeded up as it was thought there would be nothing to see. Because of the technology employed, Steve and Mary were able to examine an hour's footage in a few minutes. As they watched, the DCI shouted for Terry to freeze an image and rewind for three minutes. As the images slowly moved forward, a gold Ford Granada came into view. It was stopping and starting and going very slowly. A tailback of cars was seen snaking behind the Granada. The three police officers watched as the Granada stopped outside Crystal Motors and suddenly sped up to the relief of the following drivers. There wasn't another camera further along the road, so the Granada was lost. The time on the pictures was 11.43 on Thursday the 19th of March.

"I've seen that car before." Steve cast his mind back. "I'm sure it came from the workshop behind the showroom on Monday." He turned to Mary. "Remember? It almost caused an accident. It cut straight across the road."

"Yes, but are you sure it's the same car?"

"There won't be too many gold-coloured Ford Granadas of that vintage around. If it's not the same car, it's a hell of a coincidence."

Inspector Terry Harvey sped through the other cameras but there was nothing of interest. He had his technician load camera one from Friday the 20th of March. This was the day of the killing. Camera one was fixed but had a decent view of the front of the filling station and the surrounding buildings including Crystal Motors. As before the images were processed at speed to reduce the time spent staring at the large TV screen. The time clock quickly moved to early afternoon.

149

As the images appeared, once again, Steve called for the frames to be frozen and rewound by three minutes. An air of satisfaction suddenly arrived in the viewing room as a gold-coloured Ford Granada appeared in the centre of the picture. It stopped on the main road and a man was seen to leave the back of the car and walk into the showroom. Unfortunately, he had his back to the camera. As the three watched, the Granada suddenly moved forward and drove onto the filling station forecourt. Two small, thin men dressed in black exited the front of the car and one of them began filling the Granada with fuel.

"Hold it there, Terry. Are these the two we saw earlier?"

"Terry Harvey pressed a few buttons on his remote and the characters became enlarged.

"Looks like it could be."

"Mm, interesting. Carry on."

The images started up again. The two small men in black were seen laughing by the petrol pumps and one of them suddenly started to wave. A figure had emerged from the showroom and was facing the camera. The figure was the same as the one who had left the back seat and entered the showroom. It was obvious the new arrival had expected the car to be still by the kerb side. As one of the men in black continued to wave, the new man walked briskly toward the car. It was obvious he wasn't happy, and he appeared to pull the petrol nozzle from the car and replace it in the pump holster. Further words seem to take place and eventually one of the small men left to enter the kiosk of the filling station whilst the other two got into the car. As they watched, the man who had gone to pay reappeared holding what looked like a bag of sweets. The car started to move at a sedate pace, left the forecourt and turned in the direction of West London.

The DCI noted the time. It was 2.44 p.m. on the day of the murder.

Terry stopped the CD player. "Well, what do you think?"

Steve was thinking and Mary was giggling. "You can't be serious if you think we've just witnessed our murderer. Filling with petrol, sweeties and an old banger as a getaway car." She was beside herself with laughter. "Tell me you're not serious."

"I'm not sure." Steve saw the humour but as unlikely as it was, everything fitted. "We've seen that car before. We've seen those two clowns before and the timeline fits. Terry? Any chance you can get an ID on the third guy. The one who came out of the showroom.?"

"I can try. We got a reg number from the Granada." Terry handed Mary a piece of paper.

"Good man, Terry. Mary, run that through the database. Let's see who owns the Granada." They sat through the rest of the day's footage from the three cameras but nothing of interest appeared. They moved on to Saturday the 21st and Sunday the 22nd of March. It didn't take long to realise there was nothing of interest on the CDs for these days.

Terry had Monday the 23rd loaded. Once more using this sophisticated imagery technology, they sped through the morning until they saw themselves on the screen entering the showroom for Crystal Motors. The images were forwarded until again Steve called for Terry to freeze the play sequence. Although camera one was fixed on the filling station, a gold car could be seen on the periphery exiting from behind the building.

"Terry, can you pull up camera three and run it to the same time?"

Using his remote, Terry pressed a few buttons and once his technician had loaded the correct disk, the TV screen appeared to split in two. On the right in frozen form was the image from camera one whilst on the left the images from camera three sped forward and suddenly stopped. Both frozen images were at the same time.

"Can you run camera three forward slowly please?"

The head of Technical Services obliged.

The gold Granada was seen, having appeared from behind the filling station, speeding toward the main road. As Steve had witnessed it didn't stop to allow for other traffic but simply drove onto Mile End Road and headed towards the city."

"Terry? Can you enhance that?"

Inspector Harvey hit more keys and an enlargement of a frozen frame of the tape appeared. It showed clearly the two front-seat passengers as the pair who had been seen in the showroom on Thursday and filling the car with petrol on Friday, the day of the murder. Now here they were again.

"This is too much of a coincidence. These two are involved. We need to find them, Mary."

Steve looked at Terry. His expression almost pleading. "Terry. We need your magic. If there's any way of identifying these two, we really…"

"Yes. I know Steve and I'll get on it, but do you want the bad news?"

"No, but you're going to tell me."

"Don't bother with a PNC check on that registration DC Dougan. Look!"

Terry zoomed in on the front of the Granada. "That's a different registration number than I gave you. The buggers are switching plates."

Steve left Mary to review the VCR tapes but didn't think they'd get much more. They might get a clearer headshot of the one who bought the petrol and the sweets and that might help with identification but that was all.

In his office, he started to make notes. They had to find the Granada. There weren't many left on the road especially in gold. Switching plated wouldn't help but there had to be a way. Then they had the two funny looking blokes poorly dressed in black. They must have a record, but they didn't look bright. Steve surmised they were probably small-time petty crooks working for someone else. He knew they had a decent frontal of the person who travelled in the back of the Granada on the day of the murder. He'd been inside the showroom at the right time and for now, was the main suspect. Steve hoped Terry could work his magic.

Mary arrived back. "Not much on the VCR boss, only our man buying his sweeties." She paused and sat down. Slowly she spoke. "You don't really think that pantomime with the petrol, the car and the sweeties was the murder going down. Do you? It just looked an odd way to commit a murder, using people like that."

"I do Mary. The guy who went into the showroom wasn't a clown. He looked professional. I agree the two in black were anything but professional. Maybe our knifeman was lumbered with second-class help. Let's wait and see what Terry comes up with on his facial recognition programme."

Steve became all business thinking of what he had to do. "Mary, look into the first killing, that's Vince McGuire. Check him out, known associates, criminal record, money, everything. There's a connection to the killer and if we can find it we'll have a shot at our killer."

Mary made notes.

"Then get onto DVLA. I want the registered keepers of all gold-coloured Ford Granadas inside the M25, addresses and registration numbers. Let's see if we can find that car."

Again, Mary made notes.

"We'll have to wait for Terry, but we might get lucky."

"Right you are, Steve, I'll get on to it."

The DCI noted the use of his Christian name again. He smiled, reached for his pad and decided what to tackle next. He called in Poppy.

"We have a problem and I need all your cunning skills."

Poppy who was dressed in another figure-hugging dress sat and looked blankly at her boss.

"I can't tell you too much but what I'm going to ask you to do must remain totally private. You understand?"

"Yes. Of course." Poppy enjoyed being on the inside of investigations.

"Right. I need you to find a Russian man in London. His name is Vladimir Skoysky. That's all I have except he may be part of the Russian mob." Steve stared at Poppy looking for a reaction. He got none so carried on.

"The thing is, Poppy, you can't mention that name to anyone so looking for him means it's just you and whichever databases you can interrogate. This Russian is on a government watchlist and we are forbidden to go near him, so any sniff that we're looking, and all hell will come down on us."

Poppy looked confused. "I'm to look for this Vladimir but not mention his name. How can I do that?"

Steve laughed. "I don't know. Any reference to him outside this office could bring a load of trouble."

"But I need to ask people who know people if they know him."

"Not this time, just try. If you get nowhere, then don't worry. I think this Russian is involved with our murder case at Crystal Motors. If you draw a blank it's OK."

Poppy sat back, thinking. "Can I ask my Uncle Terry?"

"Not yet. If you get nowhere, we might try him but for now, only you and I know that name."

Poppy liked a challenge, but she was obviously stumped. "Leave it with me, boss, I'll have a good think and see what I can do."

"Good, but remember, total security."

Chapter Sixteen

The DCI called Twiggy and agreed to meet her in the canteen.

As she arrived carrying what looked like a large quantity of official-looking files, Steve stood and signalled across to a waiter for two coffees. He was, for once, sitting in the senior officers' section where table service was possible. It was also quieter, and the tables sported white crisp tablecloths and the chairs were vinyl covered instead of plain plastic.

Twiggy sat down and exhaled loudly. "These files are heavy." She pointed to the stack of brown covered files in front of her.

She had known Steve long enough to be candid with him, plus she was technically a civilian and didn't report to him. This made no difference to their working relationship which had always been close.

"Now, are you going to tell me what's going on?"

Steve looked at his watch. It was 10.47 a.m. "How long have you got?"

"Long enough. I gather it's to do with this Mile End Road killing. Poppy sent over the file with a request to look into the financials. She had pulled stuff up from Companies House on Crystal Motors Ltd but that's it."

Steve knew Twiggy was thorough but was also very determined to solve any problem she was presented with.

Steve outlined the case. He explained about the car-stealing ring and the workshop. He told Twiggy of the suspected Russian gang's involvement and how he needed to better understand how Crystal Motors was set up.

Twiggy nodded her understanding just as the coffee arrived.

"Poppy's done some initial discovery. Your victim Cameron Bowie's bank and credit cards are clean as far as they go. He has his personal account and the business account with Laxley Bank. He didn't seem to take a salary and paid no personal tax."

Twiggy raised an eyebrow." A bit unusual. He seems to have used a company credit card for everything including his meals out, his golf, his food shopping, everything. Then each month he paid off the credit card from the company bank account. Now here's the thing." Twiggy enjoyed taking her old boss through complicated financial affairs but always gave her explanations slowly. It was as though she deliberately set out to tease him.

"I've looked at the sales figures for Crystal Motors. The business was bust. It was trading at a huge loss. If I reworked the numbers the losses would be in the hundreds of thousands." Again, she paused to see if the DCI followed what she was saying.

He remained silent but had a thoughtful expression on his face.

"Bowie was charging on average around ten grand a month on his credit card. Remember he also had two employees in the showroom and a series of mechanics. His total personnel head count was 6 and he paid them a salary, again from the company, although the business was technically insolvent. He also had rates, rents, general overheads and other monthly expenses like utilities to pay. His actual generated income from car sales seemed to be around three thousand a month gross."

Steve was doing a bit of mental arithmetic. "So, he was seriously in financial trouble?"

"Yes, if his business was legitimate. We discovered the premises are owned by a company called Maple Leaf Inc. It's a shell company out of Delaware USA. I had to do a lot of digging and call in a few favours to get you this, but the only director and shareholder listed apart from the nominees is a Russian, Vladimir Skoysky." Twiggy pulled a few sheets of paper from one of her files and pushed them towards the DCI.

"That's him." She tapped a colour photograph showing a head and shoulders shot of a stocky man with dark hair.

Steve was impressed but confused. "How did you get this?"

Twiggy smiled and before answering the question produced a second sheet. It was a copy of a Russian passport in the name of Vladimir Skoysky.

"I used my feminine charms on a guy called Chuck in the Offshore Company Registration and Compliance Department in Delaware. Each listing, having any officer of a company who is not a nominee, has to register the owner and directors. That involves proof of identity and the best way to do that is by producing your passport. Chuck sent it across."

"Twiggy. You're a bloody marvel."

Miss Florance Rough, AKA Twiggy, smiled. "I know but I have more." As she always did, she was teasing Steve by slowly revealing information she knew he'd like.

"I could see money coming into the Crystal Motors account each month. It arrived from an account in the Caymans. Usually between fifty and a hundred grand. This is what kept the business afloat although your victim only left enough to cover his overheads and transferred the bulk out of the money out to an account in Gibraltar. I couldn't get anywhere with the Caymans. That's a closed shop but Gibraltar is more helpful."

The DCI sat back admiring how Florance had developed as a detective since he'd first met her.

"The account is in the name of Maple Leaf Inc out of Delaware USA. The only two signatories are Cameron Bowie and Vladimir Skoysky. As of yesterday, the account was in credit to the amount of one point seven million dollars."

Twiggy looked around for the waiter and called over, "Two more coffees please." And pointing at the DCI, she added, "He's paying."

Steve's mind began to clear. Twiggy had given him Vladimir. He had a photograph and a copy of a passport. With the passport, he could find the man. She'd also given him a direct link between Vladimir and the murder victim. The DCI wasn't happy just yet. He was convinced the Russian, if he were responsible for the murder, almost certainly didn't do it himself. The image from the CCTV of the man entering and leaving the car showroom didn't match the picture of Vladimir.

Twiggy saw the concern on her old boss's face. "What's wrong?"

"Nothing really, you've done brilliantly. It's just I know the Russian didn't actually stab our victim, but I can't see a connection between Vladimir and the car dealer."

Twiggy shrugged and drank her coffee. "I'm waiting for some tax information on Bowie and Crystal Motors but I'm fairly certain they'll just show no tax was paid."

The pair spent the next few minutes socialising before they parted Twiggy, complete with an arm full of files to a high-level fraud briefing, and Steve to his office to think.

The DCI called Poppy into his inner office. "Poppy, that Russian I asked you to look for?"

"I haven't got anywhere yet!"

"No, that's all right. Take this down."

Poppy retrieved her notebook from her desk. Steve read out the passport number from the photocopy Twiggy had provided. "It's the number from a Russian Passport, issued to a Vladimir Skoysky on the 10th of April 2018."

Poppy took down the information. "Get onto Immigration Control. Don't say too much but ask if they can trace that passport number." Steve sat forward to emphasise his instruction. "Just the number, don't use the name. If they insist make an excuse and get out. OK?"

"Yes. I've got it."

"I want to know when he arrived and what address he gave on his visa application. He's Russian so he'll have needed a visa or at least a landing card. But remember, low-key."

"Right." Poppy left and Steve locked the copy passport and photograph in the left-hand top drawer of his desk.

There was an internal envelope on his desk. He opened it and saw it was from the office of the Commissioner. "GOOD WORK IN FRONT OF THE PARLIAMENTARY COMMITTEE. YOU MAY LIKE TO CONSIDER THE COMMITTEE CHAIRMAN'S OFFER OF SITTING ON HIS SUB COMMITTEE."

Steve sat back. Was the Commissioner ordering him to accept Malcolm Freeman's offer or was she leaving it up to him? The more he thought about it, the more he realised he needed a sounding board. He placed a call to Commander Alfie Brooks.

"I need your advice. sir. Can I come up?"

"No, I'll come down." The DCI stared at the receiver. The Commander was usually more than approachable. This gruff response was out of character.

Commander Alfie Brooks arrived a few minutes later. He looked his normal self, but he had a serious face that told the DCI something was worrying him.

He closed Steve's office door, sat down and without any preamble, launched into his narrative.

"You have a problem with Superintendent Blackstone. He likes to get his own way. He told you through Terry Harvey that the CCTV images from around your murder site at Mile End Road were out of bounds. Despite that you had Terry find a back door and you've viewed them. Is that correct?"

Steve didn't want to drop Inspector Terry Harvey in it so simply responded. "Yes, I suppose that's correct." At times like this, Steve knew he was better to let Alfie have his say first before launching a defence.

The DCI was expecting a torrent of mild abuse from his senior officer for not obeying the last order but instead, Alfie smiled. "Was there anything of interest on the images?"

Steve relaxed. "Yes, we've got a clear shot of the bloke we think is the killer plus there's an old gold coloured Ford Granada involved. We saw a couple of clowns in the Granada who are clearly also involved." Steve looked at Alfie. "It was worth looking at them, Alfie."

"Yes, I'm sure it was. Do you know who these characters are?"

The DCI decided it would do no harm to tell the Commander about Terry's new facial recognition software. "Not yet but Terry Harvey's working on the identifications. If they have a record which seems likely, we'll have them."

Commander Brooks stood and paced around the room. Steve stayed quiet. As Alfie returned to his chair he asked, "So you saw nothing that you would regard as unusual apart from your three suspects?"

"No"

"Mm." Alfie sat staring obviously thinking. "I've been asking around about Blackstone. Seems he has a reputation for interfering in other people's cases using his secret surveillance as cover. He's been brought up before a disciplinary board before but they found no case to answer. I spoke to an old mate of mine who reckons he's dodgy. I also checked up on his caseload. He doesn't have anything on his plate that involves Mile End Road." Alfie stared straight at the DCI. "So, why was he so keen that you shouldn't get to see the CCTV?"

Steve was thinking and listening to his senior officer. Suddenly the penny dropped.

"Because he's involved in the killing, or at least with the people who ordered the killing." Steve stood up. "Bloody hell, Alfie, this is serious." He sat down again. The DCI had been responsible for unmasking corrupt colleagues in the past but for some reason, he was uncomfortable with this revelation.

The older policeman had a smile on his face and a glint in his eye. "That's my take. From what I hear he's a clever sod, so getting proof might be difficult. All we have is a gut feeling and little evidence." The Commander continued to smile. "What if we set some kind of trap for him and he leads us to the main man behind what's going on? We have the advantage that he doesn't know what we suspect."

Steve liked the idea. "Great, but it won't be easy and I'm not sure an unofficial investigation into a senior officer would go down well upstairs."

"Leave upstairs to me. They'll be as keen as us to weed out a bad apple." Alfie was still smiling and to Steve's eyes suddenly looked ten years younger.

"Before we go all gung-ho, there's more you should know."

"With you there always is."

The DCI set out everything they knew about the case including the rival Russian gang's involvement. He explained about the car stealing, the chop shop, the Delaware company and the definite connection between the murder victim and one Russian called Vladimir Skoysky.

"I don't think the Russian killed our victim and I don't have a connection to the first victim they found on the railway embankment but somebody senior somewhere is pulling low life criminals' strings and now it looks like Superintendent Blackstone's involved."

Alfie stood. "Come to my office at five o'clock. We'll hold a war cabinet, and I might open the single malt. This feels like something I'm going to enjoy."

Alfie marched out without a goodbye leaving Steve to wonder where this case was going.

***

The Voice was preparing for his midday call to his preferred car thief, Eddie Randall, when one of his burner phones vibrated. It was the one only used by Superintendent Blackstone.

This was annoying as he'd told Eddie to be available at 12 noon sharp. This call from Blackstone could make him late. He prided himself on never being late.

"What?" the Voice almost shouted.

"You've got serious troubles. I warned you about Burt. He's arrested the guys in the workshop and passed the whole car ring business over to Auto Crimes. Your Mile End operation is finished."

The Voice realised this was bad news but not the end of the world. He knew he was safe no matter how close the DCI got.

"I pay you to solve problems. Solve this one now. I've got an order for three Audis and I intend to deliver. I was about to order their acquisition."

"Don't you listen! I told you, the Mile End operation is finished. You can't use it again. Killing that garage owner was a mistake, you've opened a real can of worms."

The Voice wasn't interested in his police insider's conscience or opinions. "If Mile End's closed down then get somewhere else. You've got the contacts and it's time you did something more useful for your money."

The Superintendent secretly agreed. He'd been paid handsomely by the Voice for over a year and hadn't had to do too much. "Give me a minute." Blackstone had to think. The Voice had put him on the spot, and he knew he had to come up with a solution to this problem.

The Voice was impatient. He looked at his watch to learn he was late calling Eddie Randall with the car order. He held on listening to Blackstone breathing, rustling paper at the other end of the connection and obviously talking to someone on another phone.

After what seemed a long time, Blackstone was back. "I've got it sorted but it's going to cost you."

"Just tell me what you've sorted. If it works then a little bonus could be yours."

"I've just spoken to a guy who specialises in the kind of operation you had going at Mile End. I'll get him to wherever your team stores the Audis, but it can't be Mile End."

The Voice gave the Heathrow address for Eddie Randall's car emporium. He'd simply tell Eddie to store them at his place once he'd stolen them.

"Right." Blackstone was obviously writing down the address. "My guy will immobilise the trackers and sort the cars out. Get your shipper to collect all the cars on the same day. My man won't take risks. He'll turn up, do his thing and leave. The rest is up to you. I'll run interference on the trackers. That will give your boys time to sort things out."

"I'll make sure the cars are there on Friday of this week. That's the 27th." The Voice just assumed Eddie would get the cars by then.

"Fine, but it'll cost you a couple of thousand for my man, plus something for me."

"Right. You're a greedy little man, aren't you? But listen to me. Don't you ever put me under this amount of pressure again and if you ever talk to me as you have just done, I'll cut your balls off. Are we clear? Remember who you're talking to."

"Anything you say; just pay up. I'll tell my man to be at the Heathrow place at three p.m. on Friday. Make sure the cars are there." The line went dead.

The Voice felt he was coming under pressure. He didn't like this recent turn of events, plus he now had to give Vlad the news. He selected another burner phone and called.

Vladimir Skoysky answered on the third ring. The Voice took a deep breath before starting his explanation.

"The Mile End operation has been shut down. It seems the police aren't as stupid as we thought. My inside man says killing Cameron Bowie was a stupid mistake. All you've done is give the police the operation."

The Voice could tell from the silence at the other end of the phone that Vlad was not pleased to hear this news.

"So, my friend, you must now solve our problem. Our associates in Russia are unaware of your local difficulties. I prefer to keep it that way especially as we have bigger issues to deal with. The car operation can be moved but the weapon is our real prize. I hear nothing from you about the weapon."

The Voice was surprised by how well the Russian had taken the news. He decided to show himself in a more positive light.

"I'll arrange for the three Audis you want, and I've organised an alternative to Mile End." He gave Vlad the address of Eddie Randall's yard. "Have your transporter there at around six o'clock Friday evening. The cars will be ready."

"Good, but no more cars for a while. You must concentrate on the weapon and only the weapon."

The Voice found he was perspiring. His hands felt damp. He had no plan to steal this weapon and did not know where to start. He knew he couldn't admit this to Vlad and was hoping to let events play out and react accordingly.

"Yes, I know that. Leave it with me." The Voice crossed his fingers.

***

Eddie Randall was waiting in his office. His watch told him it was 12.22 p.m. The Voice was unusually late. Eddie began to worry. He was more concerned that he would lose his income from the cars than that something had happened to the Voice.

Eddie's burner phone started to vibrate at exactly 12.24 p.m. It was the Voice.

Eddie jotted down the order for the three Audis. He had decided to ask the Voice about taking over the Mile End premises but before he could touch on the subject the Voice, unusually, carried on talking.

"Keep the cars at your place. Do not take them to Mile End."

Eddie was taken aback. "Listen, I know about the trackers. The cops can trace these cars. If I keep them here, I'll be nicked for sure."

The Voice was patient. "No, you won't. Leave the trackers to me. Just get the cars. Have all three at your place by Friday morning." Just to be sure there was no confusion, he added. "That's this Friday the 27th . Got it?"

Reluctantly, Eddie confirmed he understood.

"Good. Now a man will visit you on Friday afternoon and disable the trackers and then a lorry will turn up at around six o'clock in the evening to take the cars. Is that clear?"

Again, Eddie said it was.

"Now this is our last car deal for a while. I've got something else I might need your help with, but I'll be in touch."

Eddie was left listening to a load of static. The Voice had gone.

Chapter Seventeen

Detective Inspector Peter Jones arrived in Steve's office at twelve-thirty p.m. He initially tapped on the door frame before fully entering. He had what the DCI took to be an apologetic grin on his face. Within a few seconds, it was obvious why. Inspector May Dunlop burst on the scene pushing Peter to one side.

Steve stood. "Good afternoon, May."

The DCI noted she was dressed more in regulation uniform than the last time he had met her. Her skirt was still too long and her uniform jacket still too big. However, she had disposed of the non-regulation tie in favour of the black and white check scarf specified for female uniformed officers. May Dunlop could never be called pretty or smartly dressed. She certainly didn't dress to impress. Steve noticed a stain on her scarf that looked like gravy and the stains he'd seen before on her jacket were still in evidence.

"I've come for this briefing," was all that the Inspector said.

"I told her we were getting together around lunchtime to discuss the case, Steve, and she insisted on being here." Peter Jones looked apologetic.

Detective Sergeant Matt Conway appeared and squeezed past the small rotund figure of the female inspector.

"Fine. Let's all sit down." Steve pointed to the small conference table that sat at the far end of his office. It normally accommodated four people, so the DCI stayed behind his desk and called Poppy in to join them.

Before he could start the briefing session, Steve was forced to give way to May Dunlop. "I've not heard anything for days." Looking directly at Steve. "You promised to keep me updated."

In an attempt to take control of the meeting, Steve simply said, "I think you'll find I said we'd let you know of any developments. Now, can we get on?"

May Dunlop was not appeased. She started to say something, but the DCI cut her off. "Not now May, let's take this one step at a time."

Steve knew he had something going on at the back of his mind about this case but had so far failed to bring it forward.

"Peter. What have you got?"

Inspector Peter Jones started by outlining his and Matt Conway's interviews with the missing boys' teachers. He went on to explain that nothing had been found during the searches of the three premises and house to house enquiries had drawn a blank.

Matt Conway told the room about the searches of the surrounding areas and that at one time thirty uniformed officers had been involved searching fields, old warehouses and parks. Nothing had been found. He then explained that parents who were collecting their children on the dates of the disappearances had been interviewed as had the lollipop ladies at each school. To date, nothing had shown up that might help.

Peter took over. "The interviews with the mothers were really horrible. I don't know how these people manage. The houses were all dirty and the parents are living on handouts, food bank shopping and government support. I think at least one is supplementing her income by doing tricks on the side. If these kids have run away, I really can't blame them."

May Dunlop chirped up. "Listen. Don't take a downer on these women. They're trying to bring up a kid with no father present. Some of them don't even know who the fathers are. They get involved with some low life who either gets them pregnant willingly or rapes them for his own pleasure and leaves them in the club. I agree they're not at the top of the social order but without male support, they find life difficult."

Steve was sitting back listening to the debate with his hands steepled in front of his face. He decided to let the meeting run without his input.

"I see that, but one of the boys' mothers wasn't sure who his father was."

May glared at Peter. "For good reason. As soon as these blokes have their evil way with these girls they're off. As soon as they say they're with child, these hard-hearted buggers disappear leaving the girl to fend for herself. More often than not the girls have no family to help out. It's as if they're abandoned."

"But May," Peter pressed on. "How can you defend their lifestyle? The three mothers we interviewed were all capable of working but seemed to prefer to sit back and live on handouts. Maybe it's the girls who drove the fathers off rather than the fathers doing a runner."

The debate went on until Steve called a halt. "Enough. I think it's fair to say we have nothing. Correct?"

All three officers nodded.

"May. What are you hearing? After all, you're on the ground." "Unfortunately, nothing…"

As May Dunlop spoke, Steve suddenly called out.

"The fathers, it's about the fathers!"

All four officers including Poppy stared at the DCI as though he had suddenly gone mad. Steve stood and approached the whiteboard attached to the wall.

"Do you have the kids' dates of birth?"

The Inspector fumbled in her uniform jacket pocket and produced her notebook. After flicking over several pages, she confirmed that Billy Daley was born on the 15th of March 2010. That Frank Jackson was born on the 1st of September 2012 and that William Strachan was born on the 10th of November 2013.

As Steve added this information to the board, the gathered officers looked from one to another with quizzical expressions on their faces.

"Poppy. Get onto Somerset House, I want copies of these kids' birth certificates."

"No need sir, I can get them online. Give me a couple of minutes." In the event it took Poppy nearly twenty minutes to access Somerset House's database, identify the children they were interested in and print out the certificates.

Steve examined each document and turned back to the board.

He spoke as he wrote. "Billy Daley's father was one Dwaine Russell. Frank Jackson's father was Dwaine Russell and no prizes for guessing who's recorded as the father of William Strachan."

With a flourish, Steve wrote Dwaine Russell.

"I think that's the link. Each of our missing boys has the same father."

"Bloody hell, Steve, where did that come from?" Peter Jones was impressed.

May Dunlop smiled. "So, what are you saying?"

"I'm saying what if their father wanted his kids? What if this Dwaine Russell was everything you've said about the men in these girls lives? What if he did get out as soon as they were pregnant?" The DCI paused and looked at his audience. "But what if he's turned his life around? What if he's looked at the mothers and doesn't want his kids growing up in squalor? What if he took them to live with him, and he's trying to give them a better life?"

Detective Sergeant Matt Conway looked at his boss. "That's a lot of what-ifs, boss."

"Agreed, but it's possible." The whole room felt reinvigorated. There was a new energy that wasn't there half an hour ago.

Steve addressed the room giving out assignments. "Peter, find Dwaine Russell. He's probably got a record so maybe he won't be too hard to find. Get an address but don't barge in. Put wherever he lives under surveillance. Let's see if he has the kids. If he does, you'll need May and her team with you when you go in."

Poppy was typing on her laptop. As everyone agreed with the DCI that this was a likely and legitimate theory Poppy squealed, before realising she'd done so.

Looking a bit sheepish she turned to Steve. "Sorry sir, I got carried away."

Everyone was smiling. It wasn't often a police officer squealed with surprise. Poppy looked excited. "I've found Dwaine Russell."

The room was stunned.

Steve was the first to speak. "Good work Poppy. Tell all."

"Well, you were right. He has a record. Small-time petty theft. He was released from his last stretch four months ago. But here's the thing. His address is shown as Goswell Manor, Epping. I know that place. It's in the country just outside Epping. It must be worth a fortune."

May Dunlop spoke as Poppy hit more keys. "That could fit. He was released four months ago and must have got a job at this place in Epping."

Poppy was back. "I've just checked the Land Registry. The owner of Goswell Manor is one Dwaine Russell. He bought it for 3.2 million cash two months ago."

The room was silent. If a pin had dropped you would have heard it.

"Bloody hell. How does a con, a small-time petty thief buy a £3.2 million mansion for cash two months after getting out of prison?" Matt Conway had voiced what everyone was thinking.

Poppy was still hitting keys that seemed to echo around the silence.

"Got it." She sat back with a satisfied smile on her face. Her cheeks were flushed and in her excited mood, she appeared to have difficulty controlling her overly tight dress from riding up her thighs.

"He won fifteen million pounds on the Euro Lottery."

Peter Jones, apart from admiring Poppy's long legs, could only say, "Wow, lucky sod!"

The DCI had also noticed Poppy's sudden show of thigh and vowed to talk to her about her dress code. He couldn't, however, fault her work.

"Great work Poppy. Peter. You and Matt get over to Epping. Stake it out for a few hours. Let's see what's going on. Then if you decide to go in, call May, but wait until she arrives. We haven't enough for a warrant, so tread carefully but I bet you'll find these kids there."

Steve smiled a broad smile, sighed and thanked everyone for their efforts. "Keep me posted, Peter."

Peter Jones grinned at his boss as he and Matt Conway left. Poppy returned to her desk, but Inspector May Dunlop remained seated.

"Alfie Brooks told me you were the best and he's right. I should have thought of that connection, but you did. You're a bloody marvel, Steve Burt."

As she stood, she eyed Steve with a funny stare. "Come on, I'll buy you a coffee and maybe even a sticky bun. It feels like a good day's work."

The tall DCI and the short dumpy uniformed female inspector with the overly long uniform skirt and flat shoes that were originally black but were now grey marched together from Steve's office and headed for the canteen.

After his coffee and sticky bun, Steve returned to his office to find DC Mary Dougan sitting at her desk frantically typing into her laptop.

"Got a minute, boss?"

Steve signalled her to come through to his office.

"I'm going through known contacts for the first victim as you said. This Vinnie McGuire's not an easy bloke to trace. Seems he had a reputation as a bit of a fixer. He did a three stretch for cheque fraud in the nineties but that's all we have on him. The collator doesn't have much either, but I've got a few names to chase up. Don't hold your breath, though, this line of enquiry isn't going to solve our case."

The DCI was disappointed by Mary's negative attitude but understood tracing individuals was mind-deadening work.

"I'm not sure, Mary. The two victims were killed using the same or a very similar weapon. To my mind that links them."

"But the second victim, Cameron Bowie doesn't feature in any list of known contacts for Vincent McGuire."

"Just because they didn't know each other doesn't mean the two killings aren't linked."

Steve sat back. "Tell you what. Give it till the end of the week and if we're not getting anywhere, we'll close the book on known contacts." He looked at Mary and smiled. "OK?"

The DC knew her boss wouldn't ask her to do anything unless it was useful for the case. She conceded that just because she didn't see any sense in carrying on with a line of enquiry, she thought was a waste of time and didn't mean it might not throw up a lead.

"Yes. That's fine, boss. I'll keep at it." Feeling better than she did before talking with the DCI, Mary Dougan returned to her desk and set to with renewed enthusiasm.

***

After leaving the DCI, Inspector May Dunlop called one of her colleagues and a member of the Greater London Social Care Service. Despite acknowledging that Peter Jones would call her if there was any sign of the children at Goswell Manor, she instructed the lady from Social Services to meet her at the house and told her colleague to pick her up in a police car outside the side entrance to the Yard. Inspector May Dunlop wasn't about to wait. She needed to know if the missing kids were safe.

As the Inspector squeezed into the front seat of an old pool car, a new potential recruit was walking the perimeter of Montgomery Barracks near Wetherby in Yorkshire.

He didn't really want to join the Army but as a member of a gang helping a few Russians set up an operation in London, he'd been ordered to apply to join the army in the hope he would be sent to Montgomery Barracks for assessment.

The plan had worked.

Security above ground wasn't as tight as it was in Station K. In fact, an outsider looking in might think it was very slack. The potential recruit didn't know what was below his feet. In truth, he wasn't the brightest of the gang members, but he was the youngest and qualified for military service. All he knew was he had been given a small cardboard box that had been dipped in what looked like tar. He was told this was to ensure the contents were weatherproofed.

When it was confirmed he had to report to Montgomery Barracks, his gang leader had treated him to a drink in a shabby pub in the East End. A Russian called Vlad had joined them and the recruit had noticed his gang leader had said very little. Vlad had handed him the box and had drawn a map of the barracks. The recruit was to place the package in a service box located outside what the camp called the pump building. Vlad explained the building housed all the utilities and all the heating and water came into the camp through this building before being distributed throughout the camp. The outside box the recruit was to use housed the main water valve that if it were turned off would mean there would be no water in the camp.

The recruit didn't ask questions. He was afraid of this Russian and he could tell his gang boss felt the same way.

"All you have to do is act normal for a few days. Get to know where the pump house is and find the box. It won't be locked and should be to the back of the building." Vlad seemed to know a lot about this camp.

"Once you're comfortable and know your way around put the package in the box and call this number." The Russian handed over a piece of paper with a series of numbers written on it.

"After you've done that, you can say you're not suited for the army, and you want to leave. You'll be home within a day." Vlad stared at the youth. "Is that clear? No slipups."

***

The recruit had been in the camp for two days and had reported in sick this morning. This meant that he was excused from all the hard training and was free to wander. On the first day, he'd found the pump house and the box. He'd decided now would be a good time to get rid of the box. He wandered towards the pump house without raising any suspicion, bent beside the box to apparently tie his bootlace, lifted the lid of the box just enough to place the package inside and stood up stamping his foot as though checking his boot was tight enough.

He looked around but saw no one looking in his direction. It was 14:35 in army time and most people were either listening to lectures or out on a cross-country run.

The recruit headed for the NAAFI and the payphone. He dialled the number the Russian had given him said he'd carried out his task and asked if he could now return home.

At 14:45, the recruit informed the orderly office that he wanted to leave.

Vladimir Skoysky, on receiving the call from Yorkshire, immediately called *The Yorkshire Evening News* and placed an advert in the personals section. The deadline for entries in each evening edition of the paper was three o'clock each afternoon. The Russian just made it.

***

Detective Inspector Peter Jones and Detective Sergeant Matt Conway arrived at the home of Dwaine Russell at exactly half-past three on Wednesday the 25th of March. They found Goswell Manor without any problem. It wasn't what Matt Conway had expected. The word manor had conjured up an enormous estate with high walls and electronic gates. Instead, Goswell Manor was an ordinary-looking mock Tudor house on an estate. Matt conceded it was an upmarket estate behind security gates and 24-hour manned security—but… it was still an estate.

The DS discussed this with Peter, and both concluded that prices in Epping must be high if this was all £3.2 million bought. The house was set back from the road and open to the front. A pedestrian path led to the front door and a wide drive gave access to the double garage.

"What do you think Matt?" Peter Jones was the senior officer and any decisions going forward were his.

"Steve said to stake it out and see if there were any signs of the kids."

"Yeah. But we can't see anything just sitting in the car."

Their car was parked almost directly opposite the house. They would see any movement around the building.

Peter looked at his watch. It was quarter to four. "Let's wait for a moment and see. If he isn't holding them prisoner; they should be out playing."

Matt looked sideways at his senior officer. "Look at this place, Peter. I don't think kids play outside on their bikes or kick footballs in a place like this. It's far too grand."

The DS chuckled. "At least I'm sure that's how the homeowners here see it."

Taking in the scene in front of him, Peter had to agree.

***

At 4.23 p.m., another, older car arrived and parked behind the police car. Almost simultaneously another older car appeared and parked in front of the police car effectively blocking it in.

The detectives were initially alarmed until they saw a dumpy police uniform approaching their car. It was Inspector May Dunlop.

"Well?" The inspector was a demanding lady. "What's going on?"

As Peter wound down his window, he saw another police uniform arriving to join May. "We're doing as we were told. We're checking the place out to see if there's any evidence the kids are here."

Peter was looking angry. "I was going to call you when we confirm the kids are here. You're not supposed to be here until I call you!"

Peter was even more enraged when a civilian arrived having left the car parked in the rear.

"Who the hell is this?"

May Dunlop laughed. "This, my young Inspector, is Miss Glen from Social Services. The only way to find anything out is to go and knock on the door."

It was clear May wasn't about to wait. She'd brought her team and seemed hell-bent on doing things her way. Talking directly to Peter, she said, "Come on lad. Off your bum. Let's go and get these children."

As she marched towards the house with her troops in tow, both detectives exited their car in a hurry. "She's a maniac. She's no idea what she's doing. If the kids are there, we'll have to arrest Dwaine Russell and charge him with abduction and kidnap." Peter Jones was running to catch up with May and talking to Matt who was running alongside.

"We need to do this by the book; bloody hell, Matt. We've no probable cause and certainly no evidence these kids are even here, but look at her, she's all arms and looks like she's leading an infantry charge."

Despite her bulk, May had shown an impressive turn of speed and arrived well ahead of the two detectives. She was banging on the door. All five people waited. May banged again and this time the door opened a fraction.

"Yes. What do you want?"

May took the lead, talking over Peter. "Police. Will you let us in please?"

Whoever was behind the door wasn't showing themselves. "Why? Do you have a warrant?"

"No, but in a case of child abduction we don't need one," lied May.

The door opened a little further. "I don't know what you're talking about."

"I think you do. Now are you going to let us in, or do I get my two strong friends here to kick the door down?"

Peter stood forward. He admired May's forthright approach but knew if the kids were here what had just taken place would mean the case would never get to court. He decided to salvage what he could.

"Is Mr Dwaine Russell at home?"

174

"Maybe. Why are you asking?"

Peter produced his warrant card and held it to the gap in the door. "I'm DI Peter Jones. These people with me are my colleagues. I just want to talk to Mr Russell. It won't take long. If you'll open the door, we can explain everything."

There was hesitation from the other side of the door "That woman said it was about some kids."

Peter wished May Dunlop hadn't barged in.

"As I said, sir, if you open the door we can explain."

The door was opened and a dark-skinned man with long black hair stood facing the detective. Peter wasn't sure if this was Dwaine Russell but if it was, his recent spell at Her Majesty's pleasure hadn't gone well for him. He looked thin and despite his natural colour, he was somehow pale. He looked to be in his late sixties but it was hard to tell. He was dressed in a smart t-shirt and jeans. He wore open-toed sandals and no socks.

Peter took a step forward. "Are you Dwaine Russell?"

"No, I'm his father. Dwaine's upstairs, playing with his kids." Peter wasn't sure but he thought he smelt alcohol on this old man's breath.

On hearing the news Dwaine was upstairs playing with his kids, Peter swung into action. He quietly told May that there were children in the house. He stared her out, telling her it didn't mean they were the missing kids, and she mustn't jump the gun.

"Leave this to Matt and me. You stay here with this gentleman. He says he's Dwaine's father." He lowered his voice even further. "It doesn't sound as though this bloke knows about the abductions. Keep him here and don't let him leave." May was about to say something but Peter cut her off.

"May, please, I know you care about these kids but let's do this right." He stared at the uniformed Inspector and she nodded. Deep down she knew she could have ruined the whole thing.

Peter and Matt walked up the stairs. The carpet was thick and absorbed any sound their shoes made. They stopped at the top and listened. Music was coming from one of the rooms off to the right. They stopped outside the door and again listened. The music was low, and they heard excited children's voices together with a man's voice.

175

The detectives looked at each other. The DI decided to go straight in. He turned the door handle and walked straight in. He immediately saw three boys aged between seven and ten. All three looked bright and seemed to be enjoying themselves. Shrill laughter was cut short following the policemen's appearance. Peter and Matt stood for a few seconds taking in the scene. The floor was covered in toys of various types, there were fizzy drink bottles both full and empty scattered over the floor together with bags of sweets.

The kids were sprawled on the floor and the man was on his knees obviously trying to get a toy to work. He put down the toy and stood.

"I suppose you're the cops?"

Peter answered. "Yes. And I suppose you're Dwaine Russell and these three lads are your sons." Dwaine nodded. He looked at each child in turn with a mixture of pride and regret. "I haven't been much of a father but now I can be. No more crime. I've got honest money. I can give them a decent life away from those slappers I got pregnant. They've got a future now."

Dwaine was clearly emotional but didn't seem to understand the seriousness of his situation. Peter called down for May to join them. He didn't want to upset the kids but had to take action.

May and the social worker called Miss Glen took charge of the children. They talked to them, told them they weren't in any trouble and that their school friends had missed them. It was difficult to see how this situation could play out without alarming the kids.

May approached Peter and nodded to her uniformed colleague to sit with one of the boys.

"We've got a problem. Miss Glen wants to take the three of them into care for a few days until we sort things up. Unfortunately, these boys should be returned to their mothers, but I suppose Dwaine won't like that." Peter was seeing May's caring side. She looked at Peter wearing a serious expression. She nodded in Dwaine's direction. He was back kneeling on the floor trying to get the toy to work.

"I don't suppose you've told him what happens to him next?"

"No. I don't want to upset the kids. To be honest, I was hoping you'd sort things out, you know, get the kids away before we arrest Dwaine."

"I know what the book says but if I can persuade Miss Glen to leave them here, could you hold off with the arrest?" May was pleading. "Just until tomorrow. You can see they're in no danger and I don't think Dwaine's going anywhere."

Peter's instinct was to refuse. Dwaine had abducted these children and had broken the law by doing so. He felt sympathy for the man and could see how May was thinking… but… it wasn't his decision to make. He called the DCI.

Peter explained what had happened but left out May's cavalier approach. "I don't see any harm but it's not my call."

The DCI was preparing to meet the Commander for their council of war regarding Superintendent Blackmore. He switched his phone onto speaker and sat back. "What does May hope to achieve by leaving the kids there overnight?"

"I don't know. They're clearly happy here and Dwaine doesn't seem to be a threat, but he is guilty of abduction."

"Put May on, Peter. I'll talk to her."

May Dunlop argued her case with Steve explaining why the children should be left with their father overnight. She again stated the lack of risk and the secure environment. As she was finishing her long-winded explanation, the DCI cut her off.

"Look May, now we've found the boys, our job is done. It's down to you and Social Services to sort them out. Our job was to solve the crime and clearly, a crime has been committed. I sympathise but Peter has to bring Dwaine in. I can't risk him doing a runner. I'll arrange police bail, so he'll be home tonight if you decide to leave the kids there. That's the best I can do. Who knows, the CPS may take extenuating circumstances into account and not even prosecute."

"Thanks, Steve." She sighed. "You're right of course. This is a bit of a mess, but we'll sort it. If their father gets home, I'll persuade Social Services to leave the boys here but put them on the at-risk register for now. That way we'll keep a daily eye on them." May passed the phone back to Peter.

"Well done, Peter. Try to arrest Dwaine quietly away from his kids. Get him to Central for processing and then arrange police bail. When that's done, arrange a car to take him home."

"Right and thanks, Steve. I'm not sure what I would have done if I hadn't been able to contact you."

All Steve replied was, "You'd have coped." And put the phone down.

Checking his watch, Steve realised it was 4.56 p.m. Time to go and play Commander Alfie Brooks' games.

Chapter Eighteen

As the DCI approached the office of Alfie Brooks, he suddenly felt tired. Physically he was fine but mentally he was exhausted. The past few days had been hectic, and he could feel more busy days were to come. He promised himself an early night and a good night's sleep.

Steve entered Alfie's office at two minutes past five. Alfie was seated at his conference table with his uniform jacket off and hanging on the back of his chair. Another man Steve vaguely recognised was seated opposite Alfie. Both men had what looked like tumblers of whisky in front of them.

"Ah! Steve." Alfie raised his glass in the DCI's direction. "Drink?"

"No thanks, sir. If I have one, I'll probably fall asleep."

"Right you are." Pointing with his glass, the Commander introduced the other man at the table.

"I don't think you know Superintendent Carson, from Internal Affairs."

The men nodded at each other. Steve had heard of Mr Carson and his nickname. He was known as Kit Carson because he always gets his man. Superintendent Carson was no lightweight and had ended the careers of several high-ranking officers who had flirted with the more lucrative side of policing.

"I've asked Kit to join us as I have a feeling whatever we do from now regarding Superintendent Blackstone will ultimately finish up on his desk."

Steve was surprised to hear Alfie use Superintendent Carson's nickname to his face.

"Kit has been digging since I briefed him earlier." Alfie took a sip of the golden liquid. "Carry on, Kit."

The Superintendent cleared his throat. "None of what I'm telling you goes any further than this room. Is that clear?"

The DCI nodded but also thought *Here we go again.* He wondered how many meetings he would go to that started with the same warning and if his brain was big enough to retain everyone's secrets.

"Our friend Glennen Blackstone has come and gone on our radar for years. We know he's dirty, but we've never been able to prove anything. A few months back we thought we had him. You know he runs a surveillance unit and has a fairly free hand to interfere in cases if there's a surveillance operation. You know the thing. Don't arrest Mr Big, he's under surveillance as part of a much bigger case. Sometimes it's true but on occasions, he's used the excuse of an ongoing operation as a way of stopping legitimate enquiries." Kit looked at Steve.

"Case in point, Steve. Your Mile End murder and his withholding the CCTV images. He said he had an ongoing surveillance case but in truth, he didn't. He was just running interference."

The Superintendent leant forward and took a good pull of his single malt.

"Now Alfie tells me you both think he must be involved somehow in the murder. From the evidence, I'm inclined to agree. He wouldn't chance pulling a stunt like that unless he had a good reason." Kit finished his whisky as he turned to Steve.

"Your victim was in the car trade. Correct?"

"Yes. He seems to have been involved in stealing high-end cars to order."

"Mm. Interesting. I told you we thought we had Blackstone a few months ago. Well, he was pressurising the vehicle-tracking companies to shut down their operations for up to twelve hours at a time."

Steve didn't follow. "What vehicle-tracking companies?"

"You know it's usual for high-end motors to have trackers fitted in case they are stolen? Well, that's not a police arrangement. The insurance companies monitor the trackers they've had fitted, and they always subcontract the monitoring to private companies. If the monitoring company gets an alarm call because a vehicle's been broken into or if an owner reports their pride and joy stolen, then the tracker shows where the vehicle is." Kit Carson paused while Alfie refilled both glasses.

"Some of the more expensive trackers can shut the engine down in a stolen car once it's known to be nicked. The tracking companies notify us each time a car is reported stolen and give us the location of the vehicle. Traffic usually have no problem finding the car and arresting the culprits."

Steve began to see. "So, Blackstone told the trackers that he had an operation, and their tracking system was somehow causing his operation problems?"

"Something like that. We traced back, and on each occasion, he pulled that stunt, several high-end cars were stolen but of course, with the tracker system switched off, they never recovered the cars. We went on a fishing trip and even threw a disciplinary charge at him, but he wriggled out of it."

The DCI was intrigued. He tried to put the pieces together. As he often did when deep in thought, Steve started talking to himself out loud. "We've got a killing of a car dealer involved in stealing high-end cars, and a senior police officer who has interfered in my murder case and tried to deny us access to CCTV images that have proven to be helpful to my case. Why?

Now the same officer is suspected of running interference with car tracking companies such that each time he instructs them to close their systems for a time, high-end cars get stolen and can't be tracked because the system is down; he *must* be involved."

Steve sat back staring at the wall.

"It's odds-on he's not killing people or stealing cars himself. He must be working for someone. Someone who can pull his strings. Someone who has something on him or is paying him very well to take these kinds of risks. Someone important. Maybe even someone who thinks they are untouchable."

Steve realised what he'd been doing and shook himself back to the present. "Sorry, I was just trying to fit the pieces together."

Alfie was grinning. "And you put things together nicely. Now, as Kit hasn't been able to lay a glove on him, how do we propose to bring the sod out into the open?" Alfie sipped his whisky.

The DCI was deciding how much to divulge about the murder case. He decided he could say something but held back on the Russian, bearing in mind the warning from the colonel from Military Intelligence.

"There's more but I'm not sure if Blackstone figures in it. We've established a link between the victim and a Russian gang trying to get a foothold in London. We think our victim was working for these Russians and that he was probably killed on their orders. If we're right then Blackstone must be in it up to his neck or he's working for an intermediary."

The three policemen sat in silence until Superintendent Carson spoke. "Steve, I think we'll only get Blackstone if you can tie him into your investigation. We can't set traps or entrapment comes into play. The only way to get him is evidence and you're best placed to get it."

"I agree," Alfie spoke up. "Work the case and see if you can tie Blackstone to anything. You know you have our backing but keep both Kit and me in the loop."

The DCI allowed his fatigue to wash over him. He knew he was once again being placed in an unenviable position but was too tired to argue.

After a few minutes of general chat, Steve stood, said goodbye, and left. An early dinner followed by a bath and an early night beckoned.

***

The spy at Station K was now outside the underground bunker having passed through the exit security protocols. It was early and this Thursday morning the 26th of March was cold. He shivered and surmised living underground had made him soft although he agreed with himself that March was a cold month. He was heading for the NAAFI shop as was allowed under current security rules. He'd read yesterday evening's newspaper and seen the message inserted by the Russian.

After visiting the shop, he nonchalantly strolled around the camp apparently enjoying the fresh air. He double-checked that no one was interested in him as he made his way to the utilities building and the outside valve box. He casually stretched his arms and like the recruit before him, he bent down to seemingly tie his shoelace. He extracted the parcel and, hiding it in his uniform top, he made for the communal toilets located beside the canteen.

He sat on the toilet inside a cubicle and opened the box. Inside were various plastic components all designed to fool the X-Ray machines designed to stop metal objects being smuggled into Station K. He knew 3D printer technology had produced the camera that was in the box. It was made up of three parts and each part would have to be smuggled in separately past the security system of Station K. Looking at the components the spy smiled. Each part was a work of art and would easily get past the machines. He selected the largest part. It was the body of the camera. He removed the contents of his trouser pockets. He'd deliberately filled his pocket with junk. Old pieces of string, a not too clean handkerchief and a few sticky sweets.

The remaining parts he returned to the waterproof box, resealed it and placed it in the overhead cistern.

On his return to the bunker, he went through the various security checks and simply emptied his pockets into a tray that went through an X-ray scanner. He'd wrapped the plastic part in his not too clean handkerchief to avoid any questions as to what it was and as anticipated the 3D produced part didn't set off any alarm bells.

The first part was successfully inside Station K.

***

The DCI had enjoyed a good night's sleep. He felt more refreshed but knew he was running near empty, and would need a few more early nights. He walked to his office collecting three Costa coffees on the way. As Steve was paying for the coffees the spy in Station K had just successfully smuggled the first of three camera parts into the underground bunker.

Poppy was at her desk as was DC Mary Dougan. Steve distributed the coffee and noticed both ladies already had empty cups on their desks. He thought they must have been in for a while. His watch told him it was 08.12 a.m. on Thursday the 26th of March.

Mary was first at his office door. She was carrying a few sheets of paper. "I'm still on the known associates of our first victim. As I said, it doesn't look too promising, but I have a few connections that might be something."

Steve indicated that Mary should sit down. He sipped his coffee with relish. He didn't say anything knowing Mary would tell him what she had.

"First up, he's a bit of a mystery. He seems to pop up and disappear. I've interviewed people who knew him. They all say he didn't seem to have a proper job, but lived on commissions as a fixer. Nobody I've spoken to claim to know who he was working for before he was killed. I've a list of his associates but only one seems to be in the car trade. I'm going to see a few more today and I'll see the guy in the car business. You never know. Given our second victim was into cars it's just possible there might be a connection but don't hold your breath."

Steve could tell Mary was disappointed but was pleased to see she was sticking to the task.

"Good. Well done, Mary. As I said, my gut feeling is there must be a connection between our two victims but if you find I'm wrong, I'll stand the team a round of drinks." The DCI smiled as his DC left to begin another round of interviews, she felt were a complete waste of time.

Detective Inspector Peter Jones tapped on Steve's door frame a few minutes after Mary Dougan left. "Got a minute?"

Steve signalled to the DI to sit.

"I just thought I'd fill you in on yesterday."

"Good. I presume you got our lottery winner processed?"

"Yes. That was the easy bit. May Dunlop persuaded Social Services to leave the kids in the house. The woman wasn't happy and apparently, it went all the way to the Council's Director for approval." Peter laughed. "May got the bloke at home and I hear he wasn't pleased. He said he was in the middle of his dinner." Peter continued to smile. "Poor sod." The DI obviously didn't think much of council employees.

"Anyway, the kids stayed there last night, and Dwaine got home about nine o'clock after being processed. He's bailed to appear in a couple of weeks. The kids are being collected this morning and returned to their mothers. May Dunlop's having one of her people stationed at the house in case there's any trouble." Peter looked solemn.

"You know, I feel sorry for Dwaine and his kids. Sure, he's a villain but it looks like winning the lottery may have turned his life around. He clearly loves his kids and I know he shouldn't have just lifted them off the street, but he meant well. I hope he uses his money and gets a smart lawyer to defend him. The last thing he needs is to go back inside for this."

"I agree but you did your job. All we had to do was find the kids and the person who abducted them. You did that, Peter. It's up to the courts now." Steve stood up indicating he was leaving. "It's not our problem any more. Write it up and you and Matt had better follow up with May Dunlop just to make sure everything's tied up. No loose ends."

"Right." Peter looked quizzically at the DCI. "Going anywhere nice?"

"No. I'm off to Tech Services to see if Terry Harvey has worked his magic." Steve left smiling and hoping Terry had indeed some good news for him.

Terry Harvey was Head of Technical Services. Owing to the nature of his work, very few senior officers understood the technicalities of his work. All they knew was that Terry usually got results. Because of this Terry was left to do his job without the interference from above usually experienced by other department heads. This meant Terry was more independent and therefore able to bend the rules as he thought necessary.

The DCI walked into Terry's small office tucked into a corner of a vast open-plan office that seemed full of earnest odd-looking young people typing away furiously at computer keyboards. Terry called them his whiz kids.

"I was just going to call you." Terry looked up from a large pile of computer printouts.

"Well, I'm here and looking for good news."

"Ah! Right. Let's go to the canteen and you can buy. You'll owe me big time when you see what I've got."

Both men left and the DCI was feeling excited. It wasn't often Inspector Harvey made such statements. Once they were seated and had their drinks Terry opened a file he'd brought with him.

"I ran the facial recognition protocols overnight." Terry opened his file with one hand while he sipped his coffee. "It's a wonderful piece of kit and it worked like a charm. It found our guys in minutes."

Terry went on to explain to Steve how the new system was revolutionary. He went into great detail that Steve found interesting but boring. "The great thing is we can now take a face, digitise it and run it against any number of data basis. It's bloody marvellous."

The DCI was excited to learn the names of the people the Inspector had found but knew Terry would reveal all as he went on.

When he eventually stopped his enthusiastic explanation of his new software the Inspector got to the details that the DCI was more interested in. "First, the two scruffy looking individuals. As you thought, they both have form." Terry was opening his file as he spoke.

"Albert Rogers, known as Bert." Terry produced an A5-sized photograph. "Been in and out of prison most of his life. Always small-time petty stuff but no killer." The Inspector took another sip of his coffee before producing a second A5-size photograph and pushed it across the table for Steve to look at.

"Francis O'Rourke. Same thing. Knows what a prison cell looks like better than the inside of his own home. He's spent more time inside than out. Like his mate, he's small time. All petty stuff. I pulled their prison files." Terry pushed the file he had brought to the DCI. "Nothing startling. They are both below-average intelligence, physical wrecks according to the prison doctors and are very work-shy." Terry shrugged as he sat back and drank his coffee.

Steve took the information. "You're a bloody marvel, Terry. Is getting all this strictly legal?"

"You should know not to ask questions like that, but as you ask... well not strictly. It seems our hands are tied by something called personal privacy laws and data protection nonsense. I've put using the new software down as a training exercise so if anyone asks you didn't get any of this from me and you can't use it in court if you get that far. It shows how stupid things have become. We know who the bad guys are, but we're not allowed to catch them." Terry's voice was serious. He clearly felt passionate about what he was allowed to do, and not do.

"Right. If you go to the back of that file, you'll find the real story." Terry Harvey waited while a surprised Steve flicked to the rear of the file. He found another A5-size photograph which he lifted from the file.

"That is one John Stuart McKelvey also known as The Blade. Now he is someone you should look at for your murders. He's been inside for grievous bodily harm, twice. His weapon of choice is a stiletto knife. He likes to inflict pain and has been rounded up a few times on suspected murder charges where such a knife was used. His prison record says he's clever but lacks social skills. Also, he's a nutter; his medical reports show he's a psycho, so beware."

Terry sat looking at Steve who in turn was analysing what this information meant to his cases.

"Terry? Apart from the legality of how we obtained this, was there anyone else on the CCTV who showed up?"

"No. Just the two idiots you saw hanging around and putting petrol in the car and our man The Blade. We got a clear shot of him coming out of the car showroom so before you ask. Yes… I'm 100% sure we have the correct identities."

The DCI went into deep thought mod and stared at the far wall. After a few minutes, Terry interrupted him. "I'm off back to work. If you need anything else you know where we are."

As he was leaving the Inspector suddenly stopped and turned to Steve. "Oh! By the way, I had that Superintendent Blackstone on yesterday afternoon. He's not a happy man. He threatened to report me for misconduct because we looked at those CCTV images. If you have any dealings with him, Steve, be careful." Terry Harvey was about to walk off when Steve called him back.

In a conspiratorial whisper, the DCI motioned for Terry to come closer. "It's about your niece, Poppy. I know you're close so it's better coming from you."

Terry showed some alarm at this turn of events. "Is anything wrong?"

"No, no, nothing's wrong. It's just she doesn't dress appropriately for a policewoman unless she's working undercover in Vice. Can you have a word? Ask her not to wear those tight-fitting dresses she seems to prefer."

Terry visibly relaxed and smiled. "I know what you mean Steve. She always has liked to dress to show her assets." Still standing, Terry turned to leave again. "I'll have a word."

The DCI sat for a few minutes re-examining the paperwork in the file. He knew he was close to finding the killer now, but he knew he didn't just want that. He wanted the man who ordered the second killing. He wanted the Russian.

Chapter Nineteen

After lunch at Station K, Staff Sergeant Bobby Tay had a meeting with the senior members of the research team responsible for developing the weapon delivery system Bobby was helping to design and produce. He'd mentioned something to his commanding officer and his remark had led to this meeting.

Professor Karl Symonds was present as were other research scientists.

"We understand Bobby you have once again come up with a revolutionary idea to help us develop the weapon. Care to tell us about it?"

Bobby Tay wasn't overawed by being in such august scientific company. He regarded his skills infinitely superior to these men in white coats, most of whom he didn't like.

"Well, Professor, it's only a thought. You see, when I was milling the prototype shell, I realised it will be a bugger to put into mass production because of the metal thickness or lack of it, plus the need to attach the cover plate to the cavity that holds the battery and the gas. Then there are the veins that have to open once the shell lands to allow the gas to escape. Overall, it's a bloody complicated piece of engineering."

"Yes. I think we all understand that, but we assume our engineering colleagues will find a solution." Karl Symonds was no engineer and relied on others to solve practical problems.

"I'm sorry sir, but I don't believe there is a firm in the land that could produce this shell. Each one will have to be handmade meaning there won't be a lot made and they'll be expensive."

The Professor sat back obviously taking in what the staff sergeant of Royal Engineers had said.

"So, what's to be done, Sergeant? I've told the MOD that thousands of these weapons will transform modern warfare. If we can't produce enough shells for the weapon then the thing is a waste of time."

"Exactly sir." Bobby paused before continuing. "That's why I thought of a re-usable shell. The projectiles are fired flat and are designed to hit the ground horizontally, not like a traditional shell that lands nose-first in order to activate the trigger that causes the explosion. If we put a tracker inside the cavity beside the battery and the tracker is activated when the weapon is fired, all we have to do is scan the battlefield, listening out for the signal, and then retrieve the shells. There's no reason they can't be re-used. Just a new gas sack, a new battery, a new charge and you're good to go again."

"It would certainly cut costs and mean if the projectile is difficult to produce, we wouldn't need many of them." Professor Symonds looked doubtfully at Bobby Tay.

"Bobby, are you sure this would work? We really could re-use spent shells and track them?"

"Pretty sure, sir. We'd miss a few, a few might be damaged but overall, I think we could recycle most of them."

"How long will it take you to put a tracker in the prototype?"

"Well, Professor. If I can have a pass to leave, I'll go to a local electrical wholesaler and see what they have that might be suitable for a trial. Although, if we go ahead, a more robust and secure tracker would be needed."

"Good man." The Professor looked at his colleagues who all seemed enthusiastic. "Then we are agreed. Staff Sergeant Tay can go above ground and visit the wholesalers. I'll have security prepare your pass, Bobby. I suggest you go now. I've committed to a test firing at the Army's test-firing range at Boscombe Down in Wiltshire next Thursday. That's the 2nd of April so you'd better get your skates on."

Staff Sergeant Bobby Tay was on his way. He now had what he needed. The date when the weapon would be moved.

***

Poppy appeared at Steve's door holding a cup of coffee. "I've checked out gold-coloured Ford Granadas as you asked."

"Great! Come in and thanks for the coffee." Poppy placed the cardboard cup on her boss' desk.

"You were right. There aren't too many left. DVLA say there are only just under six hundred registered but only twelve within the M25. I've tracked all twelve down and spoken to the owners. Most are in the owners' club and look after their cars. The one we saw looked like a real rust bucket so I'm not thinking it's one of them. The others are owned by what seem to be respectable citizens. A doctor, a nurse and a teacher. I don't see them being involved in our killings."

Poppy spread her arms. "I'm sorry Steve. It's a dead end."

As Steve took in this news, he saw an impish grin appear on Poppy's face. He knew she had something.

"Go on DC Cooper, what else have you got?" Steve was grinning.

"Well, sir. Despite my Uncle Terry telling me to stop wearing my designer dresses to the office." She stared hard at her boss. "And I've no idea where he got that from." She continued to stare, and Steve gave in.

"OK, guilty. I asked him to have a word. I don't think tight figure-hugging designer dresses are appropriate for the office. That's all."

"Well, I suppose I could change. I've noticed a few randy constables looking at me sideways in the canteen."

Steve was relieved. "Now, what else do you have?"

Poppy perked up. "I was thinking. If the owner of this Granada isn't an honest man, he may well not have registered the car. We know from the CCTV that he changes number plates and I bet he doesn't have it taxed or insured. The car is off the official radar."

Steve was once again impressed by Poppy's reasoning. "Good point. What's the answer?"

Poppy smiled. "Well, sir, when I was being talked to by my favourite uncle, I mentioned my problem with the gold Granada. He said he could help me and thought it would be possible to interrogate all the CCTV cameras within the M25 to look for a Ford Granada. As you know most of the cameras are old and in black and white, but I thought if we saw any and they looked like bangers we might find ours. Black and white will still show a banger."

"Poppy. You and your favourite uncle are very clever. He gave me a couple of names earlier. Looks like he's earning his salary this month. How far has he gone?"

"That's the thing. We discussed it and we know where the car was on the day of the killing. Terry says he'll track forward using the traffic cameras and try and plot its course. It headed west out of the garage so he's concentrating on cameras going west. I hope that's OK, Steve?"

"It's better than OK, Poppy. Good work. Tell Terry I'm once again in his debt. Now get off home. Have an early finish."

"But it's only four-fifteen."

"Do as you're told. You've put in a lot of unpaid overtime recently. Now go; I'll see you in the morning!"

***

Bobby Tay didn't go straight to the electrical wholesalers in Wetherby. After exiting through security and above ground, he went to collect the burner phone he had buried under one of the air conditioning housings.

With the phone safely in his pocket, he drove through the gates of Montgomery Barracks. There were only minimal security checks above ground. He drove towards Wetherby and pulled into a layby just outside the town. Sitting in the army pool car he called Vladimir Skoysky.

"It's being tested next Thursday at Boscombe Down in Wiltshire. My guess is they'll move it down the day before, the 1st of April."

Although the staff sergeant couldn't see the Russian's face, he could hear the pleasure in his voice. "Very good, comrade, I'll pass this along. Call the other number and tell him the same thing. Find out if he has a plan yet." The line died.

For only the second time Bobby Tay phoned the Voice. It took several rings before the call was answered. "The weapon is being moved next Wednesday the 1st of April to Boscombe Down in Wiltshire."

The Voice was taken aback. He'd secretly hoped this whole hare-brained scheme would go away. All he could say was, "Right."

"Never mind right, I need to know your plan. We'll have one chance at this, and we can't afford to screw it up."

"Right." For once the normally self-assured Voice was nervous. He didn't know what to do.

The staff sergeant felt the uncertainty down the phone. "Listen, it will be moved by road. There's bound to be an armed escort, but it won't

192

be too obvious. Maybe a couple of military police, that's all. They'll almost certainly take the most direct route. Get yourself a map. Check out the most likely route and plan to ambush the vehicle somewhere on the route. The weapon is only lightweight and small enough to fit in the boot of a car." The staff sergeant felt he was dealing with an amateur, not a dedicated communist like himself. "Have you got that?"

The Voice was sweating. He couldn't ambush a British Army transport especially if it was accompanied by armed guards. He realised he was in over his head but couldn't see a way out.

"Yes. I've got it."

"Good. You'll need at least four men for the job. They should be armed and prepared to shoot. Is that clear?"

"Yes, perfectly." The Voice had never been so scared in his life.

"Put an advert in the paper when you're ready. I'll try and get word to you once the weapon is on its way." Just as the Russian had done, the staff sergeant hung up without another word being spoken.

***

The Voice sat staring at his burner phone for five long minutes. He eventually closed down the open line and started to pace around his office, his mind in turmoil. If he carried out the ambush, he'd be very wealthy, but it was dangerous and who could he get to carry it out? He had connections but wasn't sure if any of them would take on such a job. He reckoned that if he found people prepared to undertake the job, they would want money and that would have to come from him, reducing his windfall. The Voice quickly realised he needed another option. He certainly wasn't sharing his million dollars.

He fidgeted as he paced around his wood-panelled office. He sat in one of his comfortable high wing leather chairs and thought some more. What if he told Vlad he'd have to pay for the team who ambushed the army car? He'd also have to provide weapons. The Voice didn't think this an unreasonable request. He rose from his chair and continued pacing. He could ask Blackstone to help. He must know some heavy underworld types who wouldn't be squeamish about such a job, but again… they'd want paying.

The Voice knew that everywhere he looked it would cost money. After an hour of soul searching, he concluded his only option was to ask Vlad to stump up the money. But how much? He had no idea what such an operation involved and of course, he'd add a commission for himself. Yes, he thought, that's the plan. He would ask Blackstone to help, find out how much the ambush gang would want and add 10% for himself. After a few minutes of review, he concluded and spoke aloud, "No, I'll add twenty per cent. After all, I'm taking risks too."

The Voice was happier now he saw a way forward plus how he'd be able to collect a sizeable commission. All he needed was for Blackstone and Vlad to agree.

**

DC Mary Dougan arrived back in the office just before four-thirty p.m. She looked windswept and a little flustered. She stuck her head around Steve's door. "Where is everyone?"

The DCI looked up from the file Terry Harvey had given him earlier. "Poppy's gone home early, and Peter and Matt are finishing up the abduction case." Mary looked blank trying to analyse why Poppy had gone home. Steve saw the confusion in his junior officer's expression. "I told her to go home. She's put in a lot of unpaid overtime." Steve knew he didn't have to explain but preferred his team to understand how he operated. Before Mary could counter, the DCI held up a hand. "Don't worry. You'll get your turn once these cases are put to bed."

Mary didn't look convinced but accepted Steve's explanation.

"How did you do?"

"Not very well. Vinnie McGuire had a lot of mates but no real friends. I've spent the day chasing down some real low lives. All I could find out was no one knew how Vinnie made his money. One or two who had served time with him thought he was a smart guy and had made a deal with someone high up. You know what these people are like. A bus inspector counts as high up in their world." Mary paused to consider. "But… it's the second time I've heard that Vinnie was involved with someone high up. I wonder if there's anything to it?"

"I suppose it's possible. I suppose it's also possible that's what got him killed." The DCI saw another possible line of enquiry opening up.

As he contemplated this, Mary carried on. "I've been all over the place. Even as far as Hounslow. It seems Vinnie spent some time with a second-hand car dealer out by Heathrow. One or two I spoke with said this bloke was as close to a friend as Mr Vincent McGuire had."

"And?"

"Well, nothing." Mary was looking through her notes. "He's called Eddie Randall. A real rough bloke. You know the thing, shaved head, tattoos, the works. Claimed not to have seen Vinnie in months. I asked if he knew if Vinnie was working for anybody important, but I only got a blank stare and a laugh. Seems Vinnie wasn't too bright, but neither was this Eddie character."

Steve was listening and thinking. "Did anybody you spoke with apart from this Eddie have any connection to the car trade?"

It was the detective constable's turn to laugh. "If you'd seen Eddie's car yard you might not have said he was in the car trade. More like the car scrapping trade. I've never seen such a collection of old rusted bangers." Mary's laughter turned to a giggle. With tears in her eyes, she carried on. "But no, from his known associates no one has any connections to cars, only Eddie."

"Does Eddie Randall have form?"

"Steve. Everyone I've spoken to over the past two days has form. I haven't checked Eddie Randall, but I bet he's seen the inside of a cell more than once."

Mary yawned and stretched her arms above her head. "What's in the file?" She was looking at the file Steve had been studying.

"It's something Terry Harvey gave me. He was able to identify the faces from the CCTV we eventually got from the Mile End Road cameras opposite the murder scene. Seems our two skeletons dressed in black are Albert Rogers and Francis O'Rourke. Both small-time crooks apparently of no fixed abode. They are registered with the probation service and should be staying at a halfway house. I spoke to their probation officer earlier. He hasn't seen either of them for months."

Steve handed over the pictures that Terry had printed.

Mary examined them and a faraway look appeared on her face. The DCI knew he went into trance like positions when he was trying to recall something so stayed quiet. Mary could take all the time she needed.

Mary Dougan eventually spoke. "I've seen these two…" She was still thinking. "But where? It had to be recently, maybe even today." Her face contorted with concentration. Steve willed her to remember.

After a further few minutes of mental gymnastics, Mary gave up. "Sorry, Steve. It just won't come. I know I didn't interview them. They must have been in the background somewhere."

"Don't worry, you've had a hard day. Let's call it a night and approach things fresh tomorrow. I'll go over this file with you in detail then."

A relieved and very tired DC Mary Dougan stood, said good night to her boss and left.

The DCI followed. He wasn't fully caught up on his sleep and looked forward to a quiet night with his wife and if he was lucky, his daughter would still be awake.

Chapter Twenty

Friday the 27th of March dawned bright and sunny although the temperature would refuse to make double figures during the day.

The DCI, after his usual breakfast with his family, got to his office early at 07.55. Finding no one else in, he wandered up to the canteen for a coffee and on an impulse bought an extra one for Terry Harvey. Steve decided it was the least he could do as Terry had been very helpful over the past few days.

As he entered the area of Technical Support, Steve was impressed to see most desks occupied and Terry's team of super whizz kids hard at work. Terry was in his small office.

On seeing the DCI, Terry waved him in. "I've got something for you." Seeing the second cup of coffee in Steve's hands, his face lit up. "Is that for me?"

The DI took the cup and relished the first sip. "Ah! That's better. The one thing about the Met is the coffee they brew in the canteen." Terry took another sip before getting down to business.

He stood up. "Come on, you'll want to see this."

Both men walked to Terry's pride and joy, his viewing room. As the pair passed through the main office, Terry called to one of his technicians, called Ian, to set up tape 6.

Steve and Terry sat in the front row of what Steve thought looked like a small cinema. The DCI noted that Terry picked up a remote-control device as they entered.

After a few minutes of lines and squiggles on the large TV screen, a picture appeared of a gold-coloured Ford Granada. The DCI was instantly enthused. Terry wouldn't be showing this unless he had a conclusion.

"Right." Terry allowed the images to slowly move forward. "This is the car leaving the murder scene." Terry pointed the remote at the TV but didn't activate it. "See it crossed the traffic and turned left heading towards the city." The image froze before another appeared. "This is on the same day but forty minutes later. It's your car on the M4 heading west." Again, the image froze before being replaced by another. "Here's the same car turning off the M4 towards Hounslow."

Terry allowed the footage to continue even though the Granada wasn't visible. "Now, this was the hard bit. Camera coverage within the boroughs isn't as slick as the traffic cameras. Plus, there are hundreds of the buggers and they're not all linked. They're more to spot muggers than identify traffic." Terry could feel the anticipation coming from the DCI.

"We got lucky, but it took hours of weeding out all the crap these cameras pick up." Steve sensed Terry was about to launch into one of his raves.

"Please Terry, just the car."

Terry knew his fondness for sounding off, so he stopped and carried on. "As I said, we got lucky." He pressed a few buttons on the remote. The picture on the TV froze until it stuttered back to life a few seconds later. Steve couldn't see the Granada and was looking at pedestrians on the pavement.

"Just wait, Steve." The DCI was on the edge of his comfortable seat peering at the screen. After a minute or so Terry called out, "There, see that?"

Steve hadn't seen anything. Terry rewound and played the footage again. As it ticked forward, he froze the image. "See, look there. On the left, you can just see a gold car turning left."

Terry rewound again but this time he enlarged each frame. The frames slowly moved forward until Terry pressed a button. On the screen but just in one corner, both men saw the rear end of a gold-coloured Ford Granada turning off the main road. Terry again froze the image and left it on the screen.

"That's your car. From the position of the camera, we know it turned into a street called Strutters Mews. It's a dead end."

Steve sat back admiring Terry's skills. "You're a bloody marvel, Terry."

Terry was pleased he was able to help but couldn't help saying, "Yes, I am."

Both men smiled. They shared a bond that verged on real friendship that seemed to grow the more the DCI asked Terry for help.

"Can you get me stills of those shots?"

"No problem. I'll send them to Poppy's computer."

As he was leaving Steve felt Terry touch his shoulder. "Have you seen Poppy this morning?"

The DCI was confused by the question. "No, why?"

Terry had a twinkle in his eye. "No reason, just curious."

A happy DCI Steve Burt made his way back to his office. Mary Dougan was waiting for him. He looked for Poppy, but she wasn't at her desk.

From Mary's body language, the DCI knew she was excited.

"Sir! I think I've remembered where I saw those two in the photographs you had last night." Steve's day was getting better, and it wasn't yet nine a.m. He indicated for Mary to sit down.

"It was late last night. It came to me in a flash. When I was interviewing that car dealer out by Heathrow, I saw two shady looking types washing cars in this bloke Eddie Randall's car lot. I didn't pay them much attention. They seemed harmless and a good gust of wind would blow them over. But thinking back, they were more curious than perhaps they should have been about my being there. They stopped washing the wreck they were working on and kept looking in my direction. As I was leaving, I saw them run into the office. I'm sure it was them."

Steve put his hands behind his head, thinking. He spoke very deliberately. "I don't suppose Eddie Randall's car lot is in Strutters Mews in Hounslow?"

Mary's jaw dropped. "How did you know that? I haven't given Poppy the notes to update the file yet."

Steve explained his meeting with the head of Tech Services and how the Granada had been tracked. "I didn't see a gold Granada in the yard." Mary was now casting her mind back to yesterday. She was silent and chewed her lower lip as a means of concentrating. Eventually, she spoke. "No, I'm certain there was no gold Granada in the car lot."

The DCI stood and walked to the whiteboard on his wall.

"Good work, Mary. It seems we're getting somewhere but I want the guy who ordered the killings." Steve wrote on the board as he spoke.

"Number one. You've shown a link between this Eddie Randall and our first victim, Vinnie McGuire. Number two. We know the car we believe was used in the killing of our second victim, Cameron Bowie, was seen in the same street as Eddie Randall's yard. Number three. You've shown a direct link between the two fools we saw at the second murder scene driving the Granada and Eddie Randall. Number four. I saw the Granada leave the workshop that was part of Crystal Motors cut and chop shop and now we have a link between the car and Eddie Randall."

Steve returned to his chair. "Look at the board, Mary. The name that appears in all four statements."

Both police officers said in unison... "Eddie Randall."

We'd better pay Mr Randall a visit this morning. I think Peter Jones should be in, so we'll take him with us." Steve looked at his watch. "Let's leave at eleven o'clock. Grab a pool car and I'll meet you in the garage." Steve looked at the file Terry gave him yesterday. "I wonder if our Eddie knows John Stuart McKelvey, AKA the Blade?"

"Let's ask him when we see him, sir. He might just admit to everything."

"Yes Mary, and he might not."

As Mary left Poppy arrived. Steve's mouth fell. Instead of the pretty detective constable with flowing locks and dresses that hid nothing, this one had her hair pulled back giving her face a severe look and instead of showing her assets she was wearing a long sack-like and shapeless dress whose only concession to any shape, was a narrow belt tied around her waist. Apart from this shock, the dress was a dark grey colour that did nothing for Poppy.

She stood by the door and twirled. "I hope this is more suitable for the office, sir?"

Steve recalled Terry's words... *Have you seen Poppy this morning?* Now he knew what the head of Tech Services was talking about.

"Poppy, you look very nice in a different way," The DCI lied. Despite her dress sense, Steve preferred the old Poppy to this dowdy figure standing in front of him.

"Yes. Well, I don't have many of what you would call office clothes so this'll have to do until I can go shopping at the weekend."

Steve didn't know how to respond. He simply brought Poppy up to speed following his discussion with Mary. The new, dowdy Poppy nodded and returned to her desk.

***

The Voice delayed calling Superintendent Blackstone. Apart from his normal workload, he wanted to be sure in his mind that he could persuade Blackstone to help.

Using one of his seemingly increasing number of burner phones, the Voice dialled and the Superintendent answered on the fourth ring. Blackstone answered as Mary Dougan was setting off to find Peter Jones and arrange a police pool car.

"We need to meet. Now!" The Voice didn't bother with unnecessary pleasantries.

"I can't. I'm busy and I've got a meeting in ten minutes." The Voice thought this was a poor excuse.

"Don't muck me about. Meet me at my club in thirty minutes." The Voice was in no mood to be pleasant. He felt Blackstone had almost outlived his usefulness and after this job, he would have no need for him.

"What's it about? I can't just up and leave, I have responsibilities."

"Yes, you do, you have responsibilities to me. Be there." The Voice ended the call.

The club the Voice referred to was a small private members-only property located within Westminster not far from Big Ben. The Voice was one of the original members and was well known to the staff. On arrival, he signed the members' attendance register and noted he had one guest. The name of the guest wasn't necessary. The club was discreet and knew the members valued their privacy.

The Voice ordered tea and set himself up at a small table set in the most private part of the member's lounge. Superintendent Blackstone arrived ten minutes later. He had discarded his uniform jacket in favour of a sports coat but still wore the rest of his uniform. The Voice thought that he still looked like a policeman especially still wearing his uniform white shirt and navy tie.

Both men helped themselves to tea. Blackstone scanned the room and was relieved to see they were the only people in the lounge.

The Voice had no idea how to introduce the subject to the Superintendent so decided just to blurt it out.

"I need you to find me probably three gangster types, big boys who know how to shoot and won't be afraid of a little fight."

Blackstone visibly shrunk. "What? You can't be serious!" He stared at the Voice. "Why on earth would you need that kind of muscle?"

"We're going to hijack a weapon and there will be military personnel guarding it."

Again, Blackstone shrunk back. "You're *what*?"

"You heard. I've been given a little job and it pays very well. All I need from you are three stout, violent types who won't shy away from intercepting a military truck, taking care of any guards and stealing what's in the truck."

"Oh! No, not me, you're mad. You can't go hijacking military vehicles in this country. I suppose you want these bandits, you think I can conjure up from nowhere, to be armed and if things get out of hand, you'll expect them to shoot."

The Voice drank his tea. He could feel his dark side rising to the surface. "My dear Superintendent, that's precisely what I want and expect."

Blackstone couldn't breathe. His throat felt restricted as his brain went into overdrive. He looked at the man sitting opposite him. He knew who he was, he knew his outward personality and had seen him charm various interviewers on television. But he knew, no one, apart from a few people, ever saw the other side of this outwardly well-respected and successful man.

"I can't do it." Blackstone was mumbling. "It's not possible." He sat looking at his hands in his lap. He decided to take a stand. "What's the cargo?"

"It's a new weapons delivery system that's been developed by the government and is to be tested next week at Boscombe Down."

"And you plan to steal it?"

The Voice simply smiled and raised an eyebrow.

"Listen. First off, any movement like this will be guarded and the police in addition to the military will be monitoring the movement of the truck from start to finish. Second, if this weapon is important, it'll be under armed heavy guard. You don't need three heavies; you need an army." Blackstone felt better, even stronger. "I want no part of it and no matter how much you're being paid, neither should you."

"I hear you but please don't take me for a fool." The Voice was talking quietly and calmly. This gave Blackstone more reason to be frightened and he quickly became less brave.

"My informant tells me there will be only one very lightweight weapon, easy to lift. There will be a box of shells also reasonably lightweight and maybe a few other boxes. One of them will be designated hazardous material. Because of the size and weight, the Army will only use two Land Rovers to transport the thing. It's going to be low-key so there won't be a heavy guard. They don't want to draw attention to the transporting of this weapon. It has been developed in secret so very few people know of its existence." The Voice paused to drink more tea which was now cold. He pulled a face at the taste of the insipid liquid.

"No one from the military is expecting trouble so we'll have the element of surprise. We'll also know their route and the best place to ambush the truck. It'll be a piece of cake. All you have to do is supply the muscle as you put it but what I really need to know is how much these people will cost."

Blackstone, despite his fear, laughed. "I don't believe this. Listen, it's not possible and I won't help; I *can't* help. A few cars and running interference on certain investigations is one thing, but not this." Blackstone was pleading. "What you're proposing is treason. Someone like you must know that! For Christ's sake man, this is the UK, not some third-world republic. People like us don't get involved with things like this." He stared at the Voice. "Forget the whole thing. Walk away while you still can. If you go ahead with it I won't be able to save you."

Blackstone stood to leave but the Voice pulled him back. When he spoke, the sound coming from the Voice was menacing. "Listen you whinger, I own you and you do as I ask. Remember I've got the evidence of all the payments you've had over the years. I know where you have hidden the money and I have the records. A simple call to your professional standards and you'd be inside with all the other crooks." The Voice wasn't smiling. "Police officers inside prison don't have an easy time."

"You wouldn't, you couldn't. You'd implicate yourself. Any investigation would show where the money came from, you'd be finished."

"Not so. You see, the source of your bribes has no connection to me. I'm clean and if you defended your position by implicating me, you'd fail. You see, I don't have to explain expensive overseas holidays that I can't afford on my salary, but you would have to, and I don't have to explain what I have done for the tax-free monies I receive every month. I have enough on you to bury you, so be sensible, do as I ask." The Voice sat back and folded his arms. He knew he had the Superintendent where he wanted him.

Blackstone knew he was caught. He was in too deep. With a sigh of defeat, he agreed, "OK. I know a few villains who might help for the right money." Blackstone looked pale and defeated. "It'll cost you ten grand a head. If you think three will be enough, that's thirty grand. You'll have to supply the shooters. These boys don't keep weapons for any longer than the last job."

The Voice lightened up. "There, that wasn't too difficult now, was it? Just one other point. I think I can provide the weapons but I'm to have no contact with these people. There is a man on the inside who'll keep us informed but I want someone in charge. I'll inform you as I receive intelligence, but you only deal with one member of this gang. Clear?"

Blackstone had no choice. "I know one of the people is usually in charge so that's no problem. When will we get the full plan?"

"In a few days. The movement of the weapon is scheduled for next Wednesday the 1st of April, so you need to be geared up before then. I'll make arrangements and be in touch." The Voice stood indicating the meeting was over. "Make sure this goes to plan. If you do, we'll not meet again, and I will have no further need of your corrupt services. You'll get a windfall bonus and that will be it." The Voice sneered at the Superintendent. It was clear he didn't think much of the man.

***

Staff Sergeant Bobby Tay was working on another prototype projectile. Professor Symonds had demanded six shells be available for the upcoming trial. Bobby had returned to Montgomery Barracks mid-afternoon yesterday and before passing through security to re-enter Station K, he'd retrieved the remaining parts of his plastic camera and replaced his illegal mobile phone in its hiding place beside the ventilator shaft.

The results of his experiment with a tracker in the shell wouldn't be known until the test but in theory, the cheap off the shelf unit he'd bought should work.

As he allowed the milling machine to continue its work, the spy, now an army Staff Sergeant, thought about his journey to his present situation. He remembered his grandfather telling him stories of the Spanish Civil war. He'd fought for the communists and told young Bobby about the struggles of the people and how wicked the regular establishment was. Bobby remembered tales of bravery that only members of the party could perform. His grandfather had passed on his communist passion to his father. Bobby's father had been branded a militant and was a leading member of the Communist Party of the UK. In addition, he was the senior shop steward in the shipbuilding works in Liverpool.

Young Bobby had been brought up believing in the rights of the working man and how only communism could save the world from greed and corruption. He recalled meeting someone from the party when he was aged twelve and told he was to be an important man when he grew up. He would be a weapon the party could deploy when they needed him, but he had to be seen not to believe in his family's views. The man came to Bobby's family home regularly and educated the young Bobby in the ways of the party. He read to Bobby from books written by the founding fathers of Russian communism, Marx and Lenin. By aged fifteen, Bobby Tay was steeped in the history of the party and willingly agreed to whatever this strange man asked of him.

He was told to join the army but to keep his political views secret. Indeed, the man told him he should be seen to shun communism in favour of western capitalism. Bobby obeyed and had become a good soldier as well as an outstanding craftsman. He hadn't seen nor heard from the man for years as he continued with his army career. Then out of the blue, the same man approached him in a supermarket as he did his shopping. Bobby had never married and lived alone. Over tea in his one-bedroom flat, the man instructed him to volunteer for difficult duties within a new and secret establishment. Bobby was told there would be a general circular seeking skilled engineers for secret work and he should apply.

As the milling machine ended its final turn, peeling microns from the round shape clasped within its jaws, Bobby's chest swelled with pride. What he was now doing was the culmination of his working life. He had served the Party and had been promised a life of privilege and status in Russia once his task had been fulfilled.

He knew his work wasn't for the present British Government nor the one in Moscow. Every suggestion on how to improve the weapon was for a new beginning in a country he'd never visited. He had been told the officials running his soon to be adopted country had been shown not to represent the true Party. The government in Moscow was full of corrupt figures who only thought of themselves. Bobby knew he was working for a purer version of communism that supported the beliefs of the founding fathers, Marx and Lenin. The new order would, with Bobby's help, sweep aside the corrupt officials and reintroduce pure communism to the masses.

He smiled to himself and shook himself back to the present. His instructions were to photograph every blueprint and plan he could. Anything that would allow other scientists and engineers to understand the weapon. If something went wrong and they could not steal the weapon then at least they would have the plans that would allow it to be copied. Bacteriologists in the research centres in Russia knew about the chemical and were already working on copying it. Bobby had been told to concentrate on the engineering of the delivery system, but samples of the gas would be welcome. He knew he was expected to deliver the entire system.

As Bobby put another slug of the experimental lightweight metal into the jaws of his machine, Corporal Edward Hicks appeared. As the keeper of the records, he was there to check when Bobby would be finished with the engineering drawings he was working from.

"Honestly Ed I think I'm in for an all-nighter. The Prof wants six shells by Monday, and this is only casing number three. I'll call you around teatime and if I'm close to finishing I'll let you lock them away but like I said. I think I'm in for a long night and I'll need the drawings."

"No problem, Bob, I've nothing else to do, I'll come back later. A few drawings and spec sheets are being used just now. I just want to keep tabs on them." With a wave, the corporal left to hunt down his precious cargo and make sure every piece of paper was accounted for.

As Bobby started his milling machine again, he spotted the auditor from the MOD walking past the window that looked from the workshop onto the main corridor. The staff sergeant didn't trust the little man and didn't believe he was an auditor. Hector Forsyth seemed to pop up everywhere. The staff sergeant thought it was as though the auditor was the spy and not Bobby. With such suspicions, Bobby was on his guard and had devised a plan to get most of the drawings photographed over the weekend. By working overnight, when everyone was in bed, he would have free access to every part of the facility. He just had to watch for the CCTV cameras and the roving security patrols. He also needed to know how to access certain areas without leaving a trace. He'd have to work on that part of his plan.

Chapter Twenty-One

The DCI, accompanied by Mary Dougal and DI Peter Jones, arrived at Eddie Randall's second-hand car lot at the same time Staff Sergeant Bobby Tay was putting the fourth metal slug into his machine at Station K.

"What a pile of crap!" Peter said as he was driving into the yard. "Everything I'm seeing looks like an MOT failure. I certainly wouldn't buy a second-hand car from this guy."

All three detectives smiled.

The DCI from the front passenger seat pointed. "But you might buy one of these." His index figure was indicating two almost new Audi A7s in dark blue. "Now I bet that's not regular stock."

Peter pulled the car to a halt away from the portacabin that was obviously the office. The door was closed but smoke could be seen rising from a rusted metal chimney sticking out of the flat roof.

"Peter, you hang around out here. Have a look around for anything unusual. I don't see the two skeletons so they must be out, but, if they show up make sure they stay."

"Right. I've spotted the first unusual thing." Peter angled his head towards the stock of bangers.

"How does that lot manage to stand on four wheels?"

Steve and Mary entered the office without knocking. Eddie Randall was dozing in his executive, cheap chair. He came to with a start, focusing rapidly on his visitors. Eddie was experienced enough to know the old bill when he saw them. He maintained a cool and innocent expression.

"Can I help you? What kind of vehicle would sir and madam be looking for?" Eddie sat straight up in his chair.

"Cut the crap. You know who we are. You must be Edward Randall, ex of her Majesty's prison Dartmoor and other such hotels across the country."

Eddie didn't flinch. "And you are?"

Both Steve and Mary produced their warrant cards. "I'm DCI Burt and this is DC Dougan. We're investigating the death of a friend of yours. One Vincent McGuire."

Eddie still didn't flinch. "Never heard of him."

"Now Eddie, we haven't done business before, so lying to me isn't the best of starts, is it?" The DCI had decided to test Eddie out to see what he was dealing with. He felt he already knew.

"Well, if you're going to be friendly, then yes, I know Vinnie, but he hasn't been around for a while."

"There, you see. It's easy to tell the truth." Steve smiled a friendly smile. "Leaving Vinnie to one side for a moment, tell me about Cameron Bowie?"

"Who?"

"Eddie! I thought we were friends, and you were going to tell the truth, but here you are lying again. Cameron Bowie, the car dealer on the Mile End Road you had killed."

Eddie moved uncomfortably in his chair. He no longer looked confident.

"Sorry, but I don't know the gent and I certainly didn't murder him."

Steve let silence fill the air for a minute before moving on. He'd decided Eddie wasn't a candidate for Brain of Britain and probably couldn't hold more than one thought at a time. The tactic was to continue to bombard him with apparently unrelated questions.

"Tell me about the car thieving?"

"The what?"

"You know, stealing cars to order."

Eddie was getting visibly more upset. "I don't know what you're talking about. I'm a legitimate businessman, running a first-class used car emporium."

"Yes, I can see that." Steve smiled at his prey. "How many cars have you nicked over the past four weeks, Eddie?"

"Mr Burt, I told you, it's not my game."

"Mm, really, tell me about the Blade."

Eddie visibly shrank, but he tried valiantly to maintain the appearance of an innocent man. "Sorry again, did you say someone called the Blade?"

"Yes. A killer for hire. We believe he killed your mate Vinnie and your associate Cameron Bowie."

The subtlety of Steve's remark went over Eddie's head. He didn't understand the significance of what the DCI had just said.

"Look. I admit I've done time, but you'll not fit me up for any of this just because I'm an ex-con."

Steve walked around the office and settled on the corner of Eddie's cheap desk. Mary was taking notes.

"I don't have to stitch you up Eddie. We know it all, even about the Russian." Steve lied but from the quizzical look on Eddie's face, he knew nothing about Vladimir Skoysky. The DCI felt he may have overplayed his hand.

"What bloody Russian?! Next, you'll be accusing me of starting a war." Eddie was fighting back. Steve had to get him off balance again.

"The two Audis outside. I suppose they're yours. New stock?" Steve gave Eddy a way to answer and he took it.

"Yeah, we're going upmarket; expanding, see? Catering for wealthier clients."

"Good to hear, Eddie. Very enterprising of you." Steve paused. "You'll have all the paperwork, invoices and so on."

"Oh yes, of course. Everything's above board." Eddie was sweating. The DCI had regained the initiative and his tactic of constantly changing subjects was having an effect on Eddie's ability to think straight.

"Can I see the paperwork, Eddie?" Steve was friendly. "Just to double-check. You understand."

"Uh... well." Eddie was visibly in distress. "It hasn't come through yet. It goes to my accountant first, but I'll get it to you in a day or two."

Steve continued to be Eddie's new best friend. "That's very kind of you, Eddie. Now tell me about Bert and Frankie?"

Another swerve in direction.

"Nothing to tell. They do odd jobs for me, that's all."

"Odd jobs like driving the getaway car from a murder scene."

"No. If they've got themselves mixed up in something it's nothing to do with me. I only pay them cash in hand. They don't work for me."

"Do you own a gold-coloured Ford Granada?"

The constant change in questioning was getting to Eddie. He sat uneasily in his chair; his top lip was wet, and he constantly played with a paper clip.

"Yes. What of it?"

The friendly DCI continued. "Well, nothing, except your two cash in hand casual labourers were seen driving away from a murder scene in your Ford Granada."

Eddie almost choked. As experienced as he was in dodging police questions, he realised this DCI knew too much. His mind was spinning, looking for a way out.

"Look Mr Burt, I'm just a lackey. I do what I'm told. I don't kill people..." The door opened, and DI Peter Jones entered holding by the necks of their shirts the two scruffiest, smelliest individuals Steve and Mary had ever seen. Peter was smiling. "Sorry to interrupt sir, but Bert and Frankie here just arrived. Bert driving a new Audi A7 and Frankie a gold-coloured Ford Granada."

The way Peter was holding them their feet were several inches off the ground. He let them go.

"So, Eddie, yet another new Audi. Care to explain?"

Eddie knew he was in a bind. He gave in. "Yeah, all right. I'll put my hands up to the carjacking but that's all."

Steve decided he didn't want to be Eddie's best friend any more. "Oh no my lad, that's not all. You'll tell us all about the murders, the carjacking and who you're working for. If you don't, I'll hang you out to dry and with your record, you'll never walk down a High Street again. Now think on, next time we meet, you tell me everything." The DCI was facing Eddie. Their faces were only inches apart. "You need me, Eddie."

Steve turned to Peter. "Get the cavalry in here and take these three in."

Steve was thinking about the new cars. He knew the Mile End Road workshop had been closed down. "What's happening with these cars?"

Eddie was passed caring. He looked at his watch. "Some expert in trackers is coming later to disarm the trackers and a transporter is supposed to be here early evening to pick the cars up."

Steve stole a glance at Mary who immediately understood.

211

The DCI had another thought about the cars and was about to go outside when he turned back towards Eddie.

"Tell me about John Stuart McKelvey?"

Eddie was sullen. He knew his time was up, but he was still trying to find a way out.

"Never heard of him." Eddie suddenly recalled it was him who told the Blade to kill McKelvey and Cameron Bowie. For the first time, he realised he was in a heap of trouble. He decided if he couldn't get a deal, he'd plead the fifth from now on.

"Eddie don't be stupid. I have a forensic team on their way here now. They'll tear this place apart and find all kinds of things like fingerprints and DNA. If the Blade has been in this office we'll know and that would give us a direct link to you. Like I said, think on and tell me everything you know."

Eddie made a decision. "Look, Inspector, I only do as I'm told. I don't even know the guy who gives the orders. He calls me on this phone." Eddie opened a drawer of his desk and produced the burner phone he'd been sent by the Voice. "Some bloke phones me and gives me orders. I just do as I'm told."

Steve wasn't convinced. "You've never met this guy, but you blindly do what he tells you, including murder. Pull the other one, Eddie."

"Honest. He calls with his orders. I've never met him, but he scares me. He uses some kind of voice changer machine, so I won't even recognise his voice. This phone came by post, and I can't call him. He calls me." Eddie looked completely deflated.

"As I said Eddie, think on. We'll have a nice chat on the record later." Steve turned from a very unhappy Eddie Randall.

Bert and Frankie had been sitting crossed-legged on the floor. Bert put his hand up like a schoolboy in class. In a weak voice, he asked "What about us? We've done nothing."

"Did you steal those Audis outside?"

Frankie decided to take over. "Well yeah, but Mr Eddie told us to."

Steve turned his head toward Eddie only to note him rolling his eyes and shaking his head, in a movement that said he was cooked.

"Did Mr Eddie tell you to steal any more cars today?" Steve felt like he was interviewing ten-year-olds.

"No." Bert was now talking. "He said he needed three Audis by today and only to nick them today because it would be safer."

Looking at the two sad figures dressed in black and barely weighing enough to register on most bathroom scales, the three detectives couldn't help but feel sorry for them.

Steve carried on. "You'll be taken in for questioning and get a ride in a nice shiny police car." Just as Steve spoke, he heard the cars arriving that would take the three to central booking and then to the interview suite at New Scotland Yard. "Mary, go with them. Charge them with car theft for just now, then get them to the Yard. We'll start later this afternoon, and get those two a bath, they stink." Steve pointed to Bert and Frankie.

As the small convoy of police cars pulled out of Eddie's yard, Steve turned to Peter.

"Get Matt Conway here as quickly as he can. He's had enough time with May Dunlop. The abduction case is over, and we need him here."

The DI got on his mobile phone whilst the DCI did the same. "Poppy, I want you to get onto crime stats. See if three Audi A7 cars have been reported stolen." Steve gave his admin assistant the registration numbers. "I'm betting they have. Then get onto the tracking company set up by the insurance boys. I don't know the name, but you'll get it easily enough. I want you to ask them if their tracking system has been switched off at any time today. If it has, who ordered it to shut down. Have you got that?"

"Yes. But what's it about?"

Steve admired Poppy's natural inquisitiveness but not on this occasion. His head was full of the case and Superintendent Blackstone. "Just do it, Poppy. I'll explain later."

The DCI headed back into the portacabin office.

Peter followed. "Matt's on his way."

Steve was holding the burner phone Eddie had handed over, now in a plastic evidence bag. "What do you know about burner phones, Peter?"

"Not much. They're untraceable because there's no contract and no name."

The DCI went into his think mode. After a few seconds, he shook himself. "There's no name attached, but are the calls traceable?" Steve looked at Peter. "Mm, I wonder." He decided he had other priorities at the moment so banked his thoughts.

213

He spoke to Peter with a renewed urgency. "You heard Eddie say someone is coming to disable the trackers on those Audis. When he gets here, I want you and Matt to arrest him whoever he is. If he's been sent because the Mile End operation has been closed down, it means whoever is pulling Eddie's string is still in business and I bet this technician knows who sent him."

"Right. What about the cars?"

"Leave them there. Eddie said a transporter was picking them up later today. We can arrest the driver, find out what he knows. Get both of them over to the Yard. We'll sweat them later. See what pops out."

"Right."

"Oh! And Peter. The forensic team should be here soon. We don't want to scare off this technician so make sure they park their vans round the back and keep them inside the office with the door closed. You and Matt had better hide yourselves somewhere in the yard. I don't think Eddie gets many customers." Steve laughed at his own joke and waved goodbye to his colleague.

The DCI drove away leaving DI Peter Jones alone, waiting for DS Matt Conway to arrive.

***

The events taking place at Eddie's yard were unknown to the Voice as he called Vladimir Skoysky using his burner phone. The Russian answered after the first ring.

The Voice explained he'd arranged for some heavy-duty muscle to intercept the weapon next Wednesday and to make himself sound important, added that he had taken personal charge of the plan.

"Very good, I'm pleased to hear it. Now, why have you called?" The Russian knew the Voice didn't call unless he wanted something.

"This operation is going to cost money, a lot of it. In this country even hardened criminals won't hold up a military truck at gunpoint for nothing. They need paying and paying big." As the Voice spoke, he saw pound note signs growing before his eyes. "I need a hundred grand just to pay off the gang and another fifty to pay off my arranger."

"You can't be serious," Vlad knew how the Voice operated. "You'll get the hundred but no more, half now, half on delivery. The first part will be in the secret account today." Vlad paused. Waiting. When the Voice remained silent, he asked, "Anything else?"

"Yes. I'll need weapons. Enough for three people but they'll have to be serious bits of kit."

"I'll arrange that. I'll have them sent to a lock-up garage in Kilburn." Vlad gave the Voice the address. "They'll be there next Monday, two o'clock. One of my men will be watching and another one will hand over the guns, so your people better not try any tricks. They turn up, my man hands over the guns and your people leave, simple. Is that clear?"

"Yes, I'll pass it on."

Vlad wasn't finished. "The weapon will leave at 11.00 on Wednesday the 1st of April. The whole weapons system will be in one wooden box. The box will be sealed. Under no circumstances will your men attempt to open the box. Understand?"

The Voice wondered how Vlad knew all this. He simply replied, "Yes."

"Good. It will be one single Land Rover with a driver, a front guard and two guards in the back with the box. The brilliant strategists in your army think a single vehicle will not cause too much attention. They think the project is secret enough so as not to need more security."

The Voice could hear the derision in Vlad's voice.

"It's good for us though. Tell your men to take the box to our warehouse in Kent. It's beside the Dartford Crossing." Again, Vlad provided the address.

"If your men do it right, the weapon should be at Dartford around two o'clock in the afternoon. Do it right and you'll be rich. Do it wrong and you could be dead."

The phone went dead. The Voice hoped nothing would go wrong.

***

The DCI returned to the Yard around two p.m. He headed straight for the canteen and a cup of coffee together with two bacon rolls. He settled down to eat and drink and run the case through his mind. He had Eddie

Randall in custody but was certain Eddie was only a middleman. Steve couldn't see any reason for Eddie to personally hire the Blade to kill the two victims. He was up to his neck in the car ring and had possibly hired the Blade, but only on someone else's orders. As he munched into his second bacon roll, his mind turned to the Russian connection. Thanks to Twiggy, he had an address but had been warned off by MI6 and Military Intelligence. The two salesmen at Crystal Motors were certain a Russian was involved in the death of their boss, Cameron Bowie. Steve's working hypothesis that rival gangs were waging a takeover battle was possible, but only just.

He finished his meal and his coffee but continued to sit, contemplating. He knew someone was employing Eddie to do their dirty work and Eddie said the only contact was with a burner phone and whoever called used a voice-distorting device. Steve pulled the phone still in its evidence bag from his pocket. He stared at it for no obvious reason. Was the reason for the voice distortion to disguise a Russian accent? Perhaps the key would prove to be the two dirty characters that worked for Eddie. The DCI smiled. "Yes." He spoke out loud. "We'll start with them. They're not bright and will be keener to talk if they think they'll get a lighter sentence."

The DCI remained seated still staring at the burner phone. Something Peter had said had triggered a thought. Steve tried to recall what was said and as he shrugged his shoulders and placed the phone back in his jacket pocket, he mouthed the words "Terry Harvey." A broad grin instantly lit up the DCI's face as he stood and almost ran to the Technical Support area.

Chapter Twenty-Two

The DCI walked into the Yard's Technical Support Unit looking for its head, Inspector Terry Harvey. Steve knew Terry and his team were experts in the field of electronics and had helped crack major cases by lateral thinking and the appliance of science. However, what the DCI was about to ask Terry to do he didn't think was possible.

Steve spotted Terry leaning over a computer screen and talking to one of his technicians. The walls of the tech support unit with their large screen TVs and flashing lights reminded Steve of pictures he'd seen of the NASA Space Control Centre during the first moon landing. The DCI raised a hand acknowledging a nod from Terry and signalling that he would be in Terry's office.

Terry arrived slightly flustered and took his seat behind his small desk. Steve sat opposite.

"Steve, I hope it's not another miracle you want. I'm up to my neck just now." The DCI was taken aback, and it must have shown. Terry relented slightly.

"OK, you are our best customer." He smiled as some of the urgency disappeared from his body language.

"Thanks, Terry." Steve produced the mobile phone. "This is a burner phone we got from a suspect in a murder case."

Terry interrupted before Steve could get into his stride. "You mean the Mile End killing?"

"Yes. We've arrested a bloke called Eddie Randall. I've still to interview him but I'm pretty sure he's just a foot soldier. The real killer is someone far above Eddie's pay grade. It seems this phone is the only way our suspect speaks to whoever is controlling him. He says it's a burner phone that can only receive incoming calls and leaves no trace of who phoned him." Steve paused. "I was wondering if that's correct."

Terry took the phone and removed it from the evidence bag. "Well…" He turned it over in his hand. "You're correct as far as you go.

Burner phones are thought to be untraceable, certainly to the individual who buys them. He can make calls and not be traced."

Steve was looking anxiously at Terry, willing him to say something positive.

"As to only being one way, well that's difficult. If this phone has had some electronic surgery, then yes, it's possible that the originator of the calls could remain invisible." Terry continued to look at the phone. "But that would take a skilled engineer. He'd have to bypass certain memory functions and re-route some of the functionality to make sure the number was blocked. Even then, he'd be working in miniature. Not an easy thing to do. However, a simpler way of achieving the same thing would be to simply remove the number function. This means someone literally cuts a line of functionality, meaning the phone doesn't display the incoming number. Easily done and relatively simple. If this was done to this phone then yes. The user of this phone would have no idea where the call originated. The number would be blocked."

Steve was amazed at Terry's knowledge. He'd heard Terry say something that caused him to think.

"You said the phone doesn't display the incoming number meaning the number the caller is calling from?"

"Correct."

Steve raised an eyebrow as he looked directly into his friend's face. Talking in a low, hopeful voice he asked. "Does that mean although the caller's number is not displayed… it might still be held in the phone?"

Terry knew the DCI was fishing. "It's possible but it's very difficult to run diagnostics on circuit boards that have been altered. Even the smallest change to the board could create problems elsewhere."

Steve was sitting on the edge of his seat. "But could you do it?"

"Bloody hell Steve. I'm up to my neck and it could be a complete waste of thirty or forty hours of work. There's no guarantee we'd get the sender's number."

The DCI persisted and in a low pleading voice asked, "But you'll try?"

Inspector Terry Harvey sat back. He closed his eyes and rubbed his temples. It was several seconds before he spoke. "Has this phone been logged in?"

"Yes, all above board, logged and registered."

"I know I'm going to regret this but leave it with me. What you owe me for the Granada is nothing to the bill you'll get for this. Success or no success."

"I appreciate it Terry and your alcohol bill is noted." As he stood to leave, he asked with a cheeky smile, "I don't suppose you have any idea when you'll know if you have the number?"

Terry laughed. "Bugger off or I won't even start."

***

Steve returned to his office with a spring in his step. He knew if anybody could crack the phone problem it was Terry. He talked to himself as he walked. "If we get the number, we might get the person pulling Eddie's strings, the real killer." Just before he arrived at the outer office Steve wondered if the number might lead them to the Russian. If it did, then all bets with MI6 and Military Intelligence were off. Vladimir Skoysky would be his.

Poppy, now dressed in less seductive clothes, was waiting for him. As soon as he walked in, she stood from behind her desk and followed him.

She got straight to the point. "First. All three Audi A7s have been reported stolen. All this morning and all from the west side of London." Poppy paused to allow Steve to acknowledge he'd heard.

He did and nodded.

"Second. The company set up by the main car insurers is called National Trace. They have one office in Sudbury that monitors their cars inside the M25. They also have offices in Manchester, Birmingham, Edinburgh and Norwich." Poppy leafed through her notes. "The system was closed down this morning at 05.30 a.m. on instructions from the Metropolitan Police. It was reactivated at 12.37 p.m. again on instructions from us."

Poppy sat down and waited. This was how she fed her boss information. A bit at a time. It was now something of a ritual and the DCI didn't mind playing the game.

"Thanks, Poppy. Now tell me you spoke to someone at National Trace?"

"Yes, I did. The Managing Director is called Edgar Wilson and he wasn't too friendly. When I was put through, he nearly bit my head off. He thought I was about to order another shutdown. He went on about twenty-something high-end cars that had been stolen while we ordered their monitoring station closed down." Poppy looked at Steve and smiled. "It took all my womanly ways to calm him down. Lucky it wasn't a visual phone. He'd have hung up on me looking like this." Both detectives laughed.

"Anyway, when I told him I was looking into car thefts and knew three Audi A7 had been stolen, I felt he thought I was on his side. I asked him how he was notified to shut down." Poppy looked pleased and conspiratorial at the same time. "He gets e-mailed."

Steve sat forward realising what this meant but said nothing allowing Poppy to continue.

"He said he was about to complain to the Commissioner. He's been told to shut down four times in four weeks and each time high-value cars have been stolen and disappeared. The insurers had to pay out and are not happy."

"Did he say who from the Met gave the instruction?"

"Yes. The e-mails came from the office of the Tactical Surveillance unit but weren't from any individual."

"Good work, Poppy." Steve assumed his admin assistant was finished.

Poppy produced from the back of her large notepad a set of A4 pages. "I got Edgar Wilson to send over copies of the e-mails ordering him to shut his system down." She passed them over to Steve.

"Poppy, you're a marvel."

"Yes, I know sir, so will you tell me what's going on?"

"How did this work?"

"You'll see from the e-mails the order says for undisclosed reasons they must shut down at a certain time. The times differ each week. They get a call from an unknown source telling them when they can reactivate the system. According to their MD — that's this Edgar Wilson, the average shutdown time has been four hours."

The DCI knew Poppy would be curious and was prepared. "All I can tell you is that we have an ongoing hush-hush investigation that's been sanctioned from the top. I'm sworn to secrecy, but I can tell you, your work on this is important."

"I thought it might be secret and nothing to do with the murders."

"Oh! It has something to do with the murders. After all, stolen cars are involved." Steve hoped this sounded convincing.

Poppy looked puzzled but resigned. "So, do you need to know who in Tactical Surveillance sent those e-mails?"

"Yes, but you said they weren't assigned."

"They're not, but each computer on the Yard's integrated e-mail system produces a unique reference that's only visible to the recipient. Look on those e-mails, top left." Poppy pointed as Steve picked the e-mails up. "See. It says MPM 10-11662. By cross-referencing that number on our resources system, we can find out which machine those e-mails came from and who sent them."

Once again Poppy was leaving the DCI speechless. All he could manage was, "Go on."

"If a computer is for open plan use it's given the code MP. If it's for the more personal use of a senior officer and located in an individual office it's given the code MPM. The extra M donates it's a management computer. The 10 says it's located on the tenth floor and the five-digit numeric code identifies the officer who has been allocated the individual computer." Poppy looked up. "For example. Your e-mail reference, if you ever send any from the machine gathering dust in the corner, is MPM 08-12875. Look it up and it says Detective Chief Inspector Steven Burt."

Steve was amazed. "I didn't know any of this, Poppy." He paused to gather his thoughts. "So, who wrote the e-mails to National Trace?"

"Superintendent Allan Blackstone."

***

At the same time as Eddie Randall and his two employees were being transported to New Scotland Yard, Professor Karl Symonds was supervising a display of the new weapons system in a conference room at Station K. He was proud of what he and his team had achieved and wanted to share their success by gathering everyone together to see the completed weapon.

The team had been slowly disbanded over the past few weeks as the project neared completion. Gone were the draughtsmen who had sweated over drawing boards and computer design systems. Gone were the technicians from Porton Down who had experimented with the chemical and succeeded in turning it into a gas. Gone were the rubber technicians who cleverly designed the rubber pouch that allowed the gas to be squeezed slowly into the atmosphere. The Professor reminisced about the team who would not be present to see this final display of success.

The main delivery system had finally been built by redesigning an existing anti-tank launcher. The engineering team had used a new composite metal that was three times lighter than the metal used in the original weapon. As the professor admired the shining metal tube, he realised how simple the project had been. Such designs had been used in World War Two, although this version was jammed with high tech electronics. However, he reminded himself, it was still basically a four-foot-long tube with a diameter of 3.5 inches They had ingeniously devised a way of hinging the long tube such that an infantry soldier could easily carry it.

He stroked the launcher before setting it into a cradle that had been set on a table covered by a shiny white cloth. The launcher was the star. Beside the launcher he set out the rubber gas sacks and the clever mechanism that would squeeze the sacks, allowing the gas to escape through the vents in the projectile.

The Professor next lifted two finished shells onto the table and placed them at either end of the launcher. He realised that if the launcher was the star, then the shells were the superstars. The skill and ingenuity needed to produce such a thing were amazing. He realised the boffins from the army engineering branch had designed something ahead of its time and that Staff Sergeant Tay had been instrumental in turning the design into reality. His idea of tracking the projectiles was brilliant as were his various suggestions on how to improve the basic design. Karl

Symonds made a mental note to mention the Staff Sergeant's efforts to his superiors.

Karl stood back to admire his efforts. He wasn't artistic in any way but felt his efforts to showcase the new weapon and its components were adequate. As an afterthought, he hefted the plastic box that had been designed to transfer the entire weapons system to Wiltshire for testing onto the table. This meant rearranging his display. When the four projectiles, Staff Sergeant Tay still had to complete were ready, everything on this table would be placed in the box and the Professor's work would be done.

As he stood admiring the results of his work, Hector Forsyth entered the room.

"Very impressive Karl. You must be very proud?"

"Yes. I suppose I am, but I'm still concerned you haven't identified the spy."

The man from MI6 posing as an auditor was taken aback by the academic's reference to the spy.

"He hasn't shown his hand. I've monitored everything I could think of, but nothing has come up. Now the headcount is smaller, if he shows his hand, it'll be easier to spot him."

"Yes, I see." The Professor turned from the MI6 man to admire his display. "What if you never catch him?"

"Two things. I'd say we scared him off because of our security, meaning he couldn't complete his task, whatever it was, and second, all those still here will be monitored for at least a year to see if they give themselves away at a later date."

"You mean all the remaining staff are suspects?"

"Exactly. If we don't unearth him and we're still sure he's here then yes, everyone left is a suspect. I'm hoping your little display here will flush him out. It's our last chance before this place gets shut down."

Although the professor had agreed to the display as a means of trying to flush out the spy, he didn't like the MI6 man's comment that this was the only reason to display the weapon. Karl felt the remaining staff should see the finished system and take pride in their achievement.

Along the corridor, Staff Sergeant Tay was busily working on projectile five and planning how to photograph the blueprints and drawings before the weapon was shipped out. He considered the plan to highjack the weapon and smiled. Everything was going to plan. Or so he thought!

Chapter Twenty-Three

The DCI saw Mary Dougan walk into his office. She looked a bit windswept and in need of a coffee. On Steve's suggestion Poppy obliged and returned five minutes later with three cups of piping hot coffee. During the time Poppy was away, Mary had rearranged her hair and was more settled as she took the first sip of her coffee.

"Right. Mary, I presume our boys are downstairs?"

"Yes. They said nothing at central, but they've been processed and charged."

"Good. Poppy, anything on this character they call the Blade?"

"Nothing so far. I've searched electoral rolls for a John Stuart McKelvey but nothing. The collator has nothing, but every station has his picture, and every beat officer has it as well. I've tried tracking him through bank accounts but again nothing. The address on his driving licence is an accommodation address and he doesn't have a passport. The man's in the wind."

"Keep trying. Get back onto the collator. We need known associates, anyone who knows him. We need to find this bloke. He's our killer I'm sure, but he's not the main man. Guys like McKelvey take orders, they don't act without reason.

Poppy stood to go. Steve saw Mary's eyes light up, seeing Poppy's dress for the first time. She stared but said nothing. Poppy recognised the look and simply turned to leave. Over her shoulder, she said, "Well, apparently it's not allowed to look your best any more."

Mary looked quizzically at the DCI who shrugged.

"Now Mary, our lads are downstairs. I think we should start with the two weedy looking ones." Steve looked up his notes. "That's Albert Rogers and Francis O'Rourke; they're more likely to say something without realising it." Steve had a sudden thought. "Did you get them cleaned up?"

Mary sighed. "Yes, their clothes have been burned so we'll have to stump up for new ones. Meantime, they're dressed in Met Police jumpsuits, very fetching but clean. I also got the doctor to give them the once-over. He says they are malnourished but fit to be interviewed."

"Good. If you've finished your coffee, let's make a..." The DCI's phone rang.

He saw it was Peter Jones. "Steve, I've got the technician who was sent to disable the trackers on the cars. He's kicking up all kinds of hell. I presume you want him at the Yard?"

"Yes. Ask him nicely to help us with our enquiries. If he says no, then arrest him on conspiracy to steal cars. How are forensic getting on?"

"The lead technician says they've got enough processing to do for a month and they're only halfway through."

"Keep at it, Peter. Is Matt bringing in our tracker guy?"

"Yes. I'll hold on here until the lorry driver turns up and then I'll bring him in. Looks like a long night."

Steve nodded. "Yes. It could be."

***

Bert and Frankie, dressed in their new attire, were in separate interview rooms under New Scotland Yard. Apart from having a bath they'd been given some food and cups of very strong tea. Both felt better than they had for a long time.

Steve and Mary entered interview room one to find Bert sitting biting his nails. He was seated at the far side of the metal table that was screwed to the floor. The usual twin recording machine was attached to the end of the table and a uniformed constable stood inside the door.

Bert looked up as the detectives entered and sat before him.

Once Mary switched on the tape machine Steve introduced themselves. Bert had declined to have a solicitor present.

"Well, Bert." Steve began, "I hope you've been well treated?"

Bert seemed alert. His long hair was combed back, and he'd been fed. The stubble on his chin made him look older than his age. "Yes Mr Burt, no complaints." He suddenly looked concerned. "I don't have to pay for the tea and sandwiches, do I?"

To his right, Steve heard Mary suppress a giggle.

"No Bert, it's on us. Now, can you help us, and we'll see if we can help you?"

From his expression, Bert clearly thought this was a good idea. "I'll help you any way I can." Bert threw his chest out. He felt important.

"Good. Now tell us about Eddie, what do you do for him?"

"Me and Frankie are his go-to people. He told us that, but we're not on staff like. Eddie explained we don't get bonuses, 'cause that would mean we was employed. We get rewarded for doing good jobs."

Steve decided Bert was a simple soul and would make a lousy witness. However, he needed to learn what he knew before tackling Eddie, so he would be Bert's friend.

"What kind of good jobs, Bert?"

"Oh! You know, driving him to places, helping with his car business. Just being helpful."

"Were you being helpful at that car place on Mile End Road?"

Bert's chest expanded as he sat back in his chair. He proudly announced that he and Frankie had 'done a good job there'. He explained how they'd been told to check on the owner and to see what he did and when. "It wasn't easy Mr Burt. Me and Frankie had to get the information for Eddie. He said it was important. The man we was to learn about wasn't even there, so we used our cunning. We got what Eddie wanted." Pride stayed fixed on Bert's face.

"And then you went back with another man?"

Bert's expression changed. He was beginning to wonder how this policeman knew about the Blade. "Well, we had to take this bloke back to the car showroom. Eddie told us to wait for him and bring him back."

"And you did. Bring him back I mean? Back to Eddie's yard."

"Yeah."

"Who was the man, Bert?"

"I don't like him. Frankie's frightened of him. Eddie says he kills people. I don't know his real name, but he calls himself the Blade 'cause he has a big stiletto flick knife." Bert was visibly shaken recalling the Blade.

Steve decided to move on. "What else have you done for Eddie when he's been working with the Blade?"

227

Bert thought for a second and without thinking blurted out. "Well, there was the body. Frankie and me didn't know it was a body till we opened the back of the van. We got a right shock I can tell you." Bert went on to explain how he and Frankie had dumped the body of who Steve now knew was Vinnie McGuire down the railway embankment. "We'd never have done it if we knew it was a dead body, honest, Mr Burt."

"So, Eddie told you to drive a van to the railway embankment and dump a body?"

"Not really. He said it was a parcel but me and Frankie recognised it." Bert gave an involuntary shake thinking about the event. "It was horrible."

Steve was beginning to see a route to Eddie. "But you are sure Eddie Randall told you to dump it?"

"Oh yes."

Steve looked at Mary who nodded. "Now Bert, tell us more about the time you took Eddie to the building behind the Mile End showroom?" Steve was recalling his first sight of the gold Granada leaving and cutting across the line of traffic.

"No, no, Mr Burt." Bert was giggling. "It wasn't like that. You see we took a car to that place. We followed Eddie and brought him back. Eddie's a very important man you know. He gets lots of money for nicking cars."

"So, when you left, you'd just delivered a stolen car?"

"Yeah, but we had to change. The guy at that place told Eddie the cars could be traced, and we should only steal them on the day they was to be sent away."

"Where were they sent, Bert?"

"The bloke at the workshop told Eddie the cars went to Russia."

"And this bloke at the workshop told Eddie only to nick the cars close to the time they were to be delivered to this workshop?"

"Yeah."

The DCI thought he'd get no more from Bert. "It was you and Frankie who stole the cars for Eddie?"

Again, pride swept across Bert's face. "Yes. Me and Frankie are the best at nicking cars."

"Thanks, Bert; would you like another tea and a sandwich?"

"Not half."

Mary followed procedure and stopped the tapes. She removed both tapes before she and Steve left to interview Frankie. Bert was sitting dreaming of his tea and sandwiches that he wouldn't have to pay for.

The interview with Frankie went much the same way as with Bert. Frankie was more of an actor and enjoyed elaborating on their time in the showroom and his efforts to get information from the salesmen he'd met. Frankie confirmed they'd dumped Vinnie McGuire's body down the railway embankment, but he couldn't confirm it was Vinnie 'cause we was really scared. No way did we open the bundle and look."

After fifteen minutes it was clear Frankie was telling the same story as Bert. As the DCI and Mary were winding up the interview and were again offering tea and sandwiches, Frankie blurted out "See Mr Burt, that guy, the Blade, he's bad news. When I was being friendly like in the car, he only wanted to talk about himself. See, I know all about how people think, it's my thing."

Steve doubted whether anything was Frankie's thing but he let him continue. It was clear Frankie regarded himself as an intellectual.

He bored the detectives with his self-taught insight into human behaviour for fully five minutes before saying, "The Blade even lives on a house bloody boat. Imagine. The big killer for hire doesn't even have a house." Frankie laughed thinking this was funny.

Steve looked at Mary, his interest suddenly pricked. "What kind of houseboat, Frankie?"

"You know, the kind that floats on water." Frankie thought his new status as an intellect gave him scope to play with the detectives.

"Very funny, Frankie. I mean did he say he moved it from place to place or is it at a fixed mooring?"

Frankie looked puzzled. His intellectual sparring with the DCI was over. Frankie didn't know what Steve meant but couldn't admit it.

"Well, I don't know 'cause he didn't say."

"What *did* he say?" Steve was gently pressing. He sensed Frankie had the information he needed.

"Well, let me think." The intellectual Frankie was back. He assumed the pose of someone deep in thought. "He said he kept it close to a good underground line so he could move around London easy like." Frankie's head was beginning to ache with all this thinking. "He said he lived where all the money lived but he didn't have to pay the silly rents people who lived in flats around him did." Frankie clearly was using all his brain cells trying to be helpful. "He said there weren't too many places for boats. I think he said berths… Oh! Yes, got it." Frankie almost jumped from his seat. "He said it was in Canary Wharf, you know. That fancy place where all the bankers make all their money."

Steve sat back and grinned at Mary. "Thank you, Frankie, I can see how you're very good at your thing. You've earned a bacon roll to go with your tea."

Frankie beamed as the detectives left.

***

Outside in the corridor, Steve compared notes with Mary. Get Poppy to check on berth owners or renters within Canary Wharf. If Frankie's right, we might have our actual killer tonight." Steve stopped to consider.

"OK. These two have confirmed what we knew. We have Eddie on the murder of Vinnie but it's thin. We need something else. As to the murder of Cameron Bowie all we have is what we know from the CCTV tapes. These two were there; they cased the place one day and drove this Blade on the day of the killing, but it's only the fact they work for Eddie and the car that ties Eddie to the killings. Their testimony helps, but not enough." The DCI sighed. "I'd hoped for more but if we've got this Blade character, that's a bonus."

"I agree, sir. These two could talk all day but we'd get nothing. I think we were lucky to get the info on the Blade. What do you want to do with them?"

"Leave them just now. We'll have a go at Eddie, see what we can get out of him then decide what to do."

Mary nodded in agreement. She phoned Poppy and forwarded Steve's instruction.

"Right. Let's see what Eddie Randall has to say." The officers headed for interview room four for a confrontation with Edward Randall.

***

Interview room four was exactly like all six interview rooms in the bowels of New Scotland Yard. Eddie Randall looked like an ex-convict. His body language said he was experienced in this situation.

The DCI hadn't decided how to play Eddie and decided to start gently once Mary had gone through the usual pre-interview under caution procedures.

"Well Eddie, you're in a bit of a mess, aren't you? We're looking at carjacking leading all the way to murder." Steve paused to make sure Eddie understood. "Anything you want to say?"

"Nothing. I've refused a lawyer 'cause I know you've got nothing."

Just as Steve had decided to go easy, Eddie had decided to play tough.

"That's your choice, Eddie but you're wrong. We've got a lot on you. Stealing cars to order is the least of your worries especially as your two less-than-bright employees have told us everything."

Eddie laughed. "Those two. If that's all you've got bring it on, they won't last two minutes being cross-examined by a defence brief."

Steve knew Eddie was right, but he pressed on, still maintaining his casual approach.

"I suppose you're right but their testimony plus the CCTV we've got is enough to charge you and if you're found guilty, you'll go away for a very long time."

Eddie remained silent. His facial expressions told the DCI he was thinking. Steve carried on.

"You see Eddie, I think you're just the patsy. We'll get you on a double murder charge, but we know you're working for someone else." Steve paused. "You've already told us the unlikely story that this big shot only talks to you on the phone—"

Eddie jumped in. "Yeah! And his voice is disguised".

"Yes, so you say, but look at it from our point of view. We've got your employees using your car as a getaway car from a murder scene and evidence that the person who actually did the killing was in your office. Now even you must see where this is going unless you cooperate."

Eddie sat back and started to think. He remembered his wake-up call in his office when he realised the Blade would say it was him who ordered both killings. He didn't know who the Voice was and had no way of knowing. He decided to play it straight. Maybe the police would believe his story that he had nothing to do with the murders.

"Look Mr Burt, I know it looks bad, but you have to believe me. I'm just the man in the middle here."

"All right, Eddie. Let's say I believe that. Start at the beginning and don't lie. If you do, I'll throw the book at you."

Eddie looked crestfallen. "I won't lie but I'm not going to implicate myself without a deal."

Steve sighed. Every prisoner at some point thought they could negotiate their way out of having serious charges brought against them. Eddie was obviously no exception.

"Eddie, you know the score. We don't do deals but if you tell us everything, I'll talk to the CPS for you and tell them how helpful you've been. That's the best I can do."

Eddie knew he had no choice and wished he knew who the Voice was. He was convinced if he had the name, his negotiating position would be a lot stronger.

Eddie reluctantly told his story. "A mate of mine, Vinnie McGuire, told me about some guy who needed someone he could trust. Vinnie was always setting up deals. Looking for an edge, anything that paid. Anyway, I said I'd be interested, and I got a package in the post. It was a phone with a typed message. It said I'd get a call and to be ready. The call came and this strange voice came over the phone. At first, I thought it was the phone but realised it was someone using one of them gadgets that makes your voice sound funny." Eddie leant forward resting on his elbows, obviously concentrating on his story.

"This Voice said the phone was untraceable and couldn't make outgoing calls. It only received calls and only from him. He said I'd be contacted by text each time he needed to give me instructions. He explained a code system so I knew when he'd call and anything else would be sent by post."

The DCI interrupted Eddie's flow. "You mean every time this Voice wanted to speak to you, he sent a coded message?"

"Yeah. He said it was security."

Steve made a note. "Carry on."

"Well. This Voice said Vinnie told him I knew cars and wasn't afraid of a bit of illegal work. He said if I performed well, I'd be well paid and wouldn't have to worry about money ever again."

Eddie didn't look comfortable. He wasn't warming to his story. The DCI let him talk without further interruption.

"At first it was a few odd jobs. A bit of housebreaking, a few petty crimes. I think this was just to test me. The two idiots were good at the small stuff so the guy I called the Voice was happy. I got money through the post, no questions asked.

This lasted a few months, then I got this call. The Voice wanted Vinnie disposed of. He said Vinnie knew too much and was a danger to the operation. He said if I got rid of Vinnie, I'd move up in his organisation and would start to earn real money. He said I'd get ten grand for disposing of Vinnie."

Eddie tried to look ashamed but failed. He'd had his friend killed for money.

"I'm no killer, Mr Burt, but I knew John McKelvey from way back. I knew he was into seriously hurting people, so I asked him to take care of Vinnie."

At this point Steve interrupted. He wanted to move things along. "The body that was dumped by Bert and Frankie on the railway embankment was that of Vincent McGuire and he was killed by John McKelvey on your instruction, based on an order you received from an unknown person who called you on the phone?"

Eddie looked smaller sat in his chair as he was forced to admit his guilt in the hope of at least getting a lighter sentence.

"Yes."

The DCI wrote one word on his pad, *unbelievable*.

"Go on."

"I got my ten grand and paid the Blade a few thousand. I knew he was trouble; he was dangerous and started coming to the office looking for other jobs. He knew I wasn't Mister Big and that it wasn't me who wanted Vinnie dead. He kept pushing to find out who the Voice was, but

I couldn't help him because I don't know." Eddie was getting animated for the first time.

"Then I got an envelope and was told to bump off some car dealer who had showrooms on the Mile End Road."

Eddie told his story including how Frankie and Bert almost blew everything by putting petrol in the car instead of waiting by the kerb. Eddie confirmed the Blade had carried out the second killing as instructed and that another ten thousand pounds had been paid.

The DCI knew all this. Eddie was only filling in details. "How did you contact the Blade to give him his instructions?"

"I asked around some of my old contacts. He gave me a phone number and I called it. The Blade turned up and we discussed things. Everything started from there."

"Do you have the Blade's number?"

"Listen! I'm no grass."

"But you kept the number?" Steve pressed Eddie who appeared to be thinking. "Look, Eddie, you're in deep here. I can't see a way of helping you. Your two employees have dropped you right in it," Steve lied. "But, as I said earlier, if you cooperate, I might just have a word with the CPS. Tell them you were helpful."

Eddie appeared to be struggling. His facial expressions told the DCI he was struggling, deciding what to do. How much to be seen to be cooperating. Eventually, a crestfallen Eddie relented. "OK. I wrote it on a piece of paper. It's in my desk drawer; it's a mobile number."

"Do you know where he lives?"

"No."

"I'll get you a cup of tea. Do you want a sandwich?"

"Yeah. I suppose so."

Steve and Mary left and went back to the office. As they arrived, Poppy jumped from her seat.

"There's a berth in Canary Wharf being rented to a John McKelvey. He also rents the boat. His lease was taken out six months ago and is for twelve months."

"Thanks, Poppy, good work. Get onto Peter Jones. Tell him the forensic team should look for a piece of paper in Eddie Randall's desk drawer with a mobile phone number written on it. Tell him we think it's the number for the killer."

The DCI turned to Mary. "With luck, we'll have Mr Blade before the day's out."

Chapter Twenty-Four.

It was just before six p.m. at Station K. The spy was busy completing projectile five and considering how to get into the document safe controlled by Corporal Edward Hicks. He'd seen the safe opened hundreds of times and knew the procedure plus the biometric requirements for smooth access. He'd run through a few scenarios, including holding the corporal at knifepoint and ordering him to help. He'd considered knocking the keeper of the documents out and somehow propping him up to get the biometric data necessary. He'd even considered murder but discounted that as an option.

His latest plan was to wait until the weapon was on its way to Wiltshire and actually break into the safe, having first stolen Eddy Hick's keys. He surmised most people would be demob happy after the project had been completed and security would be lax. The staff sergeant thought that even if the alarm were sounded, he'd have time to gather as many plans as he could and make a run to the surface before anyone realised what had happened. He visualised himself driving through the gates of Montgomery Barracks with a rear seat full of ultra-top-secret plans heading for an address in London he'd been given by Vladimir.

The turning of the fifth shell came to an end. He set about the next stage of fabricating the nose cone with its opening and closing vents, then decided to try his camera. It was quiet with a lot of people having already left and the remainder would be in the mess hall enjoying their evening meal. Now was a good time. He hadn't used it and if he got a chance to photograph the plans then he'd avoid the need to show himself as the spy.

He laid the three drawings he was using, one on top of the other onto a large workbench and adjusted an angle-poise lamp to illuminate the whole of the top blueprint. He carefully adjusted the lens on the camera to show the entire drawing and clicked a button on the side of the plastic case. Just as with a camera in a mobile phone, a shutter clicked, and the drawing appeared on the small screen positioned on the reverse side of the camera body.

Staff Sergeant Bobby Tay examined the image. It was perfect. He removed the top drawing and positioned the second. As he was focusing the camera for his second image Corporal Edward Hicks opened the door to see the spy photographing a top-secret blueprint.

"What the hell are you doing, Bobby?"

Bobby was caught red-handed. He thought quickly. "Oh, just checking some dimensions with this laser."

"Bullshit, that's a camera. Where did you get that!"

Staff Sergeant Tay was struggling to explain himself. "I got it from the Prof. He asked me to copy those plans I thought were more important to the project, in case something happened to the originals." Bobby Tay thought this sounded plausible.

"Sorry Bobby, you know the rules, no cameras. I don't believe the Prof gave you that." Looking directly at the small grey coloured plastic lump in Bobby's hand, the Corporal said. "Any fool can see that's a knocked-up piece of plastic. It's not a properly manufactured commercial device."

The Army man and the RAF man stood staring at each other in silence. Bobby took a few paces forward.

"Look Ed, this isn't what it seems. You don't know what's at stake…"

Just as Bobby was trying to explain, Edward Hicks made a lunge for the camera. Bobby, being the bigger man, backed away and the pair finished up with their arms wrapped around each other with the smaller man searching out Bobby's hand that contained the camera. Bobby pushed the RAF man away and with his free hand landed a punch on his jaw. The corporal staggered backwards and fell. As he fell, the back of his head crashed into the frame of Bobby's lathe. Corporal Edward Hicks was dead before he hit the ground.

***

Steve, Mary and Poppy were sitting in Steve's office at the time Corporal Hicks had gasped his last breath. They were discussing the case against

Eddie Randall and the lack of any hard evidence linking him to the double murders.

"The CPS and the DPP won't take the case with what we have." Steve was stating the obvious. For what seemed like the hundredth time he said, "We need this Mr Big fellow, the Voice. We need the master, not the servants. I know we've got a lead on the Blade, and we know where he lives, plus with luck, we'll have his mobile number. Let's hope he talks and gives us evidence against friend Eddie." Steve broke off his analysis.

"Mary, we'll arrest John Stuart McKelvey, AKA the Blade, tomorrow morning, say six a.m. I'll lay on Matt Conway to come with us, but can you arrange uniform back up? Four uniforms should do it."

"Will do, boss." Mary made a note in her notebook.

Just as she did this, Matt Conway arrived looking flushed but happy.

"I've got the tracker technician downstairs." He smiled. "He's not very happy, claims he's been set up. He's screaming for a lawyer."

"Right, Matt." Steve stood up. "Let's see what our technician has to say." As the DCI rounded his desk, he looked at his two WDCs. "Mary, write up your notes and have the three downstairs locked up in the holding cells overnight. If we get the Blade tomorrow, we might have more to charge them with. Poppy, update the files and get the interview tapes transcribed."

Poppy, still in her dowdy outfit, smiled and under her breath mumbled, "OK for some; I never get any of the interesting work."

DC Mary Dougan heard Poppy's remarks and in a whisper replied, "Want to help me write up my notes?"

Both women smiled at each other. There was a definite bond forming between them.

***

Steve and Matt entered interview room five. The custody sergeant had joked as he saw them approaching that Special Resolutions were his best customers.

The technician was sitting displaying all the signs of a truculent schoolboy.

The detectives sat, said nothing but stared at the technician who had said his name was Tommy Moore.

Tommy Moore was the first to break the silence. "What's going on here?" he asked, pointing to Matt. "This great gorilla grabs me as soon as I entered that car lot, and insisted I come with him to this place. You lot can't go around arresting innocent people."

Steve sighed. "Mr Moore, you haven't been arrested. You are merely assisting us with our enquiries."

"Yes. Well, I don't know why I'm here so I don't see how I can assist you."

"Oh. Come now, Tommy. I think you know exactly why you're here. You went to the car lot to disable the trackers on three stolen cars."

"You can't prove that."

"I think we can. As we speak our forensic and technical teams are going over every inch of your van. What's the bet they find equipment used to disable tracker systems?"

"That means nothing. I'm a vehicle electrician. What you've found are the tools of my trade."

"So, what were you…" Before the DCI could continue there was a knock on the door and Poppy peered around it. She signalled for the DCI to leave the room.

"What is it, Poppy?" Steve asked as they stood outside.

"I thought you'd need this." She handed over a slim buff-coloured file. "Your man in there has a record. He's been convicted three times for car theft and once as an accessory in a robbery. He fixed the alarm for a gang who broke into a high-end jeweller in Bond Street."

Once again, the DCI was impressed by Poppy's use of her initiative. He realised he'd acted too quickly. He should have checked on Tommy Moore before he interviewed him.

"Good work Poppy. I should have thought of this."

Poppy just smiled. "You're welcome." She turned and skipped off.

Steve re-entered the interview room. He handed the file to Matt.

"Right Tommy, where were we?" Steve appeared to be thinking. "Oh, yes, I was asking you what you were doing in the car lot."

Tommy smirked. "I was looking to buy a car."

The DCI looked his prey straight in the eye. "You're lying. Nobody would buy a car there unless it was one of the stolen Audis."

"Well, as I said, you can't prove a thing."

"We know about your record, and I bet if we checked we'll find you're no auto electrician. You're just an ex-con who's still using his electrical skills to commit crimes."

For the first time, Tommy Moore looked uneasy. He sat in silence.

"Come on Tommy. We're investigating a double murder. You've been around. You know we're not interested in you fixing a few trackers. We just need confirmation of what you were doing there and who is paying you." The DCI paused to let his words sink in. "Come on, do yourself a favour. Just tell us and you can go home, no charges, nothing."

Tommy knew he could sit this out, but he hadn't been paid. Also, he figured he would be back on the police's radar if they charged him. That could mean when he did his next job perhaps a charge for fixing a few paltry trackers would remind the cops that he was around. The more he thought about it, the more he realised it would be better to cooperate.

"All right, I admit it. I was sent to disarm the trackers on the Audis." Tommy grinned. "Can I go now?"

"Not quite. How come you got the job?"

"Because I'm good. Seems the regular place these cars were delivered to, was raided by your lot and closed down. The bosses didn't want to shut up shop just because you found their place, so I'm like a temporary solution. So's the guy who owns the car lot."

The DCI stroked his chin. He knew the next question and answer could open up the case. "Who sent you Tommy?"

From his expression, it was clear Tommy didn't want to answer. Steve sat patiently. No one spoke until Matt Conway spoke up.

"Look, Tommy, it's like the DCI said. We're not interested in you, but we do have two murders on our hands. If we can't get the name of your boss, we'll have to include you as an accessory. These days, anybody connected in any way to a murder case is added to the list of suspects."

Steve admired Matt's thinking. It wasn't true but sounded just plausible enough to be true.

"You can't hang a murder charge on me, no way."

Matt continued. "We wouldn't charge you with the actual murder, just being involved in the conspiracy to prevent us from identifying the killer."

Steve examined Tommy's features. He saw his jaw crunching as he thought. He'd already decided to admit to the tracker, but he hadn't contemplated naming anyone else.

"Listen, if I give you a name, you have to give me protection. This guy is dangerous and, being one of your lot, he has influence and power. I'm no grass but he'll know it was me gave you his name."

Steve's brain was already on high alert at the mention that the person who sent Tommy to disarm the trackers was a police officer, but he remained calm.

"OK, Tommy. Give us the name and I promise to keep your name out of the file. There will be no record of you even having been here." Silence fell as Tommy wrestled with his mind.

"Can't you give me actual protection?"

"Tommy, if you give us the name, we'll have this man off the streets within hours. He'll never know you told us anything. I promise."

Thomas Moore made a decision. "His name is Blackstone, Superintendent Allan Blackstone."

Steve and Matt looked at each other with a mixture of shock and horror. Steve now needed more from Tommy.

"How did Blackstone contact you and why you?"

"You've got my record. Blackstone was the senior officer on the jewellery heist. We did a deal. In exchange for a lesser charge, I'd be available to help him out with all things electrical. I thought he meant in his house, but it wasn't that. He's had me do a few tracker jobs and a few country house alarm systems that needed bypassing. I didn't ask any questions. The money was good and with him in charge, you lot were never a problem."

Tommy looked pale. "Anyway, he called me, told me he needed three trackers disarmed and it had to be done Friday early afternoon. He gave me the address, but I got caught in traffic, so I was a bit late. He told me to call him when I'd done the job."

Steve realised the importance of Tommy's last remark. He stood and as he did so, he asked, "Does Blackstone call you on a mobile?"

"Yes." Pointing to Matt, he added, "Your buddy here ordered me to switch it off."

"Turn it on; see if Blackstone has called you."

Tommy did as he was ordered. He had several missed calls from Blackstone's number as well as two voice messages.

"Play the messages and put the phone on speaker."

Tommy obliged. After the usual greeting saying he had two messages the voice of Superintendent Blackstone sounded.

"Tommy, where the hell are you? You should have called me an hour ago. Call me as soon as you get this."

The second message was again from Blackstone. "Tommy, I'm assuming something's happened, and you've been blown. Ditch your phone. I'm writing off the three Audis. I can't hold the shutdown of the tracker system any longer. Call me with an explanation and it had better be good."

Steve took the phone. He nodded to Matt to follow him out of the interview room. Over his shoulder, he spoke to Tommy. "Won't keep you long, Tommy. I'll have some tea sent in."

***

Back in Steve's office he and Matt sat opposite each other. The first thing the DCI did was call Commander Alfie Brooks.

"Christ, Steve, this better be good. I'm halfway out the door and I've got a weekend planned."

"It's about Blackstone and it's urgent."

Steve heard Alfie give out a sigh. "Oh Christ, do I have to involve Superintendent Carson?"

"It might be best." Steve knew he needed to hand this evidence of Blackstone's involvement to Internal Affairs. He'd met Kit Carson before and knew he was the right man.

A reluctant Alfie struggled to hold his phone to his ear whilst removing his overcoat. "My office, thirty minutes." The line went dead.

Steve looked at Matt Conway. "Matt, I want you to forget what Tommy told us. I'll explain sometime later but Blackstone's involvement must be kept secret."

"I'm not surprised. Whatever's going on is way above my paygrade."

"Thanks, Matt." The DCI looked perturbed. "Apart from that revelation, our man Tommy wasn't much help moving the murder cases along. Go down, give him a formal warning about his criminal activities and tell him we're keeping his phone. Give him a receipt and say he'll get it back but right now it's evidence. Also, I need his statement made official. Get it down on paper and get him to sign it."

"What about your promise that there would be no record of him being here?"

Steve gave a sly grin and shrugged his shoulders. "I did, didn't I. Tell him we only need the statement for internal reasons. Get hold of an emergency number he can dial if he feels threatened and have the patrols from his nearest nick do a drive-by his house every hour. That should satisfy him but Matt, based on what he said, we need that signed statement."

Matt stood and nodded.

Before he disappeared, Steve called out. "Don't go home once you've done that. We're not finished, and I need to brief you about the arrest tomorrow." He heard a groan come from the outer office as Matt left.

***

Steve was gathering his thoughts ready for his meeting with the Commander and Superintendent Kit Carson when Terry Harvey appeared. He was looking excited. Before the DCI could say anything, Terry launched into the reason for his visit.

"That phone you gave me, the one from the car lot, the one you want me to perform miracles on and get you a link to the person on the other end."

"Yes." Steve was sitting bolt upright, hoping Terry had indeed performed a miracle.

"Well, it got a message. I don't understand it, but I thought you might need to know about it before I start hacking into the software."

The DCI sat wondering what was going on and the penny dropped. Eddie Randall had told the officers that the Voice sent a text message before he spoke to him. Steve's brain went into overdrive. He shouted for Mary Dougan. She appeared as if by magic. Steve wanted Mary involved in this.

"What's the message?"

Terry showed the screen. It read *O-10-Sa*. The DCI wrote this on a sheet of paper.

"Thanks, Terry." Steve handed Mary the paper he'd written the code on. "Mary, go down to the holding cells, and ask Eddie Randall what this means."

Mary took the paper but didn't immediately leave. She sensed something else was happening. Terry Harvey's arrival had somehow electrified the office.

Steve sat back allowing his brain to collate this news. He was working on a few scenarios at once. Then suddenly he stood up.

"That message on the phone must be from the Voice." Steve was excited. "This means he doesn't know Eddie's been arrested. He still thinks Eddie's out and about." Steve started to pace the office seemingly oblivious of people around him. As he paced and talked to himself, he stopped, shook his head and went to the whiteboard attached to the far wall.

The DCI talked as he wrote. "This is all getting too confusing, but it should be simple. First." He looked at his two colleagues. "We've got Eddie Randall linked to the actual killer, this Blade bloke and the car ring. We'll arrest the Blade tomorrow and hope he talks. If he does then our two murders are solved. Our theory is that the Blade did the actual killings and Eddie Randall gave the orders."

Steve started to pace again as his audience watched. "Second. According to Eddie, he takes his orders from someone called the Voice. He seems to be the main man but so far we've no idea who he is." Steve looked intently at his audience. "But it now looks like this Voice doesn't know we have Eddie. This could be to our advantage but I'm missing something. I'm missing the thing that ties these people together." With more than a little frustration, the DCI asked, "But what the hell is it?"

Steve came back to the present aware he'd slipped into his theorising mode.

"Terry! If we can be there when this Voice character is on the other end of that phone, could you trace it?"

Terry felt the excitement that had suddenly built up in the office. Even Poppy had joined the group in the DCI's office.

"I could try, but if they are both unregistered burner phones, I might only get a general location. I don't think I could get an exact location unless there was only one property using the nearest mast and even then, it would be more luck than science."

"But you could give it a go?"

Terry smiled a wicked grin. "You know I like a challenge and it just happens I've—"

The DCI interrupted. "I know, you've got a new piece of software you haven't tried out yet."

With mock surprise, the Head of Tech Services laughed. "How did you know?"

As Mary went to interview Eddie Randall, and his office emptied, Steve sat down at his desk. He realised the two murders were all but solved but he needed the Voice to conclude the case. Now he also had evidence against Superintendent Blackstone who was clearly mixed up in the car ring. Steve closed his eyes trying to visualise how Blackstone could fit in.

If he were involved in the car ring, was he involved in the murders? The DCI had thought the Russian, Vladimir, could be involved in the murders but had been warned off by MI6. He wondered if the Russian might be the Voice or even Blackstone, but somehow it didn't fit. His instinct said the Russian, the Voice and Blackstone were individuals who were connected somehow. With a sigh he realised his investigations, all of them, still had a way to go. As he headed for the twelfth floor and a meeting that would see a corrupt policeman get his just desserts, the DCI had no idea what was coming his way.

Chapter Twenty-Five

At the same time as the DCI was making his way to Commander Alfie Brook's office, Staff Sergeant Tay was coming to terms with what he had done. Whilst he didn't panic at the sight of Corporal Edward Hicks' body lying on the floor beside his lathe, the spy knew he had just created a problem for himself. If he admitted to killing Hicks but claimed it was an accident, his cover was sure to be blown. There would be awkward questions and it was likely he would fail in his mission to photograph as many blueprints of the new weapon delivery system as he could. The more he considered his options, the more the spy could see that owning up to the killing wasn't one of them.

The events of the past few minutes had however put a spanner in the works. He'd planned to force his way into the vault containing the library of plans after the weapon had been dispatched. But now he knew he had to act. He finished photographing the plans he had been working with. His head was swimming with thoughts of how best to act going forward. He quickly formed a plan.

He lifted the corporal's body onto his shoulder, having first searched for and found his keys to the vault. A plan he'd considered previously of using the unconscious Hicks to trick the biometric locks suddenly became a reality; the only difference was the corporal was dead. The spy had no idea if a dead man's eye scan would fool the system, but he had to try, and hope for the best. Checking that the corridor was clear and knowing the location of each CCTV camera, he made his way quickly to the room housing the vault. He opened the door from the corridor using the dead man's key and entered, closing the door behind him. He placed the body carefully on the floor and locked the door. He also closed the blinds over the windows facing the corridor. Bobby had been in this room many times and knew the procedure for opening the vault.

Using the corporal's keys, he unlocked the three locks in the correct order. To his relief, no alarm sounded. He next lifted the body in front of the biometric retina scanner. With great difficulty, he was able to support the corporal's weight and hold his left eyelid open. He positioned the now open eye so the scanner would be activated. To his relief, he heard a portion of the locking system whirring into action and saw a green light appear on the control panel. Next, he repositioned the corpse and pressed Edward Hicks' thumb onto the reader. Again, the satisfying whirr of the locking mechanism clicked into action and a second green light appeared. With some satisfaction, and knowing he only had one more task to perform, the spy took Ed's left hand and pressed it against the full palm scanner. To his relief, the third green light was illuminated, and the door gave a gentle click. Staff Sergeant Bobby Tay was in.

He stood in amazement, looking at the task in front of him. He placed the body on the floor of the vault and systematically started to examine the rows of suspended blueprints. There was a desk at the far end of the windowless space. The action of opening the door had automatically triggered a light so Bobby had a clear view of everything inside this vault. On the table was a book marked, MASTER REGISTER. Bobby knew this was the bible that identified each drawing now suspended from the neatly installed racks. He switched on the table lamp that sat on the desk and opening the register scanned the first page. It showed the location on the first drawing, R01 meaning rack one, then the designation given to the drawing in rack one. This was shown as D/01 followed by a brief description. Without reading the description, Bobby knew this was the first drawing for the delivery system which was the re-engineering of an existing anti-tank weapon. He set to work lifting drawings from the racks and following the information in the register quickly worked his way through racks one, two and three.

Bobby Tay was exhausted. He looked at his watch. It showed 23.13 on Friday the 27th of March. With only one more rack to go, he set to again, lifting down drawings, laying them on the desk so they were illuminated by the desk lamp, and clicking his camera. It took the spy another two hours to complete everything. Despite his tiredness, Bobby Tay decided to copy each page of the register. This took a further forty minutes.

At last, the exhausted Staff Sergeant Tay was finished. He'd decided to hide Ed Hicks' body in the vault. He closed and relocked the vault door, opened the window blinds he'd closed earlier and exited the room, locking the door behind him. He returned to his workshop and rolled up the plans he'd been working on, placing an elastic band around them. He hid them behind a steel cupboard that housed various machine tools. Even in his tired state, he knew he should have returned these to the vault and placed them in the appropriate rack. He knew this was a mistake as it might alert security that apart from the murder, someone might have had access to the drawings, but he was very tired and realised there was nothing he could do. He trudged off to his bedroom to try and get some sleep.

***

The DCI arrived in the office of Commander Alfie Brooks at exactly 6.14 p.m. As he entered, he saw Alfie and Superintendent Kit Carson sitting in the same positions he'd last seen them occupying. Both men had removed their jackets that were now hanging from the back of their chairs.

"Sit down, Steve. I've got to tell you; Mrs Brooks isn't going to be happy. We were going out tonight for the first time in months and I should be dressed in my Sunday best by now, so this had better be good."

Steve saw Alfie was serious but knew he put the job before domestic considerations.

Superintendent Carson rose and shook hands. All he said was "The floor is yours."

Steve sat and opened the thin file he'd prepared. "We arrested a guy called Edward Randall and a couple of his sidekicks today. He has put his hands up to being involved in our double murder case and has given us the actual killer. I plan to arrest the killer tomorrow morning early."

Alfie spoke. "Well, that's good news, DCI Burt, but where does Blackstone come in?"

Steve noted a look of annoyance cross Kit Carson's face. He appeared to realise Steve had something and was setting the scene.

"I'm coming to that, sir. As you know, Superintendent Blackstone is suspected of arranging for the tracking service to close down just as high-end cars are being stolen."

Steve produced the e-mails Poppy had obtained from Edgar Wallace of National Trace. He slid them across the table and explained the significance of the code at the top left-hand corner of each sheet.

"You mean every e-mail I send can be traced to me and I know nothing about it?" Alfie Brooks looked confused.

"Yes sir, as the sender, any hard copy you make does not show this code. It only appears on the recipient's. These came from National Trace and definitely came from Blackstone's computer."

Alfie turned to the Superintendent. "What do you think Kit? Is this enough to nail him?"

"It could be, but it's thin. He could say someone else used his computer even though it's in his private office."

Steve watched both men think hard. He was enjoying his moment.

"There's more."

"Let's have it for Christ's sake. I can almost hear the missus shouting from here."

The DCI smiled inwardly. "This afternoon, and based on information given to us by Eddie Randall, a technician arrived at his yard to disable the tracker systems on three newly stolen Audi cars. Needless to say, we invited him in for a chat. His name is Tommy Moore, and he has form for fixing alarms to help with high-end robberies. When we closed down the cut, shunt and export operation that was part of Crystal Motors in Mile End Road, this car-stealing gang needed a quick fix for the tracking system. They'd lost their more permanent arrangement when we arrested the mechanics at Crystal Motors. Tommy told us he was instructed by Superintendent Allan Blackstone to visit Eddie's yard and take care of the trackers."

Both senior officers stared at each other.

"Bloody hell, Steve! Are you sure?"

"Certain. He should have finished his formal statement about now. He's credible and his story makes sense."

Kit Carson, as head of Internal Affairs, needed no convincing. "With this and the e-mails, we've got him. Well done, Steve."

The DCI didn't respond. Alfie who had known Steve for years suspected he had more to say.

"Go on Steve."

"It's a couple of things. First, I think he knows this Tommy Moore has been blown. Tommy should have called Blackstone when he'd disabled the trackers and Blackstone was then intending to phone the tracking company, telling them they could resume tracking. Obviously, Tommy didn't make the call."

Steve produced Tommy Moore's phone and played the two voice mail messages from Superintendent Blackstone. Once they'd heard them Kit Carson was first to speak.

"Do you think he knows we're on to him?"

"No sir. If he's wired in as he seems to be, he'll know we have arrested Eddie Randall and will have worked out the reason he didn't hear from Tommy is that we've arrested him too. I think he'll sift through our activity logs and when he doesn't see Moore's arrest, he'll feel safe. Tommy wasn't too keen to give Blackstone up."

"Mm, I agree." Kit Carson was making notes and talking. "I don't see him as a flight risk but presumably he'll be concerned that this Tommy Moore can identify him?"

"Yes. That's why I didn't arrest him. We've got his statement and we'll keep that under wraps. He's worried about his security. DS Matt Conway's getting him an emergency number linked to his local nick and he'll get regular patrols to drive by."

All three police officers sat in silence. Then the Commander chipped in. "You said you had something else, Steve?"

"Yes, but it's delicate. I don't know if or where Blackstone fits into the double murder case."

"How so." It was Kit Carson, now sitting upright in his chair.

Steve explained again the link between the stolen cars, Eddie Randall receiving his orders over the phone, the Blade as the actual killer and his theory that the killing of Cameron Bowie was linked to a turf war between the two Russians, Vladimir Skoysky and Dimitri Grochic.

"I can't put my finger on it, but I feel Blackstone's involved. I just don't know how at this stage."

The DCI didn't mention his briefing by MI6 and Military Intelligence and that he had been ordered not to approach Vladimir Skoysky.

Alfie Brooks looked at his watch. It was 7.20 p.m. "Well, there goes my night out." He gave a resigned sigh. "What do you want to do, Kit?"

"I think we have enough to pull him in. Would that suit you, Steve?"

The DCI had retreated into one of his deep-thinking periods. His mind was analysing what he knew with particular reference to Superintendent Allan Blackstone. The senior officers looked on as Steve formulated a new theory. He shook himself back to the present.

"Sorry sir, I was just wondering. You remember I told you Eddie Randall got his instructions over the phone from this electronically distorted voice?"

"Yes." Both officers answered in unison.

"Well, suppose Blackstone also takes his orders from this same Voice? As I said, I'm missing something but maybe that's it. That's why this whole thing is so complicated. If Blackstone is controlled by this Voice, who is to say the Voice isn't controlled by someone higher?" Steve looked directly at his senior colleagues. "Say a Russian doing business in London?"

Before saying anything else, Steve recalled the colonel from Military Intelligence saying Vladimir was not a small player and had someone planted inside the secret research station near Wetherby.

Steve carried on. He addressed his remarks to Kit Carson. "Sir, if I suggested Blackstone could be a person of interest in our double murder case, could you, as Internal Affairs, see your way clear to let me have first go at him?"

"What do you hope to learn?"

"With luck the identity of this Voice. He's a heavy player in this but thinking about it, maybe he's taking his orders from the Russian. We know who the Russian is, but the Voice is a mystery. If Blackstone gave us the Voice, and the Voice gave us Vladimir, we'd clean this whole thing up from top to bottom."

Kit Carson looked at Alfie with an enquiring stare. Alfie responded. "Well, I agree if we can get the top boys, we'd be doing everyone a favour. Steve has solved the double murders but putting away a few foot soldiers and leaving the top brass in place seems like only half the job. I'd trust the DCI to do it right and still leave Internal Affairs with a slice of the cake."

Superintendent Carson was a man who weighed up his decisions with care. He eventually spoke. "OK, Steve. Let me have a full report on what you have on Blackstone, not speculation. You know we only deal in facts. I'll take no action until you tell me you want to interview him or until Blackstone becomes a problem for the Force. Is that clear?"

Steve relaxed. "Very clear, Kit."

"Remember we have procedures and Blackstone has rights, one of which is he has the right to be questioned by an officer of his own or senior rank. I'll sit in on any interview but delegate the questioning to you. That gets us around that issue."

Commander Alfie Brooks called the meeting to an end. "Right, now that's settled, can I please go home to a very frosty reception?"

Five minutes later the DCI was back in his office. What seemed like a delegation was waiting for him.

"Bloody hell, folks, have none of you got homes to go to?"

The assembled officers knew their boss knew exactly why they were all still working.

Peter Jones was the first to speak up as Steve took his seat behind his desk, everyone else remained standing. Peter's gentle, lilting Welsh voice seemed out of place in this highly charged atmosphere. Everyone knew things were happening.

"I've got the lorry driver downstairs Steve, and forensics are still working the car lot. The bloke downstairs claims to know nothing. He's a contract driver for a haulage firm operating out of Harwich. He claims all he was doing was picking up cars and taking them to Felixstowe docks. He did admit it was a bit unusual to collect cars in a closed-side truck but that's it."

Peter looked tired, having been the last one to leave Eddie's yard. He carried on. "I think I believe him, but this haulage company seem a bit dodgy."

"Thanks, Peter. Get a formal statement from him and follow up with this haulage company. You never know, they might know something, and someone involved must have hired them."

"Right. Do you need me after I'm finished downstairs?"

Steve looked at his watch. "No. Go home, it's seven-thirty. We're arresting this Blade character tomorrow but Matt's on that. See you Monday."

The DI left to take his statement.

Steve noticed Terry Harvey was standing in the doorway.

Mary Dougan was the next to speak up. She took up a position beside the whiteboard and wrote the code from Eddie's phone.

O-10-Sa. "That's the message from the text. Our man Eddie tells me it's definitely from this controller he calls the Voice. It means 'be in your office at ten o'clock Saturday'. He says the Saturday in question will be tomorrow. He never gets instructions more than one day ahead."

The DCI sat forward. "How was Eddie?"

Mary gave a sly grin. "Well, sir. When I realised there was a contact planned for tomorrow, I suggested to Eddie that if he played along and perhaps took the call, we might just be able to speak to the CPS."

"Good on you Mary." Steve admired how this DC's mind worked sometimes. She seemed a natural for CID. "And what did he say?"

"He couldn't have been more helpful. He's happy to cooperate." Mary's face became more serious. "Although he did say he would have to actually *be* in his office tomorrow at ten o'clock."

"Why? It's a mobile. He could be anywhere."

"Ah! But he says this Voice sometimes posts information to him and if the call is planned for ten, then there may be something in the post tomorrow from the Voice." Mary carried on. "Eddie gets his post by nine o'clock and the Voice knows this."

"Clever. So, if Eddie's not in his office, he won't have his mail and this Voice will know he doesn't have whatever information he wants to talk about."

"That's about it, sir."

As Steve mulled this over, Terry Harvey spoke up. "If you still want me to try and trace the call, I can have a mobile tracking station set up on-site. Remember, Steve, no guarantees, but we'll do our best."

Both Terry and Mary looked on expectantly while the DCI considered his options. As he sat, he noticed Matt Conway standing beside his colleagues. Steve looked enquiringly at the DS.

"I've got the formal statement from the technician, and I've set up a surveillance patrol and emergency call number." Matt's expression was one of a conspirator. He knew the DCI wanted any reference to Superintendent Blackstone kept quiet. He deliberately avoided the use of his name. "I have the file, so I'm done. I only need to be briefed on tomorrow's swoop and I'm out of here. I'm knackered."

It was obvious to Steve that his team needed a break and that he, personally was carrying a heavy caseload.

"Right. One thing at a time. Let's deal with the swoop on the Blade first." Steve turned to the office in general. "Mary?"

"It's laid on. I've got the berth number where his boat is tied up, and four uniforms have been allocated, so that's four, plus us three. Seven should do it. I don't suppose he'll try escaping on the waterside of the boat." She indicated herself, Matt and the DCI. "Seven. You said we should start at six a.m. so I've told everyone to rendezvous in the garage at five a.m. I've booked out four cars and have a forensic team on standby."

"Well done, Mary. If all goes to plan, we should literally catch him napping. Have you got that Matt? Five tomorrow morning in the garage."

"Got it."

"OK. Now, we should be back here by seven-thirty." Steve was thinking and talking.

"Eddie has to be at his office for ten. We need to get him there and make sure we collect his post." The DCI stopped talking but continued thinking. Silently considering a plan. "Eddie's tied to the killings, so I'd better be there when this Voice calls."

Steve shook himself.

"Here's what we'll do. The three of us will get John Stuart McKelvey, AKA the Blade, back here as quickly as we can. Matt, you and Mary conduct the initial interview. Read up on the file before you launch into it. I want to be at Eddie's yard for this ten o'clock call."

The DCI paused. "We have Eddie's statement so you can use the fact we already have enough to charge him but hold off. I want the whole lot charged at the same time. Got it?"

Matt smiled at Mary pleased to be given some real responsibility. He answered for both of them. "Yes boss, leave it to us."

254

"Good. Now Terry, can you get your mobile unit set up in time?"

Inspector Terry Harvey was used to tight deadlines and nodded. "Yes. As always, it'll be tight, but we'll do it. Can we have access to the site from say six o'clock tomorrow morning?"

Matt Conway answered. "Shouldn't be a problem. The site is open, and a constable has been posted just to protect the scene until forensics are finished."

"Right. We'll be good to go before ten tomorrow, Steve."

Steve knew Poppy was still in the outer office, listening. He called her in and in a split second Poppy was there. "Get onto the custody sergeant downstairs and arrange for Eddie to be escorted to his old office tomorrow morning. If they leave at eight-thirty they'll be there well before ten. I want two officers to escort him. I'll get there after we've arrested the Blade." Steve laughed. "Where do these guys get their names? I ask you, the Blade?"

The DCI stood still smiling. "Everybody happy? Do we all know what we're doing tomorrow?"

There was a general air of expectation and a genuine willingness to get on with the job.

Chapter Twenty-Six

The DCI arrived home shortly before nine p.m. He was greeted by his wife and to his pleasant surprise, his daughter, Rosie.

Dr Alison Mills, Steve's wife, was now back practising medicine from her surgery below the family home. Although only working part-time she found she was more tired than she might have expected. She knew Steve was exhausted and that his current caseload was crippling, so she didn't mention her own mild fatigue.

Steve sat on their sofa holding his daughter, marvelling at her beauty and fragility, whilst Alison heated up his evening meal. Rosie hadn't wanted to go to sleep earlier, and Alison knew Steve liked to hold her. She'd decided not to put their daughter down until Steve had five minutes bonding with his first child. Alison presented her husband with a tray and took their daughter to bed down for the night. When she returned, she found Steve fast asleep on the sofa and his meal only half-eaten, she shrugged. Her husband looked so peaceful, but she woke him, telling him to get to bed. It suited the doctor who, to combat her own tiredness, also needed an early night, but when Steve told her he had to be out at four the next morning, she was less than amused.

***

As the DCI made his way to the underground garage at New Scotland Yard early on Saturday morning, the weather was fine but cold. He smiled to himself, happy with the thought that summer would soon be here.

After a quick briefing, the convoy, led by the DCI, set off to arrest John Stuart McKelvey, also known as the Blade. They approached the basin by Canary Wharf at slow speed. The four cars had no lights showing, relying instead on the lighting around the marina.

Mary had a map of the moorings and quickly identified berth B44. This was where the Blade's houseboat was moored. At precisely 05.52

a.m., the seven police officers exited their cars and stood on the embankment adjacent to berth B44.

In a low whisper, Steve said. "Matt, you and I will board with one of the uniformed officers. Mary, you stay here and have the other three uniforms spread out along the length of the boat. With luck, he'll be so sleepy he won't know what's happening."

Steve, Matt and a constable called Dave stepped quietly down onto the deck. Steve didn't know anything about boats, but it was obvious someone had stuck a square box on top of a barge hull. The entrance to the inner areas of the houseboat was through a wooden door set into the side of this box. Steve tried the handle, but it was locked. He motioned to the PC to use force to open the door. The PC was only too willing to deploy his fourteen stone. One good shoulder charge and they were in. Not knowing the layout of the boat, Steve told the constable to stand guard by the door while he and Matt searched the inside.

Matt found the Blade asleep on a sofa. The room that appeared to run the length of the boat stank of alcohol. There were empty beer and whisky bottles on the floor. It was obvious the Blade had had a party the night before.

Matt roused him, and realising the police were on his boat, he immediately sat up.

"Good morning, John, or should I call you the Blade? We've been looking for you for a while now so it's a real pleasure to meet you at last."

Matt was grinning as the Blade, in his hungover state, was clearly suffering and still trying to work out what was happening.

"I need a doctor; I'm not well enough to answer questions." The Blade was relying now on his old convict instincts. He knew escape was impossible but needed time to think. Asking for a doctor was always a good idea and bought time. As Matt was joined by Steve, they both wondered how this rough-looking, slim, hungover individual, dressed in a dirty t-shirt and boxer shorts, could be their killer.

"Don't worry, Mr Blade." This was the best line Steve could come up with so early in the morning. "You'll get a doctor and a lot more. Matt read him his rights and get him into a pair of trousers."

As Matt Conway did as instructed. Steve called forensics and arranged for the team Mary had put on standby, to get to the houseboat when they could. He gave the berth number and location.

Mary stood by the boat as the Blade, in handcuffs, was taken onto the dock and driven away.

"We got our man then sir. No problems?"

"No. He had a heavy boozing night and was a bit rough this morning. He's still probably over the limit to drive and he's asked for a doctor."

Matt Conway joined them. "I've told the uniforms to take him to Central. I wasn't sure how you wanted to play it. You know, charge him or just start with questioning under caution?"

"Good thinking." Steve paused to think. "Mary, you hang on here and wait for forensics. Tell them I want every inch of that boat gone over."

"Right."

"Once you're satisfied that everything here is under control, get yourself over to Central Booking. Charge our man with conspiracy to murder for now. Make sure the doctor examines him, then get him transferred to the Yard."

"OK. Are you going to the car yard?"

"Yes, we have plenty of time. Matt, you come with me. The Blade isn't going to be interviewed this morning given the state of him, so change of plan. I know I asked you two to interview him but that was before I realised the state he would be in this morning."

"No problem, boss, we understand."

Mary hid her disappointment at not getting the first crack at interrogating a murder suspect, but she hid it well. Matt Conway was equally disappointed but took comfort from the fact he was to be involved at Eddie's car lot.

With Mary and two uniformed constables left behind, the DCI and Matt Conway left for Eddie Randall's car lot.

***

The Voice had woken earlier than usual. He was struggling with his conscience and hadn't slept well. He'd alerted Eddie that he needed him and had mailed the envelope to arrive in Saturday's post. For some reason, he felt uncomfortable with what he was about to do.

Sitting in his kitchen, nursing a cup of instant coffee, the Voice knew he was giving in to his darker side. He knew what must be done and on past performance, Eddie would oblige, but realised he was about to order a third murder. He knew it was necessary if his anonymity was to be preserved but somehow it felt wrong.

The Voice agonised for an hour looking at his decision from a variety of angles. No matter how he considered his decision, he knew he was right. Another killing was necessary and having started the process, he would go through with it.

***

Steve and Matt arrived at Eddie's yard just before nine-thirty, having had time to stop at a drive-through fast-food place for coffee and a breakfast roll. As they drove into the yard, they saw a variety of vans neatly parked. One van was bigger than the rest and had a satellite dish open on its roof. It also had an array of aerials attached to the roof and appeared to be connected to a mobile generator. The generator was working hard and sounded loud despite, as Steve noted, a large silencer was attached to it.

As they exited their car, Terry Harvey appeared. He came from inside the large van and headed straight for the two detectives.

Without any formalities, Terry launched into an explanation of what was happening.

"We're all set. I've linked the burner phone that our friend Eddie has to a recording device. I don't want to amplify the speech coming from the other end in case our man hears an unusual echo. It's better if we simply record both ends of the conversation and play it back once the call ends."

Terry looked expectantly at the detectives for an acknowledgement they understood.

Steve answered, "So, you could set it up such that we'd hear the conversation in real-time?"

"Yes, but it's risky. As I said, if our man is as careful as he obviously is, he might smell a rat if the line isn't exactly as it always has been. Believe me, Steve, it's better this way."

Steve smiled. "Fair enough Terry. You're the expert."

Without responding, Terry carried on. "Now, when the call comes in, we'll start interrogating the various masts within the M25 and hope to get a ping we can isolate, but it's a long shot. To be honest, Steve, my new software is our only chance. You see, each mast handles thousands of calls a minute. Before, all we could hope for was that our caller was in an area where traffic is light, but now we can scan every mast and it's only when he hangs up that we might get a clue."

Terry was excited about his work, as always. "By monitoring the masts, we can see each call as it drops off, meaning a call has been completed. We need the exact time to the second, even millisecond when our caller hangs up, and hope no other user hangs up at exactly the same time."

Matt Conway saw straight away the significance of what the inspector had just said. He saw the confusion on the face of the DCI. "That's very clever Terry." For the benefit of Steve, he carried on. "So, by monitoring every transmitter in London, if you can pinpoint the exact second someone finishes a call, your software gives you the masts where each call finished at exactly the same time?"

"That's it, but it only applies to the numbers originating the call."

Steve was less confused but needed clarification. "Just for my simple brain Terry, if I make a call, you're saying if you know the exact time I hang up, you can identify the transmitter mast I used?"

"Not quite. But, by probability theory, if we know each call that terminated at exactly the same time, one of them must be the one we're interested in. Plus, the chances of having more than a few calls end at exactly the same time, are slim. We should be able to give you say half a dozen locations, one of which was used by this Voice character."

The DCI was, as always, amazed by Terry Harvey's level of skill and cunning.

The post had been delivered after nine o'clock and Terry had taken possession. Apart from a few junk mailers, there was one A4 envelope addressed to Mr Edward Randall. The address had been typed onto a label that had in turn been stuck onto the brown envelope. Terry had placed the mail on the desk in the portacabin office.

Eddie Randall had been escorted from his cell back to his beloved car lot. He was seated behind his desk while Steve, Terry and Matt were also present. Matt sat in the chair previously occupied by the Blade, while Steve and Terry stood. One of Terry's technicians was also present ready to operate the very sophisticated recording machine that was attached by two wires to the mobile phone Eddie would be using.

"Now remember Eddie. Play it straight, no funny business. Just act normally, respond as you would if we weren't here. Do you understand?" The DCI needed to be sure Eddie would cooperate.

"No problem, Mr Burt. You don't have to worry." In a strange way, Eddie was enjoying all the attention.

Seeing the post and the envelope Steve asked if this was the envelope from the Voice.

"Looks like it."

"When do you usually open the envelopes?"

"When he calls."

Knowing there may be evidence on the envelope and its contents, Steve made Eddie wear a pair of disposable gloves. He didn't want unnecessary fingerprints. He also didn't want Eddie to open the envelope but to follow his usual procedure. Anything out of the normal might spook their quarry.

"It's coming up to ten. Get ready Eddie."

At exactly ten o'clock, the burner phone rang. The technician pressed a few buttons and gave the thumbs-up sign. Steve indicated to Eddie to answer. He pressed 'receive' but said nothing. As before the Voice was brief.

"Have you received the envelope?"

"Yes, I've got it here." Eddie's voice was strong and clear.

"Open it."

Eddie did as, ordered, although he found the gloves got in the way. Inside the envelope was a photograph of a man and a typewritten sheet.

Steve and Terry stood by the door while Matt continued to sit in the old armchair. There was total silence apart from Eddie's voice. All three police officers were desperate to hear the other end of the conversation.

"Got it."

"The details are on the sheet of paper. I want the man in the photograph eliminated, but not before next Tuesday the 31st. I don't care how you do it, but get it done. There'll be a nice fee in it for you."

Eddie wasn't interested in the job he was being asked to perform, nor in the money. He knew this person in the photograph would still be breathing after the 31st of March and he would never see the riches promised.

"Right. Leave it with me."

The technician, who had heard both sides of the conversation, pressed a button on his recorder and started an atomic clock that was accurate to a thousandth of a second. The clock was activated before the Voice hung up and stopped at the exact moment the connection was broken.

Terry Harvey jumped into action and went back out to the large van parked outside. The technician, acting on a nod from Steve, played back the entire conversation. Steve and Matt, who had now left the armchair, stood behind Eddie. Steve put on gloves and picked up the envelope and its contents.

Without showing any emotion, Steve put everything back into the envelope. "Matt, get Eddie outside. The two constables out there will take him back."

Once Eddie and Matt had left, Steve sat in Eddie's chair and removed the contents from the envelope. Staring out at him from the photograph was an unknown face. The piece of neatly typed A4 paper had the name that belonged to the face. Steve stared at it. He was almost paralysed. The name on the paper was Allan Blackstone.

Chapter Twenty-Seven

At Station K, everything appeared normal. Staff Sergeant Tay was at his milling machine working on the last projectile. He hadn't yet decided what to do but concluded doing nothing and acting innocently was probably the best strategy. Professor Karl Symonds was fussing over his display of the new weapon and rehearsing, in his mind, the speech he would make to the remaining staff.

Hector Forsyth, the so-called auditor, wasn't happy. Unknown to the staff at Station K their movements were monitored using hidden cameras linked to a sophisticated computer-driven algorithm that counted the number of people present within Station K at any one time. Heat detectors and lung and heartbeats were used to confirm the headcount. The head of security had been briefed as to Hector Forsyth's real identity, and it was he who now sat in a small office with Hector explaining that it appeared one member of staff was missing. He further explained that no one had left the Station in the past twelve hours and as of yesterday evening, everyone was accounted for.

"Do we know who is missing?"

"No sir. We only get headcount data."

"Leave it with me. I'll talk to the Prof."

A relieved head of security left, happy to have passed on the problem.

The MI6 man sat staring at the far wall. He wondered if the spy who they suspected had been deeply bedded into Station K, had struck, or if he had somehow found a way out without triggering an alarm. Either way, a headcount was needed, and identities checked.

Hector sought out Professor Symonds and relayed what the head of security had told him.

"This is serious Hector; how could someone leave without us knowing, and do we know what he might have taken?"

"At this stage, Karl, we don't know who's missing, never mind what secrets, if any, he has made off with. I'm calling a full lockdown. There's a four-man team of Military Police stationed above ground for just such an incident as this. I'll get them down. We need to first identify who is missing, and then we'll carry out a full search of everyone's effects. You never know, our spy may not be working alone."

"Yes, yes, of course, Hector, you must do what you think best." The Professor was suddenly looking his age. He sat in an upright chair. "This is terrible. Goodness knows what we shall do now."

The auditor was now all action. At 10.27 a.m. on Saturday the 28th of March, Station K went into total lockdown and every inch was about to be searched.

**

Steve didn't confide in Matt Conway as to the identity of the Voice's target, nor that a killing had been ordered. He knew he needed time to work through what this latest piece of information meant.

They had left Terry busy checking his computers and obviously not wishing to be disturbed. All he said as they left was that he had work to do, and he'd let Steve know when he had something.

Matt was curious about the contents of the envelope but said nothing. Instead, he talked about how technology was really revolutionising police work. "Just think, if I hang up on a call and Terry knows the exact time, he can trace me to the mast I used and then to a small area. Bloody marvellous."

Steve agreed and to keep his mind on the job at hand, quizzed Matt. "If Terry can find say six masts that all cancelled calls at exactly the same time, how big an area could we be looking at?"

"Depends. I don't know enough about it, but it could be as small as a few streets if the mast is serving a densely populated area."

"We'd need to have a name; we couldn't just knock on every door."

Matt laughed. "Good idea, Steve, but I don't think we'd get very far, but yes, if we had a name and we knew the tight geographic area around a specific mast, then I think we'd have a good chance of solving any crime."

The pair drove on in silence. The DCI told himself to forget Blackstone. Despite having further confirmation that he must be more closely involved with the Voice than he'd first thought. Otherwise, why order a hit?

On arrival at his office, Steve learnt that John Stuart McKelvey had been declared unfit to interview until at least Sunday morning. The doctor had concluded his blood alcohol level was too high and would need 24 hours to return to a more normal level.

"I've left him at Central for the day, sir; I can have him brought here tomorrow."

"Right, Mary, looks like a full weekend shift."

Matt was pacing around when Steve announced. "Let's go up to the canteen. We need a coffee and see where we are."

Matt had worked with Steve long enough to become as hooked on coffee as his boss. Mary had always liked coffee but not in the volumes the DCI consumed.

The three left to drink coffee and consider the cases.

"Matt, what's your take on what we have?"

"Well, if we start at the beginning, we have Eddie Randall and his two sidekicks. Eddie has admitted he was ordered by some phantom voice to arrange the killings of Vinnie McGuire and Cameron Bowie. Agreed?"

"Yes."

"We now have this John Stuart McKelvey, AKA the Blade, in the frame as the actual killer. Eddie got the instruction and sub-contracted the murders to the Blade."

"Right," Mary spoke up. "All nice and simple and if we can get him to talk, we will surely have enough for the CPS."

Steve sipped his coffee. "I agree. On one level we have a nice open-and-shut case." He drank more coffee. "But Eddie is only a pawn; we need to find this Voice character. He seems to be the one calling the shots."

"But how do we get to him, boss? No one seems to know his identity." Matt believed they had the case solved.

"Maybe it's time to get what we have tied up and call it case closed."

The DCI saw the logic but couldn't let go of the need to discover the real murderer, the Voice. Steve also thought about the Russian.

"In many ways you're right, Matt, but the real killer can't escape. Our job is not done until we have this Voice plus, don't forget, we have the Russian who was sniffing around the garage on Mile End."

Steve suddenly stopped talking. His colleagues could see he was deep in thought. Slowly he came back to the present with a peculiar look on his face. At first, he spoke very slowly.

"Suppose this Voice is acting for someone else. Suppose he does his own thing but also takes orders from someone even further up the food chain." The DCI still wasn't fully focused on his colleagues but talking out loud but to himself. "We haven't found a connection between our first and second victim. Suppose that killing was ordered as a one-off." Thinking about the order to kill Blackstone, Steve made a connection.

"Suppose victim one, Vinnie McGuire knew too much or…" Steve's eyes lit up. "He knew the identity of the Voice!"

The DCI was suddenly very animated, with a cry he declared "That's it! Vinnie was killed because he knew who the Voice was. That's why there's no connection between the two killings. They were killed for different reasons and the order came from different people." Steve was flushed but was grinning. He knew he had it.

"So, the first killing was ordered by this Voice, because he didn't want anyone to know who he is?" Mary looked puzzled.

"Yes, look at what he does. He uses a voice changer so no one can identify his voice; he uses Eddie to do his bidding, but Eddie's never met him and doesn't know who he is, and he only communicates using burner phones and the post. This guy wants to be anonymous."

Steve had another moment of reflection. "And remember, Eddie told us the Voice ordered Vinnie's killing and Vinnie was responsible for putting Eddie and the Voice together."

"Right, so we have our first victim killed on the direct order of this Voice so Vinnie couldn't identify him." Matt was now thinking. "I suppose that's fair, but what about our second victim?"

"We've found no connection between them, other than Eddie contracted the Blade to carry out both murders. The second killing was different. It was very public and don't forget, the mechanics in the workshop definitely said a Russian had been around and they thought it was the Russian that their boss killed."

"Hold on." Matt was becoming confused. "You're saying the Voice ordered Vinnie's killing for his own ends, but the second murder was ordered by some Russian who contracted the Voice, who contracted Eddie, who contracted the Blade to kill Cameron Bowie?"

"Exactly, and my money is on a Russian called Vladimir Skoysky, although, for other reasons, we can't touch him for the moment."

"Christ Steve, that's a whole lot of story, but if it's true, we're no further forward with knowing who the Voice is."

Mary had followed the conversation. "And if this Russian is off-limits, how do we put the pieces together?"

Steve sighed. "With difficulty. Come on, let's go home. We'll meet up tomorrow at ten and talk to our Blade friend. If we're lucky we'll have the lot charged by tomorrow afternoon but don't forget, we still need the Voice."

Steve returned to his office to collect a few things before going home. It was 12.17 p.m. when Terry Harvey appeared at Steve's door. The DCI tried to gauge whether the inspector had good or bad news. His facial expression was neutral. Neither man spoke.

Steve broke the silence. "Did your magic software work?"

Terry walked further into the office and sat in the chair opposite Steve's desk.

"We got what we wanted, and the software seems to have worked. The on-site bus is great, for what it was designed for, but we need the computing power we have here to really see this new stuff at its best. Luckily, this kind of search doesn't have to be done in real-time. We got what we needed and it's now running on our mainframe."

"Sounds promising, care to share?"

"We got a lot of pings from a lot of towers, but the atomic clock gives us a bloody accurate time. We input the clock time to four decimal places plus or minus 5%. We got three people within London ending their calls at exactly the same time. Would you believe it, to three decimal places! Almost impossible."

The DCI could see Terry had something. "So, go on, tell me."

"We've got three simultaneous situations. We know the locations of the towers, but I'm running a full sweep just to be sure we didn't miss anything. I'll let it run overnight and get something to you tomorrow if you're in."

"Thanks, Terry and yes, it looks like I'll be in. Alison's not very happy that I'm never home but she knows it's the job."

"Yeah! Tell me about it..." Terry stood but hesitated. He looked shy and seemed reluctant to leave. Steve knew his friend had something on his mind.

"Come on, Terry, what is it?"

Terry got as far as the open office door. He turned to look at Steve although he was having difficulty making eye contact. "Er, well, you're married, and your wife knows you're also married to the job."

"I suppose that's right, why?"

"You know that Florance and I have been seeing a bit of each other over the past few months?"

"I heard a rumour. Flo speaks to Alison a lot."

Terry was reticent to continue but Steve pushed him.

"Well. As I said, we've been seeing a bit of each other and I'm — well — thinking of making it more permanent."

Steve was instantly overjoyed. "You old dog, you, that's great news, Terry."

Before Steve could carry on, Terry interrupted. "Do you think it's fair of me? After all, I'm a bit older and stuck as an inspector. Flo's young and climbing the ladder fast."

Steve looked at his friend and instantly remembered the first time he'd met Florance Rough. She was so large the force couldn't find a uniform big enough for her. It was this that got her into CID. Florance would always be known as Twiggy to the DCI. This was the nickname he'd given her, and it had stuck. Since they had worked their first case together Twiggy had been promoted as a civil servant and permanently seconded to the Yard's Financial Crimes Section. She was now one of the top forensic analysts in the country and certainly going places. She'd also slimmed down with Steve's wife's help and was even going to the gym.

"Listen, Terry, I can't advise you, but you both seem happy, and Twiggy knows what a copper's lot is like, so you'd have no problems there. If you feel as you do, then my friend, I'd go for it."

Terry smiled. "Thanks, Steve, we'll see." With a wave, the Inspector from Technical Support was gone.

Steve had intended to go home but sat at his desk instead. His mind was in turmoil. He'd listened to Mary and Matt and agreed that subject to John McKelvey coughing to the murders, the case was solved. The DCI knew this wasn't enough. He was sure the murders weren't linked, and that the order to commit them came from separate sources. Now he had the Voice putting out a contract on a police officer. Steve admitted the case against Superintendent Blackstone was compelling, but the contract to kill him must mean he's in deeper than anyone thought.

Suddenly the DCI sat bolt upright. Of course, he told himself he was a fool and should have recognised earlier that if the first victim Vinnie McGuire was killed because he knew the Voice, then Blackstone was being killed for the same reason. In a flash of brilliance, Steve spoke out loud: "He knows who the Voice is too!"

Satisfied he could do no more for the moment and telling himself the first priority was to get charges laid against the four people currently in custody, the DCI left his office to go home to kiss his wife and daughter and have a relaxing evening, or so he thought.

As he left, he smiled and said to himself, "Terry and Twiggy."

Chapter Twenty-Eight

At precisely 6.01 p.m. on Saturday the 28th of March, the body of Corporal Edward Hicks was discovered. Station K had been in strict lockdown for around seven and a half hours and everyone on staff was now accounted for.

"So, it's not a spy, it's a murder." Professor Symonds was talking to the man from MI6 and a Military Police Captain.

"Seems that way, but make no mistake Karl, whoever killed this boy is probably our spy." Looking at the Military Policeman. "Have your fellows started the searches?" The MI6 man knew he was out of his depth, but he was the man on the spot.

"Yes sir, but it'll be slow going."

"Better slow and thorough Captain. Our spy, and now our killer, must have something incriminating around him."

"I'll chase the lads up sir."

The captain left the Professor and the secret service man alone.

"I'll have to use your outside line, Karl."

**

Steve arrived home at 4.05 p.m., happy to see his wife baking, while his daughter was in her bouncer, sleeping soundly. He stood for a second taking in the domestic scene telling himself he was a happy, lucky man and wondered if Terry and Twiggy would be as happy. He hoped so.

He went over and kissed his wife, whose hands were covered in baking flour. "Sit down, darling and I'll make you a coffee in a minute, but don't disturb Rosie, she's only just gone to sleep."

Steve went to remove his jacket and settled down in his favourite armchair. Alison scurried around the kitchen and quickly put her baking in the oven. She tidied up, and with two large mugs of coffee, settled down beside her husband.

"Hard day?"

"Yes. An early start and a later finish than I'd hoped, but overall, not a bad day."

"I think you're working too hard; you look shattered."

"You could be right, but I think we're almost there."

Alison was herself tired but a good night's sleep the previous evening had helped to revive her. Also, for the first time, Rosie had almost slept right through.

Steve told his wife about his conversation with Terry Harvey.

"Oh, he'll be OK. Flo's been expecting him to propose for days. She'll be glad when he does."

Steve smiled a tired but contented smile. "You women." He put his arm around his wife. "You know everything."

The couple sat with their arms around each other looking fondly at their daughter who continued to sleep soundly. Alison became aware that Steve hadn't moved for a few minutes and when she gently eased away to see his face, she realised that he, like their daughter, was sound asleep.

Once roused from his sleep, Steve helped his wife prepare the evening meal. Rosie became restless and as soon as Alison had put the food on their plates, Rosie mumbled and stirred herself awake. Alison looked at Steve who, without being asked, volunteered to have his meal microwaved after he'd fed his daughter.

Family life suited the DCI, and he enjoyed everything he did for his daughter. Once Rosie was fed and changed, Steve placed her in her cot, hoping she would sleep. She didn't and it was after nine o'clock before Alison and her husband could settle down for the night. They snuggled together with a glass of wine and watched TV with the volume turned low, for fear of disturbing their daughter. Both parents were tired and opted for yet another early night. It was 10.33 p.m. when Steve kissed his wife goodnight and switched off the bedside light.

***

The lights were burning late within the vast MI6 building located by the banks of the Thames in London. The Head of the Service, Sir Patrick Bond, had been called at 6.41 p.m. to be given the news that someone in

Station K had been murdered. In normal circumstances, a killing at any government establishment wouldn't be something Sir Patrick would be made aware of. However, Station K was a top-secret facility, and the new weapon delivery system was complete and ready for testing. This, together with the existence of a spy within Station K, was enough reason to involve him and call him away from his wife's dinner party.

It was quarter to ten that night when Sir Patrick felt he had all the information available. He had called Colonel Colin Lockhart of Military Intelligence to say Station K was under a lockdown order due to a body having been discovered. On learning this, the colonel insisted on joining Sir Patrick at his office. Both men were now seated in the plush office of Sir Patrick Bond, located in the upper reaches of the MI6 building.

"You have a man on the inside?" The colonel wanted to be sure of the facts.

"Yes. A good man: name of Chalmers, although he is known as Hector Forsyth within Station K. He called me around a quarter to seven this evening. The body was found in a documents vault. At first glance, it looks like the killer whacked the victim over the head and dumped the body in the vault."

"Any evidence of anything missing?"

"Too early to say. There's an RMP squad on site but they're only searching. Chalmers has organised a search of all areas within the station, if they find nothing then he'll organise searches of the staff individually, but it will take time. The problem is none of the RMP team is trained in detective work, and Chalmers certainly isn't. I doubt they'll find the killer unless he's been really stupid."

"So, this body was found inside a vault containing all the details and top-secret documents concerning the new weapons system, and you don't think anything is missing!"

The colonel wasn't having any of it. "You're either mad, stupid or naïve and I don't think you're any of those things." Colin Lockhart stood and paced the office. "Christ man, of *course* something's missing! Has to be!" The colonel was turning red with pent up anger.

"Isn't it likely your spy has made his move! With the place in lockdown, he's trapped. The RMP might get lucky and find something incriminating on someone, but they might not. By your own admission, we've no one on-site who's experienced in solving murders and you're relying on luck to find the killer who's probably also your spy. We need a detective up there now. We need to catch the killer, and believe me, catch the killer and you'll catch your spy."

Sir Patrick was quiet as Colin Lockhart calmed down and resumed his seat. The Head of MI6 knew the military man was right. There was no one within Station K with the experience to catch a killer. When he spoke, Sir Patrick's voice was quiet. "Will they call off the test next Thursday?"

"I don't know, it's not my call, but with this spy showing his colours, I'd be concerned for the security of the actual weapon, never mind the drawings and blueprints."

"My man Chalmer isn't qualified for anything like this, but the whole thing is so sensitive I'd be reluctant to call in the local plod."

Both men agreed and Sir Patrick took it upon himself to sum up.

"I suppose the only positive is Station K is in full lockdown, so our killer come spy can't escape. He still has to be underground. The issue is the test and whether it'll go ahead plus, we don't have anybody on the inside who's remotely qualified to sort this out. I'm not keen to call in the local police. Station K is really top secret. Also, I understand from Chalmers that the professor in charge even has the bloody weapon on show. Chalmers encouraged it hoping our spy might somehow show his hand by trying to steal the thing. But now we have this." Sir Patrick looked worried.

Colonel Lockhart was studying his fingernails when he looked up. "What about that detective we read into the programme the other day. The one looking for his old commanding officer's son?"

"You mean Steve Burt?"

"Yes. He struck me as a competent investigator, and he already knows about the project. Could we get him to look into this for us?"

Sir Patrick liked the idea. "He's certainly well qualified. I suppose we could get him to go up to Wetherby, but I'd have to go through channels." Patrick Bond looked at his watch. "It's now 11.07 p.m. It'll mean getting a lot of senior police officers out of their beds!"

Colin Lockhart, ever the soldier, responded in true military fashion. "Get the buggers out of bed. We've got a national emergency here."

What he didn't mention, and Sir Patrick hadn't asked, was that Colin Lockhart had Captain Alex Hope of the Royal Military Police inside Station K.

Sir Patrick Bond made the calls.

***

DCI Steve Burt's bedside phone started ringing at 00.23 a.m. on Sunday the 29th of March. He reluctantly answered.

"Yes?"

"Steve. It's Alfie Brooks, I need you in my office in the next thirty minutes. Something has come up." The Commander ended the call without further explanation.

***

A rather untidy DCI Burt arrived in Commander Alfie Brook's office at 01.07 on Sunday the 29th of March. He'd explained to his wife he had to go into the office but had no idea why. In true form and as a doctor who used to be accustomed to early morning call outs, Alison, simply said, "OK," and turned over rapidly, returning to her dreams.

Steve could tell from Alfie's expression that he was not happy. On seeing Sir Patrick Bond and the colonel from military intelligence sitting at the Commander's conference table, the DCI suddenly became very concerned.

Without introductions, Alfie launched into his DCI. "What the hell have you got us into now?" He stared directly at Steve. "I told you before about going solo and working as a team." Alfie was standing, pacing about angrily. "I thought you understood the Metropolitan Police pay your salary, not to set yourself up as a part-time private dick. You report to *me*, and *I* give you your assignments."

Steve had been in this situation before and knew it was best to let the Commander have his say without interruption.

"You told me all this vigilante nonsense was over, but now here I am, in the middle of the bloody night, being told by these two," Alfie pointed in the direction of the spook and the soldier, "that you've been involved in some top-secret project I know nothing about, and you've had meetings with these two that again, *I* know nothing about!" Alfie was running out of steam. He sat down opposite his guests. "What the hell's going on, DCI Burt?"

Before Steve could speak, Sir Patrick tried to say something, but Alfie was in charge in his own office. "Don't say anything, Sir Patrick." Alfie's anger had not subsided. "I need to hear what the DCI has to say."

Steve took a seat at the end of the table. "If you've called me in at this unholy hour, just to bollock me, then I'm off home, sir. With the greatest of respect, you knew I was looking into the disappearance of my old Company Commander's son. I told you and as I recall, you sanctioned it, subject to it not interfering with my other cases. That's exactly what I did, and my investigation led me to these two gentlemen."

Alfie had calmed down enough to follow Steve's explanation. "And you didn't see fit to tell me you were mixing with MI6 and Military Intelligence?"

"Look, sir, I would have, but I was sworn to secrecy, plus, these gentlemen can give us the Russian, Vladimir Skoysky, who I'm sure is behind at least one of the killings I'm currently investigating."

It was clear Alfie had been given orders from above to convene this gathering in the middle of the night, but Steve had no idea why.

"Yeah, well." Alfie was a little sheepish, as he acknowledged to himself, he may have been a bit quick to condemn the DCI.

Silence descended, as Alfie realised he had torn a strip off Steve in front of strangers. He tried to recover the situation.

"Gentlemen, you have already met DCI Burt and I understand he is privy to certain secret matters that I, as his senior officer, am not. Nonetheless, I have been instructed to give you every assistance once you have told me why we are here in the middle of the night."

Sir Patrick cleared his throat before speaking. "Thank you, Commander; I'm sorry we had to disturb you, but we really do have a very sensitive situation at one of our top-secret establishments. It is a matter of national security. For obvious reasons, I can't elaborate on the work being carried out but what I can tell you is that a member of staff has been murdered at a time we are preparing to test a new weapons system. The whole facility has been locked down so the murderer must still be on site. We also have reason to believe that a foreign power may be attempting to steal top-secret material and that it is likely the killer and this agent are one and the same person."

As Sir Patrick spoke, Steve thought back to his briefing and recalled Sir Patrick and Colonel Lockhart had indicated a spy might have been embedded at Station K. The DCI assumed this was why this meeting had been called although no one had mentioned Station K, yet!

Sir Patrick was still talking. "We have our own man on the ground plus a small contingent of Military Police, but none of them is a true investigator. We don't believe we should involve the local constabulary due to security concerns and that's why I requested, through your commissioner, that DCI Burt be seconded to us to find the perpetrator of this crime."

The DCI almost choked. "What!" He couldn't believe his ears. "No way, Patrick; my plate is full at the moment and I'm sorry you have a problem, but there's absolutely no way I can just bugger off to Wetherby and drop everything here."

Sir Patrick noted Steve had dropped his title and had divulged the location of Station K.

"Steve. You know what's at stake here. You've been read into the programme..." As Sir Patrick spoke, Colonel Lockhart interrupted.

"And we're getting closer to your Russian. Don't forget our arrangement."

Steve was furious. He looked at his superior for assistance, but Alfie sat silently, just listening. "I'm sorry sir but screw our arrangement. We have the Russian's address and are closing in on an arrest. I have a murder case to solve and as of now, I'm not being held up by some promise that my suspect will be handed over when you're finished with him. For all I know, you'll do a deal with him and suddenly, he'll disappear."

Colonel Colin Lockhart wasn't used to being addressed in these terms but admired the DCI's spirit, nonetheless.

"I hear you, Steve, and you could be right, but this killing may be our opportunity to flush out the bad apple we know is working inside and may even deliver your Russian." The colonel had chosen his words carefully.

Commander Alfie Brooks was no dummy and had read between the lines.

"Gentlemen. It's very early, I need some sleep, and we need to finish this." He looked directly at Steve. "DCI Burt, I hear what you say but it sounds like these gentlemen need the help of the Metropolitan Police and you are it."

Steve stood and addressed his boss. "Can I have a word outside please sir?"

Alfie rolled his eyes and followed the DCI into the outer office normally manned by Alfie's dragon of a secretary.

"Alfie, it's impossible for me to be away from here for the next twenty-four hours."

Steve explained the events of late yesterday and the link to Superintendent Blackstone. He described his theory that the two murders weren't linked and the instruction for the killings had come from two separate sources. He explained that the technician sent to disarm the car trackers had put Blackstone firmly in the frame and Steve wanted to interview Blackstone under caution later in the day. He finally confided that if his theory were correct, Blackstone could give them the Voice.

Commander Brooks stood silently contemplating. "I see the problem, Steve. We can get Kit Carson lined up to sit in, but my orders from on high are to lend you to those two in there." Alfie pointed to the door of his inner office.

"I have an idea, sir. Can I have a free hand when we go back in?"
Alfie stood back. "Christ Steve, you put me in some awkward positions." The Commander understood Steve's dilemma and wondered why he wanted a free hand. "All right but keep it clean, no funny business. I'll let you go so far, but if you wander off script, I'll stop you. Remember, I'm under orders too." Alfie and Steve resumed their original seats. The visitors looked at them in anticipation.

Steve addressed the two guests. "Sir Patrick, Colonel Lockhart, I appreciate your dilemma. I know the sensitivity of this investigation and having been read into the programme I see that I am the natural choice to investigate. However, there are issues here within the Met, that are equally serious and need my full-time attention. I can't be in two places at once, but I can oversee investigations remotely.

I have a very competent detective inspector and an experienced detective sergeant I would suggest we second to your facility. They will investigate exactly as I would, and I'll remain in constant contact. If they haven't found the killer within 48 hours then I will travel north and take charge. They are clearly not local constabulary and know nothing about the work that's taking place within your laboratories, nor the weapon being developed."

Like Colonel Lockhart, Steve was choosing his words carefully. Without allowing a pause in case he was interrupted, the DCI carried on. "In any murder enquiry, the first 24 hours are usually vitally important, but in this case, because everyone on site is in lockdown, the killer must still be among the staff. My two officers will conduct a thorough investigation and report in, hourly, if necessary, but I'd have a lot of confidence in them finding your killer."

Steve sat back and caught Alfie's eye. The Commander nodded.

Sir Patrick and the colonel looked at each other. Colonel Lockhart shrugged his shoulders and nodded.

"Commander Brooks, does this proposal fit with your orders?"

"It fits in as much as I was ordered to give you our full cooperation. DCI Burt has explained to me the situation that means he should not be absent in the short term, and I think his proposal is sound. If I were you, gentlemen, I'd grab it."

Colonel Lockwood was about to speak when his mobile rang. Within seconds, Sir Patrick Bond's mobile also rang. Both men answered and as they listened their faces became grimmer and more serious. They both hung up simultaneously.

Colonel Colin Lockhart stared at Steve. He looked sad. "Steve, they've just identified the body at Station K."

The colonel knew he'd stated the name of the top-secret establishment but felt Commander Brooks was not a risk. He carried on. "It belongs to a Corporal Edward Hicks of the RAF." Colin Lockhart paused before announcing. "Corporal Hicks is in fact Captain Alex Hope of the RMP, your old commanding officer's son."

Chapter Twenty-Nine

Silence filled the air in Alfie's office. Everyone present struggled to take in this information especially the DCI. "I suppose you have a positive ID?"

The colonel looked at Steve sadly. "Yes, the RMP took fingerprints, and we now have a match from the military database. There's no doubt the body is that of Captain Alex Hope."

Sir Patrick spoke up as a way of filling the silent void that once more descended on the room. "As the victim is your old commanding officer's son, does that change anything as far as your willingness to travel to Wetherby?"

"No. I'm needed here for the reasons you know about. Peter Jones and Matt Conway will handle things well enough. However, they'll need a forensic team and a medical examiner." He looked at the Commander.

"I can sort that. Forensics always have a team on standby including a pathologist."

Alfie looked quizzically at his two visitors. "How do you propose to get our people to your site? I understand it's in Yorkshire."

Colonel Colin Lockhart wasn't too happy that Alfie had this information, but realised it was inevitable given the circumstances. "I'll arrange for a military helicopter to take them to the site." Addressing the room in general, the colonel carried on, "Can you have all your people at Biggin Hill aerodrome tomorrow morning at 07:00hrs?"

Steve and Alfie exchanged glances, but both said yes.

Sir Patrick and Colin Lockhart stood up and Sir Patrick spoke for both of them. "Thank you for your assistance gentlemen. This is a serious national emergency and with your help, we can nip whatever is going on in the bud. Please keep me informed, Steve, as your investigation progresses. A lot depends on finding this killer for obvious reasons."

Steve nodded his agreement. "Just one thing, Colonel. I'd like to break the news to Alex Hope's parents. I think it might be better coming from me."

Colonel Colin Lockhart was not by nature a sensitive or understanding man, but on this occasion, he saw the sense in Steve's suggestion. "Yes. I'll hold off any formal statement for twenty-four hours. That should give you enough time."

Once again, Commander Alfie Brooks realised he was out of the loop. He wasn't pleased but realised he had to accept it.

Once both men had gone, Steve and Alfie resumed their seats. "Right, Steve my boy, you'd better get your troops lined up. I'll call out forensics and the pathologist." Without waiting for confirmation, Alfie punched the numbers into his phone.

Steve called Peter Jones first. The DI eventually answered, just as Steve was beginning to think he wasn't home.

"Peter, it's Steve. Listen, something big has come up and I need you to be Senior Investigating Officer on a murder at a military base in Yorkshire, near Wetherby. I want you to take Matt Conway, and Peter, use Matt. He's more experienced and a good copper. You're to be at Biggin Hill aerodrome this morning at seven a.m. There'll be a military helicopter to fly you to the site. A forensic team and a pathologist will travel with you but remember, you're the SIO so take no nonsense. Call me when you get there, and I'll brief you on what I know. Is that clear?"

Peter Jones was now fully awake. "Right you are, Steve. How long will we be away?"

"Until you catch the killer. I'm tied up here on something else but if you're still working on this in the next 48 hours, I'll probably join you."

"Right. Will you call Matt, or should I do it?"

Steve had thought he would call the DS, but on reflection thought Peter as SIO, should do it.

"You call him Peter. You're the SIO but remember to call me as soon as you land." Steve was about to hang up when he added, "Sorry to ruin your beauty sleep."

The DCI looked at his watch. It was now 03.54 on Sunday the 29th of March.

The DCI arrived home at just after 4.30 a.m. only because, at that time in the morning, the streets were deserted. He quietly opened the front door and removing his shoes, climbed the stair to the family home. He had already decided not to return to bed for fear of wakening his wife. Instead, he settled into an armchair and was quickly asleep. He thought back to the time he spent most of his sleeping hours in an armchair with usually a bottle for company. He gave a sigh thankful those days were behind him.

He was roused from his slumbers at nine a.m. by his wife holding a cup of tea and their daughter.

"You look terrible. What was all that late-night mystery call about?"

Steve took his tea and placed it on a side table. He reached up and took his daughter, kissing her forehead and laying her on his shoulder.

"Sorry darling, it's something I can't discuss, but it was important. All I can tell you is at some point I'll have to call Robert Hope and tell him his son has been murdered."

"What! That's terrible. The poor man will be devastated. What happened?"

"I'm not sure but I've sent Peter and Matt to the scene so I should know more later today."

"You mean it didn't happen in London?"

"No. He was killed at a top-secret base in the north. The full team are being flown there by military helicopter; I presume by the RAF."

Steve looked at the time. He handed Rosie over to her mother and gulped his tea. "I'm sorry darling, but I have to go. Mary's coming in at ten and we have an interrogation to get through. Then there's something else I have to do so I may be late home tonight."

Alison, holding her daughter, gave a sad smile as she spoke to her daughter. "You see Rosie, your daddy's a busy man but we both hope he doesn't burn himself out, don't we?"

Steve kissed his wife tenderly on the lips and his daughter on the top of her head. "I'll be home as soon as I can. Promise."

***

As Steve drove to his office, Detective Inspector Peter Jones and his team were circling Montgomery Barracks. The RAF pilot was looking for a safe landing spot and after a few circuits of the base, he smoothly landed the great twin-bladed Chinook helicopter to the east side of the camp.

During the flight, Peter had decided this was his chance to prove his worth to the DCI. As SIO he would have a high profile and would be noticed by other senior officers. As a graduate entrant, his career was only assured to a certain level. Attainment of rank above his present grade of inspector would be based on merit and competence. The DI was determined to get a result.

After landing, the team of three forensic technicians plus the pathologist, together with the two policemen, were escorted by a sergeant to the entrance to Station K. Peter was amazed at the security protocols but insisted the system be overridden to allow his team easy access. This caused a bit of a problem and was only solved when the head of security agreed, based on the fact that none of Peter's team could possibly have anything to do with the killing and that the weapons system was of no interest to them.

Once inside Station K, however, the full lockdown protocols were once more instigated meaning no one could now enter or leave. The DI and his DS went immediately to the office of Professor Symonds. An army captain was with him. The head of security made the introductions as Peter decided how to begin his investigation. The forensic team and the pathologist were seated in the canteen area awaiting instructions.

Peter addressed himself to the RMP captain. "Tell me what you have done so far."

The captain was about Peter's age but looked out of his depth. He seemed a bit hesitant. "Well, you know I only have four officers?" Peter didn't answer.

Just as the captain was about to carry on, the MI6 agent known as Hector Forsyth entered without knocking. He quickly introduced himself and sat in a corner chair.

Peter turned his attention to the captain once more.

"Well, Mr Forsyth explained who he was and told me to search the premises. You know, everywhere."

Peter interrupted. "Everywhere is a big place, Captain." The captain had been introduced as Horace Dunn. He was about Peter's age and given his rank and obvious schoolboy demeanour, the DI guessed he was also a graduate entrant into the military. "Where exactly have you searched and what were you looking for?"

"We searched all the common areas and then all the occupied bedrooms. Mr Forsyth told us to look for anything that obviously didn't fit. The people who work here aren't allowed things like mobile phones or iPads so that's what we were looking for."

"I take it you didn't find anything?"

"No."

"When you searched individual bedrooms did you take out the drawers of any cabinets and turn them upside down?"

"Well, no."

"And you didn't search the empty bedrooms?"

"Er. No."

"Did you search the toilets?"

"Well yes, but there's no place to hide anything there."

"What about the cisterns?"

"No, we didn't think about that."

The SIO began to pace. Remembering the DCI's words and advice about using Matt Conway, Peter approached him. "What do you think, Matt?"

In a low voice, the DS replied. "It's a bloody shambles. We need to search again."

"I agree. Can you take Captain Dunn and his men and supervise a proper thorough search?"

"No problem."

Captain Dunn had heard Matt's remarks. "Now listen here Inspector, I'm not Special Investigation Branch. SIB are the Army's detectives. I'm not trained to search; I'm uniform, so please don't judge us on this. We were only posted above ground as extra security if we were needed."

Matt examined the captain. He thought, *Just like the police, bloody graduate entry and no clue.*

The SIO ignored the army captain's protest. "Right, Sergeant Conway, get the search underway."

As the two men left, Peter turned to the MI6 man. "Where is the body now?"

"It's in one of our walk-in freezers. It was empty as we don't go through the volume of food we used to when we had a full complement of staff."

Peter was relieved that at least any forensic evidence on the body should have been preserved.

"Professor, we have a Home Office Pathologist with us. Do you have a medical centre he could use to examine the body?"

The Professor wasn't listening but was playing over and over in his head just how this could have happened. He jumped at the use of his name. "Oh! Sorry, I was miles away. Yes, we have an infirmary. I'm sure it would be perfect for your purposes, Inspector."

"Good. Can I ask you to please go to the canteen and speak to our pathologist? Show him the location of the freezer and the infirmary. I presume you have medical staff on-site?"

"Yes."

"Can you please allocate one of them to assist our doctor?"

The Professor stood and with a slightly unsteady gait, he made to leave and carry out the SIO's instructions. "Yes of course." The Professor left.

Peter was left alone with the MI6 man. "Any thoughts?"

"None, I'm afraid. Like the Military Police contingent, I've no experience. I was sent here to ferret out a traitor, but I haven't been able to do that. Our hope is that the killer and the traitor is one and the same."

Peter knew nothing of traitors or spies but wasn't going to admit it. "Let's go and gather up our forensic team and perhaps you can show me where the body was found and where the victim worked."

"Of course."

Detective Inspector Peter Jones, now the SIO assigned to the murder of Captain Alex Hope, Royal Military Police, followed the man from MI6 into the canteen feeling he had made a good start. Now he could call the DCI knowing things were in hand and the investigation was underway.

***

Steve Burt was surprised to find Poppy and Mary Dougan in the office. Mary, he knew would be in, but Poppy had no reason to be at work today.

Seeing his confusion and before he could say anything, Poppy volunteered "I know I'm on a day off, but I knew you would be in, and I thought you might need me."

Both female detectives were drinking coffee and on seeing Steve's look, Mary piped up "There's one on your desk sir."

The DCI mumbling his thanks, retreated to his inner office for a few minutes of quiet contemplation. As he sat behind his desk, thinking of the day ahead and the phone call he had to make to Alex Hope's parents, Poppy and Mary uninvited appeared at his door.

"When do you want to get started with the Blade downstairs?" Mary was obviously keen to get started.

"Better have him taken to an interview room. Also, ask if he wants a lawyer and get a copy of the doctor's report from yesterday."

Poppy who was dressed in a loose-fitting shirt and jeans held up a piece of A4 paper. "The doctor's report is here, sir."

The DCI was again amazed at Poppy's efficiency and approved of her off-duty attire. "Thanks, Poppy."

DC Mary Dougan left to arrange for the interview of John Stuart McKelvey, saying she would see her senior officer in fifteen minutes.

Poppy remained. "We have the forensic report through from the search of the guy's boat. I knew you'd want it before you got started."

"Poppy, you're a gem."

Poppy playacted giving a sweet, shy smile. "A gem with a new wardrobe for the office. I spent a good part of yesterday after I left shopping for clothes."

The DCI was a little embarrassed. "I thought women liked shopping."

Still stifling her laughter, Poppy carried on. "I've put the forensic report into the system, but you should know they found a flick knife that they say could match the wounds on the victims, although a pathologist would have to check, plus there was congealed blood on the blade. They found several specimens, meaning he has used the knife a few times to draw blood, but they found samples that match our two victims. Also, his prints are all over the knife."

Steve was about to speak but Poppy carried on. "They also found blood inside a coat pocket that matches that of the second victim, Cameron Bowie. They say it's probably when he folded and put his knife in his pocket, the blood still on the blade transferred to the inside of the pocket. Either way, the lead technician on the forensic team says you've got your man."

Steve sat back. "Thanks, Poppy. Really good work."

"There's more. Uncle Terry wanted to see you when you came in. He's in his office but I called him and he's on his way."

"Wow. You *have* been busy."

As if on cue, Inspector Terry Harvey appeared holding a map like a sheet. "Good news I hope, Terry. Your niece has just got the day off to a bright start." Poppy blushed and retreated to her desk in the outer office.

Terry placed the map on Steve's desk and walked around to stand beside him. Both men looked at the map. It was clearly a scaled map of London inside the M25. Three circles had been drawn on the map, but no circle intersected another. Steve wondered what he was looking at but saw the circles were not connected.

"What you are looking at is the locations of the three mobile phone masts that had hang-up calls at exactly the same time as the call from your Voice man yesterday."

From his seated position, Steve looked up at Terry, willing him to carry on.

Using a pencil, Terry crossed out one circle. "We know the number and the owner of the phone that used this mast. He's respectable and over sixty. I'd wager this is not the mast you would be interested in."

Terry similarly used his pencil to cross out the second circle. "Again, this was a registered phone and unless your Voice is a twenty-two-year-old prostitute he didn't use this mast."

Terry was being very deliberate, ensuring the DCI understood the implications of what he was saying. "This third mast is the only one in the whole of the Greater London Area that cancelled a call at exactly the time your Voice hung up, and it was from an unregistered phone. A burner phone if you like."

Steve was in awe yet again of Terry's skills and his deviousness. Only a near-genius could have thought of this approach.

"So, you're saying our Voice made the call from within this circle?"

"Yes, but again, I'd wager he not only made the call, but he lives inside that circle. After all, it was ten in the morning and there's no background noise on the recording. He was inside when he called."

"I can see the area covered includes Buckingham Palace and the Houses of Parliament."

"Exactly and it's the smallest geographical area covered by any mast in London. You're looking at no more than half a mile in any direction from the mast. It's sited above Victoria Station."

Steve considered this and stood up. He walked to the far side of his office and spotted Poppy standing in his doorway.

"Poppy, have you been earwigging?"

"Sorry boss, but yes. After all, I'm officially not here."

Steve laughed. As he returned to his analysis of Terry's information, Poppy spoke.

"I could call up the electoral roll for the area inside the circle sir. We might get a known criminal on it or at least, there might be a name of interest."

Again, Steve was impressed. "Good thinking Poppy. Get to it, but Poppy, please don't listen in on our conversations. This was a mild rebuke, and the DCI wasn't sure it would have any effect. Poppy, he concluded, was Poppy. Steve looked at his watch. He was late to meet Mary, but he had more to do before he started interrogating the Blade.

He called the interview suite. "Sorry Mary, I've been held up. Give me another few minutes."

"No problem, sir. He's asked for a solicitor, and he hasn't arrived yet."

Steve closed his door in the hope Poppy was too busy researching electoral roles to listen in, even through a closed door. He smiled to himself as he thought he'd never had this problem before. An overeager detective constable!

He dialled Commander Alfie Brooks at home. He explained he intended to interview Superintendent Blackstone in the afternoon.

"I'll tee up Kit Carson, but you know, Internal Affairs will have to be seen to take the lead."

"Yes, Kit said he would sit in on the interview."

"Listen, Steve, accusing a senior officer of anything at any time is a dangerous thing. Are you sure you have enough because, if he walks, your career is as good as over?"

It was a sobering thought, but the DCI knew he had to carry on.

"Thanks, Alfie but yes, we have to see this through."

"Very well. I'll talk to Carson and ask him to bring Blackstone in. I presume you only want an interview under caution?"

"Yes."

"OK, be on standby. I know you're tying up the double murder this morning and you've got your team on the cloak-and-dagger job up north. What time do you want to start with Blackstone?"

"Better say around three o'clock. That should give me enough time and remember, it was you and Superintendent Carson who wanted any enquiries into Blackstone kept under the radar so I'm on this by myself."

"Yes. I know and I'm sorry, your workload is horrible, but you brought the MI6 thing on yourself." Alfie paused. "Look, Steve. Let's get through the day and we'll talk tomorrow. I'll come in later just in case you need anything."

The DCI next dialled the number of ex-Major Robert Hope. As it rang, he wondered how he would open the conversation. Robert Hope answered on the fourth ring.

"Ah! Steve, we were just going out to the local garden centre. You just caught us, what can I do for you?" The Major was very bubbly and bright.

Steve started to speak. Afterwards, he couldn't remember exactly what he said or how he phrased the sentences that told a doting father that his only son had died in the service of his country. Steve recalled he'd not mentioned murder until near the end of their conversation. As he was ready to hang up, a tear appeared in the corner of the DCI's left eye. "Your son's body should be brought down within a few days. A full post-mortem will be needed. I'm sorry Bob but it's standard procedure."

Once he'd finished, a mental picture appeared in Steve's mind of an elderly couple who, a few minutes ago, had been so excited about a visit to a garden centre, now sitting in their lounge, still wearing their outside clothes, contemplating life without their boy. Steve wished he could have delivered the news in person, but Major Hope lived in Wiltshire and with his caseload it was impossible. He just hoped he'd delivered the news as kindly as he could, and he knew the Army would send someone later in the day to help.

As he sat behind his desk, the DCI's resolve hardened, and he vowed to get everyone responsible for the death of Captain Alex Hope, especially the Russian MI6 and Military Intelligence were so concerned about.

Chapter Thirty

DI Peter Jones hadn't exactly followed the DCI's order to call him as soon as the team arrived at Station K. Peter thought it best to make a start and then contact his boss. From the only outside line within Station K Peter sat behind Professor Karl Symonds desk and dialled Steve's number.

"Steve, it's Peter. Sorry I've taken a while to get to you, but I thought it best to make a start and have something to report."

"Fine. What do you have?"

"As you might expect, not much. First, the pathologist has examined the body. He'll do a full post-mortem in London, and I've arranged for the helicopter we came in to transport it and the pathologist back down later today. His initial examination shows it was a severe blow to the back of the head that was the cause of death. He says it's a funny shaped wound and might have been caused by the body falling backwards onto something solid and sharp. The good news is he got skin samples from under the deceased's fingernails so we might get DNA. That can be tested in London tomorrow."

"Good work, Peter. What else?"

"The RMP contingent isn't really up to police work. They said they'd searched the place but to be honest, it wasn't much of a search. I've got Matt showing them how to carry out a proper search. They're looking at all the individual bedrooms, then the common areas including the toilets and then the offices and workshops. I've had the staff corralled in the canteen for the day while we search again."

"Right. Anything else?"

"The forensic lot are searching, looking for a likely crime scene, but they've a lot of places to look."

"Yes. It's quite a task. Anything else?"

"No. Not really."

"I'm told there's an army camp above ground called Montgomery Barracks."

"Yes."

"Do the underground staff get out to go above ground at any time?"

"Yes. The head of security told me they are allowed above ground to visit the shop to buy newspapers and the like, but they are strictly monitored in and out and are electronically searched both ways." Peter was curious. "Why?"

"Just a thought, but if you were our killer and knew you'd be searched in and out you might have stashed something above ground when you first arrived. A mobile phone for example. It's probably worth a look when the below ground search is finished. If we're lucky we might get prints."

"Right. Good thinking, sir. I'll get the lads onto it when they're done here."

"Good man. Now listen Peter, what I'm going to tell you is breaking the official secrets act but you need to know a few things."

DI Peter Jones was intrigued. He listened intently while Steve broke the law.

"You're in an underground weapons research facility called Station K. They've developed a new and secret weapon that's due to be moved to a test site on the first of April, in three days. MI6 and Military Intelligence believe a spy has been planted to either steal the weapon or the plans for it. Without telling MI6 another agent was placed within Station K to try and unearth the spy. That person was your dead body. He was posing as Corporal Edward Hicks of the RAF. He was in fact Captain Alex Hope of the Military Police. The current thinking is he discovered the spy and that's what got him killed. We think the spy and the killer is one and the same." Steve stopped his briefing and carried on.

"Has there been any attempt to steal the weapon?"

"Not that I'm aware of."

"So it's likely he's after the blueprints. He might have managed to smuggle in some kind of camera. I'd concentrate the search for that. Have the staff been physically searched yet?"

"No. That's the next thing once the team has finished searching the premises and now the above-ground camp."

"Right. Peter be careful; if we're right, this spy is dangerous. The good thing is he's locked down so can't escape but he might get desperate so watch out. You and Matt are still needed here when you've finished your Yorkshire holiday."

"Some holiday. I'll call you later in the day."

The line went dead. The DCI decided his DI had done everything he would have done. He could do no more.

A few minutes after speaking with Peter Jones, Steve met Mary outside interview room six. He handed her the file and explained the forensic team's findings.

"He's got the duty solicitor in there and I've copied the doctor's report and given him a copy." Mary sniggered like a schoolgirl. "The duty solicitor looks as though he's been brought out of retirement. He could be a hundred years old."

The DCI shrugged and thought what the younger officers might think about his age. He deliberately stretched to his full height and puffed out his chest. He told himself he only looked his actual age of forty-four but knew he was deceiving himself.

Sitting on the opposite side of the standard table that was screwed to the floor, Steve looked at his prisoner with a studied eye. He glanced at the solicitor and agreed with Mary's assessment of his age. The duty solicitor was dressed in an old tweed suit and was slouched in his chair. He gave the impression that he didn't want to be here and given the size of his belly he might be worrying about missing his lunch.

With the formalities covered, the DCI began the interview.

"How are you feeling this morning, John?"

"No comment."

"When I saw you yesterday you were a bit hungover. You must have had a really great party the night before?"

"No comment."

Steve moved in his chair. "OK, if you want to play the no comment game, we'll just get you charged with two murders plus any others we can link you to."

Like all professional criminals, John Stuart McKelvey had been through the system and thought he knew how to handle himself in these situations. He knew 'no comment' meant he couldn't be tricked into incriminating himself.

"We have enough to get a conviction, John. You can help yourself by telling us what you know and who put you up to the killings."

"No comment."

"John! You're an old hand. You know juries usually convict when they hear me tell them that you refused to cooperate. We have you bang to rights for the murders, but a bit of cooperation now might persuade the judge to go easier on you."

The Blade sneered. "No comment."

"Have it your way, but just so you know, Eddie Randall has admitted to paying you to carry out the killings. Also, we have DNA from the second victim on your knife and inside the pocket of your jacket, and just to round it off, we found DNA from your first victim inside your knife." Steve paused and stared at the Blade. "So, you see John, you've nowhere to go. With your record and certain conviction for these two murders, you'll be a very old man when you get out this time."

Steve knew the tactic of reminding suspects of the consequences of their crimes usually brought a response even from someone using 'no comment' as his answer. This was no exception.

The Blade was clearly thinking and hadn't jumped in with his predictable response. He realised the police had the evidence to convict him and he didn't fancy spending longer inside than he had to. His brain was whizzing, looking for a way out but finding there was no reprieve. He surmised that on balance he'd better cough up.

"OK, but I want a deal."

Steve was happy to be making progress. "Tell us what you know, and we'll see. You know we don't do deals, but I can have a word."

John Stuart McKelvey looked long and hard at both the DCI and Mary who had her notebook out and had already made a few notes. The Blade looked at his solicitor who seemed to be asleep. The duty solicitor simply nodded.

The Blade sighed and asked for a cup of tea before beginning.

"It was Eddie Randall what asked me to do the first murder. He said it was a mate of his, but he'd been told by some geezer with a funny voice to get rid of the poor sod. The bloke's name was Vinnie McGuire. He seemed a nice guy. I'd seen him around a few pubs, so it was easy to get close to him. I just got him a bit drunk one night and offered him a run home in the van I'd borrowed from Eddie. I stopped behind a row of shops that was on his way home. That's where I done him. He didn't know a thing."

Steve interrupted. "How did you kill him?"

"Oh! I slit his throat." The Blade stopped his tale to think. He contorted his face in the process before adding. "Funny thing. Eddie wanted the body kept so he could bandage it up like. You know, one of them Egyptian mummy things." The murderer shrugged and continued. "I took the stiff back to Eddie and that was me done. See I only gets paid, when the job is done."

It never failed to amaze Steve how hardened criminals often saw nothing wrong in committing their crimes and showed no remorse when telling their stories.

John Stuart McKelvey's tea arrived. He took a sip and carried on with his narrative.

"The second geezer were a bit different. Eddy said he was told to kill this car dealer out by Mile End Road, but it had to be public." The Blade paused to sip his tea and think. "See, I prefer to be a bit discreet like. You know, nothing too showy, but Eddie says the body has to be found in public and in his showroom."

The Blade was warming to his tale. "Well, that's not easy, so Eddie has these two idiots stake the place out so we know the geezer's movements. I tell you, Mr Burt, these two clowns almost landed me right in it. They're bloody useless but I suppose that's another story." John McKelvey drank his tea before carrying on. "It was easy like. I just went into his office and stuck him near his heart, straight in and out. He fell back into his big fancy chair, and I was gone."

"And it was Eddie Randall who ordered the killing?"

"Yeah. He got a package in the post. It had a photograph and all the details. Eddie likes to play the big man, but I knew somebody else was giving the orders and providing the cash."

Steve knew he'd get no more from the Blade. He now had all the confirmation he needed, and nothing that had been said changed his working theory that the two killings were connected by anything other than the actual killer.

The DCI nodded to the uniformed officer who was standing by the door. "Take him back to the cell." The Blade and his elderly solicitor left. Steve sat back as Mary put her notebook in her handbag.

"That's it, Mary, as far as it goes. We can get the whole bunch charged. John Stuart McKelvey with the two actual murders; Eddie Randall with the same murders and conspiracy plus car theft and the two idiots with conspiracy and aiding and abetting. I need you to pull everything together and get it over to the CPS as soon as. Poppy can help with the documentation. Get the lot of them over to Central and see when you can get a court date. They'll all be held without bail."

Mary Dougan had reclaimed her notebook from her handbag and made notes. "Right boss, well done. That's a double murder solved, and I think the charges are watertight. We've got confessions from the lot of them."

"Yes, you're right, but we don't have the main man, this Voice."

***

It was after two o'clock when Steve got back to the office. Mary was now processing the prisoners and wouldn't return to the office today. Poppy was still at her desk typing away furiously at her keyboard. She looked up as he arrived and followed Steve into his office.

"I've got the electoral roll as I said. There's a lot of important people live in that area but none of them jumped out. I did a database search and apart from a few speeding fines and a couple of driving under the influence, they're all clean." Poppy stood by the open door as though she had more to say. Steve recognised the signs.

"Go on Poppy. What else have you done?"

Relieved that the DCI had opened the door for her, Poppy continued. "I asked Uncle Terry what he would do to try and narrow down the list of people living in the area of the mast."

"And your Uncle Terry suggested what?" Steve didn't like where this conversation could go.

"He said he would check their financial records. Look for mysterious money appearing in their accounts. He said if any of them are this Voice then there must be a money trail."

Once more Steve admired how Terry Harvey's brain worked. He relaxed a little thinking this was a good idea but he'd no idea how to get the information until Poppy spoke again, this time a little sheepishly.

"Terry suggested there is a computer programme that would throw out the data in hours even though we need to look at well over 20,000 bank accounts. He said that Financial Crimes could help so I've e-mailed Florance Rough and asked her if she could help."

This was the news Steve didn't want to hear. Digging into the financial records of some rich and influential people could cause all sorts of problems. Whilst he admired Poppy's initiative, he knew such a decision had to be his. He remained calm.

"Well Poppy, that's very good, but don't you think you should have discussed it with me first?"

"Absolutely sir!" Poppy obviously felt the best form of defence was attack. She was standing upright full of self-confidence. "I know the decision on things like this has to be yours, that's why I only asked if Miss Rough could help. She's not in today but will get the e-mail tomorrow."

Steve relented. "OK, Poppy. It's a good idea but we'd better see what Flo thinks before we push any buttons." Steve needed to think. "Can you give Mary a hand with the paperwork on the double murder case tomorrow? If you're staying just now maybe you can make a start. You know the thing, big files for the CPS and the DPP." Steve threw a tape cassette at Poppy. "That's the interview with this character who calls himself the Blade. Get it transposed and include it in the files."

Poppy nodded and as she left, Steve called out, "Shut the door behind you please. I need to think."

Left alone, the DCI once more mentally went over his caseload. He knew the double murders were now done. They had all the players except the main man, this Voice. Thanks to Terry Harvey they knew the area the Voice had called from yesterday at ten a.m. It was a fair assumption that he had called from his residence meaning he lived within the circle on Terry's map. Poppy had the electoral roll list so all they had to do was identify a name. Steve puffed out his cheeks. He knew this was impossible but if Twiggy really could identify and interrogate the bank accounts of everyone on the electoral roll, they might get lucky if this Voice was moving money.

Steve's mind drifted to Superintendent Blackstone and his upcoming challenge. He was convinced Blackstone knew the identity of the Voice and that's why he was a target for the Blade. But would Blackstone talk, and what was the connection to this Russian Vladimir Skoysky? Did Blackstone know the Russian or only the Voice?

As Steve sat pondering, he had a sudden flash. What if it was the Russian who was giving this Voice character his instructions? What if the Russian had something on a high-ranking official? After all, the Russian gang was new to London and would need a member of the establishment to smooth the way for them. Steve's brain was in overdrive. What if it was the Voice who ordered the killings only to protect his anonymity and he and the Russian were involved in the Station K spy thing and that's why MI6 were supposedly keeping tabs on the Russian?

The DCI pulled out his phone and dialled Sir Patrick Bond, the Head of MI6. He didn't answer which was no surprise. It was after all nearing three o'clock on a Sunday afternoon. Steve left a message asking Sir Patrick to call him.

DCI Steve Burt stood and stretched. He knew he was tired, and he felt dirty. He realised he'd slept in the clothes he was wearing and hadn't shaved. He once again thought back to his life before he was drafted in as head of the Special Resolutions Unit and smiled. He was reliving old times.

Chapter Thirty-One

The Voice sat in his home office in his luxury apartment which was a stone's throw from the Houses of Parliament. Crammond Gardens was a block of eight upmarket properties that had been redeveloped only three years ago. As he sat at his desk catching up on his legitimate work his burner phone rang. He knew immediately it was Vladimir. He thought about not answering. It was three o'clock on a Sunday afternoon. It would be perfectly legitimate to be taking leisure time. This thought only lasted a few seconds before he knew he had to speak with the Russian.

"Is everything ready?" Vladimir didn't waste time on small talk.

"Yes. As far as I know. I've heard nothing to suggest we are not ready."

"Good. I just wanted to check."

The Voice liked to hear the uncertainty in Vladimir's voice.

"Everything's fine. The thugs will collect the weapons and ammunition from your boys as planned. They are driving the route this afternoon to be sure they have everything covered." The Voice was lying. He'd told Blackstone to survey the route but hadn't heard back.

"OK. Have you heard from our man inside the place?"

"No, but he said he wouldn't be in touch until he had the whole plan." The Voice detected an ongoing edge to the Russian's voice. Calming words of reassurance didn't seem to be working.

The Voice tried to sound confident, but it was a confidence he himself didn't feel. "Look Vladimir, so far everything's fine. Don't worry, I'll call you when I hear something."

"Good." The call was broken off.

The call brought the Voice back to thinking of the wealth that awaited him. He fantasised about large boats and pretty girls, about expensive holidays and a villa in the Caribbean. As he thought about his future, he realised his present might be in danger. He knew the plan to heist the weapon was not well thought through and he didn't trust

Vladimir to pay him. He'd ordered Eddie to kill Blackstone next week after the heist and that at least would protect him. He smiled as he thought no one knew who he was. His dark side had kicked in more often of late and still, he was invisible. With Blackstone gone, he could relax.

He turned once more to the papers on his desk and carried on doing his day job. He put his dark side back into its box.

***

As the Voice was trying to reassure the Russian, Steve walked into the reception area of the interview suite under New Scotland Yard. He was met by Commander Alfie Brooks and Superintendent Kit Carson. Without any formalities, Kit Carson as Head of Internal Affairs opened the conversation.

"We lifted Blackstone just after lunch. As you can imagine he's not happy. We also did a preliminary background check." The Superintendent handed Steve a slim file.

"We didn't have much time but what's in there is quite revealing. It's clear he's living beyond the means of a superintendent. Neither he nor his wife comes from money, and it seems he has no other source of income that might explain his lifestyle. His house is valued at over a million and he has two classic cars registered to him plus a new Range Rover."

Steve was perusing the file while Kit Carson continued. "We'll get more background stuff tomorrow, but I'm satisfied that apart from what you have, we have sufficient grounds for this interview today."

All three policemen were standing outside interview room three. Steve had scanned the file whilst listening to the Superintendent. He felt confident with the contents and saw how he might frame the interview.

"Right Steve, I'm going to observe from the observation room. You and Kit will take the interview." Alfie, dressed in his tweed suit and looking like an out-of-work farmer, smiled fondly at the DCI. "He turned down the offer of a fellow officer to be with him, but he has called in a high-priced lawyer. They're in there now." Alfie started to leave, heading for the entrance to the observation room of interview room three. "Good luck."

Kit Carson and Steve watched the Commander leave.

"Now Steve, you know the drill. Under the rules, you cannot ask him any questions. Only someone of his own rank or senior can do that but I'll explain it's me asking the questions, but I've delegated the job to you. We usually get away with it but this one's a bit different. I just hope his brief agrees."

The DCI nodded and both men entered interview room three.

As they were about to sit in front of Superintendent Blackstone and his expensive-looking lawyer, Steve's mobile sounded. He quickly snatched it from his pocket realising he should have switched it off before entering the interview room. He glanced at the screen. It was Sir Patrick Bond.

"Excuse me, sir," Steve said to Kit Carson. "I'm sorry but I have to take this. It's important."

Outside in the large reception area, Steve explained where he was and what he was doing.

"My reason for calling was to see if you still had the Russian Vladimir Skoysky under surveillance?"

"Yes. Of course, but he hasn't made any moves."

"How long have you been tailing him?"

"I don't know exactly but over three weeks. Why?"

"It's just a hunch but I think it's possible my murder case and your spy case might be linked. I can't say too much now but could you get any surveillance video or pictures over to me first thing tomorrow?"

"Well… as it's you, I suppose I could but what are you looking for?"

"I'll tell you when I see it." The DCI hung up and re-joined Superintendent Carson.

Once the formalities had been satisfied and Superintendent Carson had explained Steve's role, the interview began. Steve had never met Superintendent Colin Blackstone before but on first inspection, he concluded this was an arrogant but self-confident individual who was too well dressed to be a policeman. His sports jacket was tailored to fit as was his shirt. His hair was immaculately groomed, and Steve noted his fingernails had been professionally cut and polished. The DCI decided his best technique would be to catch Blackstone off guard.

"Who do you work for, Superintendent?"

Blackstone wasn't expecting this. He knew Steve Burt by reputation and knew he was a formidable foe and he'd have to be careful, but this first question was unexpected. He'd role played this meeting in his head and this question hadn't been considered.

Stalling for time, Blackstone answered, "I beg your pardon?"

"It's a straightforward question sir: who do you work for?"

"Well, if I may say so, Superintendent Carson, this is a silly question that doesn't even deserve a response."

Steve noted that Blackstone had replied to Kit Carson who sat stone-faced and said nothing.

Steve held his tongue as Blackstone turned to his lawyer.

The lawyer spoke with the clipped upper-class tone of a public-school education. "I believe my client doesn't understand the question."

The DCI launched in. "Oh! I think he does. He's not stealing cars himself and standing down the tracking system himself, so someone must be employing him. So, I'll ask again, sir, who are you working for?"

Steve noticed sweat beginning to form on Blackstone's upper lip. The arrogant policeman of a minute ago didn't look so sure of himself.

"I don't know what you're talking about."

"Oh, come sir." Steve tapped the thick file he'd brought with him. Under it was the thinner file prepared by Kit. "In this file, I have all the evidence I need to show you must be taking orders from someone." The DCI produced a series of photocopied sheets. "This is an e-mail from you instructing Edgar Wilson of the National Trace company to close down his operation."

Steve placed it on the table in front of Blackstone and explained the coding system that was only shown on the recipient's copy. He then produced a second paper that Poppy had prepared. "This shows the makes and models of three very expensive cars that were stolen while the tracking unit was shut down on your orders."

The DCI produced a second similar combination, then a third. "Every time you ordered National Trace to shut down, high-end cars were stolen never to be seen again. A bit of a coincidence, don't you think?"

Blackstone was now on more comfortable ground, although he didn't know about the codes on his e-mails.

"I can explain all that. We had very sensitive operations going on and the tracker system interferes with our CCTV and other listening devices; it's all above board. As to the stolen cars then yes, it must be a coincidence." A satisfied smile appeared on Superintendent Blackstone's handsome features.

"We have a sworn statement from Edgar Wilson, the Managing Director of National Trace, that it was you personally who phoned, telling him to restart operations. We've worked out the timeline and your call always came after cars had been stolen and the trackers deactivated."

Blackstone was again suddenly on the defensive. "Another coincidence." He hadn't been subjected to this type of interrogation before and found the constant switching of topics disturbing.

Steve changed tack again, knowing he had Blackstone on the defensive.

"What do you know about a car showroom called Crystal Motors on Mile End Road?"

Blackstone answered too quickly. "Nothing."

"What do you know about the murder of the proprietor of that showroom?" Steve knew he didn't have anything to back up this question but felt it might upset Blackstone.

It did.

"Murder! Are you mad?" The sweat on Blackstone's upper lip was back. "I know nothing about any murder."

"Then why did you put a stop on our Technical Support unit from accessing the CCTV tapes from opposite the murder scene?"

"I didn't; don't be silly. Why would I do something like that?"

Suddenly, Steve knew he had him. "I have a sworn statement from Inspector Harvey, Head of Technical Support that says that's exactly what you did. You've lied to us, sir, and I'm sure you're astute enough to see why we think someone told you to withhold those images, and that brings us back to the first question. Who are you working for?"

"I've told you, no one."

Once again, the DCI changed direction.

"Is the person you're working for the same as the person who is paying you?"

Superintendent Blackstone began to realise this interview was turning against him. He needed time to think but this DCI kept throwing more seemingly unrelated questions at him.

"I've told you…" Steve noted Blackstone was now avoiding eye contact. "I'm not working for anybody nor am I receiving money from any other source than the Metropolitan Police."

Steve knew Blackstone was crumbling.

"How do you explain your house move approximately twelve months ago from a three-bedroom semi-detached property in Acton to a one million four-bedroom detached villa in Chigwell?"

"None of your business." Blackstone now had beads of sweat on his forehead.

"We haven't completed our financial checks, but we know you should not be able to afford the Chigwell property on a superintendent's salary especially as the land registry shows it was a cash transaction. Also, there's the question of your two vintage sports cars and the new Range Rover you bought last month. Unless you've found a money tree, I think you need to explain where the cash came from." Steve allowed a sarcastic edge to enter his voice.

Blackstone sat back and remained silent. His head was in a spin as he searched for a way out. The DCI was relentless. "Do you know a Thomas Moore?"

Again, Blackstone answered too quickly.

"No."

"You may know him as Tommy Moore."

"Never heard of him."

"Strange, because our technical wizard whom you threatened when he asked for the CCTV output from Mile End, looked into Tommy's mobile and found you had called him on Thursday the 26th and the call lasted four and a half minutes."

"I can't remember." Blackstone was tiring and was making mistakes.

The DCI sat back preparing to hit the Superintendent with his coup de grace: the contract to kill Blackstone.

The room filled with silence until the DCI spoke again.

"Look, sir, I'm only interested in finding the person responsible for ordering the killings. Personally, I'm not interested in a car-stealing ring or you making a bit on the side—"

"Just a minute Inspector. I'm your senior officer and will not be spoken to like that!"

Steve shrugged in a theatrical way and carried on. "As I said, my interest is in finding this Mr Big and I think you can help."

The DCI turned to Kit Carson. "I'm sure Superintendent Carson and Internal Affairs could find a solution to your present predicament if you were to cooperate and give us the name."

Blackstone glanced at his solicitor who didn't acknowledge him.

Steve carried on. "This person you work for has a reputation for removing people who know his identity. We believe our first victim was killed for exactly that reason." Steve paused to remove the photograph the Voice had sent to Eddie Randall. "We intercepted an envelope yesterday addressed to Eddie Randall. We know he is the person your benefactor goes to when he needs something done. He's ordered another killing of someone who knows him."

The DCI paused and slowly turned over the photograph. Blackstone immediately recognised himself. All colour drained from his face as Steve continued.

"The instruction is to kill you after the 1st of April. Any reason for that?"

Blackstone was in shock. His hands were shaking, and his stomach was doing somersaults. He couldn't focus and appeared to have difficulty breathing. Without thinking, he blurted out, "That'll be because of the ambush."

The Superintendent didn't realise he'd spoken. He started to cry and put his head in his hands.

Superintendent Kit Carson spoke for the first time. "We'll leave it there for now. We'll get you a cup of hot tea." He indicated to Steve that they should leave.

Alfie Brooks was exiting the viewing room as the two detectives entered the reception area.

Alfie was grinning. "Well done, Steve, that was about as good a penetrating interrogation as I've seen."

Kit Carson chipped in. "Yes, Steve, well done. You've got him, but now we need to decide what to do next."

Steve thought for a moment. "I think we should hold him overnight and start again tomorrow. I know it's not normal and we haven't arrested him, but we could hold him in protective custody. We know there's one contract out on him but there could be more."

Kit Carson liked the idea. "Let's do it. I'll take the flak if his lawyer cuts up rough. Let's say we reconvene here at ten tomorrow morning."

It was agreed and as Kit left to make arrangements, Steve and Alfie went home.

***

As he was climbing wearily into his car, Steve's phone sounded.

"Evening sir. It's me, Matt."

"Hi, Matt. How's it going?"

"The body and the pathologist are in the air as we speak on their way to London. The pathologist says he'll do the full post-mortem tomorrow morning. He has the nail scrapings and says they'll be processed overnight for DNA. We should get something by midday tomorrow.

"Good. Anything else?"

"Yes. The forensic boys think they've found the murder site. Peter Jones is with them now. They've found blood splatter in one of the workshops and blood on a lathe. The working theory is that there was an argument and our victim either fell or was pushed and caught his head on the edge of the machine frame. I've contacted the local force so you may be getting a call. We need their lab to confirm the blood matches our victim. I hope that's OK, sir?"

"Yes. Yes. Good thinking, Matt. What else?"

"We found technical drawings stuffed behind a cupboard in the same workshop. According to security, they should have been locked in the vault that our victim was found in. The workshop is the domain of Staff Sergeant Robert Tay of the Royal Engineers. Can you call up his service record?"

Steve made a mental note as Matt carried on. "We've finished the internal searches and we'll start above ground tomorrow, then we'll conduct individual strip searches of the staff."

"Good work, Matt. I'll call in the morning with this soldier's particulars and keep me posted. I've got Military Intelligence to keep sweet."

The DCI set off for home after a very long but productive day. He had no idea what tomorrow would bring but felt his search for the Voice was almost over.

Chapter Thirty-Two

The DCI had no problems sleeping on Sunday night. Having arrived home before eight, he had his evening meal, showered and went straight to bed. He slept for ten hours straight and had to be woken by his wife otherwise he would still be asleep.

Monday the 30th of March had dawned bright but cold. Steve hardly noticed the weather as he walked to the Yard. His mind was on the day ahead and his hope that Blackstone would crack and give him the name of the Voice.

As he walked, his mobile sounded. It was Peter Jones.

"We've found a phone up top. It was hidden under an airshaft. God only knows how the search team found it, but Matt had them at it since the crack of dawn. The forensic guys have it and are dusting it for prints. They'll get them to Poppy."

"Good. When they're finished get that phone down here pronto. I want it with Terry Harvey ASAP."

"Got it. I'll lay on a motorbike. Should be with Terry by lunchtime."

"Right. Anything else?" Steve felt he was beginning to sound like a stuck record. This seemed to be his only question.

"Yes. I've declared this place a crime scene, so it's now shut down for the duration. I've posted extra bodies at the exit. I've told Professor Symonds he can't move his weapon out on the 01st of April unless we have the murderer in custody."

"Good work. Anything more?"

"No. The teams are still searching above ground. The blood forensics took from the kill site is with the local lab. We should get something within the hour."

"When you do get the results to Poppy. She'll confirm if the body is Alex Hope although, with a fingerprint match, it must be."

Peter detected the sadness in the DCI's voice.

Steve arrived in his office at 08.51 a.m. Mary was busy at her desk as was Poppy. The DCI walked into his office to find an internal envelope sitting in the centre of his large blotter. He cautiously opened it and sat down. A scowl appeared on his face as he thought this was no way to start the week. It was a note from Human Resources reminding the DCI he had been invited to sit on a House of Commons Committee and the Commissioner was keen he should accept. It went on to remind him he was invited to attend a drinks party at the House of Commons as a guest of the Chair of the Committee on Policing, a Mr Malcolm Freeman. It said several senior police officers had also been invited and he was ordered to attend.

The DCI screwed the paper into a ball and threw it into his wastepaper basket. "Bloody cheek! As if I didn't have enough to do."

Poppy appeared bearing a gift of a cup of piping hot coffee. "Miss Rough's on her way to see you and I've completed the electoral roll check."

No sooner had Poppy spoken than Twiggy appeared. Steve had to admit she was much trimmer than a few years ago but Twiggy would never be slim.

Looking at Twiggy reminded the DCI he hadn't noticed what Poppy was wearing. He quickly realised this must be a good thing, otherwise, if she were dressed oddly, he would have noticed.

Twiggy sat and eyed up her ex-boss. "You look terrible. I hear you've been putting in the hours."

"The workload just now is horrible. I just have to work through it."

Twiggy, or Miss Florance Rough, got straight to the point. Steve recalled this was one of her annoying habits when she was first assigned to the Special Resolutions Unit on its creation. He sat back enjoying his coffee.

"I got an e-mail from your girl Poppy. She said you might need some financial background checks."

Steve explained the case to Twiggy. How Eddie Randall didn't know the identity of his controller and how Terry Harvey had cleverly discovered the area where the Voice almost certainly lived. "Poppy got the electoral roll for the area and hit on the idea that our man might be involved in illegal financial transactions."

"Good thinking. Usually, these high-power criminals do it for the money and it has to be moved."

"Right, but here's the problem. The area is one of the most upmarket and expensive in London. It not only covers Buckingham Palace but the Houses of Parliament. The residents include cabinet ministers, judges, celebrities and editors of national newspapers. I'm worried that if any of them discover we're looking into their bank accounts I'll be on point duty until I draw my pension."

Twiggy smiled as only she could. Her face lit up with that smile.

"Don't worry. We can interrogate remotely but we'd better get a warrant." Twiggy had a sudden thought. "There are no Treasury politicians on your list are there?"

Steve handed Poppy's research's over. Twiggy scanned the names and looking up gave out a soft whistle. "I see what you mean." She stood full of purpose and folded the list into her handbag. "I'll get a warrant and let you know. It may take a while though."

Steve held up his hand. "Anything you can do can only help."

***

As ten o'clock rolled around, Steve was alone in the interview suite's reception area. After a few minutes, Commander Alfie Brooks and Superintendent Kit Carson arrived together.

The interview of Superintendent Blackstone was reconvened and commenced at exactly 10.12 a.m.

Steve started straight away. "Well, sir, have you had time to think?"

A more belligerent Blackstone faced them today. "Go to hell." It was clear a night in the cells hadn't softened him up.

Steve now tried the nice cop approach.

"Look sir, whatever the reason you are sitting here, you know what you could be facing. You've seen the evidence. The fact you called Tommy Moore from your own listed cell phone was stupid and ties you in to the car-stealing ring. That, in turn, ties you in to Eddy Randall who ordered the killings of our two victims and that means we have you on a conspiracy to murder charge."

Steve leant forward putting on his most friendly face and in a soft voice continued. "All that can go away if you give us the name of the person you work for. You don't owe him any loyalty. For Christ's sake, he ordered your murder. Superintendent Carson will work something out with you to minimise the damage you have done to yourself. All we need is a name."

Blackstone sat back and looked at his lawyer who nodded. It was clear Blackstone was tempted but surprisingly said, "No, not until I know what's on the table."

Kit Carson, as head of Internal Affairs, signalled that he and Steve should leave. Outside, Kit got straight to the point. "How badly do you need this Voice character?"

"I believe he's behind the killings and the car-theft ring." Steve stopped to consider how much else to say. He decided to tell as much as he could. "There's something else. I'm afraid I can only tell you so much as national security is involved but I believe this Voice is being controlled by a Russian who may be responsible for another murder involving the son of a friend of mine. Getting the Voice is the main objective, but MI6 are after the Russian and I believe there is a connection."

"You realise we'd potentially never prosecute Blackstone?"

"Yes." Steve had a sudden brainstorm. His memory banks went into overdrive. "What did he say last night when we told him he was on a hit list? It was something about an ambush."

Both men looked at each other. The DCI carried on. "Maybe he has more to tell us. Maybe you can leverage more out of him in exchange for a deal?"

Kit Carson's eyes lit up. "Let's go back in and find out. You lead as before."

Once everyone was seated Steve opened the interview again. "Anything to tell us now, sir?"

Blackstone looked to have a cunning glint in his eye. "I'll give you the name and I walk out of here. I resign from the Force on medical grounds and with a full pension. There will be no reprisals and I keep my assets and money."

"That's one heck of an ask, sir, but if you also tell us about the ambush, I'm sure your request could be considered."

"What ambush?" Blackstone in his shocked state the previous evening had no recollection of saying anything about an ambush.

"You mentioned an ambush when I showed you the note saying you were to be murdered only after the 1st of April."

"No comment."

This sudden refusal to talk when a deal was potentially on the table told Steve there was something very serious going on. He looked at Kit who nodded Steve should continue.

"Look, sir, you know we have you and you'll probably get five years. As an ex-superintendent five years in prison will not be a happy experience. We can cut you a deal, maybe even the one you've asked for." Steve felt Kit Carson wriggle in his chair as he lied. "But we need it all. Otherwise, there's no deal and you will come out of prison a broken man."

Steve sat back, letting his words sink in.

Blackstone whispered to his solicitor who whispered back. After a few whispered exchanges, Blackstone seemed to come to a decision. "I'll tell you everything including the ambush, but I want a legally notated document confirming my deal before I say anything."

The DCI didn't think this unreasonable in the circumstances. "If we agree you must realise that if the information you give us is false or out of date then your deal will be off?"

"Yes." Blackstone was once again the smug, arrogant police officer that Steve had first met.

"You know I can't authorise this? I'll have to take it upstairs."

Superintendent Carson looked pleased despite the circumstances. As Head of Internal Affairs, he had taken part in ferreting out another corrupt officer. That was his job, not obtaining convictions.

Blackstone was returned to his cell as Kit Carson went to arrange the paperwork for the deal. Alfie Brooks left the viewing room and he and Steve went to the canteen for a coffee. Kit would call when he had everything in place.

**

At Station K, Staff Sergeant Bobby Tay was a worried man. He'd carried his camera with him since finishing photographing the entire set of blueprints plus the log. He'd been lucky so far but had heard everyone was to be strip-searched. He knew he had to get the contents of the camera out. But how?

He had been locked down with his fellow staff members and held in the canteen since the arrival of the team from London. If it were just the MPs conducting the enquiry, he would feel better, but this London lot seemed to know what they were doing. Bobby Tay consoled himself, sure they couldn't trace the murder to him. His concern was the camera.

He knew all the common areas had been searched and cordoned off except one toilet. As the staff were all men, this was considered workable and secure. A plan was developing. If he could find a polythene bag he could place his camera in it, make an excuse to go to the toilet and put his phone in the cistern before the body searches began. It wasn't perfect but at least they wouldn't find the camera on him, and he could retrieve it before he left Station K.

He had heard the transportation of the weapon had been delayed. His fellow comrades might never get their hands on the actual weapon. He pondered this and concluded that the images in his camera were even more important than ever. He had to get them out.

***

Steve was in his office chewing over what he knew when his phone rang.

"Did you get the images?" It was Sir Patrick Bond.

"Not so far. When did you send them and where?"

"They went about twenty minutes ago and were addressed to your assistant Amelia Cooper."

"Ah! Poppy. If they had arrived, I'd know about it. Give it another ten minutes and I'm sure they'll be here."

"Remember you getting them is highly unusual. There aren't many pictures I'm afraid. Most of our reports are verbal. Our Russian has led a quiet life of late, hardly going out. We've tried to monitor his phones but with all these unregistered phones, it's near impossible to track who he's talking to."

"Don't worry Patrick. It's a long shot but it's worth trying. I'll let you know."

Steve next called Colonel Colin Lockhart and as promised gave him a briefing as to events at Station K. The colonel said he was grateful but in true military manner, was all business and didn't sound overly grateful to Steve's ear. Steve noticed when he had returned from his coffee with Alfie that Mary wasn't at her desk. As he was thinking this, she appeared at his door. She was smiling and Steve thought it was good news. She closed the door and sat.

"You know there are few secrets in this office sir?"

"Yes, but that's how I like it."

"Even when it is supposed to be a secret?"

The DCI was following but didn't fully understand. "Go on."

"We know about the body in Yorkshire and that the DI and Matt Conway are there now. We also know the body has had its post-mortem. Poppy has the results, the pathologist thought you'd want them."

Steve was amused by the cloak-and-dagger. Even by the closed door. Mary carried on. "I went to the lab to speed up the DNA results."

"What! How the hell did you know about that?"

"I just did, sir. I've got the results and Poppy ran them against the military database. I've just been upstairs to collect the results. The skin fragments under your victim's nails belong to a Staff Sergeant Robert Tay of the Royal Engineers."

Steve wasn't happy that Mary knew so much about a top-secret operation but was pleased by her initiative. He also thought Poppy's eavesdropping talents had been put to good use. He smiled.

"There's no doubt?"

Mary handed over the certificate confirming the DNA match.

Steve wasn't about to congratulate his DC on her initiative. She had, after all, overstepped the mark.

"Thanks, I'll pass this on to Peter." Without smiling, as a way of showing his displeasure, he angled his head toward his door.

A slightly contrite Mary Dougan left without the praise she had hoped for.

The DCI dialled Peter Jones. "The DNA from under the victim's nails is a match for a Staff Sergeant Robert Tay."

"Really!" Peter sounded pleasantly surprised. "The crime scene is his workshop. That's where we found the blood."

"If we're right and the killer and the spy are one and the same then you have your man. DNA evidence isn't easy to wriggle out of. I'd say this Staff Sergeant is our…" Poppy was at Steve's door looking flushed and urgent. "Hold on, Peter."

Steve looked expectantly at Poppy. "The techs sent through the fingerprints from the phone Peter found, you know, the one that's being sent down by fast bike? I ran them against all military databases. They belong to Staff Sergeant Robert Tay." Poppy nodded to the phone in Steve's hand. The DCI knew she'd been earwigging again but despite his annoyance laughed.

"Thanks, Poppy. Peter, are you still there?"

"Yes."

"Poppy has just confirmed that the prints on the phone you found hidden above ground belong to the same guy. With the DNA match as well that's enough to arrest him for murder. Get him and your team back here as soon as. Leave the forensic boys behind if they're not finished but I want that guy here. Be careful Peter. We don't know how dangerous he is."

Steve hung up. He felt he was getting close and went out to check on Poppy and Mary.

***

"I went shopping Saturday afternoon. I hope this is what you call more suitable sir?"

Steve knew better than to comment as Poppy carried on. "It cost me a fortune. I bought five outfits just like this one but in different colours. I've a good mind to put them on expenses!"

"You can try Poppy and I'd sign it, but I fear it wouldn't be approved by upstairs." The DCI decided to carry on, hoping to clear the air with Mary. "You both look very nice and do the women's detective branch proud."

Both lady detectives grinned at each other.

Just as Steve was about to re-enter his office, a police motorcycle rider arrived with a parcel containing Staff Sergeant Tay's illicit phone. Wasting no time on ceremony, Steve told Poppy to log it in and then immediately headed for Tech Services and Inspector Terry Harvey.

"Terry, I need you to interrogate the log on this phone. I need to know who was called not just the number called. Can you do that?"

"You know we can. I suppose you want it yesterday?"

"You know me, Terry. If it wasn't urgent, I wouldn't ask."

With a promise from Terry that he'd get the information as soon as was possible Steve returned to his office. He revisited the two murders. He had the culprits in custody and charged. Mary was completing the files for the CPS, but no one saw any problems with the case. All four suspects would be in court later in the day and the DCI knew, bail would be denied. He allowed himself a sly grin as he remembered Blackstone had all but admitted he knew the Voice. If Blackstone talked, the DCI would have the Voice. He didn't know where this would lead but Blackstone had spoken about an ambush. There was clearly something afoot and it involved the Voice and Blackstone.

Just as Steve was nodding off, comfortable in his large chair, his internal phone sounded. It was Kit Carson. "Right Steve. We're on. Downstairs in five minutes."

The DCI roused himself and looked at his watch. It was 2.18 p.m.

The by-now-familiar interview room was manned as before. The formalities having been completed, Steve took up where he left off. Kit Carson handed Blackstone's lawyer the agreement not to prosecute in exchange for information. The lawyer read it, noted the caveat concerning the accuracy of the information and nodded to his client.

The DCI began. "Right sir. Your solicitor seems satisfied, so the floor is yours. Let's have it."

Blackstone was back looking like his old arrogant self. He told himself he'd won and was happy to cooperate, but he still wanted to look good.

"I'm not a corrupt cop, at least I didn't start out that way. This MP approached me over a year ago. I was involved in a surveillance job in the Houses of Parliament, and we caught this guy doing something he shouldn't have been doing with his secretary. It was only a minor thing and didn't affect why we were there." Blackstone sat back recalling the events. "For some reason and I suppose for a bit of fun, I showed him the footage. The guy is always on TV, you know the type, holier-than-thou in public and on the box but getting his leg over on the side. As you can imagine, he wasn't too pleased to see himself on film. He offered to buy the tape and pay me to keep quiet." Blackstone looked at his inquisitors with a small smile creasing his face. "It was easy money and there was no harm, so I took the money. What I didn't know was he recorded our conversation and a few months later he called me, told me he needed some dirt on a political colleague and played the tape over the phone." Blackstone was now in the groove. His narrative was flowing. No one spoke.

"That's how it started, small favours, then bigger ones, but each time the favour got bigger, my payments also became bigger. Soon I was earning more from giving this guy information than I was getting from my police salary. The car-stealing ring was my biggest payday. I was told a Russian had approached him and told him to make sure cars could be nicked safely. It would be about three to four high-end cars a week. He said I was his fixer and I had to fix this." Blackstone was trying to frame himself as the innocent party.

"I had no choice. I knew these cars would have trackers, so I simply got in touch with the tracking company and told them to close down their operation while the cars were being stolen." Blackstone looked directly at Steve. "I was a bit shocked when you produced the e-mails and told me they had been traced to my computer, very clever."

He paused the story to gather his thoughts. "Anyway, that's how the car thing started. I was getting well paid. He told me about the murder of Cameron Bowie at Mile End and that he was doing it on behalf of a Russian who was setting up an operation in London. That's when I knew I had to get out. I told him it was trouble and when you closed down the workshop, he had me send Tommy Moore to that car lot beside Heathrow to fix the trackers."

Blackstone leant forward and talked in a softer voice. "But when he told me he needed a group of heavies to ambush a military convoy, I told him no. I said he was going too far. Unfortunately, he's not the kind of guy you say no to once he's got you. He said it would be the last thing he'd ask me to do."

Steve decided he had to break Blackstone's concentration. "What military convoy and what ambush?"

This intervention threw Blackstone momentarily, but he soon recovered his composure. He explained about the telephone conversation with the Voice and his reluctance to get involved. He told Kit Carson and the DCI that all he knew was that a secret weapon was being transported to a test site and it was to be stolen. "He said it had to be at least three heavies who didn't mind shooting and that the Russian would supply the guns."

"When is this to happen?"

"The ambush is set for the day after tomorrow. Wednesday the 1st of April." Blackstone wasn't aware of how important this information was to Steve as he carried on. "It's to happen up north around Wetherby. The gang have a spot picked out on the route the convoy will travel. They're going to nab the weapon soon after it starts its journey."

From the expression on the DCI's and Superintendent Carson's faces, Blackstone realised they knew nothing about this.

Steve had to get out of this interview and get in touch with Colonel Lockhart as soon as he could. However, he still hadn't heard the name.

"OK, sir. We've got that and you've got your amnesty. Now, who is this Member of Parliament you've been working for?"

When Steve heard the name, his heart missed a beat.

Steve sat through the formalities that Superintendent Carson was duty-bound to perform and when Chief Superintendent Charles, head of the Met's Human Resources Unit arrived, Kit and Steve left. They stood outside the interview room.

"I hope you got what you wanted?" Superintendent Carson was looking serious.

"Oh yes, sir, and more."

"You know who this MP is?"

"Yes, I do." Steve looked at his watch. "I'll have to hit the phones and pass on the info on the ambush. I promise I'll give you the full story when I can, but you have been a great help, sir."

Steve rushed off, satisfied he could now close the case.

317

Chapter Thirty-Three

The DCI didn't go directly to his own office, but to that of Commander Alfie Brooks. Alfie hadn't been in the observation room for the second interview with Blackstone and Steve thought he should be put fully in the picture.

Once Steve had finished briefing his senior officer, Alfie stood, flabbergasted at the revelations. He slowly analysed the implications of what he'd been told as he paced his office.

"You're saying you've got Blackstone to confess in exchange for immunity to prosecution and he's given you this Voice person plus the scheme to steal the weapon developed at the top-secret station where your old company commander's son was murdered?"

Steve knew Alfie was running everything through his brain and the question didn't need an answer, but he replied "Yes."

"And this Voice is involved in the car thieving ring and the heist of this weapon?"

"Yes."

"And the ambush is to take place this Wednesday the 1st?"

"Yes."

Alfie sat down. He was clearly taken aback at the news and the speed of events. "You are sure you've got this spy for Sir Patrick and he's the killer up at Wetherby?"

"We know he's the killer, whether he's the spy, well that's for Sir Patrick, but it seems likely. Peter Jones should be here with him any time soon."

"It's your show, Steve. Tell me what you need?"

"Thanks, Alfie but I'm not sure. I'm still working it out and where jurisdiction lies. All I know is I want the Voice and the Russian. Everything else isn't any of my business so I need to pass the information on. I've got the names of the three heavies Blackstone has hired for the heist. The problem is the Russian is supplying them weapons and ammunition. If we lift them too soon, he'll realise the game is up and might do a runner back to Mother Russia."

"Agreed, but if you wait too long before doing anything, the whole lot might disappear. Remember, if you've got the spy, the Russian might find out and run anyway."

Alfie looked concerned. "Steve?" He had a pained expression on his face. "I know you want to tie everything up, but you've solved the murders, you've got the culprits behind bars, why not hand this over to someone else?"

"It's tempting, sir, but the main culprit is still out there, and the Russian is responsible for the death of Alex Hope. Unless you order me to hand this over, I'd like to see it through."

"You're either a brave lad or a fool, DCI Burt, but whichever it is, time will tell. Keep me posted." Alfie stood up and formally extended his hand to be shaken. "Good luck."

Steve hurried to his office to find Twiggy and Terry Harvey waiting. His mind fleetingly pictured the pair walking down the aisle but quickly dismissed such images. He knew he had to stay focused.

Twiggy spoke first. "I've run that search of the bank accounts of people on the electoral roll Poppy gave me."

Steve was still standing as were his guests. "And?"

"There's one who stands out. Lots of money movements to and from dubious sources. The name on the accounts is—"

Steve answered before Twiggy could say whose account it was. "Malcolm Freeman MP."

"How the hell did you know that?"

Steve gave a quick laugh. "As Mary Dougan said earlier today, I just do." Twiggy placed a large file on Steve's desk.

"If you're so bloody clever, I presume you don't need me to tell you whose details were on that phone you gave me?" Terry Harvey was joking and seemed to be in a good mood.

"Unless I'm wrong, the only number that was dialled from that phone has been traced back to a Vladimir Skoysky."

"Christ. How do you do that? You're absolutely right, but also absolutely wrong. The Russian's number is registered to him, but your spy also called a burner phone." Terry looked smug. "I took all the phone numbers we have for these cases and guess what?"

Terry didn't wait for a response. "The burner phone number that your Voice used to call Eddie Randall is the only other number this spy of yours phoned using this phone." Terry held up the evidence bag containing Staff Sergeant Tay's illicit mobile.

"Good work Terry, so we now have a link between the Voice and Staff Sergeant Tay and a further link between the staff sergeant and the Russian."

"Looks like it to me."

Steve sat behind his desk and considered this new information. He knew it was important but stored it in his brain to be used later. He told Terry and Twiggy what he could of the events of the day so far. "So you see, what you have given me is corroborating evidence. The DPP will need it all."

Terry sat and looked at Steve. "What are you going to do?"

"I'm going to ask Poppy to get me a coffee and sit here and think."

***

As Steve was sipping his coffee and thinking, Matt Conway and Peter Jones appeared. Both looked tired and slightly untidy. "We've got Staff Sergeant Tay downstairs. He's been tight-lipped so far. All he says over and over is one day the world will belong to all of us." Peter and Matt exchanged knowing glances. "I think he's a nut job."

"Could be Peter, but he's a nut job who killed the son of a friend of mine."

Once more Steve explained the happenings of the day and once again received the same response. "What are you going to do?"

"Keep your man Tay on ice downstairs. I'll let you know."

Steve returned to his coffee and his thoughts. He examined all the options and soon realised he needed not only help but advice. He called Sir Patrick Bond, Head of MI6.

"Patrick, we've got your spy."

Sir Patrick was taken by surprise at this stark statement. "Not over this line Steve. Come to my office now if you can."

"You'd better get Colonel Lockhart to join us. I'll be there by five o'clock." As Steve put the phone down, Poppy and Mary stood in his doorway.

"The four prisoners were remanded and are being held in Broadmarsh. The CPS says we have more than enough. They've got the full case files so there's no more for us to do." Mary looked tired but Poppy in her new clothes looked ready to party.

Steve's admin assistant added, "Of course that is unless the events of the day throw up more evidence against this Voice and Eddie Randall."

The DCI saw the two ladies glance at each other, and smile conspiratorially. Poppy had been earwigging again and sharing her news with Mary.

"Poppy, I swear I'm going to have this room soundproofed."

He had too much on his mind to be angry with her. "In answer to your question, no, it's unlikely we'll be adding to the files on the murder case as far as our four prisoners are concerned."

Steve stood up. "I have an appointment at five, but I suppose you already know that?" The question was directed at Poppy who simply looked down at the ground and said nothing.

***

Steve arrived at Sir Patrick's MI6 office at exactly 5.07 p.m. He was greeted by Sir Patrick and Colonel Colin Lockhart. Both were seated in the comfortable club chairs favoured by whoever furnished senior civil servants' offices and both were drinking whisky. For once, Steve accepted the offer of a 25-year-old single malt. He told himself he had earned it.

"We have the person we think is your spy in the holding cells below the Yard. He's also the person who killed Captain Alex Hope. We have more than enough to charge him with murder and that's as far as I'm going. Spying charges are down to you."

Steve had decided to feed his information slowly to the pair in order they fully understood the complexity of the case and how he intended to deal with the suspects.

"Well done, old boy." Colonel Lockhart of Military Intelligence was glowing at the news, as was Sir Patrick.

"Thank you but you should know I intend to charge him as a civilian. He's a murderer and will do his time in a civilian prison."

Colin Lockhart looked at Sir Patrick. "Well Steve, I think you know we will have to speak to him, interrogate him even. Find out what he knows, who he's working for, that kind of thing, so maybe you can hold off doing anything rash."

"Colonel, I've stated my position. Once he's been charged and is in the system then of course we can't stop you questioning him but he's my prisoner."

Sir Patrick admired Steve's calmness and his actions. He had outflanked the soldier from Military Intelligence and the Head of MI6.

"I can see you have more, Steve." Sir Patrick sipped his whisky while Colin Lockhart fumed.

"Yes, I do, Sir Patrick." Steve paused. "Your spy is called Robert Tay. He's a staff sergeant in the Royal Engineers. We're doing background checks now. He had a mobile phone that he'd stashed above ground in Montgomery Barracks. We found it and interrogated the memory. He only ever called two numbers and one of the numbers belongs to your Russian, Vladimir Skoysky. We've a direct link to the murderer and the Russian."

The DCI had decided to hold back the information on Malcolm Freeman for now.

Colin Lockhart spoke but was rushing his words. "But you're not going to arrest him I hope?"

"Not at the moment, but we have another connection that could involve the government." Sir Patrick was all ears. Any mention of government involvement frightened him.

"We had a case of two murders that we traced back to a couple of low life want to be gangster types. They are on remand and that case is closed. However, during our investigation, we discovered that one of our senior officers had a connection to the person who had ordered the two killings."

Steve paused again hoping his audience of two were following him. Satisfied they were, he carried on, "This officer has taken a deal and has given up the person he was working for. That person is Mr Malcolm Freeman MP, Chair of the All-Party Committee on Policing."

Sir Patrick took a large pull of his whisky. "Dear God! Are you sure?"

"Absolutely. We believe Malcolm Freeman has been involved in criminal activities for some time now and has had people killed to preserve his anonymity. As a result of our investigations, we've established a link between Malcolm Freeman and your Russian, Vladimir Skoysky."

Steve waited before continuing, knowing his next statement would shock the pair.

"The other number on Staff Sergeant Tay's phone has been traced to Malcolm Freeman."

This blunt statement seemed to paralyse both men. Their mouths opened to speak but no sound came out. The DCI continued. "That's a direct link between a Member of Parliament and a spy who has a connection to a Russian mobster."

While his audience was clearly in a state of shock and both seemed deep in thought, Steve went on to explain how he had examined the photographs taken by MI6 when they were shadowing Vladimir. He explained there was a shot of the pair talking inside a coffee shop. "That's our first link. The second is much more conclusive." Steve suddenly realised he hadn't taken any of his whisky. He took a mouthful, letting the golden liquid slide down his throat before continuing. His audience was spellbound.

"Based on the evidence from the mobile phone your spy had stashed inside Station K, we believe he got word to both Vladimir and Malcolm Freeman telling them that the weapon was to be moved on Wednesday of this week." Steve spotted the two men glance at each other.

The DCI was firmly in control. "Malcolm Freeman ordered our bent senior officer to hire three seriously violent criminals to intercept the convoy transporting your weapon and hijack it. The real connection is that the Russian is supplying the guns to carry out the heist and the weapon is to be delivered to him." Steve sipped his whisky.

"In other words, we have evidence of a direct link between Malcolm Freeman, Vladimir Skoysky and your spy, Staff Sergeant Tay. As your spy appears to be working for Vladimir it means that Vladimir is, at the least, an accessory to murder and probably a threat to national security." Steve awaited the reaction from his audience. There was none. Both men appeared still to be in shock or calculating how to resolve the issues Steve was presenting.

Steve, having thought through his options, carried on. "I'm going to arrest Malcolm Freeman for murder and conspiracy to commit murder plus bribing a public official and conspiracy to steal cars. He won't see the outside world for a very long time."

Before the DCI could continue, Sir Patrick spoke. "What about the Russian?"

"Despite your best efforts to thwart my investigation, I have his address. We're still looking at the connections but, once I have enough, I'll arrest him on conspiracy to murder, corruption and firearms charges."

"I don't suppose we can interrogate Malcolm Freeman before you charge him. After all, national security is involved and if he's been working with Russian agents, we need to know about it." Sir Patrick was now fully focused.

"As I said, Sir Patrick, he'll be arrested and charged tomorrow morning. Like your Mr Tay, I can't stop you interviewing him once he's been remanded."

"When do you think you'll be ready to arrest Vladimir?" Sir Patrick was showing undue interest.

"Within the next 36 hours. My first job tomorrow is to arrest the three thugs and Malcolm Freeman. That means your weapon is safe. After that, who knows? We'll build our case against the Russian and go from there."

Sir Patrick refilled his glass and topped up the other two.

"Well Steve, it sounds like this country owes you a debt of gratitude. Our new weapon is safe, and you appear to have unearthed a spy and a murderer, uncovered a corrupt senior policeman and given us a headache concerning a Member of Parliament and a Russian mobster. I only wish you'd give us first crack at Mr Tay and Malcolm Freeman, but I see your point.

"As to Malcolm Freeman, I'd ask you to hold off until the Prime Minister is informed. There'll be a lot of damage limitation to be done plus of course we need to be sure Vladimir Skoysky is really involved.

I'm not sure if the case against Malcolm Freeman will stand on the murder charge but if he has connections to foreign governments, we need to know."

Steve smelt a cover-up was being hatched, so he stated his case. "Sorry Patrick, you can brief the PM and anyone else you want, but Freeman is being lifted tomorrow morning and I'll have his place under surveillance as soon as I leave here, just in case one of his government friends slips him the wink that we're on to him."

"Of course, Steve, nothing like that. We fully appreciate your position. It's protocol to inform the PM if bad publicity is coming his way."

Steve having briefed the head spy and the senior intelligence officer, left Sir Patrick's office with a nebulous feeling of doom. Something wasn't right.

Chapter Thirty-Four

On returning to his office, Steve briefed his team on the operation to arrest Malcolm Freeman the next day. "We'll go in at six o'clock tomorrow morning, the usual drill. Peter, I want you to arrange for a forensic team and a search team to be present, and can you also take care of the uniform presence? Matt, you and Mary will be with me and we'll carry out the arrest together. We'll all meet outside his flat just before six."

Everyone agreed and began to disperse before Steve called them back.

"We'll have to do this by the book and then some. Poppy, get a search warrant for Freeman's house and his office at the Houses of Parliament. This guy is an important figure, and no doubt has important friends so let's cover all of our bases."

As his team left, Steve phoned Commander Alfie Brooks and updated him on his meeting with the Head of MI6. "I can't explain it sir, but I don't trust Sir Patrick and certainly not that Colonel Lockhart. I'm sure I was given a polite goodbye before they started something underhand."

Alfie was quiet still digesting what the DCI had told him of his meeting. "You're absolutely sure you've got enough for this, Steve? Malcolm Freeman has a lot of friends in the force and they can hurt you."

It was clear to the DCI that his superior officer wasn't interested in his feeling that something wasn't right. He was more concerned about the possible repercussions of Steve's actions.

Saying good night, the DCI terminated the call.

With everything laid on for the morning, Steve left his office in New Scotland Yard at 8.22 p.m. and headed home.

***

At the time the DCI was leaving his office, Sir Patrick Bond and Colonel Colin Lockhart welcomed a guest at Sir Patrick's private members' club located in Jermain Street. The visitor, who had received the invitation less than thirty minutes before, was shown to a private room on the first floor.

Sir Patrick and the colonel had discussed the implications of the DCI's actions immediately he had left and quickly realised they could not allow everything Steve proposed to happen. Furious phone calls had been made after Steve's departure and senior civil servants, government officials, police officers and even a member of the American CIA had all been roused from their evening meals. A meeting of this very select and secret group was immediately arranged and took place in Sir Patrick's office less than an hour after the DCI left. Sir Patrick briefed the group and plans were put in place. The dark and dirty world of international politics and devious dealings all made in the name of national security and world peace was on show at this meeting. No one outside the meeting would believe what was being proposed. The American CIA agent had to obtain clearance from his bosses in Langley, Virginia before he could agree to the plan, and even they were surprised at what had been agreed within this group.

The most obvious result of this meeting was that the plastic camera that Staff Sergeant Tay had used to photograph the blueprints of the weapon was now in Sir Patrick's jacket pocket.

One of the people at the meeting was the Deputy Commissioner of the Metropolitan Police. Sir Patrick explained the plan in detail and the importance of the role he, as the Deputy Commissioner, had to play. Based on the agreed plan, the Deputy Commissioner had arranged for a runner to sign out the camera from the Met's evidence locker and had it delivered to himself at Sir Patrick's office.

"DCI Burt told us about this phone and its contents." Sir Patrick was talking with the Deputy Commissioner. "I appreciate your help and as I said it is a matter of national security. You'll be aware of the real world we work in and that sometimes we have to do things for the greater good." The DC nodded his understanding as Sir Patrick continued. "Your DCI Burt won't be happy about our course of action but I'm sure you'll be able to explain it to him."

There had been five people at Sir Patrick's meeting including the Deputy Commissioner and a senior civil servant from the Foreign Office. All five endorsed the plan and agreed it should be actioned immediately.

The visitor to Sir Patrick's club was impressed by its opulence and the very English feel. Once everyone was seated and drinks had been served, Colonel Lockhart opened the discussion.

"Mr Koptic, I'm pleased to be able to tell you that your investment in our new weapons delivery system has helped us develop the weapon." The colonel knew about the money Koptic had secretly given to the new weapon project and that, in return, he expected to receive supplies of the weapon.

Koptic, the Russian Arms dealer, gave a broad smile as he recalled his promise to the President of his country that he would deliver a new weapon, proving to everyone that he still had the technical ability to keep his country out front in the arms race.

"That is indeed very good news, Colonel." Koptic's English was only slightly accented.

Silence fell on the room. Koptic was quick to feel that something wasn't right. He decided to put the two men he'd come to meet to the test.

"My government will be delighted you have developed a weapon and even more delighted when we can take deliveries. After all, our money helped finance the programme and we have in effect already paid for the weapons we will receive."

Koptic knew that, by stating what had been agreed, he would require a response.

Sir Patrick sat back in his comfortable club chair. "What you say is correct, or at least it was when we last met. However, things change, and I have to tell you that you will not be receiving any of the new systems. Our government will not agree to an export licence for this weapon to be seen to be sold to your country."

Koptic was used to dealing on the international stage and knew how such games were played. Instead of becoming angry and accusing his hosts of dealing in bad faith, he simply smiled and sipped his drink.

When he spoke, his tone was very measured. "Gentlemen, you know that when you took our money there were no official pieces of paper. Why? Because you needed to keep such a transaction secret, and this suited you. Now it is time for you to honour your commitment, you are hiding behind official pieces of paper and export licences. This I understand and I also understand there are ways to meet your obligations without the need for pieces of paper."

Koptic sat back in his own comfortable club chair before adding. "So, I await your proposals."

Sir Patrick looked towards Colin Lockhart before speaking. He was rolling his brandy glass around between his hands.

"Very well put, Mr Koptic, but it doesn't change the fact that Her Majesty's Government cannot be seen selling weapons to your government."

Koptic was still smiling. "And the solution, Sir Patrick, is?"

Patrick Bond knew Koptic was a smart operator. He slowly produced the plastic camera from his jacket pocket. It was still inside the police evidence bag. He gently swung his arm sending the bag towards the Russian who caught it one-handed. Both men looked at each other although Koptic's face had a look of shock and lack of understanding. He looked quizzically at Sir Patrick.

"Contained on that phone are the blueprints for our weapon. The one you helped fund. We cannot be seen to export the actual weapon but in that camera is everything your engineers will need to build your own weapon." Patrick Bond sipped his brandy. "And I understand you already have the formula for the gas that is delivered by the weapon." Sir Patrick had no desire to prolong this meeting. He stood, offering his hand to Koptic. "I believe this concludes our business, Mr Koptic."

Koptic stood and shook Sir Patrick's hand. Colonel Lockhart remained seated. He didn't like the deal that had been agreed earlier and he didn't like Russians. He didn't mind being thought rude in the eyes of Koptic.

"I have your word, Sir Patrick, that everything is in this camera?"

"Yes, Mr Koptic, you have my word."

Sir Patrick touched a bell push and a white-jacketed steward appeared as if by magic. "Please show our guest out."

Koptic left holding the camera and the entire portfolio of blueprint drawings for the new weapons delivery system Captain Alex Hope had given his life to protect. The inner workings of the dark world of dirty politics and espionage had just made his sacrifice unnecessary.

***

Just before six a.m. on Tuesday the 31st of March, DCI Burt, accompanied by DC Mary Dougan and two uniformed officers, entered the luxurious apartment of Mr Malcolm Freeman MP.

Freeman had been in bed when the night porter on duty in the apartment block had phoned to say the police were on their way up. Malcolm Freeman, dressed in pyjamas and a silk dressing gown, answered the door as Steve rang the bell.

"Good morning Chief Inspector, it's a little early but you are very welcome."

Malcolm Freeman was very smooth. His accent was lush and was the sincerest voice he used when giving televised interviews. "How may I help you? Our drinks party isn't till this evening."

Steve wasn't persuaded by the smooth talk. He could see this man was worried.

"I'm sorry, sir, but your drinks party will have to be cancelled. I'm here to arrest you for conspiracy to murder and other as yet unspecified charges." Steve read Malcolm Freeman his rights. The prisoner chose to say nothing except to request he be allowed to get dressed.

Before Matt Conway, assisted by a uniformed constable, escorted Freeman to a waiting police car, Steve ushered him to one side. "Get him over to central booking and get him processed. I want you to stay there and start things off with our staff sergeant. He's had a night to kick his heels so hopefully, he'll want to talk." Steve considered his next remark. "Don't get dragged down the spy thing road. All we're doing is getting him on the murder charge and we're pretty solid. The spy bit is for others, not for us. Understand, Matt?"

"Yes. Got it, sir."

"Have Central ship Freeman over to us as soon as he's processed."

"Will do, Steve."

"Good lad and give Poppy a shout. Get her to sit in with you, it'll be a good experience for her. I don't think she's been to Central booking before." After Freeman had left, Steve and Mary began to look around the spacious apartment being careful not to disturb anything. Neither spotted anything that might be incriminating.

Inspector Peter Jones arrived with the search team and three forensic technicians who set to work immediately they arrived.

Talking to Peter and Mary, Steve said, "I think that went better than I'd hoped. Peter, you stay here and keep an eye on proceedings and then get over to his office. You may need to call in another search team. Mary and I will go back and start the interview, as soon as Matt gets our MP through processing."

***

Matt Conway was escorting Malcolm Freeman into the Metropolitan Police's Central Booking Station at the same time as two MI6 agents were knocking on the door of Vladimir Skoysky's rented villa in Hammersmith.

Vladimir was shocked to see the agents as he opened the door and learnt who they were.

"We'd like you to come with us please, sir." The senior agent had been briefed by Sir Patrick personally and wanted to make sure everything was done properly.

Vladimir was wearing boxer shorts and a t-shirt. "I'm not dressed and it's still the middle of the night. I don't get up until at least nine o'clock."

The senior agent noticed that he hadn't asked what this was all about.

"Please just get dressed, sir. We have orders to transport you to a meeting."

"What meeting?"

"I'm not at liberty to say sir, but can you please get dressed?"

The junior agent pushed past the Russian and using his outstretched arm, indicated that Vladimir should come inside and comply with the instruction.

As Vladimir was dressing, his wife arrived dressed in a floral dressing gown and offered the two MI6 officers, coffee. They declined but thanked her.

At 8.04 a.m., an MI6 pool car carrying Vladimir Skoysky drove away from his rented villa.

***

Steve and Mary were in Steve's office awaiting the arrival of Malcolm Freeman.

Steve still felt uneasy but couldn't tie his thought down. Mary had gone for two coffees from the canteen and both officers sat in silence, sipping the hot liquid and waiting.

Mary was reluctant to break the silence but had a question she needed an answer to.

"Sir, Malcolm Freeman, what do we actually have on him?"

"Good question, Mary." Steve sat back and placed his overly hot coffee on his desk.

"We know he's the Voice who gave instructions to Eddie Randall. From Eddie's evidence, we know Freeman ordered at least two killings. He didn't actually carry them out but by ordering them he's guilty of murder or at least conspiracy to murder. The DPP will sort that out. Then we've got Blackstone's confession naming Freeman as the person who issued the orders for the car-heisting business, and remember that Freeman, as the Voice, ordered the killing of one of the people involved in the car business." Steve sipped his coffee.

"Then we've got the connection to the Russian, the spy and the planned stealing of this weapon. We've got phone evidence that Sergeant Tay spoke to Freeman and Tay certainly killed Captain Alex Hope. I think we need to untangle a few things but I'm sure we have enough."

"Well, sir. It all sounds great but I'm glad I'm not leading the interview."

Both smiled and allowed silence to once more fall over them. The only sound was one of coffee being slowly sipped and enjoyed.

***

The MI6 pool car pulled into the underground car park of MI6 headquarters just before nine a.m. The two agents escorted Vladimir up to Sir Patrick's office where he and Colonel Lockhart sat in wait. After a few minutes of pleasantries, Sir Patrick got down to business. He'd never met the Russian and didn't like what he was seeing. The man looked evil, and his dark brown almost black eyes didn't help this impression.

"May I call you Vladimir?"

The Russian was worried. He now knew who he was sitting opposite and recalling what he had ordered, he knew this would turn out badly.

"Yes. Of course."

"Vladimir, we, and you, have a problem. Our wonderful police service is, as we speak, gathering evidence implicating you in the murder of a car dealer in Mile End Road and involvement in running a carjacking ring in central London."

Vladimir's face suddenly took on a sneer that really did make him look evil.

"Your Metropolitan Police can't prove anything. They are wasting their time."

"That's as may be, but they know about your involvement with one of our Members of Parliament, Malcolm Freeman."

At this statement, the Russian turned white. The sneer and confidence had gone. It was clear he hadn't expected this news. He sat still and didn't answer.

As if doing a double act, Colonel Colin Lockwood took over. "We have your man from inside Station K."

This bland statement sent Vladimir's mind spinning. He opened his mouth to speak but nothing came out.

"We also know of your plan to hijack our new weapon."

Vladimir could take no more news. He closed his ears and his eyes. He knew he was caught and could see no way out other than to deny everything and let the British prove his guilt. As he opened his eyes, he saw his two enemies smiling at him as though he were a naughty but likeable schoolboy. He sat in silence. He was stunned by this turn of events, but he couldn't fathom why his two inquisitors were looking so pleased with themselves.

Sir Patrick took up the interrogation. "Do you deny your involvement in a spy ring at one of our secret bases?"

"Of course I do." The Russian was delivering his strategy to try and survive this.

"Do you deny ordering Malcolm Freeman to kill Cameron Bowie of Crystal Motors?"

"Yes. I deny it."

"Do you deny ordering the hijacking of a military convoy in order to steal a new secret weapon?"

"Who do you think I am? Some master criminal?"

Sir Patrick sat back, and Colin Lockhart took over.

"Well, Vladimir. Firstly, we know you are guilty and if you go to court, you will likely get thirty years, so please don't take us for fools. Secondly, we know you are the frontman in London for a group of Russians who want to overthrow your government. Your criminal enterprises are only a sideshow. The real Russian mobster in London is Dimitri Grochic but he's no revolutionary.

"Thirdly we believe you were planning to steal the plans and the weapon to arm your comrades back home and give them an advantage." The colonel paused. "Are these not the real facts?"

Vladimir was amazed at how much these two knew. He also had a feeling this interview was leading somewhere. He remained silent and waited.

"Vladimir." Sir Patrick was back as the frontman. "We have a policeman, a very good policeman, who intends to arrest you any day now and charge you with murder. He's not interested in espionage charges. He'll leave that to us."

Vladimir didn't understand why he was receiving all this information. When he was told why it came as a bolt out of the blue.

"You see Vladimir, Her Majesty's Government and our American cousins wouldn't mind if your revolutionary pals succeeded in overthrowing your government, and given the lengths you've gone to, to steal this particular weapon, we have concluded that if you had this weapon, your quest might be easier." Sir Patrick stared an unsmiling stare at the Russian.

Vladimir couldn't think straight. Slowly he was making sense of Sir Patrick's words. Speaking in a loud whisper he stammered. "Y-y-you mean… You will give us this weapon to help in our cause?"

The colonel sat forward. "In a sense, yes, but it would be top secret. You'll leave the country this morning. There's a flight to Moscow from Heathrow at 12.35. You should be on it. That way the police might be able to build a case against you, but you'll never stand trial. We'll arrange to deliver weapons to you over the next nine months or so. Enough to arm a regiment. You can never return to the UK and you and your comrades can have no connection to this country. Is that clear?"

Vladimir was speechless. He stood and approached the colonel ready to give him a bear hug in gratitude, but Colin Lockwood, still sitting, fended the Russian off.

It was clear that Vladimir was excited and relieved. He'd got away with murder and an espionage charge plus arranging to hijack a top-secret weapon.

Sir Patrick pressed a bell recessed into the wall. The senior agent who had escorted Vladimir to the meeting appeared. "Simon, Mr Skoysky is leaving. See he gets the flight to Moscow as we discussed."

Vladimir wanted to say thank you, but Simon took his arm and gently guided him from Sir Patrick's office.

***

Mary and Steve were well into their third coffee when they heard voices coming from the outer office. As the DCI stood to investigate, his phone sounded. It was Commander Brooks. "Steve, my office in twenty minutes." The line went dead.

Such a summons from Alfie wasn't unusual so Steve put it to the back of his mind as he entered his outer office. Matt and Poppy were standing in the middle of the room.

Steve hadn't expected to see them. "What are you doing here? You're supposed to be interviewing Staff Sergeant Tay."

"We know boss, but he's not at Central."

"What!" the DCI exploded, "what the hell do you mean he's not there?"

Matt tried to explain in such a way as to avoid his DCI having a stroke.

"We got there with Malcolm Freeman. He was charged and being processed when Poppy arrived. We finished with Freeman and arranged for his transfer here. I checked and he's downstairs. We asked the duty sergeant to bring up Tay and he said he'd been moved. He said two MI6 agents arrived, just before we got to central with Freeman and handed over a warrant transferring Tay into their custody."

Steve was calmer. "Didn't the duty sergeant think it was odd?"

"Apparently no. He followed procedure, double-checked their IDs, confirmed the signature on the warrant and handed Tay over."

Steve started to pace the floor. "Bloody hell Matt, did the sergeant say he knew where they were taking Tay?"

"No, sorry sir." Matt Conway was crestfallen.

If Steve didn't already have an appointment upstairs, he would by now have been at Alfie's door.

"It's not your fault. I have to see the Commander now, so all of you go to the canteen, have a break. We'll pick this up once I get back."

The DCI set off to the twelfth floor intending to have serious words with the Commander.

***

The two MI6 agents driving Staff Sergeant Tay were seated in the front of the pool Rover 75. It was unusual as a pool car as it was almost clapped out. It was the oldest car within the pool and should have been scrapped years ago. However, the agents knew why they had this particular disposable car. The agent driving checked his rear-view mirror and saw a much newer and smarter Honda Accord following them.

"Where are we going?" Staff Sergeant Tay was glad to out of his cell but was nervous being in this car with two obviously armed MI6 agents.

From his back seat, he had followed the signs and noted they were heading into Kent. They were travelling at speed along the old Thanet way before the second agent spoke.

"A nice day by the sea, Sergeant, what could be better?"

Tay thought this fellow seemed friendly enough and relaxed a little. His last sight of anything on earth was a view of the English Channel. As he marvelled at its beauty, the agent in the front passenger seat turned fully round and shot Staff Sergeant Robert Tay in the centre of his forehead. Blood splattered across the rear window such that the driver now had to rely on his wing mirrors.

The two-car convoy pulled into a remote disused industrial estate just outside of Margate. The agents opened the boot of the old Rover, removed two cans of petrol and poured it inside and out taking care to totally douse the corpse in the rear. The junior agent threw a match into the car, and they stood watching it burn.

"They'll be lucky to identify the poor sod once the fire has done its job." The senior agent had seen it all before. As the younger MI6 operative turned white and looked like he might be sick, the older man continued. "Don't worry lad, the first is always the worst."

The two agents from the tail car stood and watched before signalling that they should all leave. The Honda Accord was spotted by a roving speed camera van on the M2 at ten o'clock on Tuesday the 31st of March. It was doing 67 miles per hour and the police speed check crew didn't give it a second glance.

***

The DCI arrived to find a delegation waiting for him. Apart from Alfie, he recognised Sir Patrick, Colonel Colin Lockhart, the Deputy Commissioner resplendent in what could have been a new uniform and a civilian whom he recognised but couldn't put a name to. He recalled the civilian was with the DPP.

Sir Patrick invited everyone to sit around the Commander's boardroom table. Steve noticed Alfie sat glum-faced in the large armchair he was presently occupying.

Steve sensed a tension in the air and knew better than to challenge the removal of his prisoner until he saw how the land lay.

"Gentlemen," the Deputy Commissioner was speaking, "I think we must recognise the efforts Detective Chief Inspector Burt has put into not only solving a double murder in double-quick time but also working with MI6 on an unrelated episode that led to him solving a third murder." The Deputy Commissioner looked directly at Steve. "So well done, DCI Burt.

337

The Commissioner is very pleased, and I wouldn't be surprised if a commendation wasn't coming your way."

Steve knew bull and flannel when he heard it. He knew his previous feeling that something was wrong was about to be explained and he wouldn't like it. He glanced at Alfie who had stubbornly refused to join the table. He sat with a pained expression almost painted onto his face.

The DCI held his own counsel and gave the table what they wanted with an embarrassed, "Thank you, sir."

Sir Patrick was next to talk. "Steve, you have done outstanding work and at any other time, you'd be showered with awards. You unearthed a spy working against our government and you prevented what would almost certainly have been a firefight on public roads in England. By preventing this, you also stopped the hijacking of our latest secret weapons system. All round a brilliant job." As Sir Patrick paused, the DCI knew the real reason he was here was about to be divulged. He sat passively awaiting the worst.

Sir Patrick continued. "Unfortunately, Steve, we don't live in a perfect world. If we did, we wouldn't do the work we do. So in our imperfect world and in an effort to make it a little more perfect, we are drawn into circumstances we would rather not be in." A pause. Despite the severity of the topic, Steve was enjoying Sir Patrick's attempt to sound sincere. "Your recent efforts have led us to such a circumstance."

For nothing better to do, Steve decided to participate. With a sarcastic edge to his tone, he said, "Go on. This is fascinating."

Sir Patrick was clearly not comfortable. "Your arrest of Staff Sergeant Tay for example. There is no doubt in any of our minds that he killed Captain Hope." Sir Patrick pointed to the civilian. "Giles, here from the DPP's office, is in no doubt a conviction was certain."

The middle-aged man now identified as Giles nodded and added, "Yes, no doubt at all."

Colonel Lockhart took over. "Unfortunately, Steve, he was a spy, and we can't have people like that in open court not knowing what they are going to say. He might take the opportunity of using his trial as a platform for his extremist views; he might spout something that the government wouldn't want in the public domain. You do see that?"

"What I see, Colonel is a murderer who has been caught, but he's gone missing. I told you last evening I was only interested in the murders, not your cloak-and-dagger games and you're right. He may blurt something out in court but so what? All I'm interested in is that we get a guilty verdict, after that, I personally don't care what you do."

Steve hadn't meant for his outburst to be so fierce but listening to this crowd around Alfie's table was beginning to get to him.

The man from the DPP spoke. "DCI Burt, as much as we agree with you, it has been decided that for reasons of national security, Staff Sergeant Tay will not stand trial."

"What!" Steve was on his feet. He stood with such force his chair almost fell over. "What is going on here?" He turned to the Deputy Commissioner. "Sir! Are you going along with this?"

"I'm afraid DCI Burt that there are certain things that have to be done secretly for the national good." The Deputy Commissioner looked at ease surrounded by these high-powered agents of doom. It led Steve to the conclusion this senior police officer was involved in their decision-making. The Deputy carried on. "As we have stated…" This speech by the Deputy Commissioner sounded to Steve as though it had been rehearsed,

"…your work in solving the double murder case was outstanding. Unfortunately, you were unwittingly drawn into an area that is significantly above your level. We appreciate it was at Sir Patrick's behest that you became involved in the goings-on at Station K but nonetheless, you must be happy you solved the case you were originally given. Now you must leave everything else to others."

The DCI again glanced at Alfie Brooks who continued to sit in his armchair, apparently taking no part in this meeting.

Steve saw he was getting nowhere and realised he had been ambushed. He decided to pass on the Staff Sergeant Tay situation. He sat back in his chair.

Silence descended, and in an effort to lift the mood, he said, "I suppose you're going to tell me Malcolm Freeman is also going to walk?"

A sudden pain appeared in the DCI's gut as he realised that his attempt at lifting the mood was in fact a reality. The looks on the faces staring at him told a story. No one reacted to Steve's comment, but silence said it all. Malcolm Freeman would not face justice.

"Please tell me Freeman is not getting a walk?"

Giles from the DPP's office spoke up. "Your admin assistant does a remarkable job in updating your case files. I've never seen such up-to-the-minute reports. From the file you have on Mr Freeman, we consider you don't have enough evidence at this point to achieve a conviction. Mr Freeman is a man of some standing and influence not to mention a public figure. We believe that prosecuting such a person based on the likely charges you may bring is not in the public interest."

Steve was calmer now he realised he was in the middle of a set-up. "My lads are even now searching Freeman's home and office. It's almost certain we'll get forensic evidence, plus physical evidence, which will tie him to the murders and everything else." Steve turned his focus towards the colonel. "Colonel, a young man gave his life to prevent your weapon falling into the wrong hands. I have evidence of contact between Freeman and your Russian, Vladimir Skoysky, and the planned heist. I have evidence linking Freeman to my original murder case. How the hell can any of you not see that this man is evil and needs to be put away?"

Colonel Colin Lockhart was dressed for the first time since Steve had met him, in his army uniform. He looked every inch the professional soldier except for his lack of medal ribbons. It was clear to the DCI that the colonel was a desk soldier.

The colonel didn't meet Steve's gaze. "I sympathise Steve but as has been said here already, sometimes we have to deal with issues in a way we would rather not, but if national security and the good name of the government are involved, we have to take action that doesn't sit well with us and certainly wouldn't sit well with the public. Hence, public trials have to give way to other forms of justice."

The DCI didn't know how to respond. It was obvious that this committee had powers he couldn't imagine. He felt drained having worked almost around the clock over the past few weeks. His brain gave conflicting messages. Then a flash of light appeared as he recalled something that had been said earlier.

"You've assassinated Bobby Tay." A surprised look appeared on Steve's face as he realised for the first time what was not being said at this meeting. "You've all spoken of other forms of justice and you, Colonel, referred to Tay in the past tense. He's been killed, hasn't he?"

The Deputy Commissioner stood and glared at the DCI. "Gentlemen, I think this meeting is over. DCI Burt, you are not to repeat what you just said, is that clear?" He continued to lift the files he had brought with him as the others present stood ready to leave. Steve remained seated. He didn't reply to the Deputy Commissioner.

A hasty and embarrassed set of senior officials exited Commander Alfie Brooks' office, leaving the Commander and the DCI alone. Neither man spoke.

Eventually, Alfie left his armchair and stood beside Steve. "In all my years as a police officer, I've never heard anything more disgusting. I'm sorry, Steve. When the Deputy Commissioner told me the DPP wasn't going to prosecute this spy or Freeman, I felt sick. It's obvious something is going on but we're not privy to it. Try to forget it. You got a result on the murders. The rest is out of our hands. Get the team together, go to the pub and celebrate your success. Leave the spooks and the wheeler-dealers to their own world."

The DCI thanked Alfie for his words. As he left the office on the 12th floor of New Scotland Yard, he turned to Alfie. "Is it all worth it, sir?"

***

Not long after the team learnt that Staff Sergeant Tay had been removed from Central booking, Malcolm Freeman had been delivered to the holding area below New Scotland Yard in anticipation of being interviewed by Steve. His delivery to the holding cells was timed at 09.55 a.m. At precisely 10.22 a.m., two MI6 agents authorised the release of Freeman into their custody. The sergeant in charge of the holding area vetted the paperwork and seeing it all in order, handed over his prisoner.

The journey to Freeman's expensive flat took only twenty minutes in another old MI6 pool car. This one was a Ford Cortina, and the agent driving wasn't sure if his chariot had an MOT.

At more or less the same time the DCI was learning that Malcolm Freeman MP would not be prosecuted, he was lying dead below the balcony of his expensive flat. The verdict would be suicide based on his inability to live with himself after being arrested.

At 11.09 a.m., the MI6 Ford Cortina was being crushed by giant jaws at a scrapyard in East London.

Coincidently this was also the exact same time Steve was leaving Commander Alfie Brooks' office.

***

Although Peter Jones and his search and forensic teams found enough evidence to secure a conviction against Malcolm Freeman, his apparent suicide closed the case.

With a heavy heart, Steve explained as best he could that the investigation into Captain Alex Hope's murder was closed.

Sir Patrick had informed Steve that Vladimir Skoysky was no longer in the country and would not be returning. Steve told the team what he could about Vladimir but again had to say there would be no case.

He told everyone to knock off for the day and he himself went home to his family. In the dirty world that Sir Patrick lived in, Steve was glad he was no part of it. His family was all he wanted.

***

Sir Patrick and Colonel Lockwood were once again in Sir Patrick's office at the top of MI6 headquarters in London. Both men had said little on their journey from New Scotland Yard, having said goodbye to Giles and the Deputy Commissioner as soon as the meeting with the DCI was over.

"Well, I suppose overall it's not a bad result." Sir Patrick was sitting behind his vast desk. "We're in the good books with our American allies by pitting the would-be revolutionaries against their government. I've no idea how that will work but at the least, it'll cause a few problems that'll keep them out of our hair for a while." Sir Patrick was relaxed in his chair.

The colonel was sitting in an armchair away from Sir Patrick's desk. "I hope you're right. I don't like giving these Communists our latest weapon but if it serves a purpose then I suppose it's worth it. I just hope the bloody test goes OK."

Sir Patrick sat forward. "I presume you removed Staff Sergeant Tay's records from the military personnel database?"

"Of course. It's as though he never existed. He wasn't married and was an only child so no family problems to deal with."

"Good. I'll brief our press people to put it out that our man of the people, Malcolm Freeman, jumped to his death due to overwork. That's always a tearjerker. The press will love it."

The colonel stood and asked, "What about your assassins?"

"All four have been posted individually to overseas embassies. I've had their files marked as no UK postings for six years. That'll keep them out of the way."

"Looks like that's it then. We're in the clear; the government has been saved from having to explain about Freeman and our weapons programme serving more than one purpose." Colonel Colin Lockwood headed for Sir Patrick's office door. "Until next time then, Patrick."

With a flourish, he left, leaving the head of MI6 to relax and contemplate recent events.

***

A few weeks later Steve's team, together with partners and other guests, were celebrating the engagement of Inspector Terry Harvey to Honorary Inspector Florance Rough. They had hired a pub close to Florance's flat and as Steve stood next to his wife, he was pleased to see everyone enjoying themselves. Poppy was once more dressed to impress and obviously having a good time. Peter and Matt were not big drinkers but were laughing and mixing with other guests. Mary was dancing with her partner that she had brought along, and Steve realised for the first time that his detective constable might be gay.

As he finished his beer, Alison set off to get him a refill and he allowed his mind to wander to the recent case and the disappointment of not being able to see Staff Sergeant Tay, nor Malcolm Freeman in the dock. Alison had helped him rationalise the events and Steve now saw the sense of the actions Sir Patrick's committee had taken. He couldn't condone the murder of Tay or of that of Freeman. It was obvious Freeman had been pushed to his death probably by MI6 agents and Steve had no idea what had become of Tay. He also knew nothing of the weapon or of how Station K could or would recover from recent events, but he didn't care. The case was closed.

Alison helped him forget his disappointment by announcing she had booked a two-week holiday in Italy. Steve felt life was returning to normal and hoped he'd never again be drawn into the murky and dark world of Sir Patrick Bond.

He could hope but there was no guarantee.

THE END

If you enjoyed reading *The Voice* then look out for the next novel in the DCI Steve Burt Murder Mystery series. See how Steve's career progresses after he has cracked this case.

The Norwich Murders

DCI Steve Burt is sounded out about a promotion to become Head of Norfolk CID but before he is given the offer officially, he is seconded to the Norfolk Force to solve the murder of an elderly police officer.

The victim is a female detective sergeant called Elsie Brown, who was close to retiring. It was known she had become obsessed by an eleven-year-old cold murder case and the DCI soon realises it is this obsession that may have led to her murder, especially when another body with a connection to Elsie turns up.

Before being seconded to Norfolk, Steve's team had started to investigate the case of a young woman whose headless body had been pulled from the Thames. So begins a dual investigation involving seemingly unrelated events. The cases prove to be the most complicated investigations the DCI has ever had to deal with.

During his hunt for answers Steve and his team become involved with London's criminal underworld, big business fronting criminal activity, sophisticated drug barons, money laundering on a commercial scale and corrupt officials.

As the investigation into the headless girl's murder gathers pace, the DCI is drawn further into London's underworld and begins to realise there is a connection between this murder, the killings in Norfolk and even the eleven-year-old cold case. Sifting through the evidence and proving the links becomes a challenge for the DCI and his Special Resolutions team.

Made in United States
Orlando, FL
19 May 2022

17999673R00189